Oldearth

ISHTAR

—ENCOUNTER—

By A. K. Frailey

Hardcover Edition

Cover design: A.K. Frailey and James Hrkach
Photo credit (of man): Juanmonino (Istockphoto)
Photo credit (of canyon): 4nadia (Istockphoto)

ISBN Hardcover edition: 979-8-9861803-7-3

The Writings of A. K. Frailey

Books for the Mind and Spirit

https://akfrailey.com/

Contact

akfrailey@yahoo.com

Historical Science Fiction Novels

OldEarth ARAM Encounter

OldEarth Ishtar Encounter

OldEarth Neb Encounter

OldEarth Georgios Encounter

OldEarth Melchior Encounter

Science Fiction Novels

Homestead

Last of Her Kind

Newearth Justine Awakens

Newearth A Hero's Crime

Short Stories

It Might Have Been—
And Other Short Stories 2nd Edition

One Day at a Time and Other Stories

Encounter Science Fiction
Short Stories & Novella 2nd Edition

Inspirational Non-Fiction

My Road Goes Ever On—
Spiritual Being, Human Journey 2nd Edition

My Road Goes Ever On—

A Timeless Journey

The Road Goes Ever On—

A Christian Journey Through The Lord of the Rings

Children's Book

The Adventures of Tally-Ho

Poetry

Hope's Embrace & Other Poems 2nd Edition

**Audible Versions Now Available.
Check book details on Amazon
for current listings.**

Dedicated to our human family;
we do not journey alone

PROLOGUE

—TEMPLE CITY—

WORTHY OF RENOWNED

Chai's fingers stuck together as he clutched a bloodstained knife at his side. His unruly black hair, muscled build, wide stance, and flashing black eyes proclaimed his dominance. He swept a long flowing cape over his shoulders and watched an enormous shadow slither forward. His heart pounded. The deed had been done.

The body of a young man was lowered into the pit.

For a horrifying moment, Chai stiffened as he beheld a vision: His mother's face as she lowered him onto his soft bed, cradling his body and crooning in her sweet voice.

Chai froze. The knife slipped from his fingers and clattered on the stone floor.

A circle of robed figures turned toward him.

He raised his head, searching wildly for direction.

The stone carving of his god—a man's head with the body of a great cat and the wings of an eagle—stood in the center of the cold room staring sightlessly through blood-red eyes.

Chai exhaled a long breath. Squaring his shoulders, he forced himself to look into the pit one final time. A dead body. No personality, no family, no loving mother—no grief.

The shadow followed the body into the black depths.

A servant tiptoed near and retrieved the knife.

Chai grunted, and the knife was slapped into his hand. He held it aloft, his crimson sleeves flowing in rippled folds down his arms. His heart thudded against his chest.

The dazzling fire flared in front of the stone god and burnished the blade a deep bronze.

A new vision framed itself in his mind.

He sat on a high seat above every mortal man. Every being on Earth shrunk from him in terror. His will reigned supreme. He could feel a smile creep across his face, but the burning in his heart seared all joy.

As he stared at the stone figure, his vision widened. A wall of impenetrable mountains opposed him. Suddenly, he flew aloft and with a bird's-eye view, vast rolling hills and open grasslands slid away under him. Clans huddled against the foothills and nestled between the shoulders of the great mountains. Chai caught his breath. A great throng—people from all over the mountainsides, hills, and valleys—gathered. Finally, a conquest worthy of his skill!

He dragged his gaze from the vision and stared at reality. In utter silence, the pit consumed his offering. He lifted his gaze to the blood red eyes. "I will bring more…and become worthy of renown."

With a guttural command and a sharp gesture, he ended the ceremony. His quick, sharp steps echoed through the dim temple hall. When he reached the open doorway, he halted on the threshold. Peering into the black night, a sensation so riotous it could not be controlled rose up inside him and demanded release.

He burst into wild laughter.

Chapter One

-Lux-

Test a Theory

Ark, his fleshy white potbellied body encased in a somber gray bio-suit and brown boots, stood aside from the main crowd in the domed Luxonian chamber. He blew bubbles through his breather helm, wrapped his four tentacles behind his back, and tried to ignore the bright light streaming in from above. *Planet Lux has altogether too bright a sun. They ought to shield us from the blasted thing.* He squinted and averted his eyes.

The Luxonian meeting hall, punctuated with purple-veined marble columns and glorious fountains shaped like creatures from every planet in the district, was filled to capacity with representatives from four races: Crestonian, Bhuaci, Luxonian, and Ingoti.

He studied a Luxonian Lightbird sculpture, as it appeared to fly into the air, spraying clear water from its beak. With a shrug, he shifted to the more fascinating Crestonian Sandfish, spouting green liquid from its razor-toothed jaws. A shiver rolled down his spine.

Dragging his gaze away, Ark nonchalantly shifted his stance and waited for his superior to approach. It would never do to appear hasty.

Ungle, a Crestonian with bright red cilia swaying on top of his plump head and dressed in a spring-green bio-suit and matching boots, meandered the circuit of the room with two tentacles wrapped behind his back in a contemplative manner. A third tentacle held a long-stemmed glass filled to the brim with blue gelatinous goo. With his last tentacle, he shook appendages—or mechanical armatures—as the occasion required, with various Luxonian and alien representatives. His perpetual smile never wavered.

Ark slumped and caught the eye of a young Luxonian who stared directly at him. Ark patted his breathing helm as if stifling a yawn.

The Luxonian's gaze delved deeper, his obvious curiosity breaking to the surface.

Annoyance broke Ark's placid mood. He discharged a narrow-eyed glare at the Luxonian, who soon turned away. *Idiot.*

"So you finally made it."

Ark's head jerked so hard as he twisted around to face his superior that he felt a crackling in the bone holding his spine erect. *Blast. I'll have a muscle spasm from that.* He clasped Ungle's tentacle from which dangled a gaudy bracelet. Ark blinked and swallowed. *Better not expect me to kiss that thing—like some weird Bhuaci sign of obeisance.*

"Not for kissing, just admiring."

Ark swallowed convulsively. *Uh-oh.*

Ungle laughed, nearly spraying liquid over the top of his breathing helm. "I can't read your mind—but really—Ark, you've become practically translucent. Been among humans too long in my opinion."

A Luxonian waiter in humanoid form, as befits the theme of the meeting, and dressed in an embroidered gold tunic and lavender leggings, glided in close. With a bow, he offered a tray of pink, blue, and green drinks.

Ark glanced at Ungle.

Ungle poured blue goo into his breathing helm, slurped, and shivered. "Not bad. But I'd recommend the green. Not authentic green, you understand, but less of a kick than the blue."

Ark swiped a blue drink off the tray and poured it daintily into his breathing helm. Like a connoisseur savoring an ancient wine, Ark sipped his liquid while his gaze wandered the room.

Ungle waved the servant away.

Ark turned to his superior. "You were the first to recommend Earth observation. Have you changed your mind?"

"Not at all. I think humanity will have a great deal to offer—in time. But I also realize there are many complications that must be considered—"

A bell tinkled.

"Bothmal those bells!" Ungle tapped Ark on the shoulder. "Meet me in my chambers after the meeting."

"You aren't staying for the Balatin Reenactment Festival?"

Ungle gurgled. "I'm a Crestonian. Science, not pleasure, dictates my schedule."

Ark took the hint.

~~~

Ark settled in a plump chair and hated the hiss of his bio-suit as it wedged between the stiff arms. *Dark waters, I'll never get up without help.*

The Crestonian chambers included a mini-pool built into the back wall, cushy, white furniture, and a simple cleansing and dressing closet.

Ark glanced over as Ungle tapped a console, lighting up a holopad.

"Pay attention now. I've done careful research, and I think I have just the solution we need."

Ark grunted as he tried to wiggle out of the chair. "What…is…the…problem?" Popping like a cork, he sprang to his feet.
~~~

Ungle straightened, and a hologram of the Luxonian guardian stationed on Earth—Teal—appeared before them. His slim, well-balanced figure, straight light brown hair, piercing blue eyes, and firm jaw emphasized his determined personality.

Ark shrugged and clumped forward, his embarrassment forgotten. "Teal?" His gaze swiveled to Ungle.

"As I mentioned earlier, science dictates the direction of my life. I believe that humanity has a great deal to offer Crestonian studies. Not the least of which is their obsession with good and evil."

Ark wrapped his tentacles behind his back, arched his neck forward, and meandered in close. "Surely, we understand the concept as well as anyone. Why—?"

"We don't experience the polar opposites as humans do. It makes quite a difference. Consider—" Ungle tapped the console. Teal dissolved, and Chai appeared beautifully dressed in crimson robes embroidered in gold. "A dangerous—by all human standards—evil force controls this man. It's a force I've rarely encountered before. Yet, this human believes he'll benefit from the experience."

Ark's tentacles wiggled nervously behind his back. "What does he have to do with Teal?"

"This being—calls himself Chai—will cross paths with the one you call Ishtar. It doesn't take serious extrapolation of data to figure this out. Their paths must intersect."

"So—"

"Teal will be watching. He'll care what happens. He might even attempt to interfere."

"That goes against all his training."

Ungle shrugged. "Given proper motivation, we all go against our training. Don't be obtuse, Ark."

"What do you want?"

"I want to see the natural exchange between Chai and Ishtar. I want to witness a soul damned to—"

“Hell?”

“Yes, I believe that is the term.”

“You want me to keep an eye on Teal—is that it?”

Chuckling, Ungle tapped the console. “Not primarily. I want you to keep your eye on her.”

The holographic image of Chai dissolved, and Sienna, a Luxonian beauty with reddish hair, golden eyes, and a slim figure appeared in all her radiant glory on the holopad.

“Sienna? She cares for Teal, but—”

“She’s a Luxonian with a healer’s soul. She wants to help so badly; she could do a great deal of harm in the process.”

Ungle tapped the screen and Chai, Teal, and Sienna appeared together on the holopad facing away from one another.

“They’re each convinced that they know what’s best for humanity. I’m convinced that they have no idea what’s in store for them.”

“And you want me to observe and collect data?”

“I want to test a theory—about good and evil.”

Ark waited.

Ungle smirked. “You’ll see.

CHAPTER TWO

—GRASSLAND—

BEGIN AGAIN

Jonas, in a simple gray dress with her black hair flowing over her shoulders, cupped her hands around her mouth and called. "Onia! Where are you?" Anxiety fluttered in her chest.

No answer.

Curious villagers weaving baskets, stirring bubbling cooking pots, tending to lines of dried fish, and other daily tasks swung glances her way.

After circling around her large thatched dwelling, she heaved an exasperated sigh and brushed strands of hair out of her sweaty face. Strolling through the dusty village of rounded huts and storage sheds, she continued the hunt for her youngest son.

Several heads lifted. Smiles crinkled in the corners of eyes, and lips curved in response to her plaintive quest.

A short, plump woman straightened before her loom and rubbed the small of her back. "If you find your son, maybe, you could find mine also? Send him home if you do."

One grandmother called out in cheerful teasing. "Lose that youngest one again?"

Jonas controlled an urge to roll her eyes and merely shrugged.

The old woman pointed south. "When Eoban returns, he's like the rain after a long drought—they flock to see what he's brought and hear the news. I've seen many pass by this morning."

Turning her head aside, Jonas caught her loose hair and braided it into a tight bun. She wrapped it with a dark woolen tie she pulled from her belt, squared her shoulders, and trudged on.

As the sun beat down, sweat trickled down her back. Her irritation building to the breaking point, she scowled. When she reached the edge of the village, a cacophony of voices met her ears, deepening her scowl. *What on earth—?*

Numerous boys and young men bustled around the framework of a new dwelling. Each youth appeared busy with a task. Two stacked mud bricks by an unfinished wall, three thatched a low roof, one braced a stout door, while two others dragged a wooden bench to the shaded side of the house.

Jonas stared, and her mouth fell open. As her gaze wandered, she found Onia, high on a rafter, patting thatch firmly into place. Her lips pursed, and she glanced about. *Where is—*

Eoban's voice rose above the tumult.

With a quick shake, Jonas marched around to the back of the dwelling. She blocked the sun from her eyes.

His broad muscular shoulders barely covered by a sleeveless tunic, one hairy arm akimbo, and the other waving like a leaf in the wind, Eoban's bushy beard moved in time with his words. His face crinkled in a grin. "Keep working, boys. That roof won't thatch itself. Watch yourself there, son. Lay those bricks carefully. They're worth all the time and energy it took to make them."

Jonas's hand dropped to her side as tension seeped from her body.

"No, be careful there, Malib! If you don't do it just right, you'll end up like a man I knew in Asher." Eoban scratched his beard and propped one hand on a post. "He built his house so quickly; he thought he was a god, and everyone spoke of the marvel. Until the rains came and woke him from a sound sleep."

Eoban turned his voice high and squeaky. "'Never mind, I'll fix it tomorrow.'" His voice returned to its usual rumble. "Then a cold wind blew and his walls cracked." High and squeaky again. "'I'll take care of that in the morning.'"

Eoban spat on the ground. "Finally, the ground shifted, and the fool was just about to close his eyes—when the house fell in."

The boys chuckled, all eyes fastened on Eoban.

Jonas's irritation vanished with a laugh. She strolled over to Eoban. "You're a wise teacher, my friend." She swept her hand in the direction of the new dwelling. "Have you decided to move? Or do you build with someone else in mind?"

With a teasing sneer, Eoban waved her questions away. "No and no."

Jonas poked his arm in mock severity, her tension rising again. "Don't make me angry, Eoban. Tell me, why is every boy, including my son, helping you make a new house?"

Eoban stared at the sky, shrugged, and clasped Jonas's arm. He led her aside, out of earshot of the bustling workers.

A gentle wind rippled the grass, and the smell of ripening wheat filled the air. A hawk soared across the sky and screeched as it dove toward a grove of trees in the distance.

"All right, I'll tell you, but I wanted it to be a surprise." Straightening, Eoban met Jonas's gaze and puffed out his chest. "Lud and his family are moving here. They'll be my neighbors."

Her skin tingling pleasantly, Jonas inhaled. "Lud? And his family? That's wonderful!" She squeezed Eoban's massive hand. "I am so glad!"

Eoban grinned, his eyes beaming with joy.

With a quick pat, Jonas dropped his hand, and stared over the horizon. "I only hope—"

Images flashed into her mind: Ishtar struggling with Haruz, and then her bloody body sprawled on the ground. Jonas swallowed and wrapped her arms around her middle. "After that awful night, I was afraid he'd never return. You know he only came for Pele. He couldn't reconcile himself to her death."

Eoban's gaze floated west, across the river toward Ishtar's village. "I wonder where he is now?"

She shivered. "She's dead, and he's gone. That's all we need to know. I'm still frightened by the memory of that night. I'll never forget it."

Eoban ran his hand through his thick, disheveled hair. "It still baffles me too. But then, I never pretended to understand such things."

"I had hoped that Lud would help Ishtar, but he left as quickly as he came."

Eoban snorted and glanced into the sky. "No one could've helped Ishtar. Lud was right to return home." He shifted his gaze to Earth and squeezed Jonas's shoulder. "Lud's a smart man—even though he is too skinny." A smile twitched his lips.

Rolling her shoulders to release the tension yet again, Jonas faced Eoban. "So why does he want to move here, so near you, of all people?"

Eoban rubbed his nose like an abashed child and glanced about. "He never fit in back home. He's seen too much, been too many places. He likes to welcome strangers and travel. His people don't understand. They're so suspicious. Even when I visited, they glared at me—like I was a monster from the deep. Can you imagine!"

A villager strolled by and waved.

Jonas waved back, glancing at Eoban. "Well, you've

been known to intimidate even—"

Eoban raised an eyebrow and turned back to the half-finished structure. "We're lucky that Lud married well. Dinah is a sensible, hardworking girl. They have three children all ready. Lud wants to enjoy the world as a gift, not a threat."

Jonas chimed in, "A gift from God."

With a noncommittal shrug, Eoban lifted a load of thatch and balanced it over his shoulder. "They'll be good neighbors. Obed agrees. He says Lud is a unifying force since he's been the slave of one clan, the rescuer of another, and a friend to all."

Dropping the thatch against the west wall, Eoban lowered his voice. "I'll stay closer to home now anyway. There's more to life than trading and riches." His eyebrows danced as his head tilted toward the assembly. "Someone has to train up the youth. Good warriors are good workers first."

A cool wind swept through, and relief spread over Jonas, relaxing every muscle in her body. Affecting nonchalance, she suppressed an exuberant smile and merely nodded.

A shout and a sharp yelp turned every head.

Eoban jogged forward as a crowd gathered inside, under a hole in the roof.

Jonas skirted around with one trembling hand clasped over her mouth and the other over her pounding heart.

Onia lay on the ground, peering through a mask of straw and mud. He attempted a brave grin. "Just slipped through a little hole."

Eoban cleared his throat as he glanced from the broken roof to the boy. "Tell me, Onia, do you remember what I told you about laying thatch?"

Onia blinked, his mouth dropping open.

Eoban waved a finger, his voice rising. "What happens to the foolish builder?"

Onia's eyes screwed up as he recited from memory. "Without a strong frame, the builder builds in vain."

"Yes, that's right." Eoban swiped straw from the boy's hair and pulled him to his feet. "Now go make bricks."

Onia glanced at his mother and shrugged helplessly.

Jonas sighed as she watched her youngest son amble off to his next duty, knowing full well that by the time he got home, he would be too tired to be of any use to her.

She gripped Eoban's arm. "You may have him until noon, but then I need him back. I have work for him as well. And feel free to tell your workers a little story about boys who help their mothers being the best of sons."

Jonas and Eoban locked eyes in a struggle for dominance. Eoban broke first, and they both grinned.

Jonas turned toward home and peered over her shoulder. "You might want to check this house before Lud moves in, or he'll be in for a few surprises."

Eoban folded his arms high across his chest and surveyed his confused crew. He called after Jonas. "They do great work—you'll see!" He nodded to the boys and lifted his hands like a warrior readying his men for battle.

Jonas walked backward, watching and grinning.

A fresh smile broke over Eoban's face. "Back to work, everyone. Did I ever tell you about the Sun Keepers? No? Well, there's a lesson in perseverance, let me tell you! You see, long ago…"

Jonas turned and strolled toward home, her arms swinging at her side.

—LAKE LAND—

Barak clasped his hands around one knee as he sat on a bench leaning against the back wall of his dwelling. His work-worn, patched tunic and leggings rippled around his thick, muscled body. He tipped his head up.

Brilliant stars twinkled overhead in miraculous glory. Inside a nearby dwelling, a child murmured plaintively, and a woman crooned a baby to sleep.

Barak sighed as his gaze wandered the heavenly sphere. He whispered. “Aram, where are you now?”

Stretching out, he sprawled on the bench, one leg hanging over the side. “There’s so much I don’t know.” His brows furrowed. “I’m not alone.” He waved a finger at the sky. “Your God follows me everywhere, but He won’t speak to me!”

Clasping his hands over his face, he groaned. “If your God spoke to Eymard and comforted you, why won’t He do the same for me?” Barak ran his fingers through his hair. “By the cat’s paw, can’t He choose someone else? Eoban would make a great leader. He’s forever telling me what to do.”

A soft wind with a spicy, resin scent stirred his hair, sending a chill over his body. Sitting up, he snapped a broken twig off the bench. “Eymard, can you hear me? I can’t lead all these people! If Ishtar can return to evil ways, who can I trust?”

Slumping in exhaustion, Barak lay back down, pillowing his head with his arm and closing his eyes.

In a dreamy haze, Aram appeared before him, standing with a lean, sober-eyed, black-haired man, who looked somewhat familiar yet unknown. The stranger reached out with his palm up.

Fear warring with excitement, Barak lifted his arm. He clasped the man’s hand, and lightning raced through his body.

Jerking awake, Barak bolted upright and opened his eyes.

A pinkish hue on the horizon signaled the start of another day.

—GRASSLAND—

Obed stepped away from his rolled-up bed, pulled an embroidered tunic over his broad shoulders, and let it fall gently over his white leggings. With care, he slipped his feet into a pair of new sandals.

Jonas stood near the doorway, her arms folded. "And about Tobia—"

Rounding on his wife, Obed glared, hot fury flushing his face. He slapped the wall post. "Why are you bringing this up again? It's the best thing for the boy, and well you know it. He's too retired and shy. He's a man now, but he doesn't seem to know it."

Jonas clenched her jaw, her lips in a tight line.

"He spends all his time carving figures and dreaming. I can't find him when there's work to be done, and when I ask why he's not at the field, he shrugs. He doesn't seem to know that we need

to work…to build homes…to trade and acquire the items that we can't make for ourselves."

Jonas glared, her eyes narrowing as she gripped her waist.

Obed swiveled away and pounded to the other end of the room. He waved and knocked a bowl of fruit askew, spilling a cluster of grapes. Ignoring the mess, Obed refocused his gaze on Jonas. "He's consumed with carving, and even when he makes something decent, he's reluctant to trade it for anything useful. He needs to grow up!" Obed folded his arms over his chest in a precise manner, his heart pounding against his ribs.

Readjusting the bowl and settling the grapes in place, Jonas, stiff as a board, choked out her words. "He is doing something important—his carvings speak to the part of us that makes us more than beasts." She closed her eyes and swallowed. "Onias believed in the value of art. Tobia is following in his father's footsteps."

Obed's jaw clenched. "Since I'm not his blood father, I can't see his worth—is that what you mean?"

Her anger flashing, Jonas plunged forward. "I never said that! You've been a wonderful father, but Tobia is different from you. Even from me. Is that wrong?"

A knot forming in his stomach, Obed shook his head. "You and I hold this village together. What'll become of our people if Tobia dreams his life away—even in the noble pursuit of becoming more than" —he gritted his teeth— "a beast?"

Jonas lifted her hands as if in a truce. "Stop! Please." She sucked in a shuddering breath. "You're right. Traveling and trading will probably do Tobia good. I just don't think that Vitus is the right man to lead our son into manhood. He'll never confide in Vitus, and Vitus will never understand him."

Sensing victory, Obed's heart leapt. "My point exactly! Tobia has been coddled for too long. He needs a man's influence. A man who will not coddle him. Vitus knows a lot of people along his trade routes, and that'll force Tobia out of his shell. He won't stand by and let him stare aimlessly with those sad eyes, carving useless pieces of wood."

Jonas wrung her hands and meandered to the open window, staring ahead. "Vitus is not the man you think."

Swallowing his doubts, Obed hesitated a moment. But as irritation welled, he leaned against the wall and struck again. "Vitus will do more good than you or I. We've almost ruined the boy." He slapped his hands together, lacing his fingers in a stranglehold. "Boy! Why, he's a man in size and strength, but we speak of him as a child!" Pushing off the wall, Obed started for the door. "No, my mind is made up. Tobia is leaving with Vitus in the morning." Looking back, Obed felt his stomach crunch.

Standing stiff and unyielding, Jonas blinked back tears.

With a shake of his head, Obed charged through the doorway and sped through the village.

—WILDERNESS—

Ishtar halted and stared ahead at a barren landscape. His long, unkempt hair blew around his dirt-smeared face. A rough beard sprouted along his jawline, accenting the hollows of his cheeks.

The sun rose into a hazy sky. Clouds swirled through the red glow of an angry firmament that bespoke of troubles in the heavens. A sharp breeze blew, and a line of pine trees behind him groaned in warning.

His toes bled onto the hard rocky ground. Ishtar peered at his torn skin and clothes—a ragged loincloth and a sleeveless tunic—hung loosely about him as if they might sail into the wild wind. Long strands of hair obscured his vision, but his ears thrilled to the howling wind through the heavy pine boughs. His lean body, sunken to near emaciation, bowed to the tempest. Neither fear nor pain accosted him.

He waited. But death did not come. Pain did not come. Sorrow did not fill his heart. He felt nothing. He cared for nothing. He wondered if he had, in fact, become nothing. Was he a man or had mere shadow engulfed his very being?

Without thought, he strode on.

The sun crawled overhead as he paced out his measured steps. Slipping on an incline, he instinctively grabbed hold of a rock embedded in the dirt to steady his balance. He climbed for time uncounted and, without interest, crossed a flat expanse.

Finally, the fog-ridden landscape cleared. To his utter amazement, he peered across an enormous desert. After an entranced moment, he glanced down at his torn feet and realized with the first tremor of fear that he stood with his toes pointing over a vast and mighty cliff edge. If he took one more step, he would fall to a bone-crushing death.

In the distance, mountains dwarfed the hills he had already ascended. Purples, blues, and pinks vied with one another to create a rainbow landscape over the barren land.

He gasped, sucking in the breathtaking beauty. Tears coursed down his cheeks. Grimacing in pain, he curled his toes around the rocky ledge. Birds, swirling in the heights, crisscrossed one another in innocent delight, dancing for him alone.

Ishtar raised his hand to his face and brushed his hair behind his ear. He stared at the glorious sky, never looking down to the depths that beckoned.

A vision of Pele, her gentle eyes set in her perfect oval face, wisps of hair swirling as if in the evening breeze, swayed before him. But unlike the birds, she gazed upon his troubled face. A faint message traveled through the harsh wind. “You live, Ishtar. Begin again.”

Ishtar’s heart pummeled his chest. *Begin again?* He was an exile, an outcast—no longer a man. Twice cursed. Was redemption possible after such a fall?

The birds faded like specks of dust into the horizon as his vision paled into vaporous clouds. He stared into the suddenly clear blue sky and wiped away fresh tears.

He took one more step back.

CHAPTER THREE

—HILL LAND—

NOT SET IN STONE

Lud, skinny but stalwart, watched his eldest son, Gilbreth, as they trudged over flat grassland.

Though small for his age, Gilbreth's heavy frame gave him a robust appearance. His little brother, Ham, bumped into him and fell backward, sprawling flat on the green expanse. Gilbreth stared at his brother and smiled. He plucked the little boy out of the grass, easily swung him onto his hip, and continued his march. "Ham, look where you're going. This is the third time you have run into me."

As his little brother's dark eyes filled with tears, Gilbreth's voice softened. "I can't be picking you up all the time. We have to travel far today." By the last word, Gilbreth's tone had lifted to a gentle croon.

Lud stifled a laugh. He dared not look at his wife.

Dinah clasped a hand over her mouth while a grin peeked out from her eyes. She carried her baby, Deli, in a sling wrapped over her shoulder.

Lud wrapped his arm around his son. "You'll make a good father someday."

Gilbreth rolled his eyes. "More than that, I hope! The new boys will think I am a nursemaid." He met his father's gaze. "Please, keep Ham and Deli away from me when we arrive."

Lud grinned. "You think I'd be so cruel? When the others see what a good-natured boy you are, the whole community will speak of it. They'll say, 'Gilbreth is a boy to be trusted!'" Lud pointed from Ham to Deli. "Besides" —he cringed in mock fear— "what would they do to me if I kept you away?"

Gilbreth pursed his lips, set Ham on his feet, and readjusted the bag slung over his back. "You can at least tell me why we're leaving. Did we do something wrong?"

Lud glanced at his wife, the dull thud of reality bringing his soaring spirit back to earth.

With an understanding nod, Dinah strode ahead. A sack strapped across her back bounced with each step. Deli swayed on her hip, and she gripped Ham's small hand.

Lud cleared his throat and clasped his staff tighter. "My father thinks I'm soft in the head because I'm so friendly with everyone. I told him that we want to see the world, but that's not the whole reason we're leaving." He peered into the distance. "My people won't last much longer. They've refused visitors, and they view every new idea with suspicion. They cloud their minds with doubt and fear. Even their blood grows weak because they allow no new members to replenish the spring. They're dying." Lud sucked in a deep breath and hurried his pace.

Gilbreth frowned, gazing at his feet as he kept pace with his father.

"That's why your mother and I decided to leave—so we could join with a different clan. They're kind, like to travel, and they're willing to learn about the world. Despite her upbringing, your mother has an adventurous heart. Look at her. Does she seem in the least bit afraid?" A warm burst of joy spread over Lud as he stared at the woman marching before him. "With each step, she soars—an eagle on an updraft—like an old friend I once knew."

Gilbreth bit his lip. "But will I never see my grandparents or the rest of my family again?"

Lud glanced away and picked up his pace. "I can't say. The future is not set in stone."

Gilbreth glanced from his mother to his siblings, grief entering his eyes.

Lud pressed his son's shoulder gently. "It is hard, but we must grow into a new life or die in stagnant waters. I'd not have you endure such a fate." Hurrying forward, Lud caught up to Dinah and grinned in her direction.

Dinah smiled back.

As Gilbreth ran ahead, Lud watched him. "You'll enjoy meeting Eoban. He came to visit just as your mother and I made our decision. I never saw a man so well pleased."

When Ham tripped and squalled, Lud scooped the little boy into a comforting embrace.

With a harrumph, Gilbreth lifted his arms like a bird with wings slicing through the air. His bag bounced across his back.

Lud murmured under his breath, "Nothing is set in stone."

Chapter Four

-OldEarth-

By Nature Fleeting

Teal peered into Sienna's eyes as they lay on a grassy plain before a mighty cliff. A hot sun beat down on them from a clear sky. Propped on his arms and knees, he hovered over the length of her body.

Sienna waited, grinning.

Teal lowered himself.

A flash of fear rippled over Sienna's face.

With a groan, Teal tipped his head back and plopped onto the grass beside her, sprawling out like a broken toy.

Sienna jerked up, pouting. "What's wrong?"

Teal rubbed his eyes. "You still don't trust me."

Yanking herself to her feet, Sienna brushed grass and dirt from her tan leggings. Her long-sleeved tunic rippled to the ground. "You don't trust *me*—rather."

Rolling to his side, Teal peered at her. "I'd like to. By all that is good and holy, I want to." Rising, he slapped dry stems from his gray tunic.

Sienna's lips quivered.

Exhaling a long breath, Teal stepped closer and caressed her arms. He tilted his head to meet her downturned gaze. "I've never wanted a woman as much as I want you."

Swallowing and batting back tears, Sienna shook her head. "I've never been this—"

Teal quirked a smile. "Vulnerable?" Impulsively, he pulled her into a tight embrace and tucked her head under his chin. "Me too." He ran his fingers over her hair, across her shoulder, down her arm to her waist…and forced his trembling hand to stop. He lifted his eyes to the setting sun. "We're in the midst of an interplanetary struggle. No one knows who to trust or what to believe."

Sienna sniffed and pulled away. "You seem ready enough to trust that Crestonian and Ingot."

"They're Crestonians and Ingots. I know their true nature and their peoples' hopes for this world."

Snorting, Sienna turned her back on Teal. "Then you can't trust them at all."

With a chuckle, Teal glanced aside and froze.

A ragged figure, bent forward, scrabbled down a steep incline, grasping at rocks and tough weeds to keep from sliding.

Teal exhaled a low breath. "Ishtar?"

Racing to his side, Sienna followed his gaze. She clutched his arm. "How'd he get here? It's well beyond —"

Suppressing even the hint of panic, Teal swiveled around and surveyed the area. With a grunt, he grabbed Sienna's hand and gestured with his chin. "Over there, under that rocky ledge."

They scampered forward and hid in the deep shadows.

Ishtar scrambled to the bottom of the incline and turned aside. He padded on bleeding feet toward the desert.

Sienna frowned. "Where's he going? There's nothing on the other side but barren lands. He'll die there."

Teal stepped out from under the stony ledge and peered at the emaciated figure striding purposefully away. "He's pursued."

Sienna's eyes widened as she glanced around. "By whom?" Snatching up a rock, she crouched for battle. "Can they see us?"

"No. And we can't see them. But they are here nonetheless."

With a snort, Sienna tossed the rock to the side. "You're a regular Bhuaci with all your riddles."

Teal watched Ishtar stumble. *I should've seen this coming.* A stabbing pain tore through his chest. "We need to return." He glanced at the sky. "Officially, I shouldn't even be here without Zuri and Ark. Luxonian Guardians should respect our own treaties."

Sienna huffed and crossed her arms. "It was your idea. Don't blame me if—"

"Don't start." Teal pulled her closer.

Relenting, Sienna placed her hands on his chest and started rubbing in slow circles.

Teal peered down, clasped one of her hands, and examined it. "Never any jewelry. Why?"

With a teasing grin, Sienna slipped away. "I don't need any. My mother taught me that a woman is enough in herself. My father agreed." Her gaze softened. "He used to bring me autumn flowers. Said that beauty is fleeting."

Teal glanced back to where Ishtar had rounded the rocky crevice, his voice dry and distant even to his own ears. "You believe that?"

"Of course. If something lasts—we don't appreciate it."

Teal locked his eyes with hers. "I disagree. Beauty is eternal. It's our gaze that is fleeting."

~~~

Ark sat on a log next to a rippling stream and slapped his fleshy, three-toed feet into the flowing water. He shivered in delight.

Zuri crouched on a boulder, his black bio-armor including headgear, body suit, and hard-toed boots, glinted in the bright sun. As he hunched over a handheld screen, his gaze scrolled over a data-stream.

Ark scratched his neck. "By all rights, we shouldn't even
~~~

be here without Teal. Cresta Accords are nothing to splash at, especially when they're backed up by a Luxonian treaty and your Ingoti Magisterium's seal of approval."

With a grunt, Zuri scrunched his face and peered closer to the screen. "You gonna tell him?"

"Ahhh!" Ark swung his dripping toes from the water and dropped them on the end of the log, tipping backward precariously. Using two tentacles for support, he leaned further back and stretched out, pillowing his head on two other tentacles. "Perhaps I shall. I really feel I must. After all, he's our friend. We don't want to break trust with him."

Zuri peered at Ark, grimacing. "Friend? What makes you think he's our friend? He never believes anything we tell him. He always checks our data after the fact. And he reports every bloody word we say."

"As do I. As do you." Ark lifted his head and glanced at Zuri's bent figure. "There's more to friendship than trust, you know."

The datapad slipped from Zuri's grasp and dropped to the ground. "Blast!" He scowled at Ark. "You want to explain what your idea of friendship entails, exactly?"

"Endurance." Ark groaned and rolled to a sitting position. "No Cresta worth his cranium capacity would ever bother with trust. We're not like that." He waved a tentacle in the dim light. "You've been reading too many memes on the Inter-Alien bulletin board."

"Don't be ridiculous. I'm suspicious of everyone."

"Even yourself—I hope."

Zuri smirked. "I just told Teal where we are." He strode to Ark and stared down at his limp figure. "I contacted him as soon as we arrived and told him that *you* wanted to follow up on Ishtar." His eyebrows rose. "How do you like that—friend?"

Ark shifted aside, pulled one of his boots forward, and wagged it at Zuri. "Fine with me." He grinned, quite pleased with himself. “I told him where we were going even before we left Crestar.” He wagged the boot again. “You know how these things pinch. Do be careful this time.”

CHAPTER FIVE

—AMIN'S VILLAGE—

MY ENEMY'S SONS

Amin, with his sharp, chiseled chin and pointed nose, stood in front of a grave mound with his hands clasped behind his back. Tears clouded his vision.

Villagers strode by—unaware or uncaring—never once looking in his direction.

Shuffling footsteps neared.

Amin scowled.

A small brown hand clasped his. Amin peered down and met the sad-eyed gaze of his little brother, a red-cheeked child losing his bloom too early. He swallowed back a lump and cleared his throat. "Caleb. What're you doing here?"

A slight shrug hinted at a deeper ignorance.

"Did you eat yet?"

Caleb drew one hand from behind his back. A half-eaten piece of bread crumbled beneath his grasp. "It's all she could spare—at the moment."

Amin nodded. "Finish it."

Caleb frowned. "Half's for you."

"I already ate. Got some broiled fish off one of the men. Threw it at me like I was a dog."

Caleb's eyes widened, his tone a pitch higher. "Fish?"

"I would've saved it for you, but it fell in the dirt—wasn't more than—" He shrugged, clasped his brother's shoulder, and turned away from the grave.

Caleb turned back, staring at the mound. "Hagia would

want flowers."

An ache throbbed in Amin's middle. "If she were alive. No need of flowers where she's gone." He pulled his brother along.

Caleb followed with a sigh. They wandered to the center of the village.

A young couple bustled in serious industry outside a large, sturdy dwelling. The woman shifted a bench from the right to the left, while the man strung a rope taut from one pole to another. They stopped and peered with sour expressions as the two boys shuffled closer.

The woman waved toward a boulder surrounded by rank grass. "Go over there. That woman left you a tray. Eat the leavings and move on." She glanced to the hills as if indicating the way.

On the boulder, a tray of gruel lay broiling in the hot sun.

Amin's frown deepened as he stared back. "What woman?"

The man marched forward, his face flushed, and his brows arched. "Namah. But why she should care for you—after what your father did—is beyond me." He spat on the ground. "I'd have slaughtered my enemy's sons. Not fed 'em."

Caleb trotted over to the food and sniffed. The gruel had jelled into a thick gelatinous mass.

Amin peered over his brother's shoulder. "Disgusting."

The woman's hand fluttered like a garment in a strong breeze. "Not so loud. She's over there. Discussing you two, no doubt."

After settling on the ground cross-legged, Caleb pulled the tray onto his lap and shoveled the messy mixture into his mouth with his dirty fingers. He glanced at Amin while dribbles leaked down his chin. "Want some?"

Amin's gaze fixed on Namah's back as she stood across the village chatting in a company of other women.

"Wonder what she's saying."

The woman straightened a blanket on the line. "She wants someone to adopt you." She thwacked the heavy cloth with a stick.

Amin whirled around. "Adopt me?"

The woman pounded in a steady rhythm, sending billows of dust into the air. "You and him." She gestured with her chin. "You've got to live somewhere."

Amin glanced at the dwelling, fury rising like hot liquid in his stomach. "This used to be our home."

Dropping an ax on the bench, the man turned around, glaring. "Not anymore. Ishtar's disgraced himself—exiled to his doom, far as I care." He slapped the doorpost. "But it's a solid house. I've as much right to it as anyone."

Caleb peered up, licking his sticky lips. "Why?"

With two strides, the man leaned forward and cuffed Caleb on the head. "No more questions. Be on your way now. You're lucky I didn't let the dogs have that mess."

Whimpering, Caleb dropped the tray in the dirt and covered his head.

Growling like a chained animal, Amin gripped his brother's hand and lurched him to his feet. Tugging him along the path between the buildings, he glanced around. No Namah. "Curse that man! He's no right to hit you. Or order us away."

Caleb sniffed as he rubbed his ear. Tears welled in his eyes. "Everyone hates us."

Amin lead Caleb to a grove of trees beside a rushing stream. "Not everyone." He frowned and glanced at Caleb as he settled him under the shade of a large tree. "Rest. We'll sleep here tonight."

Caleb's eyes rounded. "But animals come at night."

Amin tugged a piece of flint from a small wallet tied around his waist. "I can make a fire." He glanced around. "There's plenty of tinder, and we can gather bigger pieces before dark."

Caleb's sniff turned into a shudder. "I wish Hagia were here. She loved us."

"She did. But" —Amin shrugged away his helplessness— "at least Namah and Jonas leave us food."

"Why? I mean, why do they?" Caleb peered up, squinting into the light filtering through the branches.

"Barak probably tells them to. He's a good man. Or so I've heard."

"Hagia said Namah would follow Aram to the grave. How can she?"

"It's just a saying." Tousling his brother's thick, curly hair, Amin worked up a crooked grin. "No more questions, all right?"

Caleb ran a filthy hand over his sweaty face, smearing streaks of dirt over his head and neck.

Amin's stomach churned. "Go wash in the stream. I'll get some wood." He sucked in a deep breath. "Maybe I'll even catch a fish for tonight, and we can roast it."

A new light entered Caleb's eyes. Turning on his heel, he scampered away.

Amin watched the boy leap like a frisky puppy into the bubbling stream. He sighed and turned to the woods. As he stepped into the cool shade, he glanced back at his old dwelling. Setting his jaw, his eyes narrowed.

CHAPTER SIX

—GRASSLAND—

THAT GOD OF YOURS

Jonas stood outside her dwelling and hugged Tobia in a tight embrace, an ache building behind her eyes.

Vitus, dressed in a short gray tunic, matching leggings, and with a dark red cloak flung over his shoulders, stood aside, tapping his foot and drumming his fingers on his walking staff. As he looked to the sky, he exhaled a long-suffering sigh.

Tobia, wearing a new long-sleeved white robe over tan leggings pulled back and chewed his lip. His gaze flickered to Obed out of the corner of his eyes.

Jonas glanced from her son to her husband and back to her son. Her stomach clenched into painful knots. She caressed the side of Tobia's face, letting strands of his fine brown hair stream through her fingers. Staring into his eyes, she tried to memorize every feature.

Obed turned away.

Like children at play, birds swooped and circled in the sky above.

Vitus drummed his staff faster, louder. His sighs turned to huffs and were not encouraging.

Pulling away, Jonas released her boy. "I've lost one son—and your father. I cannot bear—"

Vitus lifted his hand. "We're not going to the earth's edge, woman. Just the trading circuit." He slung a limp bag over his shoulder and peered at Tobia's bulging bag. "We have a long road before nightfall, so if you don't mind?"

Jonas forced a smile despite impending tears. "I'm sure you'll do well." She smashed down a rising nausea. "Vitus is a good man of business, and he'll teach you a great deal. And" —she dropped her voice to a whisper and leaned in— "you'll teach him a thing or two, no doubt."

With a grunt, Vitas whapped Tobia on the back and looked up. "The sun is far higher than I intended for our leave-taking. Come

now, you've said enough farewells for six sons." His scowl swung from Tobia to Jonas. "Let's go!"

Tobia nodded and shifted his bag over his shoulder. "I'll do what I can."

Vitus stomped off in haste.

Tobia trotted after him.

Wiping her face with the back of her hand, Jonas glanced around. Villagers scurried in their daily duties, no one noticing a mother's tears. Her shoulders sagged under a hidden weight as she turned to her dwelling and stepped into the cool interior. Slicing roots and vegetables for the mid-day meal, she muttered under her breath. "If that man—"

"Talking to someone?" Obed stood in the doorway, his face draped in shadow.

A stream of light broke through the window and fell across Jonas, making her blink.

With a headshake, Obed grinned and strode to her side. He sniffed the pot. "I hope you're making something good. I'm starving."

Her irritation frothing into righteous indignation, Jonas scowled. "Everything I make is good." She swept the sliced pieces into a pot. "And yes, I am talking to someone. And no, I'm not overprotective." She sloshed water from a pitcher into the pot and plunked it on the table.

Obed lifted his hands. "I didn't say anything." He snatched a date from a bowl and chewed.

Pulling a tray close, Jonas flipped a cloth off a rounded ball of dough. She flattened the dough with her fist and began kneading it with her palms. "You don't need to say anything. The look in your eye is enough."

Obed's eyes widened. "What look?"

"The look you gave me when I hugged Tobia goodbye. The look you make every time Tobia and I pray to God." She laid the dough aside.

Shaking his head, Obed retreated to the other side of the room, folded his arms, and leaned against the wall. "I won't deny that your private conversations do seem rather childish, and you did act like Tobia was being sent to his death this morning."

With deliberate jerks, Jonas wiped the dough off her fingers and rinsed them under a stream of water from the pitcher. "First things first. Our prayers are childish?" Jonas dropped the washcloth on the board. "How about Eymard? Was he a foolish old man? Or Pele? Was she being *childish* when she appeared out of nowhere and stopped the sacrifice?"

Pushing off the wall, Obed sauntered to a corner and plopped down. He plumped the pillow beside him and peered at Jonas. He waved her over. "Let's talk without all the dramatic fury—if that's possible."

Her shoulders drooping, Jonas stepped over and plunked down stiffly at his side.

"I'm willing to consider what you have to say, but it'd help if you weren't bristling like a pine tree in high wind every time I talk to you."

Tears threatening, Jonas closed her eyes and clasped her hands. After a deep breath, she opened her eyes and met Obed's gaze.

Obed wrapped his arm around her and drew her to his chest.

"I'm sorry I insulted your faith. I shouldn't say anything"

—he grinned— "even with my eyes." He peered at her. "But you know perfectly well that Tobia's journey will be good for him. You were suffocating him, treating him like a child." He squeezed her shoulder playfully. "I bet that God of yours would agree."

Her stomach unclenching, Jonas relaxed and sighed. "You might be right, but I wish you'd talk to Tobia about his beliefs—and his work. It means so much to him."

With a chuckle, Obed pulled his arm free and laced his fingers together. "What's there to talk about? How to hoe a field or watch over a flock?"

Her chin hardening, Jonas nudged away. "I mean his carvings. Tobia's art speaks to the human spirit."

With a grunt, Obed shook his head and rose. "Men don't need to trouble themselves with spirits. I have no wish to become like Ishtar—or any of his kind." He took Jonas's hand and pulled her to her feet.

Jonas slapped dust off her dress. "I'm not asking you to become like Ishtar—God forbid. But don't you ever wonder where the soul goes at death? What other world we might enter? What happened to Onias and Aram?"

Clenching his jaw, Obed slapped a post. "Onias is dead. Aram is dead. Ishtar might as well be dead. It's time you moved on." He swung around. "I can't live in two worlds. One is quite enough for me." He glared at Jonas, his nostrils flaring as his breathing quickened. "There is no other world." He bent over and pinched a smidgen of dirt, sifting it through his fingers. "After death, there's nothing more than this."

Jonas stomped across the room and stared Obed in the eye. "How can you be so blind? Don't you see that we have a Creator—a great being beyond us?"

A grin played on Obed's lips as his gaze roamed over Jonas. "I see greatness before me. I don't need to look beyond."

Blushing, Jonas dropped her gaze. "You're just being stubborn."

"No, I'm being honest. I've more useful things to do than worry about other worlds and gods beyond my sight."

"Aram believed in God. He told Tobia so."

Obed grabbed another date and studied it as if it contained a secret. "When a man is dying, it's comforting to think such things—great banquets in the sky, meeting old friends. I'll probably want the same comfort when I'm on my death bed."

"Why wait till then? Talk to God now. Just once—pray."

With a groan, Obed popped the date in his mouth, chewed, and swallowed. "I'd feel like a fool."

Defeat bowing her shoulders, Jonas dropped her head.

Obed rolled his shoulders. "All right. If it'll make you happy, I'll try." He blew air between his lips and peered at his wife. "But you've got to stop babying Tobia. He's a man, and he must grow up. Carving is fine—but he needs to support his family and this clan."

Jonas nodded.

Stepping forward, Obed ran his fingers over her hair, caressing her neck.

A pleasant shiver ran down Jonas' back.

Obed whispered in her ear. "I'm still hungry. You won't let me starve?"

Jonas rolled her eyes. "If you catch a couple fish, I'll do my best to keep you alive another day."

"Now I can thank your God."

Jonas returned to the lump of dough, her stomach still in knots, but her shoulders relaxing. "Poor man, I should've sent you on a journey."

With a chuckle, Obed started for the doorway. "Not a bad idea. You think Vitus would wait up while I got ready?"

Jonas watched her husband, with his broad shoulders and straight back, saunter into the sunlight. She glanced up to the rafters. “You may have created him—but I have to live with him.”

CHAPTER SEVEN

—LAKE LAND—

MAKE YOURSELF AT HOME

Eoban's booming laugh reverberated through the trees. He stood in front of a new dwelling and watched Gilbreth try to free himself from his two younger siblings who clung to him like creeping vines in midsummer. Eoban stepped closer.

The children's eyes widened in stark terror.

Loping forward, Eoban scooped Ham into his arms and swung him high into the air.

Screaming bloody murder, Ham struggled for a handhold, using Eoban's nose for support.

Eoban laughed louder. He flipped the child around to face his mother and father.

Lud smiled and waved.

Dinah held out her hands, ready to receive her baby boy. She grinned as she took him her arms. "Does Eoban the Giant scare my baby?" Standing next to Eoban, she tapped his arm. "He's a good man." She kissed the little boy on the nose.

With a new light in his eyes and mad glee in his heart, Eoban strode toward Deli.

The little girl scampered into her brother's arms in a desperate attempt to flee from the approaching menace.

Lud laughed so hard, he bent double and lifted one hand in surrender. "Deli, don't be afraid. He's a friend. He wants to make friends with you."

The little girl peeked around Gilbreth's neck and pointed

an accusing finger. “He’ll throw me up in the air and drop me!” She nuzzled her head against Gilbreth and murmured into his neck. “You won’t let him get me, will you?”

Gilbreth managed to gasp. “Don’t worry. But please, I can’t breathe!”

Eoban shuffled to a halt and chuckled.

Lud strode over and rescued his eldest son.

Gilbreth offered wide-eyed gratitude as his father pried his sister from his body.

Eoban pointed at Gilbreth. “You have a remarkable son, Lud. Few boys could take such treatment without complaint. I bet he’s as fearless as he is good-natured.” Leaping forward, Eoban grabbed Gilbreth by the waste and then swung him over his shoulder. He peered from Ham to Deli. “See, little ones. I swing children into the air.” He swung Gilbreth around and then placed him gently on his feet. “But I do not drop.”

Red in the face, Gilbreth readjusted his tunic.

Eoban patted Gilbreth on the back, best of buddies.

Lud grinned. “You’re a man of many talents! As I remember, you used to tell entertaining stories, too. Maybe, if my children are very good, you’ll tell a few tales today?”

“To be sure!” Eoban smiled broadly. “Even if they are not so very good.” He stepped forward and waved to the dwelling before them. “So, how do you like the house?”

A rosy sun settling on the horizon, a cool breeze, and evening bird song set a peaceful scene.

“It’s beautiful.” Lud glanced at his wife. “We’d like to build one very much like it.”

Eoban rubbed his chin thoughtfully. “Build? This one is vacant, and I know the owners. I’m sure they’d offer a fair deal.”

Dinah’s face lit up. “We’d be neighbors then?” She glanced at her children. “But we might get a bit noisy.”

Eoban ran his fingers through his wild, unkempt hair. “I’m easily bored. I enjoy hearing laughter—or screams—as the case may be.”

Dinah giggled, nestling her baby against her shoulder.

Stepping forward, Lud peered at the framework and slapped a post with a firm hand. “Could you introduce us to the owners tomorrow? We’ll make camp for the night and meet them in the morning.”

“Make camp? Perish the thought. I’ll introduce you to the owners tonight, though” —Eoban jogged a few paces away and waved at distant figures shuffling in the center of the village— “it might take me a few moments to gather them up.” He flung a grin at Lud. “Make yourselves at home. I’ll be right back.”

~~~

Lud’s eyebrows rose.

Dinah sighed, strode to her husband’s side, and clasped his hand.

Carrying the little ones and with Gilbreth in tow, Lud and Dinah circled the dwelling.

Lud stroked his chin. “It’s new. A few rough spots but generally well-done.” He nudged his wife. “Eoban’s a bit of a mystery, isn’t he?”

Dinah’s gaze roamed over two matching front benches. “I trust him. A man without guile.”

Lud nodded. “Honest to a fault. You’ll never wonder what he thinks.” He glanced at the sinking sun. “It’s getting late. Let’s get supper.”

Gilbreth jumped forward. “I’ll start the fire. Man’s work. Finally.”

Lud unrolled mats, and Dinah pulled provisions from
~~~

their bags.

A rumble of murmuring voices rose in the distance.

Dinah glanced up as Lud turned to face the approaching throng. She edged closer to Lud and gripped his arm.

A crowd of young men ambled forward chattering in high-spirited exuberance.

Eoban led the group, his voice rising above the rest. "Remember your manners. They're new here, and their children are a bit skittish. Don't talk too loud or make foolish jokes. Just smile a lot. Understand?"

The assembled heads nodded. One voice lifted above the rest. "Just don't tell them who made the roof, whatever you do!" Laughter soared like a flock of excited birds.

Eoban tapped the speaker on the head. "You know who'll be doing all the repair work if there are any problems, right?"

The boys chorused as one voice. "Eoban!" A roar of approval met this comment.

Lud glanced at his wife and grinned.

Eoban and his troop halted in front of the stupefied family. Silence ensued as the two groups stared at one another.

Lud laid a comforting hand on his Gilbreth's shoulder.

Eoban nudged one young man forward. "Go on, Tannit."

A handsome, dark-haired lad of fifteen stepped forward, his gaze skittering from husband to wife. "You and Dinah were expected, Lud, and your children too, of course. We wanted to make you feel welcome. It was Eoban's idea, but he made us feel like it was ours, since we did all the work." He blushed. "Though he worked, too. He had to tell all those stories!" Tannit grinned. "So, we built you this house. We figured it was something you'd need right away, and it wouldn't spoil if you were late in coming." He glanced at the house. "Hope you like it." Biting his lip, he stepped aside.

Giving Tannit a firm pat on the shoulder, Eoban spoke up. "The boys worked very hard." He flashed a grand smile.

Lud stood frozen and wondered if his heart had stopped beating.

Dinah smiled, her eyes round with shock.

Attempting to make his mouth work, Lud swallowed and sucked in a deep breath. "You mean…this house is ours? It's too much. How could we ever repay such generosity?"

A younger, slighter-built youth stepped forward and stared boldly at Lud. "My name is Onia, son of Jonas and Obed." He brushed a stray lock of hair from his eyes. "Truth is, we're only paying you back for all you've done for us. Didn't you lead the slave revolt? Wasn't it you who befriended Pele so she could warn us about the Giants? You helped a whole passel of children during the great fire and brought the vision that stopped Ishtar." He shuffled his feet, his gaze dropping to the ground. "It seems to me that we'd have to build many houses—and better ones than this—to repay all you've done for us. We're just being grateful…as all worthy people are grateful." With a little shrug, he stepped back among his peers.

Mouths fell open across the assembled group.

Tears ached behind Lud's eyes. Straining, he swallowed and clasped his hands together. "I accept your gift then, and my family and I will treasure this house as a warrior treasures his finest weapon." He glanced from one face to another, finally landing on Eoban. "We thank you from the depths of our hearts."

His eyes gleaming, Eoban squeezed Onia's shoulder. "Breeding is in the blood." He glanced around. "Boys, show Gilbreth around while I help Lud and his family get settled. We ought to celebrate!"

Dinah's face blanched. "I don't have enough provisions to feed the whole clan."

Onia turned on his heel and called back. “Don’t worry. Mother and the other women have been preparing a feast for days. It’s their surprise.”

The troop of boys galloped away, laughing and shouting.

Looking like a proud father, Eoban stared after the boys.

Lud took his wife’s hand, and they laced their fingers together. His heart swelled, joy flooding his whole body.

“I want to see!” Ham scampered to the doorway and peered inside with Gilbreth holding Deli on the other side. Lud and Dinah stepped closer and leaned over them, glimpsing the dim interior.

Lud felt a hand on his shoulder.

Eoban nudged him forward, nearly tumbling the whole family. “Go on! It’s your house now. Make yourselves comfortable!”

Before stepping over the threshold, Lud glanced back at the glowing horizon. The same horizon he knew as a boy in captivity. The same horizon he shared with his family in the hills. The same horizon he shared with his wife and children while traveling. Tears slipped down his cheek. Forever, now, this horizon would glow in splendor…just outside his home.

CHAPTER EIGHT

—WILDERNESS—

BEYOND MORTAL STRENGTH

Ishtar stumbled over the barren lands, sending stray pebbles skittering in all directions. He barely had the energy to lift his feet. Since there was no point in dying among the barren rocks, a life must be forged from the nothingness of his existence.

He traveled north over the great mountains. Ancient stories told of a great civilization that once built stone monuments to gods more powerful than any ever imagined. Rumors whispered that the inhabitants of a stone city knew the secret to immortal life and could help a man enter the world beyond in safety—and style—if he had the wealth to make it happen.

After ascending a steep rise, Ishtar crumpled to the ground in an exhausted heap while the sun beat upon his bare, blistered skin.

Pain woke him. Scratching at the sandy ground, he crawled beneath the shade of a boulder and closed his mind to all agony and thirst.

Dreams haunted him, filling his mind with horrifying images of his father and grandfather. The spirits of the dead called to him. Claiming him. *I have nothing. I am nothing.* But the netherworld did not take him. With eyes squeezed shut, Ishtar scoured the ground with his fingers as if digging his own grave, but he found neither death nor relief.

After the sun settled behind the mountain, a chilly wind

sent dust rising into whirlwinds. Shivers wracked his body. Groaning, he sat up, leaned against the warm boulder, and rubbed his blistered face. He winced in pain.

Exhaustion, hunger, and thirst tormented him. Staggering to his feet, he threw back his head and stared at the pink and golden firmament. As darkness descended, uncounted stars blinked into view and hung in the sky like bright jewels beckoning his soul. Bowing his shoulders, he dropped his gaze, fixed his eyes on the distant mountains, and let his feet lead the way.

When the pink rays of the sunrise once again shimmered over the horizon, he listened for signs of life. A faint birdsong twittered in the distance.

He staggered on.

The sun rounded and glowed in bright white glory, small insects flittered from boulders to thorny desert plants, and lizards and tiny rodents scampered under rocks. A scent of foreign blossoms floated to his nose, awakening his senses.

Tears trickled down his face.

When the sun's heat burned too fiercely, he followed the lizards and small creatures into crevices and shadows. Scooping sand aside with his torn fingers, he smoothed a soft bed and rolled under a ledge, safely hidden for a few hours from the burning glare of the sun.

Beyond count of days and nights, he couldn't remember how many rocks he crawled under or how many lizards he caught and ate. Ignoring his revulsion, he ground in his teeth and swallowed whatever he could catch.

Thirst tormented him.

In a delirium, he reached a pass and scuttled into a valley where a strip of green broke the monotony of the scorched earth.

Three tents rippled in the evening breeze, sending shivers of expectation running through his worn and exhausted limbs.

Crouching low, and feeling more like a wild dog than a human, he limped to a watering hole.

A wide, stone well within a circle of palm trees and verdant grass appeared like a vision from another world. His cracked lips stung at the very thought of liquid.

As the sun descended behind the mountains, he felt his face break into a grimace. He searched for a bucket or a ladle of some kind.

Nothing.

Digging his toes into the shifting sand, he pressed on the heavy stone lid. His blackened arms splotched by scorched skin and shredded by fierce winds trembled when he tried to lift the lid.

It would not budge.

A moan escaped his lips.

Madness gripped his mind. Fear and agony tore his soul. He would die of thirst beside a well. *Would this be justice—at last?*

A young girl in a long-sleeved embroidered dress humming a strange tune and swinging a bucket in one hand sauntered forward.

He tried to rise, but his body shook so violently that he merely staggered and fell.

The child's eyes widened in terror. She froze. Her mouth opened. Without a sound, she turned on her heel and fled, the sand spraying behind her.

Ishtar felt heaving sobs break inside him like waves on a distant shore. But no tears came. He could no longer even cry like a man.

A few moments later a brawny, dark-skinned man with curly black hair, wearing a white tunic with a gray robe thrown back over his shoulders, jogged forward. He halted when he met Ishtar's gaze.

Ishtar closed his eyes.

A shadow covered the glare of the sun. A hand clasped

Ishtar's shoulder. Water brushed his mouth.

His eyes fluttering open, Ishtar opened his cracked, bleeding lips and, with the last of his strength, lifted his hand to direct the cup.

He drank until the man told him to stop and pressed his shoulder. "Come. I'll take you to my father. He's always glad to meet travelers and hear news."

With the help of a pair of strong arms, Ishtar limped to the largest of the three tents. He stopped. Fear enveloped him. Choking him.

The girl stepped out of the tent and smiled. With a nod, she lifted the door flap wide open and stepped aside.

Ishtar stared at the child. His heart squeezed so tightly, he could not breathe.

The man touched his elbow, edging him forward.

Ishtar stumbled inside.

A thin, elderly man with piercing black eyes and a gray beard, wearing the long white robe of a Bedouin, stood in the middle of the tent straight and tall. His gaze scoured Ishtar no less than the brilliant sun.

A scent of stewed goat meat, spices, and something sweet almost overpowered Ishtar as he waited, trembling, just inside the doorway.

The elderly man drew near, one hand extended, as if to catch Ishtar should he fall. "You've come at a good moment, my friend, for I have too much food for one man. My wife wishes to fatten me up, but I can never do justice to her ample portions. Perhaps you could assist me?"

Ishtar wasn't sure if the quirk of a smile he thought in his mind actually appeared on his face. He followed the man across the room and nearly collapsed on a large comfortable pillow. He swallowed a sharp pain in his throat. "It—it'd be an honor to eat with you. Thank you." He grimaced at the sound of his reed-thin voice.

The heavyset man who had helped him drink, settled to

his left and handed him a bowl of water.

Ishtar frowned.

The man laid the bowl on the pallet, dipped his fingers in, washed and dried them on a cloth. He gestured from Ishtar to the bowl.

After Ishtar washed, a dish of beans and rice with spicy meat was placed before him. He waited for his host to begin, and then dug in, pinching clumps of the savory food with his fingers and carrying it to his mouth. His stomach clenched, and he heard a whimper break from his throat in relief as the delicious food met his teeth and lips and traveled down his throat.

The girl sashayed into the tent again, balancing a tray of cups filled with wine. She placed one cup in Ishtar's hands.

He trembled.

With a glance, the older man nodded to the girl. She knelt at Ishtar's side and directed the cup to his lips. He sipped, peering over the rim into her wide black eyes. Warmth spread through his body.

The older man leaned back and gestured to Ishtar to keep eating. "Please, take your time. Enjoy. My wife will be pleased to have it so well appreciated." He gestured from the young man to the girl. "You have met my eldest son and youngest daughter. We welcome you to our home. It's clear that you've traveled long and hard. From some misfortune, perhaps?"

As Ishtar swallowed the last morsel, his whole body relaxed.

Undisturbed, the old man rested his hands on his lap. "My name is Alanah Matalah of the tribe of Sirah men Talah. I have the fortune of traveling the lands of my fathers and grandfathers, going back generations untold. We are a simple people who look for nothing more than to tend our flocks and care for our families in peace."

Ishtar leaned back, his mind dizzy with the joy of food,

wine, and comfort. He rested his gaze on his host.

"God-Above-All has been most generous. I have four sons and three daughters, all healthy and strong. They care for the flocks, and my sons travel to neighboring lands and trade and learn the news of the world. Many things have I seen, and many stories I could tell—" Matalah lifted his hand as in an invitation. "But if you have a story to share, I would gladly hear it."

Ishtar peered down at his bruised, torn hands clasped on his lap. Peace settled over him. He lifted his eyes to his host. "I have lost my way in the wilderness. My story is a bitter one, which I'd rather forget. I can share nothing but the pain of my past and a future shrouded in darkness." Without warning, Ishtar felt flames lick his body and searing pain stab his innards.

Matalah sat silent and still. His children's eyes grew large and anxious.

Ishtar swallowed a lump rising in his throat. "If I told you what I've done, you'd gather your sons and throw me out your tent. I do not deserve to live." Staring at the ground, his vision blurred, and his voice cracked. "I certainly do not deserve your kindness."

Matalah motioned to his children, and the two rose and left the room.

A tear meandered down Ishtar's cheek and slipped off his chin.

Matalah spread his hands wide. "I'm not a man of great wisdom, yet I believe in wisdom, and I know there is a force beyond mortal strength that calls each soul forward into the light of truth."

The image of Pele flashed before Ishtar's eyes, and he stifled a gasp.

"In truth, you may have done terrible wrong, but I suspect that there is more to your grief than your own chosen evil. I have learned that evil begets evil, and I acknowledge the source of all evil is a constant temptation to the soul of every man."

Ishtar squeezed his eyes shut, and the face of his father appeared in his mind's eye.

Matalah's voice lowered to a gentle invitation. "Each man must learn where his evil comes from…and to whom he passes it."

Like roaring waves, sobs crashed over Ishtar. Covering his face with his arms, he rocked back and forth. Grief and pain warred with shame and humiliation.

With a light touch, Matalah clasped his shoulder. "You are wounded. And true healing cannot be rushed. May I make a suggestion?"

Ishtar stopped, frozen, like a child awaiting his punishment.

"Stay with us for a time. Assist my sons for the season."

Ishtar glanced up, afraid to hope. Afraid to breathe.

A smile flashed over Matalah's face. "No one in love with wisdom can ever have too many sons. My daughters enjoy fussing over strangers, and my wife lives to cook enormous meals. Rest, work, and grow strong again."

As if rain fell on his blazing body, Ishtar felt relief wash over him.

"If a troubling memory disturbs you, come to me. I may not have a sagacious remedy, but perhaps that does not matter so much. Let the Lord God heal you."

The memory of being rocked in his mother's arms unclenched Ishtar's body. Peace entered his soul. He met Matalah's unwavering gaze. "You would let me stay…without knowing my past and what kind of man I truly am?"

"I will let you stay as long as you allow yourself to stay."

As a hot flush burned his cheeks, Ishtar bowed. "I will do whatever you ask. I am your servant."

Matalah rose. A smile hovered on his lips. "I consider

you my guest. My sons will show you where to sleep, and they'll assist you for the remainder of the evening."

Ishtar stood with his back straight once again.

Matalah stepped to the doorway. "I must get an early rest for the Lord awakes me early with the quiet beauty of His creation."

The son and daughter opened the flap and stood on each side.

Matalah gently gripped Ishtar's arm. "You have nothing to fear."

~~~

Ishtar lay awake while the four brothers slumbered in quiet repose. He could glimpse the starry sky through the open tent flap. Rolling on his side, he stared into the night and savored a sensation he could hardly recognize. Peace felt so strange and unfamiliar that he could not sleep for want of basking in its presence. The madness swirling in his mind had vanished like early morning vapor under a hot sun.

The image of Pele floated before him. Matalah's gentle touch still tingled on his arm. The memory of the young girl's piercing black eyes sent a pleasant shiver over his arms.
~~~

CHAPTER NINE

—AMIN'S VILLAGE—

YOU MEANT WELL

Amin stood in the center of the village with his hands on his hips and his mind reeling in fury. He squinted in the mid-day sun. If someone had told him that his father was living among nomads of the desert, he would have shrugged the information away. He had troubles of his own, and no one, especially not his father, could help him now.

Namah stopped in front of him. Her gaze surveyed his face, and she frowned. "Amin, may I speak with you?"

Clenching his hands at his sides, Amin turned abruptly and strode away.

With an intake of breath, Namah pattered after him, her feet slapping the dusty ground. "Amin! You know who I am and why I'm here. I've found a family—"

Amin halted and spun around, his whole body stiffening against the desire to strike. "Caleb is my family. I want no other."

Namah panted, her face flushing and strands of loose hair falling into her face. "Jared and his wife, Lia, have agreed to adopt you. They'll take—"

Amin's rage burst from all constraint. "Take? Yes, they'll take! Do you know how they treat us? Like dogs. They don't care for us. They hate us."

Namah shook her head, her eyes wide with wonder. "I just spoke with them this morning. Their parents are old, and they need help. Would it be so hard to assist—?"

"Who are you to give me away like a goat?" Amin growled deep in his throat. "You're not even a member of this clan. You have no authority here. Leave me and my brother alone!" Jerking around, Amin sped toward the tree-lined stream.

Clamping his arms over his chest, he stared at the foaming water as it crashed against rocks and gurgled through narrow channels.

Flapping footsteps stopped at his side.

Amin clenched his jaw tight against a scream.

Namah's voice rose. "Like it or not, Amin, I do have a part to play in your life. Your father nearly murdered my daughter, but I have never blamed you or your brother. You're victims of his madness as well."

Amin turned slowly. "I'm not a victim! I take good care of Caleb, and we're fine. We don't need you. And we certainly won't be enslaved by Jared and his wife."

"But you're living like animals!" Namah sucked in a deep breath and pressed her hands against her chest as if to alleviate a sudden pain. She breathed slowly, in and out, and straightened her shoulders. "What has Jared done so terribly wrong—?"

Smacking one hand against another, Amin stomped forward and glared into Namah's eyes. "Jared hardly feeds his own father. He had him working out in the sun the other day until the old man collapsed. And Lia's mother isn't allowed to do anything without asking for permission first." He swung his gaze to the village. "No one dares speak of it because Jared is a cruel man." He swung around and faced the water again. "Even Caleb feels sorry for the old people. He wants me to free them from their misery."

Namah padded around and faced Amin. "How could this be true and yet no one has warned me?"

"What happens to Caleb and me is of little consequence. Most of the clan wishes we were dead. They hate being reminded of my father's disgrace."

"But many of your people supported Ishtar."

"They supported him when he made the clan rich. No one supports a man in exile."

Clasping her hands over her mouth, tears swam in Namah's eyes. "I only want to help."

"By sending us to Jared, you'd send my little brother and me to misery and an early death. For which of these expectations do you wish me to give you thanks?"

Namah backed up and plopped down on a log jutting into the water. "Am I so blind?" She shook her head and met Amin's gaze. "I never thought to ask…you."

Amin crossed his arms and glared.

A tear slipped down Namah's face.

Scurrying up a tree, a squirrel waved its tail and clicked in warning. Two crows cawed and burst from the branches overhead.

Amin heaved a deep breath, his chest tight and painful.

Namah jerked to her feet, her eyes wide and anxiety wrinkling around them. "I should've asked Barak's advice. He'll be furious with me."

Amin's arms fell limply at his sides, his anger seeping away like the heat from a gray campfire. "Why do you care anyway? We're nothing to you. Only a painful reminder."

Namah turned to the bank and stared ahead. "A long time ago, almost a lifetime, I made a terrible choice. I regretted it—" She choked. "Aram forgave me." She glanced back and peered at Amin. A bitter chuckle broke from her wobbling lips. "Everyone forgave me." She wiped her face and stepped nearer. "I pity Ishtar. He fell, and no one cared to pick him up again."

Amin dropped his gaze. A sharp pain lodged in his chest.

Namah laid her hand on his shoulder. "Though he's gone into exile, I believe your father still cares for you." Her voice dropped to a husky whisper. "I do."

Amin lifted his eyes. "Perhaps, if I speak with Barak, he'll understand. Perhaps, he'll think of a solution."

One of Namah's eyebrow rose. "You admit there *is* a problem?"

"I admit that Caleb needs more than just an angry older brother."

A smile quivered on Namah's lips. "First I must see Jared and his wife and rescind my agreement."

"They'll be furious."

"Not as furious as Barak will be."

A splutter of relief surged through Amin's middle. "Maybe you need my help?"

Namah patted his shoulder and grinned. "Caleb has a very astute brother."

Amin shrugged and squinted through an upturned gaze. "I know you meant well." He looked toward the mountains. "If my father still lives and learns of your kindness, he'll be grateful."

With a nod, Namah stepped away. "I'll leave you for now, but we'll meet again. In the meantime, keep your brother safe."

Amin watched until Namah rounded a corner and was lost from sight. He scratched his jaw and glanced around, a dart of concern jabbing him. "Where is Caleb?"

Chapter Ten

–Lux–

Legitimate Concerns

Sterling lifted a trailing purple vine from a deep pot and carried it beyond Teal to an ornamental box hanging outside his open apartment window. "By the Divide. You don't honestly believe that I'd want to go to that barren wasteland you describe in your reports?"

Shoving loose soil aside, Sterling nestled the plant roots in a wide hole. "Why, I'd rather be eaten alive by Crestonian dissection maggots."

He patted the dirt around the plant stem and laid the vine runners across the box so they dangled artistically. "At least they do their work quickly and leave you in peace when they're done." Holding his hands out like a surgeon ready to perform surgery, Sterling marched across his living room and slapped a wall panel with his elbow.

A glossy white sink and accompanying faucet emerged from the wall. He waved his dirty hands under the faucet.

Nothing happened.

Sterling glanced at Teal.

Teal tapped his fingers together and pursed his lips.

Sterling swung his gaze from Teal to his hands and whined. "You could help, you know."

Marching across the room, Teal slapped the wall console. Hard.

High-pressure water rushed from the faucet and nearly cut Sterling's hands from his wrists.

"Aw! Damn it, Teal. You want me to go to that hideous

planet, but you nearly maim me first." Sterling eyed the wall console. "Your Ingot friend said he fixed it."

Teal snatched a blue-green oval fruit from a bowl on an end table and chomped. He talked around a chew. "Ingots like high-pressure water."

Sterling ripped a towel from the sink rack. "Ingots like high-pressuring everything." He jutted his jaw at Teal and patted his hands dry. "You've been around Zuri too much. I'm beginning to notice a resemblance." He waved his hand in a circular fashion before his face. "Especially around the eyes. You're glaring like he does."

Teal finished chewing and swallowed. "I'm not glaring. I just made a simple request."

Sterling returned to the window box and peered at the transplant.

The vine lay limp, wilting before his eyes. *How very depressing.*

Teal stepped up and eyed the pathetic foliage. "I think you need to water it."

Sterling glanced at the high-pressure sink and bit his lip.

A chime sounded.

Teal and Sterling turned to the door.

Exhaling a long exasperated breath, Sterling shrugged. "Come in." He glanced at the vine. "I'm not doing anything…worthwhile."

With an eye roll, Teal swept a tall, square glass off the liquor cabinet, adjusted the water pressure, and filled the container.

The door slid open and Ark ambled in. He waved a tentacle. "You called?"

Teal watered the vine, waited, and then faced Ark.

Ark eyed the glass, his brows rising, a smile quivering on his thick lips. "Having liquids, are we?"

Sterling's gaze swiveled from Ark to Teal. "You invited him here?" He marched to the liquor cabinet and pulled down three glasses. "Let me guess. The Ingot is on his way."

Ark eyed Sterling's actions with obvious interest and sidled closer. "Actually, he's still on Earth." Twining two tentacles over his middle like an abashed student before his learned master, Ark glanced at Teal. "He's keeping an eye on Ishtar. And taking copious notes, I hope."

Teal chuckled. "And taking a few ore samples, if I know him."

Sterling lifted two full glasses and strolled across the porcelain tile flooring to Ark. "Here, you can have these since the Ingot isn't coming."

Teal stepped closer and extended his hand. "You aren't having one, sir?"

Sterling swiped the last glass off the counter and poured himself a full measure of golden liquid. "Don't be ridiculous. I'm having three before the day is out. You need to stay alert. There's a pot of swill over there" —he nodded toward a vessel on the counter— "that's got enough stimulants to keep a dying rhinoceros on his feet." He glanced at Ark. "They do have feet—don't they?"

Ark poured both drinks into his breathing helm and slurped noisily. "Not my area of expertise." He glanced at Teal who placed the water glass in the sink, pointedly ignoring the swill.

Sterling harrumphed and tossed back his drink in one swallow. He closed his eyes. *Picture the sea. Calm waves rolling on the shore.* He held the moment and then, opening his eyes, he peered ahead. "So, Teal, why did you come today and invite your nice friend?"

Teal strode to the window and peered at the now bright and swaying purple vine. He grinned. When he faced Sterling, his smile vanished. "Someone is trying to kill me."

Sterling shook his head and marched directly to the

cabinet. "I can think of many reasons why…but not who." He turned around swinging his empty glass in the air. "I hope you don't suspect me?"

Ark's golden eyes rounded on Teal. "Or me."

Teal rubbed the back of his neck. "Neither of you." He glanced out the window and sighed. "I might be mistaken. Someone might be trying to kill Zuri. But someone is definitely—"

Ark choked. "I left him alone on the planet!" He huffed sending bubbles through his breather helm. "Why didn't you tell me?"

"He's not alone. Sienna is watching him. From a discreet distance."

Sterling slapped his glass on the counter, his composure cracking. His imaginary rolling waves rose to pounding surf. "Do you mean to tell me that you have Sienna watching Zuri who is watching Ishtar?" He laughed. "Getting rather redundant, aren't we?"

Teal stepped forward and dropped his voice to a whisper. "I want the three of us to return to Earth, undetected, and find out who's trying to kill me—or him."

Ark tapped Teal on the shoulder and imitated his whisper. "Don't bother. I already know."

Sterling froze. His body actually felt numb. "Know what? That someone is trying to kill Teal? Or that a plot's afoot?" *Distractions always help.* He returned to his empty pot, yanked it off the shelf, hefted it to the wall disposal unit, and dumped it down a shoot. He clapped his hands free of every blasted particle of dirt. "Personally, I think Teal needs a vacation. He's getting paranoid."

Ark glanced from Teal to Sterling and wrapped all four tentacles around his thick waist. "How did you know we're focusing on Ishtar?"

Freezing, Sterling felt his chest tighten. *I can't actually have a heart attack. It's impossible. This body is a facsimile*— He glanced at Teal.

Teal stared him into the ground.

If that were possible.

"Oh, bloody Bothmal!" After pacing across the room to an arrangement of plush chairs and a couch, Sterling plunked down on the sofa and stretched out. "Mind if I collapse? It's been a long cycle."

Teal sauntered over and perched on the arm of a chair opposite his superior.

Ark plodded to a slightly wider chair and squished into place. He stared at Sterling. "Ungle?"

Teal frowned. "Who's Ungle?"

Ark waved the question away. "Shhh! Wait your turn."

Rubbing his brow, Sterling realized that he felt completely drained. *Maybe I'm not suited to this line of work.* "Can't I just say that Teal put it in his reports?"

Ark snorted.

With a grim expression, Teal slipped onto the chair and laced his fingers behind his head. "Start talking."

As if ready for his analyst session, Sterling lay back, crossed his feet, and placed his hands on his stomach. *I could be buried in a tomb in this position.* "Yes, Ungle came to see me. He thinks he knows who has turned out the lights on Earth."

Bright sunlight filtered through the window and the purple vine swayed in a soft breeze. A spicy scent wafted through the air.

Teal's voice seemed to echo across a vast distance. "From Earth's vantage point, our world has vanished into darkness."

Sterling tapped his fingers together and relaxed, seeping like a puddle into the ground. "Yes. This mystery race has surprising abilities. They engineer new life forms, terra-form entire planets, and much more." He shrugged. "While we Luxonians and our sometime-allies have our own unique abilities, these beings can do everything we can—but better—with more flare."

Ark harrumphed.

"Truth is…they're extraordinary. But they aren't particularly social. They need a lot of elbowroom. We've only discovered a few pockets of their kind. The ones your people irritated" —he swiveled a glance at Ark—"must've been rather high strung. Very private. Hence their desire to keep Earth in the dark."

"What does this have to do with—?"

Ark speared Teal with a frown and nodded to Sterling. "Go on."

"Ungle believes that their race is obsessed with the nature of good and evil. So, he wants to learn everything they do…and more. Apparently, your studies caught his attention. He wants to know more about Ishtar and someone called Chai."

Teal jerked to his feet and paced across the room. "Chai is dangerous. He's mad."

Ark's head swiveled from Sterling to Teal. "Evil like Ishtar?"

Freezing, Teal glared at Ark. "Ishtar isn't evil. He's just—"

Sterling lifted his head. "How about his father, Neb? You called him evil."

"I can't debate that now. I want to know why Ungle wants to kill me. Or Zuri. We're the ones investigating—"

Sterling sighed, swung his legs off the couch, and sat up. "He isn't trying to kill you! Why do you keep insisting on making things more dramatic than they really are?"

Ark shrugged. "Ungle specifically stated that he wants your work to continue—" His pink cheeks blanched as he sat bolt upright. "Uh-oh."

Sterling jumped to his feet.

Teal pelted across the room and gripped Ark's shoulder.

"What?"

"Ungle doesn't want you to become distracted by anything…or anyone."

"Zuri is annoying, but he's not a distraction. He's—"

Sterling closed his eyes. His throat felt very dry. "Not Zuri. Sienna. He wants her to leave the planet—quietly." He swallowed. "I tried every argument I could think of."

Teal's gaze fixed on Sterling. "Then?"

"I tried to arrange a little accident. So, she'd go home."

"A *little* accident? I was nearly crushed by a boulder, my food was poisoned, and that wasn't a natural lightning strike."

"She's Luxonian. She would've survived." He scowled at Teal. "It wasn't *your* dinner by the way—it was hers."

Teal leapt at Sterling, grabbing him by the neck.

Ark sprang forward. Slapping Teal's hands off Sterling's neck with three tentacles, Ark wiped sweat from his face with another. "I'll need a swim after this."

Glaring, Teal jerked away and spat his words. "How could you? Sienna is completely innocent. I thought we trusted each other." He squared his shoulders. "I'll know better from now on."

Ark shoved them further away from each other and glanced from Sterling to Teal. "You don't understand. Ungle has a very persuasive nature. He can make a person's life remarkably challenging. He's quite capable of creating an interstellar incident and making it appear that a certain judge" —his eyebrows wigged in Sterling's direction— "is long overdue for a spell at Bothmal."

Teal wiped his hand across his mouth. "Seems to me that Ungle wouldn't be far behind."

Ark laughed. "Perhaps. But our Crestonian leadership has legitimate concerns. This mystery race will dictate the Universe's parameters…if we let them." His eyes widened as his voice rose. "It's one thing for Earth to face a hidden universe. What would happen to Lux if someone put your planet in the dark?"

Sterling collapsed on the couch. "Oh, God. I really will have a heart attack."

Teal shook his head and ran his fingers through his hair. "Not possible. Though, I rather wish…"

Sterling peered at Teal. "All right! I should've told you. Ungle's talk of good and evil…a life of heaven or hell. I didn't know what to do. Frightening Sienna seemed like child's play. An easy way to keep an ally happy."

"Easy way to lose a friend."

Sterling groaned. "I'll have to go to Earth now—won't I?"

"Someone has to keep an eye on you."

Ark swung his tentacles in various directions, clearly facing an impossible reality. "How will I ever keep you all in line?"

Sterling sank onto the chair. "Give me a moment."

Teal glanced at Ark. "At least Zuri and Sienna are safe."

Sterling closed his eyes.

Ark poked him in the back. "What?"

"Ungle warned me that if I failed, he'd take care of the matter himself."

Teal groaned.

With a long huff, bubbles swarmed through Ark's breather helm.

Sterling stood and pressed Teal's shoulder, meeting his gaze. "Sienna is safe. Really." His eyes wandered to the purple vine; it appeared to be waving goodbye.

Oh hell.

CHAPTER ELEVEN

—MOUNTAINS—

PROVIDENCE OF GOD

Tobia tried to sound curious. "So, where do we go next?"

Peering blankly ahead, Vitus frowned. "I'm thinking, you stupid oaf! If you'd be quiet, I might be able to come up with a solution to this problem!"

Tobia bit his lip. *I knew it. We're lost.*

Vitus tapped his foot and scratched his head. "I've been through here before, but someone's changed things.

Choking on a snort, Tobia clenched his hands. *Changed what? The trees?* He exhaled a long breath and stared at the woods before, beside, and behind him. No path. No village. No sign that a human being had ever trekked through this wilderness before. "Maybe we should go back to the last village and—"

Vitus swung around and glared at Tobia. "Those idiots don't know anything. Scoundrels. Worse than slinking wolves. They would've robbed us if given a chance."

Tobia closed his eyes to the memory of Vitus shuffling up to the village leader, his gaze darting every direction, and stumbling through a request to speak to the clan. A shiver ran down his spine. A rough shake made him blink back into the world.

"Don't think you can take a nap. We've got a long way to go today."

Always a long way. But we never get anywhere.

Vitus swung his loaded bag over his shoulder and started tromping to the right. He stopped short and turned to the left.

Tobia lopped along beside, peering out of the corner of his eye at Vitus. *He's more than lost. He's terrified.* He ducked under a hanging branch.

"Ouch!"

Tobia stumbled to a halt and looked up.

Vitus stood frozen in the middle of a briar patch. A vine of sharp nettles clung to his hairy arm.

Tobia swallowed. A veritable wall of needles blocked their path in nearly every direction. "I guess we'd better —"

With a grunt, Vitus slipped his knife from his belt and began hacking.

Tobia's throat went dry. "I don't think that's a good idea."

Vitus grunted and swore as he hacked right and left, sweat dripping down his arms and legs.

Tobia stood his ground. "You'll only get—"

"Oh, by the gods! It's got me."

After inching forward, Tobia stopped behind Vitus and peered over his shoulder. "Oh, Creation of God."

Blood seeped from uncountable scratches and cuts as thorns and vines gripped Vitus' arms and legs.

"Demon woods!" Vitus tried to shake loose but screamed with the effort.

"Stop! You're only making it worse." Tobia carefully and painstakingly pinched each vine and tugged it to the side.

Vitus fumed and whimpered.

Finally free, Tobia gripped Vitus by the arm and helped steer him backward, clearing the way as they went.

Once out of the brambles, Vitus threw himself on the ground and covered his face with his hands, groaning.

Tobia's gaze lifted from the pathetic figure to the glimmers of sun through the branches. The sun had lowered considerably since they halted for their mid-day meal. He sighed.

"I think I left something back at the last village. Would you mind if we retraced our steps, so I could enquire about it?"

Vitus lifted his arm and peered at him in a grieved manner as if Tobia were the stupidest boy on the earth, but he rolled to his side and staggered to his feet.

"It is getting late, and I don't want to get caught out in the middle of nowhere with you crying your head off over some little thing."

Tobia grimaced and turned around.

After some time, they ended up back in the village they had left that morning. Tobia strode to a woman he recognized.

"Hello, my name is Tobia. We were here this morning, offering trade goods." He flashed an embarrassed smile. "I accidentally left something behind. May I look for it?"

The woman nodded. "Certainly, Tobia. My name is Kamila. I'll help you look. What was it?"

"Oh, uh…something my father made for me before he died. My mother will be so—"

Kamila smiled and lifted a hand. "Say no more. I understand."

As they searched across the village and in the various dwellings they had visited that morning, Kamila asked Tobia about his family, and he described the members of his clan like warriors from songs of old.

When they came to the end of their search, Kamila perched her hands on her hips and frowned. She stood before Tobia in the village center and shook her head. "I hate to say you've lost it for good, but it's certainly not here."

Tobia shrugged. "It may turn up yet." He glanced at Vitus sitting under a tree in the distance, chewing moodily on a crust of bread. "Perhaps Vitus packed it up with the trade goods and forgot."

Kamila squinted at Vitus. Her mouth pursed in distaste.

Tobia stepped between Vitus and Kamila, blocking her view. He peered into her lovely eyes. “You know, Vitus has had a very hard life. He lost his wife and entire family to sickness some years ago, but he’s carried on the trade despite his loss and suffering.” He glanced at the sky. *God forgive me.*

Kamila tipped her head and leaned so as to peer around Tobia at Vitus. She smiled.

Tobia glanced over his shoulder.

Vitus met Kamila’s gaze. He sat up straighter.

Kamila swung around Tobia and sauntered over to Vitus.

Vitus scrambled to his feet.

Kamila extended her hands. “I’m sorry we were not more welcoming to you this morning.” She glanced aside and frowned. “There’s been trouble in the area, and it’s hard to know who to trust.”

Vitus, appearing very much like a rat caught in a trap, stared wide-eyed.

Tobia stepped to his side and locked on Kamila’s face. “It’s getting late. Is there any hope you could direct us to a safe place for the night?”

Kamila shifted her gaze to Tobia and smiled. “You’ll stay here, certainly. My family and neighbors would enjoy hearing about your people and adventures.”

Vitus’ mouth dropped open. His eyes shifted from Kamila to Tobia.

Tobia clamped his hand on Vitus’ shoulder as he spoke for both of them. “We’d be very happy to accept your invitation.”

~~~

Tobia sat next to Vitus as dusk settled into night. He rubbed his hands against the evening chill.
~~~

A short, stocky man with a thick beard and gray eyes, wearing a sleeveless tunic and a wide belt, sauntered near. He crossed his arms over his chest and peered first at Vitus and then at Tobia.

Tobia held his gaze.

"I'm Kamila's brother, Remy." He gestured to three other men assembled a short distance away. "We were hunting earlier. She told us about you." His gaze swept over Vitus again, and he scratched his chin. "She'll bring dinner out soon, but in the meantime, you can tell us about yourselves and your people."

Vitus lifted his head and opened his mouth, but Tobia gripped his hand, squeezing hard. "I'd be happy to."

Describing the best parts of their clan's nature and leaving out everything to their disadvantage, Tobia retold the story of Neb's invasion, the great drought, the terrible fire, and Ishtar's madness and exile.

The entire village assembled in a ring around the flickering fire as Tobia regaled them with the tales. Kamila brought venison, fruit, and stewed roots.

Vitus ate with alacrity, only glancing up now and again to grunt in agreement with something Tobia said.

His belly full and his story told, Tobia wiped his mouth with the back of his hand, sighing in gratitude and relief.

Remy chuckled. "You've told a wonderful tale, young man. Any ancient would be proud of such a recital." He glanced at the throng, his gaze lingering on his sister, Kamila, longer than the rest. "But I should warn you, there's been trouble around here of late." He wiped his hands on his tunic. "There're men who say they've come to trade, but instead they observe and later return to steal what they could not obtain through honest means."

Tobia looked at the assembly. Weariness and sadness enveloped him. "I'm sorry. I can see why you didn't trust us at first." His gaze wandered to Vitus who was now leaning on a larger man, snoring in a deep slumber.

He rose and edged Vitus to the side so the villager could slip out from Vitus' weight.

Remy shook his head and wandered over. Together Tobia and Remy led the sleepy Vitus to a grassy spot under a tree.

Vitus grunted and curled up, laying his head on his arm.

After plucking Tobia's sleeve, Remy gestured back to the circle of firelight.

Many clansmen and most of the women shuffled off to their evening duties and their own beds.

Remy perched on a log next to Tobia. "That sleeping fool can't help you through your travels." He glanced at Vitus slumbering form, little more than an outline of a shadow in the darkness. "Much as I hate to be the bearer of bad news, it behooves me to tell you that you have aligned yourself with either a wicked deceiver or an incompetent idiot." He clasped his hands over his knees. "That man knows nothing about trading."

Tobia sighed. "I realize that—now."

Remy shook his head. "How could your father let you go with such a fool?"

"He believed his wonderful stories. Somehow, Vitus managed to succeed when he followed in the footsteps of other clansmen. But this time, he thought he'd find his own way and start his own trade routes."

"That man" —Remy pointed to the snoring figure— "is no more capable of good business than a fish of walking about on land." Remy shook his head. "Take a word of advice. Go home and leave him to find his own way." He shrugged. "He might live." Remy met Tobia's eyes. "But at least, you'll survive."

Warm gratitude flooded Tobia. Someone actually cared about him. After Vitus' abuse, it felt like a gentle rain after a severe drought. He stood, stretched, and peered at Remy.

"I trust in the providence of God. We'll make it home again. I agreed to this journey, now I must see it through."

Remy glanced into the night sky. "Perhaps your coming was ordained from on high." He stood and pressed Tobia's hand in his own. "I hope we meet again."

Tobia nodded and glanced at Kamila's dwelling in the distance. "Me too."

CHAPTER TWELVE

—LAKE LAND—

DO THE RIGHT THING

Barak stood outside his home and stared at the mountains in the distance. Bright sunlight glinted off the peaks and colored the crevices with a blue tinge. Pointy evergreens lined the west side. He could almost feel the breath of the big cat, as it chased his clan from their ancient homelands, curl up his nose. A mad desire to run into the mountains shivered down his spine.

His shoulders slumped. "Do Aram and I share the same fate? I can't make sense of anything, but I'm supposed to lead others! Hah!"

A high, childish voice echoed. "Hah!"

Barak spun around so quickly he tripped over a root and fell backward. He searched wildly for someone to fix upon, but all he saw was the same thin air he had been talking to a moment before. Rising, he tapped his ears and shook his head.

At the base of the tree in front of him, a brown foot gripped an exposed root as if clinging to it for dear life.

Relief flooding his body, Barak heaved a sigh and grinned. "All right. Who are you? Heath?"

Silence.

"No? Then Lamech. Come on out, son." Barak took a step closer.

A whimper.

Barak stopped. "Eber? You know I'm not really mad." He frowned. "Yet."

Silence.

"All right, Shad? Rula? Come out here, or I'll come get you."

The foot retreated behind the tree.

Barak tiptoed forward and leaned around the tree.

The child backed up and bumped against Barak. He screamed.

Barak clutched his chest and spun around, ready to grab his miniature tormenter. He froze. His mouth fell open. "Who are you?"

The little boy wrapped his arms over his head and burst into sobs.

Barak closed his eyes, mumbling, "I will be calm," and then inhaled a deep breath.

Continuing to cry, the child's whole body shook.

Barak laid his hand on the boy's shoulder and led him to a bench. He went inside, poured a cup of water, returned, and put the drink into the child's hands, guiding him to drink between sniffles.

A few hard sniffs jerked the boy into apparent calmness.

Barak crossed his arms. "So tell me…who are you?"

"I'm Caleb."

"And why have you come, Caleb?"

"My brother told me about you. He wants to talk to you."

Barak rolled his eyes skyward and rubbed his forehead. "And who is your brother?"

"Amin. He's older than me and very wise. He's talking to Namah. He wants to work everything out, but I want to talk to you first."

Barak tapped his fingers to his lips, holding onto his calm demeanor by sheer force of will. "So, what do you want to tell me?"

Caleb laid his cup aside and propped his head on his

hands like a weary old man on the brink of despair. "Amin and I should go far away—maybe follow our father into the mountains. When everything is better, we can come back. But for now, we should leave."

A sharp pain stabbed Barak's chest as he plunked down at Caleb's side. "By Aram's soul—you're Ishtar's son."

Caleb blinked. "Father left. Mother died. Only Hagia wanted us—" He swallowed and shivered.

Barak rubbed his eyes. He patted Caleb's shoulder. "Well, about your leaving... Ishtar might come looking for you. Or you could get lost...or hurt...or something."

Caleb peered at his feet dangling over the edge of the bench.

Barak glanced into the blue sky. *Help me.* He tapped his fingers together. "Listen, Namah is a good woman, and perhaps she and your brother will—"

Caleb shook his head. "Amin said that Namah wants to sell us into slavery. Not everyone is nice, you know. Some people are very bad. Amin told me."

Stroking his short beard, Barak's eyes narrowed. "But not everyone is evil. Many people will do the right thing, if given the chance."

"Do you?"

"What?"

"The right thing."

Barak opened his hands expansively. "I do pretty well. My family seems to think so."

"And your clan made you their leader."

Barak ruffled Caleb's hair and grinned.

Two voices meandered close.

Barak and Caleb turned.

Namah and Amin strode around the dwelling ignoring the mother who suckled her baby, a young girl tending a stew pot, and four men who hefted a boat on their shoulders and headed toward the lake.

Amin stopped in mid-motion and scowled at Caleb. "What're you doing here?"

"Talking to Barak."

After offering Amin a reassuring pat on the shoulder, Namah strode forward and met Barak's gaze. "I know you're busy, but we need to discuss something important."

Barak glared at Namah and snorted. "I'd say we do. The last I heard, you were bringing food to these two. Now, I hear they're being sold into slavery?"

A rather alarming smile spread across Namah's face. "Yes, you're right. I admit my mistake. I apologized to Amin for my interference, and I ask for your forgiveness as well. As clan leader, you should've been consulted. These boys need a home, but very few people—"

His pent-up frustration flaring into rage shot Barak to his feet. "What? One can never have too many sons! Any man would be blessed to have these boys at his side." He patted the top of Caleb's head.

Caleb grinned.

Amin leaned against a post and folded his arms.

Barak puffed out his chest. "Tell me. Who's the lucky man to inherit such stalwart sons?"

Namah pointed at Barak. "You!"

Barak froze. He glanced from Amin's cold stare to Caleb's beaming face.

Caleb's eyebrows lifted as he stood and clasped Barak's hand. "So? Will you do the right thing?"

Barak closed his eyes. After a long silent moment, a chuckle bubbled up from deep within. He opened his eyes.

Without warning, two boys raced around the dwelling and careened into Barak. The first boy, laughing, pointed at the second. "I won!"

A sudden, surprising joy flooded through Barak. He tousled the two boys' heads.

Milkan strode into view, caught Namah's eye, and

nodded. “My friend, how good to see you.”

Namah smiled and bowed her head.

The first boy shuffled over to Amin. “Are you hungry?”

His gaze remaining steady, waiting, Amin glanced at Barak.

Barak locked eyes with the boy.

Milkan gestured to the door. “There’s food enough for all. Go inside, and I’ll arrange things.”

Still gazing at Amin, Barak cleared his throat. “Take Caleb and get something to eat.”

Amin nudged his little brother, and the two boys followed the others inside.

Milkan watched the children tromping into her house. “Will they stay long?”

“As long as need be.”

Patting Barak’s arm, Milkan followed the boys. “We’ll need more fish.” She stepped into the house.

Exhaling a sigh of relief, Namah clasped Barak’s hand. “You don’t know what this means to me. My heart can rest easy tonight.” She waved goodbye.

Barak watched Namah stroll away and listened to the happy chatter inside the house. He glanced into the bright sky and shook his head. “Hah!”

Thanks.

CHAPTER THIRTEEN

—DESERT—

FOREVER IN YOUR DEBT

Ishtar stared at the bleating herd of sheep and sighed. "Move on, you stupid—" He glanced aside. Not another soul on the horizon. Three distant tents, green fields, and plenty of rocks.

He set his jaw. "Not your fault." A memory flashed through his mind. His warriors lined up at his command as they faced the giants from the north…he and his men hunting for game…his men lounging around a sizzling fire, laughing, teasing, eating…" He closed his mind.

No!

Still, memories tore through his brain, searing all other thoughts.

He could feel his sweaty body steaming in passion as he and Haruz embraced on their first night together…the birth of his son with his head full of black hair…the ore-empty earth slipping through his fingers…the glinting knife in Haruz's hand—

He screamed. "Noooo!"

The startled sheep scattered, their bleats high and terrified.

His eyes snapped opened, his whole body shook.

Matalah stepped outside his tent and glanced up, shading his eyes from the sun.

Ishtar unclenched his hands and sucked in deep, calming breaths. He dropped his voice to a coaxing whisper. "Come, sheep. Green pastures…just ahead."

A fleecy lamb scampered near and wagged its tiny tail.

Running his fingers along its back, Ishtar surveyed the landscape. All lay quiet. No Matalah. No memories.

For the moment.

He struck the ground with his staff and started climbing. The sheep trailed along behind.

~~~

Ishtar stopped for a rest and stretched across a level spot. He opened his satchel, and slowly chewed his bread and cheese. Watching the rosy sunset deepen to black night, he battled every memory of his father. Neb in battle, jabbing a man with his spear…Neb sneering at Haruz, shoving her into a corner with an angry retort…Neb grasping Ishtar's knife and plunging it deep into his own breast.

Ishtar choked, his head dropped to his chest, and his bread crumbled in his fisted hand.

A lamb rose and sauntered near, butting its head into his arms.

Ishtar clasped the lamb and sobbed on its shoulder.

~~~

Ishtar led the sheep to greener pastures as days passed uncounted. The tents moved with them. He ate his allotment of bread and cheese and sipped at the single stream that gave life to this barren land. His tears joined the stream.

One hot day, two lambs frisked in innocent joy and bumped into each other. Their collision sent them careening backward where they sat down hard.

Ishtar laughed. "You are like Caleb and Amin—children at play with no notion of—" A burning flush worked up his cheeks.

Fresh tears flowed.

~~~

Ishtar stood on the top of a hill and glanced at an approaching figure. He swallowed back a sour taste and tried to ignore a disconcerting tightening in his stomach.

The eldest son of Matalah wound his way toward him.

Ishtar tipped his head in courtesy. “Abdul.”

“Ishtar.” Abdul did not incline his head but, instead, folded his arms across his chest and narrowed his eyes. “I’ve been watching you.”

Ishtar waited. He squinted in the bright light, watching the sheep, wary.

“You know your way in the world.” Abdul turned his focused gaze to the east. “Tending animals is hardly a fitting occupation for a man of your skill and intelligence.”

Ishtar’s fingers tightened around his staff.

“I’m sure my father didn’t mean to insult you, but he doesn’t understand the greater world. He travels but never goes anywhere.” A grin quirked on Abdul’s lips. “I’m a more fortunate man.”

“Fortune can be deceiving.”

A twinkle sparkled in Abdul’s eyes. “I’ve seen glorious horizons. There is a great deal to desire in this world.”

Swallowing, Ishtar shifted. He glanced at the three tents at the bottom of the hill.

“My family served you well in your hour of need. Perhaps you could render us assistance in return.” His broad smile flashed and disappeared.

A lamb butted Ishtar’s hand. He stroked its soft head.

“Of course, this is just between us.”

Ishtar glanced at Abdul. Their eyes met and fought for supremacy.

Neb’s gaze glowed through Abdul’s eyes.

Ishtar stiffened.
~~~

"Accidents happen. You understand." Without another word, Abdul turned and strolled down the hill, his garments billowing in the stiff breeze.

~~~

Ishtar led the sheep back to the Bedouin's camp, the cool evening air tingling over his arms. After washing at the well and nodding to the brothers around the fire, he made his way to the central tent.

Matalah sat cross-legged before a simple meal.

Ishtar remembered their first meal together. Weariness enveloped him.

Matalah's eyes lit up with an inner fire. "Ah, my adopted son. Come, sit, and enjoy a well-earned rest."

Ishtar offered a deep bow and sat by the old man. He leaned back on a firm pillow and stared at the array of food. "You are ever a kind host." Ishtar clasped his hands in his lap and looked down. "I was never so good to my guests…not even to my own family."

Matalah pressed his hand over Ishtar's. "Kindness is a gift, given to me, which I pass on to you." He smiled and met Ishtar's gaze. "Share it well." His smile vanished, replaced by a shadow of doubt.

As they ate, Ishtar peered out of the corner of his eyes at his host's worried face. His stomach clenched even as the good food nourished his exhausted body.

When they leaned back and sipped wine, Ishtar wrapped his fingers around the vessel and lifted his eyes from its depths to Matalah. "My friend—for so I dare call you—it's clear that something weighs heavy on your mind. If there is anything I can do—"

"I thank you, Ishtar. You've become like a son, though I hope not like some sons I must claim, though I'd rather not."

A murmured conversation passed outside the tent flap,
~~~

and Ishtar glanced over. The voices faded into the evening.

Matalah dropped his tone and leaned forward, tapping Ishtar's knee. "You're a more honest man, despite your troubled past, than my sons who, though they have been raised with love and security, are little less than cheats and thieves."

Ishtar sat up. "I'm here to listen…though I may know your story in part."

"My sons plan to gather men and take by force what would have been theirs if they had but waited for the proper time. I am not yet dead, but they wish me in the ground."

Ishtar shook his head. "Why? They are free men in charge of a prosperous territory."

"They wish to acquire more land and grow rich and mighty." He spat to the side. "It is no use telling them that a man's wealth grows cold and more heartless over time."

"They're willing to battle for more territory?"

"It's what they look forward to the most." He gulped the last of his wine and placed the cup aside. "My two eldest, Abdul and Wasim, asked permission to scout out the weakest tribes in the area, gather a strong force, and put our friends and neighbors to flight. Once the land is abandoned, they'll claim the herds and servants for their own."

Like a man witnessing before God, Matalah waved his hand high. "It is an evil plan, which under any circumstances would be difficult, but as they have little experience in battle, it's preposterous. They received no permission from me."

Closing his eyes, Ishtar clenched his cup. "But they did not listen?"

"Worse. They convinced my third son, Assam, to join them, and they're gathering such a force that it makes my blood boil. Every day they bring in strange men, insisting that I am too feeble to manage matters. They invent troubles that never existed."

Rising, Ishtar paced before the old man. "Your sons can't control what they are setting into motion."

Matalah waved to the doorway. "I told them—no one would be left unscathed by their evil ambition."

Ishtar stopped and stared at Matalah. "Such was my father. A curse he passed to me."

A shadow wavered at the door.

Matalah frowned. "Come!" His youngest daughter scampered forward with a full carafe of wine. Matalah gestured toward Ishtar, but Ishtar refused with a soft smile. Sending the girl away, Matalah wrung his hands. "Everyone must endure the battle between good and evil."

Kneeling before his friend, Ishtar peered into his eyes. "But you don't deserve such a fate. You are innocent."

Using Ishtar's arm as a brace, Matalah rose and strode to the doorway. He stared at the starry sky. "Innocence does not protect us. It only offers alternatives."

Standing aside with his hand on Matalah's shoulder, Ishtar gazed upon the same sky. "I will do anything you ask. Such ambitious plans take time. Perhaps your God will intervene in some way we can't yet see.

Matalah turned and stared into his eyes. "If you don't side with them, they'll turn on you." He gripped Ishtar's arm. "You must leave—soon."

Weaving around his friend, Ishtar crossed the room and turned at the doorway. "I'm not dead—thanks to your kindness. If it's not disagreeable to you, I'll stay a little longer. Let's see what the future brings."

Lacing his fingers together before his face, like a man in earnest prayer, a tremulous smile crossed Matalah's face. "God sent you." He peered at the twinkling sky. "My kindness has been repaid a hundred-fold."

"Yet I am forever in your debt." With a nod, Ishtar padded into the dark night.

CHAPTER FOURTEEN

—GRASSLAND—

INSECURE, HESITANT, AND UNWILLING

Lud sat hunched on a bench next to Obed, in the center of the village. He glanced at Eoban who stood before them. *They're going to fight. I know it.* He scooted to the edge of the bench.

Eoban faced Obed with his chest out, head up, and feet firmly planted on the ground. "I'm not going to continue in the trade business, and I never travel for fun. I plan to settle down. Who knows? Maybe I'll get married." He glanced at a group of women off to the side and grimaced. "Jonas will be *so* happy."

Obed rose, slapping his hands to his sides, and faced Eoban. "So why—?"

"I must." Eoban glanced around and met Lud's gaze. *You* understand, don't you, Lud?"

Obed stomped closer. "Why are you asking him, since I'll have to bear the burden—"

Eoban nudged Obed in the shoulder, one eyebrow rising. "A little adventure wouldn't do you any harm, either." He turned away. "I don't trust things as we left them, and besides, Barak has taken responsibility for Ishtar's sons. They have the right to know what happened to their father."

Obed's eyes narrowed as he placed his hands on his waist. "I never had much faith in Ishtar, and his degeneration merely proved his real quality."

A memory flashed through Lud's mind…Ishtar patting his arm, comforting and encouraging him on the day they walked away from bondage. Lud straightened and refocused his attention. "It's true, Ishtar did disgrace himself. But Eoban has a point. When Ishtar helped free the slaves, he defied not only his father but also an evil within that would've doomed a lesser man. His bravery and decency saved my life." He dropped his gaze. "The fact that he fell to the charms of an enchantress was partly my fault. My family rejected him. The insult was more than he could bear."

Obed flicked his fingers dismissively. "From father to son. Who could trust such a man? I know I can't!"

Exploding into wild arm waves, Eoban pounded forward. "Obed, you don't have to trust Ishtar! I just want to find him, and if he's alive, learn his plans. We've got to forge a new future without the fear that he might return someday. Certainly, his sons need to know the truth."

Obed tilted his head, a wary expression in his eyes. "I never noticed you giving them much attention."

"I've watched and listened. They're better boys than I had dared to hope. They must've inherited their temperaments from their grandmother. They're nothing like Haruz or even Ishtar, for that matter, though Amin does tend to brood at times. Who wouldn't under such a cloud? That's why I must go."

Obed shrugged. "It'll be a waste of time, but let's tell Jonas and see what she has to say." Obed strode sedately across the village, toward his wife.

Locking his hands behind his back, Eoban paced before the bench.

Lud glanced at Eoban. "You knew he wouldn't like the idea. Why didn't you just go alone on one of your famous journeys? You're a free man."

Bending low, Eoban met Lud's gaze. "Because I don't know what I am getting myself into, and I'd like traveling companions."

Lud's heart lurched into his throat and lodged there.

Obed followed behind Jonas. She marched up to Eoban, her brows furrowed, and her arms swinging like scythes ready for harvest. "What madness! You want to look for Ishtar? A risk for no gain—it's not like you."

Standing his ground, Eoban drummed his fingers on his leg. He turned to Obed. "If you're going to call in Jonas, I'm calling in Namah." He huffed, clearly put out. "While we're at it, we'll call in Barak and Amin…and Caleb too."

Lud dragged a hand over his mouth, smothering a sigh.

Eoban swung his glare from Obed to Jonas. "What do you say? I'll gather everyone, and we'll meet tonight."

Jonas nodded.

Eoban nudged Obed. "Mind if we convene at your place?"

Obed shrugged. "You're playing with fire, Eoban. But fine. The outcome will affect us all."

Lud slipped off the bench and watched as Obed and Jonas strolled away. He turned to Eoban. "Why make this even bigger…and harder?"

Eoban sighed. "It's not going to get any easier for a long while yet."

Lud lifted his hands in surrender. "Long as I don't have to join in your madness."

~~~

Jonas peered at a spectrum of colors ranging from pink to purple. She exhaled a long, slow breath. Tree branches stretched into the sky, creating a vision of contrasts. The black horizon etched the contour of the low hills, while the world around blended all the hues of the universe into one vast sheet of darkness. She murmured under her breath. "If other beings do exist, we'll learn the truth of it…whether
~~~

we hope to or not."

Obed strode up from behind and squeezed her shoulders. "Chatting to your invisible friend again?"

Jonas stiffened and faced her husband. "A blind man doesn't know what he can't see."

~~~

Barak stood outside his house, his thoughts trailing into the distance.

Eoban, silhouetted against the dark sky, strode forward. "Contemplating your existence?"

Barak rubbed his jaw. "As a matter of fact, I was just wishing for warriors."

Eoban grinned. "Now you're speaking my language!"

Pointing to the bench, Barak paced before his house. "Sit down, and we can discuss the foolishness of being unprepared."

Eoban clapped his hands. "You've spoken the desires of my heart! But I know a better place…with an appreciative audience. Come, let's go!"

A sudden pain twitched. Barak rubbed his neck and rolled his shoulders. "What're you talking about?"

"I am talking about whatever it was you were talking about—but with more details. Don't argue. Come on! Namah is already waiting, and it's getting dark."

"Eoban?"

"Don't ask! Just call those two boys. Where are they?" He cast his gaze around the village. "Amin and Caleb?"

"What do you want with them? They're fine. I've never seen them so happy."

Eoban lifted his hands. "Don't worry. I'm not about to put them in any danger. We just want to speak with them about their father."

A rock settled in Barak's stomach. He glanced at the
~~~

children playing in the distance. "Amin! Caleb! Hurry up, boys! We have business to attend to."

Amin and Caleb raced forward, grinning. "Hello, Eoban! Yes, Barak?"

Eoban's voice boomed. "We have a long journey before us, boys, adventure!"

Amin's eyes narrowed. "What do you mean?"

"I'll explain later. If I don't gather everyone now, it'll never happen, so hurry."

The three traipsed to the lake.

Namah sat in a small boat gripping the edges. Eoban ushered the rest in and rowed across the lake at an alarming speed. By the time they reached shore, the sun had set, and the glowing full moon rose.

Jonas laid wooden trenchers of minced goat meat, bread, honey, olives, dates, cheese and vegetables on a spread cloth. Carafes of spiced wine stood at the center.

Amin and Caleb dispensed with all formality, gathered what they could hold, and ate to their heart's content. Eoban followed, gesturing for Barak and Obed to hurry.

When everyone had eaten their fill and became acquainted with Eoban's plan, they fell into silence.

Pacing before them, Eoban clasped his hands behind his back. "So, who will come with me in search of Ishtar?"

Amin stood, his gaze following Eoban. "I will."

"Then I go too." Caleb gripped the edge of Amin's tunic. "To keep you safe."

Amin pried his brother's fingers off. "No! You can't. You're too little."

"Don't leave me!" Caleb broke into sobs.

Jonas hustled closer and wrapped her arms around the child. "Don't worry, Caleb. You must act like a man now and help keep the home fires burning. Milkan will need you more than ever if Barak is going away."

The settled rock exploded in Barak's stomach, and his

eyebrows shot up as he glanced around. "Am I going somewhere?"

Jonas peered at Eoban. "If you're determined to go, then you must take Barak along." She looked Barak full in the face. "I know you have a lot to do, but please—" She glanced at Eoban. "He might wander places where wiser heads would avoid."

Eoban winced and snapped a piece of thatch from the low roof. "Thanks for your confidence."

"Oh, Eoban, you know you want Barak to go. Obed would be of no use. He'd think too much and drive you mad."

Eoban tapped his fingers together, nodding. "I have no objection to Obed joining us. It might be good to have a thinking man along."

Rising, Barak tossed a branch on the fire. "Thanks for your confidence."

Eoban rolled his eyes and threw a stick at Barak.

Obed chuckled. "Contrary to all expectations, I'll take up the challenge and go with you, Eoban."

Jonas stared at Obed, her mouth dropping open.

Nausea rising, Barak folded his arms over his chest. "With Ishtar gone, I've been the leader of two clans. Would it be right for me to leave? And if Obed leaves…"

Eoban leapt forward. "No better time! Things are peaceful. Harvests have been good. We're doing well."

Obed nodded. "We'll have to appoint someone to lead in our absence."

Barak wiped sweat off his brow. "Who's strong enough to manage three clans, wise enough to keep everyone calm, and completely trustworthy?"

All eyes swiveled toward Lud.

Lud raised his hands in protest. "Oh, no! I'm a former slave, and I have no experience. Please, you'd be mad to leave me in charge!"

A gleam sparkled in Eoban's eyes. "Insecure, hesitant, and unwilling? You have all the qualifications, Lud. Congratulations!"

Lud glanced around with imploring eyes. "Eoban? Obed? Barak! You can't be serious. Think what this could mean?"

Eoban patted his shoulder. "Lud, can you honestly tell Amin and Caleb that we can't go in search of Ishtar because you're afraid of managing things for a few days?"

Lud glanced from Amin's sober face to Caleb's red-rimmed eyes.

"Oh, all right." He shot a glance into the darkness. "But I won't know what I'm doing."

Straightening, Barak heaved a long sigh.

CHAPTER FIFTEEN

—MOUNTAINS—

WHAT HAVE YOU DONE?

Tobia leaned against a fallen log and closed his eyes. The hot sun sent beads of sweat dripping down his face. Images of the villagers he had met and the trades he had made brought a smile smuggling up from his middle. He pictured Obed's surprised expression when he returned home with a bag stuffed with noteworthy goods.

Someone nudged his foot. He opened his eyes.

Vitus peered down at him, a sour expression making crow's-feet at the corners of his eyes. "Where's the bread?"

With a grunt, Tobia rose to his knees and fumbled through the smaller of the two bags at his side. He found a healthy chunk of bread and tossed it into Vitus' hands. "Here. But eat slowly. We won't get any more until we find the next village."

Tearing into the loaf, Vitus sank to the ground and leaned against a tree trunk. He chewed noisily and wiped the crumbs from his face with the back of his hand.

Swallowing back disgust, Tobia plucked another piece from the bag and took a sensible bite. Alternating bites of bread with sips of water from his skin bag, Tobia stared at the lush green valley spread before them.

Vitus rolled his finger around his mouth to clear out the last vestiges of his meal. He rose and tromped to the gurgling stream and splashed water on his face.

With his eyes, Tobia followed the man's every move.

Returning, Vitus plopped down and stared at Tobia. "Tell me about this God of yours."

Tensing, Tobia ran his tongue over his teeth and waited.

"I'm not teasing." Vitus shrugged. "I'd like to know where you get your power."

Tobia tilted his head and considered the man before him. "What makes you think I have power?"

"You make deals faster than anyone your age has a right to. Villagers fall under some kind of spell the moment you walk near."

"I'm just kind and honest."

Vitus shook his empty water skin and frowned. Scrabbling to his feet, he returned to the stream and filled the bag. He peered over at Tobia. "There's more to it than that. Your God aids you."

"I won't deny that's true. But only because…" Tobia's gaze wandered to the valley. "I don't know why. He just does."

Vitus lifted the dripping bag, tied a leather thong around the neck, and hooked it to his belt. Then he eyed Tobia. "I'd like some of that power myself."

"God does what he wants."

Vitus sat down and folded his hands over his knees. "I'd like to speak to Him face-to-face, as a man who contracts with a man."

His heart thudding in his chest, a hollow sensation shot through Tobia's middle. "I don't think you can do that. God is…big."

Vitus waved Tobia's concern away and snorted. "I have plans. Good plans."

"I'm not sure. I mean, you might offend Him and—"

"Don't be an idiot." Vitus snapped his fingers at Tobia. "Just tell me where He lives."

After sipping the last drops of water from his bag, Tobia

squeezed it flat. He glanced at Vitus, stood, and ambled to the stream. He laid his bag in the flowing water. "I don't really know. I've heard that He resides on the high mountains."

Peering into the distance, Vitus stared at the chain of mountains. He grinned.

Tying the mouth of the water skin tight, Tobia clenched his jaw. "We need to get to the next village."

Vitus rose and shoved Tobia in the shoulder. "We need to understand each other." He bent in closer, his eyes narrowing to angry slits. "I've let you lead because everything seems to work in your favor. But that's going to stop—today. I've been trading longer than you and if you've received help, I deserve the same assistance." He pointed to the mountain. "Since He lives there, that's where we're going."

Tobia gathered his bags and shoved them over his shoulder. Anxiety boiled in his stomach and dread weakened his knees. But as Vitus headed for the mountain, Tobia followed.

~~~

Tobia's shaky legs slowed to a crawl. The mountains loomed closer and more forbidding as the evening wore on.

Glancing back, Vitus frowned and stomped back to Tobia. He shoved him hard and knocked him backward. "Listen, idiot, we're not going anywhere else until after I get up that mountain and speak to your God. So you might as well move a little faster."

Evening turned to twilight and soon faint stars appeared between wispy clouds. They trudged on until Vitus' steps stumbled, and Tobia felt like he would collapse in an exhausted heap.
~~~

After dropping his bag beside a boulder, Vitus rolled into a ball and slept.

Dizzy and weak from hunger, Tobia crept to a tree and laid his bags aside. He rested his head on his knees. A black hole of depression swallowed him.

A sharp pinch on his arm forced his heavy eyes open too soon. Swallowing a sour taste and feeling like rocks were tied to his arms, he peered at the sky. A clear expanse of glorious stars twinkled down and a chill rippled over his body.

"Get up. We still have a long way to go."

Tobia shook his head and rubbed stinging sleep from his eyes.

"If you're hungry, good. All the more reason to move." Vitus stumped away. "You won't eat again until I say."

As the sun broke over the horizon behind them, the mountains loomed straight up ahead. Like a man possessed, Vitus climbed the nearest slope.

"Oh, God." Tobia's head swam. "We can't get up to the top. It's too high. We'll never make it."

"Who said we have to go to the top? You just said He's on the mountain. I can talk to Him when we get high enough. A God as powerful as yours will be able to hear me."

"He won't hear you! Or even if He does—"

Vitus climbed faster.

Scrambling for handholds and footholds, Tobia followed. His fingers tore against the rough surfaces and bled. His aching head threatened to burst.

As the sun climbed, dark clouds rolled in. A rumble in the distance warned of an impending storm.

Tobia stopped on a ledge about a third of the way up and wiped his sweaty brow. He peered up at Vitus. "It's almost noon. How long before we stop?"

"There's a wide space just ahead. We can climb up there

and rest a bit. It looks like the perfect spot for a private conversation."

As he scrambled over the lip of the edge, Tobia felt a dream-state block his vision. The eerie green expanse swirled into a nightmare, wavering and hovering like a roving monster.

Vitus dropped his bags and chuckled. "At last!"

Tobia fell to his knees and dropped his bags at his side. Hanging his head, he sucked in long draughts of air. A gust of wind whipped through his hair, sending a chill over his body. He glanced up.

Mountainous dark clouds roiled overhead.

Vitus peered at the sky and laughed. He pointed to the dreadful storm. "I think someone is waiting for me."

With a whimper, Tobia crumpled on the ground, his gaze riveted on the man before him.

Vitus threw his arms straight into the air, his wide eyes glaring like a madman at the turbulent sky. "Oh, God, I'm here! Listen to me!"

A zigzagging flash of lightning exploded from the sky. Enveloped in brightness too intense to stand, Tobia covered his face. A crack of thunder split the air and rumbled across the firmament.

Tobia rolled onto his face and squeezed his eyes shut. "I'm sorry. I'm sorry!"

Even with his hands over his face, Tobia saw another bright flash and heard another crash of thunder. He curled into a tight ball and rocked, moaning apologies.

After the third flash of light and deafening crack, silence fell.

Tobia stopped rocking and waited.

A pounding rain lashed his body. He lay still, exhausted, and frozen with fear.

When the downpour decreased to drizzle, a cool wind swept through and caressed him. Tobia relaxed and fell into a deep, dreamless sleep.

~~~

Tobia awoke with a neck ache and tasted grit between his teeth. Sitting up, he stretched and glanced around. The sun, rising in the east, pinked the mountainside. He looked around. "Where—?"

Only a few feet away, Vitus lay face up with his arms outstretched. His eyes stared without moving.

Tobia shuddered. He scrambled to his knees and scuttled closer.

Vitus lay frozen.

Poking Vitus' shoulder, Tobia tensed. "Vitus?"

Not a flicker.

Climbing to his feet, Tobia hovered over Vitus and tapped his face. His skin felt warm to the touch and there was a faint blush on his cheeks. But not a hint of movement.

"Vitus? You all right?"

Nothing.

Tobia surveyed the land before him with a sweeping gaze. Not a cloud in sight. He stepped to the edge of the path they had climbed. He shook his head and glanced aside.

A rocky ledge edged around the mountain. A goat trail? He trotted over and peered along the distance. It sloped downward. With a sigh of relief, Tobia returned to Vitus. He knelt by the man's side and shook his shoulder. "You've got to get up, Vitus. We need to get down the mountain."

Vitus rolled like a ragdoll. When Tobia pulled on his arms, he slumped to a sitting position, but his eyes remained fixed and unnaturally wide, staring at nothing.

A chill prickled Tobia's arms. He croaked his words, his throat dry and scratchy. "Oh, God, Vitus. What have you done?"
~~~

Chapter Sixteen

-OldEarth-

Your Intensity Disturbs Me

Ark crouched over Ungle's sprawled, green-splattered body and checked for life signs. One of Ungle's tentacles ended in messy pulp. Ark snatched a tube from a bag slung over his shoulder and tore off the seal. Lifting Ungle's unconscious head from the ground, Ark pulled on the breather helm and carefully poured the murky green liquid into the repository.

Standing beside Ark, Teal peered down at the scene, tense and waiting. Nearby, Zuri paced before a large boulder next to a winding stream. Sterling sat limply on the boulder, his head propped in his hands, looking sick and weak.

With a jerk and a snort, Ungle's eyes fluttered open. He stared at Ark, a puzzled frown rippling across his face. "What're—" Wincing in pain, he writhed, groaned, and lifted his injured tentacle. His eyes widened in obvious disbelief. "How—?"

Glancing aside, Ark barked an order at Zuri. "Get that medical kit you always carry around."

Zuri froze, peering at Ark. "It's for Ingots, not Crestas." Glancing at the writhing tentacle, he shook his head and swallowed. "But I've got a decent sickbay on board. Let's go." He glanced at Teal. "It's not far, hidden in a cave."

Ark backed out of the way as Zuri and Teal lifted Ungle's body and half-led, half-carried him over the stream to a large cave.

Sterling followed, his head bowed and his hands clasped behind his back.

Snug in the cave, the ship gleamed like an oval blue-black jewel. The dripping walls housed colonies of bats and lichen. A few stalactites hung from the ceiling on the right, while broken stems showed where the ship had barreled through.

After tapping a key code, Zuri stood aside and the shiny bay door rose from the cave floor. A bright shaft of light directed their steps to the interior.

Once inside the Ingot ship, Zuri pointed to a small niche in the rear. A reclining chair with armrests embedded with wires, tubes, and assorted medical gear stood prominently in the center. A large console with three colored panels arched from the left wall.

Zuri adjusted the seat, and he and Teal dropped Ungle in place, directing his tentacles to the side and laying the injured limb on a rolling side table. Zuri waved Ark to the console. "It's set up for Ingots, but there are overrides so it can be adjusted for the needs of other species. He glanced at Teal. "Though, I don't know if we've ever used it on a Cresta before."

Ark nodded, his gaze sweeping over the instrument panel. "I'll make do." He glanced up with a wavering smile. "We scientists are ingenious at this sort of thing." He locked eyes with Zuri. "Don't worry. It's not as bad as it seems. Our tentacles grow back."

Zuri closed his eyes and exhaled a long breath. "Yes, of course. I should've remembered."

Teal strode up and peered at Ungle's closed eyes. "I think he's out again."

Ark nodded. "Certainly hope so. I gave him enough painkiller to knock out the entire Cambial Zoo." He rubbed two tentacles together and scanned the console. "I'll just trim off the nasty bit, and in a few days, he'll feel as good as new, though a little off balance until it grows out again."

Sterling plopped down on a swivel chair near the front and called back. "So, you want to explain what happened?"

Zuri ran a hand over his gleaming helmet and sighed. "I didn't know what he was doing. At first, I just figured he was another Cresta scout…odd after everything, but then I'm not always kept informed of changes. Still, he was out of order."

Ark glanced up.

Frowning, Teal stepped over to Zuri, his hands on his hips. "So you blasted him? Why?"

"He kept shooting at birds. I couldn't understand what he was doing. But then I remembered that your friend, the cute little Luxonian, liked to transform into an eagle—"

Ark dropped the scalpel, and it clattered onto the tray. "Oh blast!"

Teal pounded the wall console with his fist and the bay door slid open.

Sterling jogged forward. "Wait! You don't even know if he actually hit her or where—"

Teal swung around, his eyes glowing in rage. "Then where is she?"

Sterling clutched his arm. "I'll come with you."

Teal shook Sterling away. "Not likely. You'll only slow me down." He swung out the door and charged into the glaring sunshine.

With an explosive huff, Zuri slapped his hand against his thigh. He glanced back at Ark. "I'll go. You stay and keep an eye on these two." His gaze swiveled from Ungle to Teal. "We've had enough accidents this cycle."

Ark retrieved his scalpel and started trimming. "I'd say."

~~~

Teal lifted Sienna's limp body off the dusty ground and
~~~

followed Zuri back to the ship.

As the two crossed over the threshold, Ark closed his eyes and muttered a long slew of Crestonian curse words.

Sweat poured down Teal's face as he stumbled forward. Sterling jumped in to assist.

Zuri jogged to the right and pointed. "Here's another pullout chair—for emergencies." He gripped a red handle and yanked it down. A smaller version of the chair Ungle occupied unfolded from the wall.

Cradling Sienna, Teal laid her down and brushed strands of hair from her face. "I don't see any injury, but she won't wake up."

Sterling placed his hand on her forehead, closed his eyes, and frowned in concentration. With a long exhaling breath, he opened his eyes. "She's still alive." He nodded while his gaze rolled over her. "It's good instinct to maintain the shape of your host environment." He glanced at Teal. "She's clever; I'll give her that. Most would've panicked—but she knew it would be safest to appear human if she was injured and couldn't travel."

Teal glanced over at Ungle's slumped form. "Is he going to live?"

Sitting in a padded chair against the wall, Ark waved a tentacle in droopy-eyed weariness. "Of course. It's not a life-threatening procedure, just rather painful." He yawned. "And tedious."

Zuri fell into a chair on the opposite wall. "My body can take almost anything but—by the Divide—I'm emotionally exhausted."

Sterling glanced at Teal. "Go pace around the ship or something. Your intensity disturbs me."

Teal stalked over to Ungle and glared at his sleeping form. "I ought to kill him."

Ark leapt to his feet. "Oh, no, you don't! Not after I just spent worthy corpuscles keeping him alive."

Zuri's eyebrows rose.

Ark puckered his lips. "I had to give him a transfusion—to counteract the shock." He blinked. "We're a brilliant race but not terribly resilient."

Teal nudged Ungle's shoulder. "Wake up, Cresta. I have questions you need to answer."

A long, drawn-out sigh from across the room turned their heads. Sienna whimpered and shivered.

Teal raced across the room and gripped her hand. "Sienna?"

Sterling stepped out of the way.

Her eyes blinking open, Sienna swallowed and opened her mouth to speak. No sound came. She frowned.

Sterling shrugged and glanced at Teal. "She'll be fine. She had a hard landing but no serious injury. She'll mend."

A rush of relief flooded Teal as he caressed her hand. "You understand, Sienna? You'll be all right."

Sienna stared at Teal as if she had no idea who he was, her puzzled frown etching deeper into her forehead.

Sterling laid his hand on her forehead and whispered under his breath.

Sienna closed her eyes, and her head fell gently to the side.

"Let her rest. She'll tell us what happened when she's feeling better."

Teal glared at Sterling. "I want answers—now."

Ungle's ragged voice rose like a cracked flute. "And you shall have them."

CHAPTER SEVENTEEN

—DESERT—

SHADOWS OF THE PAST

Ishtar stood, using his advantage in height, and bore down on Matalah's second son, Wasim, staring fixedly into the hard face and squinted eyes. "I understand your position, but I accept it only on my terms. I'll not oppose you, on the condition that you leave your father in peace. Keep your conquests to yourself and don't lure your sisters and younger brother with stories of power and wealth. Stay away and keep your glorified visions far from here."

Puffing out his chest, Wasim crossed his arms. "The power and wealth you speak of will be mine—and no illusion." His eyes wrinkled in amusement. "All my brothers and I ask is that you keep father from opposing us. Will you do this little thing?" All amusement died. "Consider your answer carefully."

Anger coursed through Ishtar's blood as he bit off his words. "I will stay at your father's side and do nothing to stop your treachery."

Wasim nodded and turned away.

Ishtar called after him. "Others may oppose you, though."

With a disdainful wave, Wasim paced away. His figure shimmered into the scorching heat.

~~~

Ishtar, calm and free from terrifying memories and
~~~

having put all thought of Wasim from his mind, climbed the hills to greener pastures. As the days slowly passed, he watched the lambs frolic in innocent abandon. One persistent yearling butted against him repeatedly.

"All right, you win!" Ishtar bent down and rubbed her thick fleece.

Contented, she ambled off in search of new pleasure.

Ishtar threw up his hands. "So like a child! You plague me for attention, and when I'm finally willing—" His gaze fell on a group of men climbing the hillside. He braced himself.

Matalah's third son, Assam, strode at the head of the assembly and stepped up to Ishtar with a hand extended.

Glancing away, Ishtar rebuffed the gesture.

Unruffled, Assam grinned. "My eldest brother, Abdul, requests a meeting before we begin our conquest." The lines of his face tightened into dread seriousness. "You must come. We're not far."

Ishtar nodded, and using his staff, he descended the hillside. As he glanced back, his eye caught the lamb that had nestled in his arms and was only now beginning to make forays into the wider world. He felt a pang in his chest as he considered her response when she came seeking him, and he was no longer there. Caleb's face floated before his eyes. Ishtar stumbled.

Assam turned and frowned.

Irritation washed over Ishtar, and he waved the man on.

The group wound down the hillside onto the barren plain. Ripples of sand and dots of desert weeds covered the landscape. No insect or animal movement caught his eye, except a large bird soaring above. *What could it possibly hope to find here?* Ishtar shook his head and dropped his gaze as they marched along.

As the sun began its descent, Assam's voice rose in a business-like tone. "We're making our final plans, and we'll leave as soon as everyone is ready."

Ishtar squinted in the afternoon sunshine, using his hand to block the blinding rays. Like a splash of cold water, the sight before his eyes sent a rippled shock over his body.

A large assembly of men busied themselves in battle preparations. The sight of so many weapons and hardened men stole Ishtar's breath away. This was hardly the idle fantasy of mere boys. Matalah had been right—his sons were the tools of a much greater force.

Assam flashed a grin and gleefully shouted a battle cry as he lunged forward to greet his comrades.

Ishtar followed more slowly, his heart pounding.

In the center, dressed for battle with a long sword hanging at his side and knives tucked in his belt, stood Abdul.

Ishtar halted on the periphery, watching the excited men boast and gesture, building themselves into a fever pitch. Pounding blood coursed through his own veins. Faces floated before his eyes—Neb, Hagia, Aram, Obed, Tobia, his wife and sons—as if there were no past but only a great muddle of present moments involving all the people who had been important to him. How could a man build a future when the past would not leave him be?

Abdul peered at Ishtar, and for a moment, they were alone in the world, staring at each other, taking one another's measure. A gleam entered Abdul's eyes. "So, my father's friend has joined us at last. Good of you to come."

Ishtar inclined his head. "Your invitation could not be ignored."

Abdul gestured curtly. "Come then, we'll get started. I have a few men I want you to meet. They're assembled in my tent."

Ishtar followed as the sun touched the horizon.

Abdul plunked down on a pile of pillows, leaving Ishtar to stand. He waved to the assembled men, hardened warriors every one of them. "Our plans are complete, except for one small thing. We'd like your cooperation in a simple matter."

Ishtar clasped his hands, his patience wearing thin.

"Your part is most important, for it will help us in all our future plans." Abdul waited.

Ishtar pursed his lips. "Speak plainly. What is it you want from me?"

"Lead my father into battle against us." Abdul grinned, apparently amused by Ishtar's frozen reaction.

His throat tightening, Ishtar swallowed against a choking sensation. His words dropped to a whisper. "You want your father out of the way."

"Just so."

Ishtar's hands trembled. "In this, I am your equal at least." He clenched his jaw. "But I never wanted my father to die—only his evil to end."

A scowl rode across Abdul's forehead, one eyebrow rising. "There is no other way. If you lead him into battle, he'll have the honor of a valiant death. If you abandon him, it'll be mindless slaughter. Which would you have? Honor or disgrace?"

Ishtar's voice rose to a fevered pitch. "Is it your father's disgrace to be murdered by his son?"

Abdul poked the air before Ishtar. "Unless my father confronts us honestly, our mission cannot succeed. I wouldn't be a worthy son if I didn't give him the opportunity to defend himself."

Ishtar unclenched his teeth and sucked in a deep breath. "He is no threat to you! Why must you make such an evil choice?"

"The future is unforeseeable. I cannot always watch my back, uncertain of his loyalty."

"You can speak of loyalty? You, who have *none?*"

"My father must see—he has no choice. He can't remain

hidden in the folds of his tent, embraced in self-righteousness. We are the heirs of this land. We must decide the future. I am not content to die as I was born."

"You want me to convince your father to go into the open battle and be killed by your men?"

"Yes."

"And this seems *honorable* to you?"

"How does an old man wish to die? No valiant tales are told of quiet lives endured in peaceful times. Better to die in a struggle for home and position than to die mourned only by the plaintive wailing of a few old women."

"Even when that struggle is against his own son?"

"We are all brothers…or sons under the same sky."

Ishtar shook his head. "I could reason better with the sheep."

"The sheep are mine."

All emotion burning into ashy cinders, Ishtar squared his shoulders. "I will tell your father what you've said. Whether he comes to offer battle or self-sacrifice is more than I can say." Ishtar turned to leave.

Abdul called after him. "Ishtar! You'll ride out with him."

The flap fell back into place as Ishtar stepped into the dim light.

~~~

Ishtar rose from his bed of softened earth in the crook between two sheltering boulders, blinked at the rising sun, and dusted off his tunic. He tromped over the hillside while the sheep gamboled along behind. Once on the plain, he blocked the hot sun with his arm, and directed his steps to Matalah's tent.

Outside, a low fire smoldered under an empty pot. Camp activity had stilled to a deserted silence. Only one
~~~

attendant came and led the sheep to their enclosure.

Ishtar passed around the fire and entered the tent.

Matalah, in his usual place, sat still and quiet. His shrunken frame bowed as if to reflect the breaking of his heart.

After embracing the old man, Ishtar stood aside and told his dreadful news.

Matalah's head dropped lower on his chest. His eyes were open, but his gaze remained unfocused.

Pacing closer, Ishtar crouched and peered into the old man's face. "So, what now, my friend? Will we go out together and meet the enemy?"

Matalah lifted his head and raised his hands in as if in supplication. "Against my own sons? My flesh is taken from my frame and attacks me! Those I held as babes and loved as boys now hate me as men."

Swiveling on his heel, Ishtar turned and pounded to the other side of the tent. "But they'll destroy you if you do nothing."

Matalah rocked back and forth, his arms wrapped around his middle. "My heart beats by some command that is not my own. If I could fight a heartless enemy, I would be satisfied, but how can I wish to murder a part of myself?" Peering up, Matalah locked his gaze on Ishtar, and tears filled his eyes. "I love them—even yet. They are my second self. They look like me; they sound like me. Though they have forsaken me, they cannot forget me altogether. They, too, will grow old and have sons, and my countenance will accuse them through innocent eyes."

Ishtar bowed his head, pain searing through his middle. "Your words ring more true than you know. My sons will inherit my guilt without knowing the reason or the price paid for my pride and ambition."

Matalah sighed. "Ever is it so."

Returning to Matalah's side, Ishtar gripped his friend's

arm. "But I have outlived my horrors, and the shadows of the past no longer claim me."

"God is gracious to those who repent—"

"It was *your* goodness that set me free. If I can offer my life to you in gratitude for your generosity, I only help myself to decency and peace."

Matalah groaned. "It is my hour to wish for a quick death."

Ishtar strolled to the doorway, lifted the tent flap, and peered out. "Death will come soon enough." He glanced back. "Let's go out and discover what awaits us."

Matalah's hands spread wide. "I have nothing to offer that will gain us time or strength…or imbue them with forgotten decency."

A strange, unexpected peace settled over Ishtar. "There are things your sons do not know. Even things that you do not know. The goodness you bestowed on your neighbors—even on your herds—will return to you in the end."

"What you say may be true, but my sons won't care for such philosophy. They want a quick gain, no matter what the cost." He rose and tottered to the opening, standing next to Ishtar. "All my life is to be thrown to the wind."

"You were brought into the world for a purpose and shall be held accountable for your part only."

Matalah's arms reached into the air beseechingly. "But they are my sons. Surely, I share the guilt in what I have helped to create? Has my life not been made worthless?"

Ishtar clenched his hands and stared at his friend. "*You* are not worthless."

Matalah closed his eyes and dropped his head to his chest. He murmured under his breath and then opened his eyes. Straightening, he started forward. "I still have a few attendants and camels; they will lead us to my sons."

Ishtar laid his hand on Matalah's shoulder. "You have

less to regret than most mortals."

Matalah sighed as he stepped outside. "But my heart is broken, nonetheless."

Ishtar understood the feeling.

CHAPTER EIGHTEEN

—WILDERNESS—

A SINKING FEELING

Eoban laughed as he slapped Barak on the back. "Just like old times! I remember hearing stories about the great cat hunt—" He yanked a tree branch out of his face. "And I've always wondered how you managed to survive. You must carry some special charm to keep you free from harm."

Barak frowned and hoisted his pack over his shoulder as he climbed over a fallen log. "You hardly know the whole story, or you'd never say that I stayed free from harm. On that particular occasion, I was mauled by a ferocious cat and abandoned by my friends. Hardly a charming experience, I assure you."

Eoban winked at Obed. "I'm sure that if Aram were here, he'd have a few details to add."

"If Aram were here, he'd probably knock you on the head."

Eoban burst out laughing. "Oh, how I wish he were here. He'd add a dash of excitement to our dreary wanderings." Eoban turned just in time to have a branch slap him in the face. He swore, bringing a smile to Barak's face.

Obed hustled past Eoban and gripped Barak's shoulder in a brotherly fashion. "Don't let him bother you. I remember the time I took Onias to the wilderness for a cure. It wasn't easy, but we both returned better for it. There's a great deal in the natural world that can benefit us."

Amin jogged along behind, a frown building between his

eyes. "You told Jonas that you didn't believe—"

Obed turned around and walked backwards, his eyes narrowing. "What?"

Amin quickened his step and brushed past Obed. "Oh, nothing. Just, Jonas told Namah that you couldn't see anything beyond your reach."

Obed swiveled around, his gaze following the boy. "You shouldn't listen to women's gossip. It'll lead to something unpleasant."

Silence ensued as the three tromped through the tree-filled hillside.

Amin bent his head and pursed his lips tight.

Eoban broke the heavy silence with a chuckle. "You remember Gimesh, Barak?" He gave Obed a friendly shove. "There's a story worth retelling."

Barak picked up speed.

They broke free of the trees and turned straight toward the summit of the hill. Eoban panted as he climbed. The air grew heavy and moist, sending perspiration slipping down his face.

Barak pointed ahead and nodded. "Eoban's right. I'd never seen a man like Gimesh before." He glanced aside. "You may not believe in unseen powers and miracles, Obed, but I don't know how anyone could explain Gimesh's sudden appearance. It was more than mere luck."

Obed rolled his eyes. "I beg you, please don't start. So a man appeared at an opportune moment and decided to help you. What's so strange about that? It doesn't take an act of God to have good luck, surely."

Barak grinned. "If only you saw Gimesh!"

Once they reached the top, Eoban threw down his walking stick, bent over, his hands on his knees, and took long, slow breaths. "There'll be time enough to chat about mysteries and miracles, but right now, let's eat." He glanced aside. "Obed hurried us on so this morning that I barely got a morsel in my poor, parched mouth." He flopped onto the ground.

Amin laughed and then dropped to the ground in a fair imitation of Eoban.

Obed glanced at Barak and shook his head.

Sitting up and leaning against a tree, Eoban sighed in contentment. *So far…so good.*

Barak stood with his hands on his hips, much like a mother hen ready to scold her unruly brood. "I suppose it won't do any good to mention that the sun will set soon, and there is no decent shelter around." He swept his hand from side to side as if to emphasize his point. "No rocks or caves or—" Barak's scowl deepened. "What's that?"

Obed placed his packs in a neat, orderly pile. "What's *what?*"

Barak pointed into the distance; a plain lay before them with the mountains as a backdrop. "Look over there. Is that a migrating tribe?" He glanced aside. "You know the people in these parts, Eoban?"

Amin's eyes widened as he peered at Eoban.

Eoban slapped his forehead and ran his fingers down his face. "I knew people in these parts a long time ago, but things change. By the blazing sun, even the hills seem to move around. It could take weeks to locate a friendly clan." He sniffed and rubbed his nose. "If they're migrating, they have bigger worries than we do."

Obed studied the distant tribe. "It might be wise to know who is traveling so close, especially as we have no real defensible—"

Eoban rummaged through his bag. "Defensible? What're you worrying about? You think someone's going to attack us? Here?"

Obed shrugged. "It's been known to happen." He glanced at Barak. "And I doubt any miracle would save us."

Amin turned on his side and perched his head on his hand, a scowl darkening his face.

Eoban rose with a groan, munching on a piece of stale bread. Sweaty and feeling rather put out by their attitude, he strode to Obed's side overlooking the plain. "If Barak thinks a bird from the sky will rescue us from danger, I say good for him as long as he lets me sharpen my spear. After all, he might be right. But unless you see—" Scanning the horizon, every muscle in Eoban's body froze. "You idiots! That isn't a migrating clan—*that* is a war party!"

All eyes turned toward Eoban. Obed lifted his hands. "We tried to tell you."

Barak nodded. "We did."

Amin scampered to his feet.

"Stop blathering and get your stuff. This is no place to stop and rest. What were you thinking? Didn't you hear Amin sigh in consternation when you fools started complaining about your bellies? Act like men, would you?"

The war party below turned and started up the hill.

Eoban thrust his bags over his shoulder, helped Amin load up, and gripped the boy's arm.

They all scrambled around to the far side of the hill and then slid their way down to the dusty plain.

Stark mountains rose up in the distance.

As they hurried across the barren land, long shadows loomed on their left. Dust rose in the wake of their footsteps. All afternoon, they trudged—marching, walking, stumbling, and limping. As the sun dropped near the horizon, they began to climb the slow, winding way up the mountainside.

At a steep juncture, Amin slipped backwards, rose too quickly, offset his balance, and fell on his back. He cursed under his breath.

Hustling forward, Eoban extended his hand. "Hold on,

Amin. You are moving too fast for your elders. We don't want anyone to think we're running away." He hefted Amin to his feet, but the boy jerked his arm free.

"I'm not running *away*. I am running *to* something."

Obed pivoted on his heel and scowled. "Don't take that tone—"

Barak lifted his hand in concession as he laid his bundles on the ground. "We all need a rest. Besides, we should discuss where we're heading. Last I heard we were just going to look around these hills and perhaps up in the mountains a little ways." He glanced at Eoban. "You're not thinking about going all the way to the mountains, are you?"

Obed stowed his things in a pile next to Barak's and sat down. "We're liable to kill ourselves, running around out here in the dark. We need a fire and some food. I'll get a blaze going if we call it a night."

Eoban nodded. "A fire out here won't alert anyone. Make it a modest blaze, Obed." He dug a stone out of his sandal and glanced at the boy.

Amin stood stoop-shouldered, still frowning, his bags high on his back.

"What's bothering you, Amin?"

"We can't go back until we find my father."

Barak shook his head. "We don't know when or if we'll find him." He waved Amin closer. "You know as well as anyone, Ishtar may be dead—"

Amin grimaced. "I know. But Caleb needs to know the truth."

Obed snorted. "Oh, *Caleb* needs to know."

Eoban flicked the stone at Obed. He turned and beckoned Amin closer. "A good meal will make us all feel better." He glanced up. "Obed, start a fire, and I'll take a look around. Maybe some delicious dinner is traipsing around these woods just waiting for us." He squeezed Amin's shoulder playfully. "You gather wood while Barak and I see what we can find."

With a shrug, Amin nodded.

Barak ran his fingers through his hair as he surveyed the dim twilight. "It's pretty dark out there. What do you think we'll see besides glowing eyes surmising whether we'd make a decent meal?"

Eoban snorted. "Barak! You are embarrassing yourself." He glanced at the boy. "Amin, don't listen. Any animal that wants to come my way is welcome. I love meat of all kinds."

Barak chuckled and rubbed his tired legs. "All right! But please don't attack anything bigger than the two of us combined."

Eoban snatched Obed's spear and handed it to Amin. "I'll leave you in charge." He nodded, one warrior to another. "Protect those that need protecting."

Amin took the spear with the hint of a grin.

Obed waved Eoban away and proceeded to clear a space for the fire.

Barak nudged Eoban with his spear.

"Come on, Brave Hunter! It's nearly dark, and every animal with decent hearing knows we're here."

The two moved into the twilight.

~~~

Amin watched Eoban and Barak traipse away with a sinking feeling in his chest. He shook himself and turned his attention to Obed.

After gathering a handful of tinder, Obed pulled out his flint and forced a spark. After a moment of smoldering, a flame broke to the surface.

Amin scampered to the edge of the small circle of light and gathered twigs. He bundled them into his arms and
~~~

started back to the small blaze when a large, bronzed hand gripped his arm. Thrashing, he tried to escape but the hand gripped tighter. Suddenly, he found himself facing the torso of a giant. With a quick thrust, he was forced to turn around. He called out, but it was too late.

CHAPTER NINETEEN

—MOUNTAINS AND DESERT—

BURY THE DEAD

Tobia glanced over his shoulder and shuddered.

As if tied to an invisible thread, Vitus traipsed blindly behind Tobia's footsteps. It appeared as if he had no other purpose in life than to keep in step with his companion.

Tightening his jaw, Tobia changed direction suddenly, but Vitus, apparently seeing through his unseeing eyes, stuck close, like a chick to its mother. "Seven days of this. I'll soon go mad." Tobia stopped and shaded his eyes, surveying the mountainous landscape. He licked his parched lips. A sound turned his gaze.

Trickling water gurgled over the never-ending buzz of insects.

Tobia sighed and closed his eyes a moment in relief. "Thank God." He rushed forward, scurried around a boulder, and encountered a tiny waterfall and a thin green patch growing from the mountainside. After slapping water into his parched mouth, he unslung his water bag from his shoulder and laid it on its side. Still licking his lips, he watched fresh clean water flow into it. Then he fell back against the white cliff side and drank a long slurping draught to his heart's content.

After wiping his mouth, he peered up. There stood Vitus, heaving deep breaths, stoop-shouldered, his clothes stained with sweat. His lips cracked.

"Oh, God, yes." Tobia led Vitus to a shady spot and pulled the water bag from the man's shoulder. After filling it, he put it to Vitus' lips, praying that he'd drink willingly. Some days, Vitus let the water pour down his chin like a naughty child.

With his trembling hands limp at his side, Vitus tipped back his head.

Tobia directed the water into his mouth.

Vitus slurped and drank readily, an occasional grunted moan escaping his lips.

Tobia eyed the man. "That enough?"

Vitus didn't answer. He never answered. He just stood and stared vacantly ahead.

With a quick shake, Tobia lifted the water skin again and held it against Vitus' mouth, but this time Vitus didn't respond. The water merely dribbled down his chin. In resignation, Tobia slung the water skin bag over Vitus' head and laboriously gathered his own bags. He didn't have much left. Just a few trade items and what scraps of goat meat he had saved from their last meal.

Trudging along an animal track, they wound northward. When they finally reached the other side of the mountain, Tobia felt relieved, as if he had actually accomplished something. "There's surely a clan around here somewhere…"

But there never was. Another bend, another vista, another trail to follow. But no sign of another clan.

Struggling forward, they passed between the mountains and wandered downward into a drier, desolate land where fine sand shifted underfoot.

Tobia stopped and wiped his brow. "The blind leading the blind."

The land stretched before him as a vast panorama of open space. The intense blue sky spread wider than he had ever imagined possible.

In exhaustion, they stopped in the shadow of a high slope and ate the last of their food. They soon gulped the last of their water. Tobia's heart clenched. He searched but found no stream or watercourse in sight.

With no other options, Tobia rose and started forward, always toward the falling sun.

Soon, his tongue felt thick and his lips bled. He glanced aside at Vitus. The man drooped like a wilted flower, his eyes as vacant as ever. "At least, he's not complaining." But a headache pounded in the back of Tobia's head, and he groaned.

A dark speck in the distance caught his attention. Bracing his hand on his forehead as a shield against the light, he squinted. He knew it was useless, but he felt the need to speak out loud, as if it might light the spark that would ignite Vitus' intelligence. "What's that?"

Forms wavered ahead.

Tobia forced himself to stand, though his legs begged to crumple. Dread warred with excitement, raising nausea from his middle. He glanced at Vitus. "How am I going to explain you?"

The shapes of men on plodding camels grew larger and more distinct, heading slightly to the north of his statuesque-like position, but suddenly they altered course and headed directly toward him.

Sweat trickled down Vitus' flushed face, his back bent low, and his hands hung limp at his sides.

Draped from head to foot with a thin white material, the figures appeared to be heading some place but not anxious to get there.

Tobia stepped closer to Vitus.

A tall, thin man with a dark complexion and black hair halted before them. "Hail, stranger. My master would like to know what brings you out in the heat of the day without beast to carry you or friends to protect you."

Tobia cleared his parched throat, but his voice sounded raspy even to his ears. "We're lost. My guide here" —he pointed to Vitus— "has been injured, and I am not fit to lead anyone—even myself." He tried to smile but failed.

The men, looming so high above him, exchanged amused glances. The old man beckoned another to his side.

This companion, his lower face covered in a cloth, appeared younger and more robust, though from his narrowed-eyed expression, Tobia sensed the wariness of an experienced warrior.

Tobia offered a respectful bow and nearly tumbled over with the effort.

The shrouded figure spoke in a husky voice that tingled in Tobia's ears. "You're not the first to get lost in these lands. But don't despair; it's possible to survive and even grow stronger though the journey." He waved with a light flit of his hand to the north. "We're meeting the sons of my patriarch here, but it may not be a happy reunion, or we'd take you with us."

Desperation rose to a shriek in Tobia's mind.

The man leaned forward. "Perhaps we could direct you home again. Where do you live?"

Griping Vitus' arm, Tobia struggled to stay on his feet. "If I knew that, I wouldn't be here. Please, we're exhausted and near death. Take us as slaves if need be, but don't abandon us here."

The old man nudged his mount forward. "We'll assist you then, for it would be offensive to God to do any less." He commanded his men to assist Tobia and Vitus to mount.

Like a weak child, Tobia straddled the camel behind the shrouded figure, and Vitus was set behind the old man.

As they started forward, the old man turned to Tobia. "Your name?"

"I am called Tobia, son of Obed of the Grassland, though we are now in alliance with the clan of Barak."

The shrouded figure turned suddenly, his eyes widening.

Tobia frowned, and his pounding head swam in the heat. He closed his eyes and prayed for mercy.

~~~

Tobia awoke to a delicious coolness caressing his aching body. He propped himself on one elbow and glanced around. In the darkness, the light of a full moon slanting into the tent aided his sight. Sleeping forms lay near. He leaned closer and recognized Vitus' emaciated frame and his familiar snoring broken by short bursts of blowing air.

After throwing off the light blanket, Tobia rose and started toward the open flap. He stretched and licked his dry lips. Rubbing his arms, he emerged from the tent into the chilly night air.

A silent figure stood alone, peering into the starry sky.

Stepping quietly, he made no discernible noise, yet the still form shifted as he drew close. They stood together for a moment in silence. The stars, clustered in milky splashes, spread wide across the sky.

Without turning, the figure spoke. "I was hoping you'd awake before the others. The sun will rise soon, and then we must accomplish our journey."

"You wish to speak with me?"

"I do, very much, though I doubt you'll feel the same."

Tobia swallowed a sudden fear.

The figure turned and faced Tobia. "Don't you know me?"

Tobia stood his ground though his legs trembled. "Your voice sounds familiar, but so much has happened in these past months—I might not recognize my own family."

The figure unwrapped the cloth that hid his face. Ishtar opened his hands, palms out, as if in surrender.

A jolt surged through Tobia's body. "I thought you were dead." He choked. "I didn't mean—" He clenched his
~~~

hands. “But no one could survive—”

Ishtar placed a gentle hand on Tobia’s shoulder and steadied him. “I did die. At least the man you knew died.” He let his hand drop to his side. “I am not the man I was.” His gaze returned to the horizon, now turning rosy with the hint of day.

Following Ishtar’s example and facing the new day, Tobia shuddered. “I’m glad to hear you say that. I couldn’t manage—” He glanced back to the tent where Vitus lay sleeping. “Another problem.”

“I didn’t say your problems are over. By coming with us, you join a doomed expedition—a father facing death by his sons’ treachery.” A bitter chuckle rose in Ishtar’s throat. “Fate never ceases to amaze me.”

Tobia’s eyes widened. “I once believed that growing up meant I would have more say over my life, but I was wrong.” He pointed to the tent. “But what about Vitus?” Stepping closer, he gripped Ishtar’s sleeve. “He can neither run nor fight. He’s as helpless as a child. Is there no safe place for him?”

Ishtar glanced aside. “I’ve prayed for an escape, but I’ve found no other path than the one we’re on.”

The murmuring of men’s voices turned their attention. Matalah’s men pointed to the horizon.

Tobia and Ishtar stared as a cavalcade of hazy silhouettes rose into view.

Ishtar licked his lips, and Tobia held his breath. “Who?”

Suddenly, from the right and left, armed warriors sped into view, surrounding the approaching group, thrusting their spears and swinging clubs.

Matalah’s men shouted and chattered, pointing at the battle playing out before their eyes in the distance.

Tobia frowned. “Are those men being attacked?” He swallowed hard and peered at Ishtar. “Are we being attacked?”

Folding his arms, his legs spread and braced, Ishtar watched the scene. A slow smile crept across his face.

Shouts rang through the air.

Matalah sprang from his tent and gripped Ishtar's arm. "Must they rush the hour? Is there not time enough for our destruction?"

His voice low and controlled, Ishtar glanced at his patriarch. "They are the ones being destroyed."

Matalah leaned forward, squinting into the rays of the rising sun, his lips compressed and his jaw ridged.

Suddenly, the lead rider turned and faced his pursuers. The pursuers encircled their quarry. A quick spear thrust missed its target. More spears loosed as camels were driven into the fray. Warriors swung clubs with abandon, many finding their mark and sending men tumbling from their mounts.

Tobia, Ishtar, Matalah, and his faithful men watched in heart-stopping silence.

Men and beasts lay sprawled on the desert floor. Only the loudest shouts and clinks of battle could be heard as the shapes rose and fell.

Matalah's face drained of all color. "My sons! Are they among them? I must know!" He staggered toward his camel.

Ishtar gripped his arm, holding him back. "This morning your sons wanted to destroy you, but now you to rush to their rescue?"

Matalah tried to shake free. "They are flesh of my flesh. I cannot stand by and watch them be murdered."

Ishtar glanced from Tobia to Matalah. "I'll go. Stay with the boy." Without waiting for further argument, Ishtar swung on his mount and trotted into the distance.

The battle appeared to end as quickly as it had begun. Ishtar approached slowly. A thick man from the second group advanced and a discussion ensued.

After a few moments, Ishtar broke away and turned back, though now the thick warrior followed close beside him.

Tobia rubbed his dry lips. “What does it mean?”

The old man stared in mute misery.

Ishtar drew near with his companion close behind.

The tall, heavyset man wearing a blood-smeared cloak stopped before the small group. As he descended from his camel, he nearly slipped, but jerked himself upright. He strode straight to Matalah and bowed his head in respect.

His whole body trembling, Matalah returned the bow.

“My friend, it is my sad duty to report the death of your eldest son at my hands. I did not wish it but was forced to such action. If I did not act, your sons planned to kill me and my family.” He took Matalah’s hand in his own, pressing it firmly. “I do not hold his crimes at your door. I feel only your shame and loss.”

Matalah’s head dropped to his chest, tears trickling down his burnished cheeks. “I’m glad it was you who administered justice, for you would be neither weak in the face of a necessary duty nor excessive in revenge.”

Tobia stepped into the background.

Ishtar reached out and gripped his shoulder, holding him steady. He looked to the warrior. “Where are the others?”

“They, too, were set upon by neighboring clans.” He shook his head in shared sorrow and glanced at the old man. “I do not believe you have many sons yet alive, Matalah. I am truly sorry for your loss.”

Matalah choked out his words. “They met their chosen end.”

~~~

Ishtar stood aside as the body of Matalah’s eldest son was brought and laid before them.
~~~

As the young man stained his garments with his own blood and his head lay twisted at an unnatural angle, so Matalah seemed to bleed tears while his body contorted in agony. “Take me from this earth! I no longer wish to inhabit the land of the living. I have failed, and my sons will not join us in the place of rejoicing.”

Ishtar nudged Tobia forward. “Come, we’ll do this together and bury those past healing.”

~~~

Tobia swept his sweaty hair out of his eyes and leaned on his shovel.

Ishtar set a marking stone in place before the grave mound and stepped back. His long black hair clung to his cheeks and neck as drops of sweat trickled down the side of his face.

“What next?”

Ishtar glanced at the high sun. “We’ll take Matalah home.” He shrugged. “His wife and surviving children await his return.”

“If I knew nothing of you, I’d think you a marvel among men for what you’ve done for you friend. Because I know what you’ve been through, I’m even more amazed.”

Ishtar turned and stared at the flames of a fire that still burned in the remains of their camp.

Tobia followed his gaze and grew uneasy as Ishtar walked to the fire pit, seemingly entranced by the colorful flames. With his foot, he scattered the coals. “Don’t be impressed with me, for I’ve given back but a tiny portion of the kindness Matalah has shown me.”

Tobia peered back at Vitus, who stood aside staring vacantly into space as Matalah’s men readied for the return journey. “We buried the dead. But what will I do with the living?”
~~~

CHAPTER TWENTY

—MOUNTAINS—

TO BE THE ONE

Amin squeezed his eyes shut. Crack! The sound of wood smashing against a skull was as distinct as it was nauseating. He turned to see a towering figure swaying like a tree in a mighty breeze clutching his wrist.

Obed, sprawled on the ground, lay stunned.

Eoban, rearing back for a swing, soon became pinioned by three of the largest men Amin had ever seen.

"Stop!" Amin tried to wrench free.

A new figure lumbered forward. "Enough!" The stranger stood a head taller than Eoban, but he made no attempt to physically interject. Slewing his gaze from Obed's still form to Barak standing behind Amin and then to Eoban, he merely shook his fist like an angry parent. "You're trespassers here! By all rights, I should put you to death!" He dropped his hand to his side. "But that is not my way."

Grumbling erupted from the other warriors.

"I am Luge. I decide!"

Obed roused and shook his head. Eoban marched to his side and pulled him to his feet.

The stranger propped his hands on his hips. "Leave these mountains. If you disobey, my men will have their way."

Obed staggered, rubbing his head with one hand and lifting the other in apparent surrender. "We've no wish to offend. We'll leave."

Enraged, Amin's body trembled, his voice dropping to a growl. "I won't go."

Luge grabbed Amin's tunic and shook him. "No?"

A wall holding back fear and fury burst, flooding Amin's system. "I can't leave! I've come so far to find my father—I won't turn back now."

The giant warrior's eyes narrowed as he studied the boy in his grip. "You're looking for your father?" Another shake, gentler this time, followed the question.

Amin nodded and sniffed, wiping his face with the back of his hand.

Freeing Amin, Luge glanced at Eoban. "Who is this man you seek?"

Eoban rubbed his jaw. "Neither friend nor enemy. He's this boy's father—the leader of a neighboring clan."

Luge scowled at Amin. "Why did he leave? Why do you seek him here—in the mountains?"

Amin shrugged. "He was lost—out of his mind…"

Barak stepped forward. "Why waylay us? We've done you no harm."

His gaze still fixed on Amin, Luge tilted his head as if appraising the boy. "I had a son about your age." His voice grew thick. "We were attacked by raiders from over the mountain. Now my boy is gone—forever."

Eoban leapt forward. "Have you seen a man with long black hair, slender body, and dark haughty eyes?"

Luge shrugged. "That describes many men." His gaze slipped from Amin to Eoban. "If I found such a man, I'd send him home. This is no place for strangers. Treachery is afoot."

With a snort, Obed glanced from Barak to the giant. "Is that what you fear? Why you attacked us?"

Luge stepped over to the smoldering fire, grunted, and gestured to one of his men.

The warrior squatted before the fire and blew the feeble flames to life. Another warrior gathered kindling and twigs and arranged them, building the flames into a small blaze.

As the fire grew, Luge crouched before it and studied the flickering light. "Few of us are left. Once we were a mighty clan, fierce hunters and warriors. Our leader was a brave man, much revered by all, near and far. But he fell at the hands of the enemy."

Eoban stepped closer and squatted on the other side of the fire. Barak followed, sitting on his left while Amin crouched on Barak's right. Obed remained standing, a shadow among the other men.

Luge rubbed his forehead. "They attacked at night, killed four men, and took two women and three children as slaves. We tried to follow, but they went into the desert and disappeared in the distance." He closed his eyes. "A kingdom lies beyond the desert—I traveled there and saw it for myself." He dropped his head to his chest. "They are like gods—living in a world beyond description."

Obed shuffled near, his face unnaturally bright in the firelight. "I wouldn't mind seeing that for myself."

Luge shook his head. "Not if your son was there—forever beyond your reach." He glanced around. "Now, we wander, aimless and hopeless. We treat all strangers as enemies because we have no friends. Our days draw to a close. We'll pass away with no sons to mourn our loss."

Eoban sighed. "I knew a mountain man once—a great man among great men. Gimesh led a large and vigorous clan. I cannot imagine he would let things come to such a pass. You know him?"

"These mountains are vast, but I have heard the name. As far as I know, he too bowed to this superior race. The days of the mountain men have come to an end."

An owl hooted in the distance.

Amin twisted his hands together and peered at Luge. "My father would've fought. He fought against slavery and freed innocent people. He'd help you too, if he knew your troubles."

Obed snorted. “Your father was deranged. He couldn’t even help himself.”

Eoban glared at Obed as he stood up. “You talk too much, Obed.” He turned and rubbed his stomach. “I’m starving. What if we get some food, Luge? We could help each other survive the night at least.”

Rising, Luge meandered to Amin and tapped him on the shoulder. “I’d like to meet your father.” With a sigh, he glanced at the uneasy assembly. “As for food, yes, there is plenty—if you have the skill.”

Chuckling, Eoban slapped Luge on the shoulder. “Skill? Barak and I are two of the greatest hunters in the grasslands.”

Barak choked.

Eoban’s eyes widened, staring hard at Barak. “Barak even fought two man-eating cats and has their skins hanging in his dwelling to prove his worth.” He flexed his arms. “And I certainly never come home empty-handed.”

Barak and Obed stared at Eoban. Amin’s mouth dropped open.

Eoban grabbed his spear. “Let’s go. I’ll wither to a mere shadow of myself.”

After Eoban, Barak, and a few of Luge’s men started away,

Amin stretched out before the fire, his head heavy with exhaustion. He closed his eyes and let sleep steal every worry from his mind.

~~~

Amin felt rested as he sat up and rubbed his eyes.

After a night of indiscriminate gorging on undercooked venison, the two groups assessed each other groggily in the early morning.
~~~

Obed staggered up to Luge. "Where are you going from here?"

Luge shrugged. "Doesn't matter. We'll live as best we can until our end comes."

Eoban slapped his hand over his bag. "Wouldn't it be better to attack your enemies and release the prisoners? Perhaps you could get your son back."

Luge crossed in front of Eoban, waving his hand. "You've never seen this enemy. The vastness of their fighting force is beyond—"

Barak propped his hands on his hips. "Perhaps that's your problem. If you would stop thinking about your doom and death and think about your life and what it means, then you could do something useful."

Luge closed his eyes. "Our people were defeated. You have yet to experience that."

Obed rubbed his chin. "Could you bring us to that land—the one you described last night?" He glanced at Eoban. "We've come this far—there's no reason why we shouldn't see this through. Show us your enemy—then we can talk of death…or glory."

As Luge's men broke into discussion, Luge lifted his hand. "You have no idea what you are saying!"

One of Luge's men strode over to him and argued in a husky undertone.

Luge glanced from the speaker to his other men, who waited expectantly, eagerly. Then his gaze rolled over Obed, Eoban, and Barak. Finally, it rested on Amin.

Anxiety twisted his innards and Amin's heart pounded so hard he grew dizzy.

Luge lifted his voice. "You want to see the enemy? We'll take you, but we won't engage in battle. We'd be slaughtered."

With a grin spreading wide across his face, Eoban sauntered forward. "Who said anything about an attack?"

He shrugged. "It'll be enough to see this amazing city as you described at our hasty— though delicious—dinner. Besides, Ishtar may be among the slaves." He glanced at Amin. "No turning back now."

Luge swiveled around and glared at the boy. "No, he must not go! They would see a healthy boy and steal him away."

Amin gripped his spear, squashed the tumult in his stomach, and pointed at Luge. "I won't abandon my father. If you tie me up and drag me away, I'll escape and follow you."

One eyebrow rising, Eoban glanced at Barak.

Barak lifted his hands in appeasement and stepped over to Amin. "Luge is right, Amin. We'd get sidetracked trying to keep you safe." He glanced at Luge. "I'm sure you could stay with his clan until we return."

Panic flooded Amin, making it hard to breathe. A cold sweat broke over his skin. "But you could be killed, and I'd be left alone! Besides, I know my father better than anyone, and he'd do for me what he'd never do for you."

Obed nodded. "If Ishtar is alive, he may not want to come with us. But if he sees Amin…" He shrugged. "It's the boy's life."

Spluttering, Eoban jabbed Obed in the shoulder. "His life? Obed, take a closer look! He is a child! Children don't think things through. That's what adults are for. If Ishtar is alive and we find him, having Amin away will be the greatest inducement for drawing Ishtar out—assuming that's what we want. We don't know what he's like now."

Amin pounded his spear on the ground. "No! I won't—"

Luge twisted the spear out of Amin's grasp.

Amin clawed at Luge, wrestling for his weapon.

Barak grabbed Amin from behind and pulled his arms behind his back in a tight grip. "Stop it, Amin! You're behaving like a spoiled child."

Amin spat his words, his whole body trembling. "You'll regret this, Barak."

Reaching around, Barak grabbed Amin and turned him so that they stood face-to-face. "Only a child would put his pride above the safety of one he professed to love. You came all this way to find your father and for once we have a real lead, but now you stand here threatening us and making demands."

Tears started in Amin's eyes, his heart contorting as if it was being torn to pieces.

Barak loosened his grip. "A lot of good men are going far out of their way to help a man who doesn't deserve such kindness. For love of you and your little brother, we're risking our lives to find your father." His jaw clenched as he gave Amin a slight shove. "A little cooperation would be helpful."

Heaving sobbing breaths, Amin hung his head and tears coursed down his cheeks.

Luge strode over and laid his massive hand on Amin's head. "A son's love for his father goes beyond reason. And so should a father's love for his boy. I'm ashamed. I'll go with your friends. You wait for your father, and I'll look for my son." He called to two of his men. "You two take him home. My wife will watch over him and await our return."

The men packed the leftover venison into skin bags and filled their water pouches.

Amin sat against a tree and watched through a glassy stare. The familiar feeling of abandonment swept over him. First his father…now this.

Before leaving, Barak crouched at Amin's side and squeezed his arm. "Don't be angry. We'll return soon." He stared at the boy's unwavering expression. "You're still mine by adoption. Whatever happens, you and Caleb are dear to me."

Swallowing back the ache in his throat, Amin nodded. "I wanted to be the one to find him."

Barak sighed. "It is every son's wish—to do something wonderful for his father. That may yet come to pass. But for now, use this time well. Learn from these people. New experiences are worthy teachers." Rising, Barak shouldered his pack.

Amin stood and watched the men assemble with Luge in the lead.

Obed sauntered close and ruffled Amin's hair as he went by.

Eoban stopped and knelt before him. He held out a bone spear tip. "I was working on this, but now I don't have the time to finish it. Perhaps you could do the job for me?"

Taking the piece, Amin studied the carved point. He nodded.

Grinning, Eoban patted Amin's shoulder. Then he started away, whistling a happy tune.

Luge turned and frowned.

Eoban stopped abruptly. "Oh, you don't like whistling? Well, if that's no good, I can always sing."

A glint of joy sparked in Amin's middle as he watched his only hope traipse into the wilderness.

CHAPTER TWENTY-ONE

—LAKE LAND—

A NATURAL PART OF MOTHERHOOD

Namah smiled at Milkan and patted the wooden bench next to her. The sun shone hot though a cool wind ruffled her hair as she leaned against the woven reed fibers making up the wall of her home.

Milkan settled down, perching her youngest child, Rula, at her side. "I wish I brought news, but we've had no visitors."

Namah exhaled a slow breath. "Nor us." She closed her eyes. "I'm so tired." She shifted her weight, straightening. "I shouldn't complain. It's Jonas we should think of. She's been having a streak of ill luck, the like of which she's never experienced before. Though she hates to admit it, she misses Obed as much as you miss Barak and I miss my Aram."

Milkan surveyed the yard, counting her children on her fingertips. She frowned. "I'm one short."

Rula climbed into her nap and pulled at a bag slung around Milkan's neck. She reached in, drew out a piece of dried fruit, and chewed it lustily.

Milkan peered ahead and started a recount.

Jonas strode into view with Onia following behind.

A burst of pleasure swept over Namah. She nudged Milkan. "See who's coming."

Milkan smiled and moved aside to make room. "Good morning, Jonas! We must all be feeling weary and bored."

Jonas stopped and motioned for Onia to join the other

children. She faced the two women, a frown etched into her forehead. "I wish I had good news, but—"

Milkan clutched Rula. "Why? What's happened?" She stood up. "Barak? Obed?"

Jonas shook her head. "No, not them."

Namah rose to her feet. "Let's go inside where it's cooler."

The three women trailed into Namah's dwelling. The space between the wall and the overhanging ceiling allowed a slight breeze and a slanting light to filter through.

Before anyone sat down, Jonas faced her friends. "Runners came late last night to warn us—invaders are destroying villages to the north and west." She squeezed her hands together, her face pale and pinched. "They're taking slaves."

Namah closed her eyes. "Not again!"

Trembling, Milkan clutched Rula to her chest, forcing the child to whimper in reaction. "But what about my children? What protection do we have?" Milkan stepped to the threshold and started counting again.

Jonas laid her hand on Milkan's shoulder. "Stay calm. The runner said they're still some distance away and may decide to go another direction."

After ticking the last number off her finger, Milkan nodded, satisfied, and motioned for the children to continue playing.

Jonas smiled at Onia as he led a chase across the village. She glanced back at Milkan. "We won't allow our children to be enslaved as long as we have breath in our bodies. I spoke with Lud this morning. He's organizing the men to watch for trouble from every direction. We'll also send scouts north and west to discover news. Men from all three clans will prepare their weapons. We must trust in Lud's wisdom and direction." She sighed and glanced outside.

“But I had to warn you.”

Namah wrapped her arm around Milkan. “We’re not alone.”

Jonas pointed out one window. “There are caves in the north. We could find shelter there—if need be.”

Milkan clutched the table edge as she slid onto the bench. “I feel sick. I’ve been dreading something like this ever since Barak left.”

Namah and Jonas smiled at each other. “A natural part of motherhood.”

Jonas turned to the door. “We will not be defeated. For our own sake and those who return.”

Milkan drew Rula back into her arms. “I just want Barak home again.” After rising, she stepped out into the sunshine, slung her bag over her shoulder, and clapped.

Her children turned and gathered before her.

Her head down, Milkan started away with her throng trailing behind her. She turned. “Send word—anything—so I know.”

Jonas nodded and waved. She stepped outside and faced Namah. “I must go too.”

Onia stepped patiently to his mother’s side.

“I’ll send word if I hear anything.” Jonas peered around the village and sighed. “It’s at times like these that I miss Aram the most.”

Namah clasped her hands before her. “Yes, he was a wise man—more so than I gave him credit for while he lived.” She peered at Jonas. “Time helps us see more clearly.”

Jonas patted her friend’s arm. “Lud will be a good leader. We must not be afraid.” She turned and started away with her son following in her footsteps.

After watching her friends traipse out of the village, Namah glanced at the sky. “I’m not afraid.”

Chapter Twenty-Two

-OldEarth-

We Still Have Free Will

Zuri hated emotional chaos. He clumped to the base of the cave and plunked down on a rock. Propping his head on one hand, he stared at the creek rippling by.

A squirrel hippity-hopped along the water's edge, then scrambled in the dirt, discovered a half-buried nut, and leapt forward. It dug furiously. A darker squirrel scampered from behind, chuckled, and sent the first squirrel, humpbacked, straight into the air.

Zuri laughed. "So, little quadrupeds, who's stealing from whom?"

Ark meandered forward, rubbed his bulbous eyes in the bright light, and harrumphed. "Not me. Certainly."

Zuri peered over his shoulder, one eyebrow rising. "You'd think we were all planning to kill each other the way Sienna acts." He rubbed his neck. "I wish Sterling would send her back to Lux."

"He would, if Teal would let him. Ungle would love to end her searing glares."

"She's only mad because he shot at her."

"Yeah, but she never actually got shot—whereas Ungle—" Zuri dropped his gaze and sighed.

"You didn't know." Ark wrapped his tentacles across his lap. "Ungle justified his actions under the Crestonian rule of law—extreme measures are acceptable in the pursuit of knowledge." He shrugged. "Hardly Sienna's chosen creed."

Zuri shifted and clasped his hands. "Are females on Crestar as…you know—?"

"Emotional?"

"I was going to say unpredictable. On Ingle, our girls are raised so much like the boys, that we're almost interchangeable. They're as strong as we are and have all the same technological advantages. There was a time when our race almost did away with sex types altogether."

Ark's eyes rounded. "You don't say? I never read that."

"It's not one of our happier chapters. We almost killed each other."

"Ah."

He prodded Ark. "Like when Crestar did all that cloning—"

"Miserable affair." Ark lifted a tentacle as if reciting a pledge. "Mutations are our salvation." He chuckled. "How could we have been so naive?"

Zuri wiped his face and slipped off his helmet.

Ark nearly fell backwards. "Oh, seamuck! I didn't know you could do that. I thought you were losing your head."

Zuri ran his fingers over the blond fuzz crowing his cranium. "I'm trying to grow hair." He looked around. "Don't tell anyone."

"Why? For darkness sake, your race advanced beyond body hair ages ago."

His gaze darting to the cave entrance, Zuri practically tiptoed to Ark's side. He dropped his voice to a whisper. "There's this Ingot woman—"

Ark frowned. "I thought you said there's little discernible difference?"

"I said interchangeable—in respect to our professional life." He sucked in a deep breath. "When it comes to our personal life…there's a big difference. Trust me."

Ark nudged him playfully, his smooth eyebrows waggling. "You like her?"

Zuri sunk onto the boulder next to Ark. "Passionately. She's intelligent and funny…and very unpredictable."

Ark leaned in, his gaze watery. "And beautiful?"

Zuri shrugged. "I don't think about that. We're all assembled parts…natural and otherwise." Heat rose to his face. "The only thing that really matters is what's inside—you know what I mean?"

Ark nodded. "I do. Unfortunately, I only experienced an attachment once…and it nearly killed me."

"She left you?"

"Poisoned me." Ark shook his head. "I gave up such associations after that."

A shuffling near the cave entrance sent Zuri scuttling back to the other side of the cave, frantically tugging on his helmet.

Ark turned, his tentacles crossed just so.

Sterling staggered forward, bumbled to the creek fully clothed, and waded in.

Zuri straightened, his mouth dropping open. He started forward.

Ark reached out and held him back. "Let him be. Water is very soothing to a troubled soul." He glanced at his terrestrial boots. "I should know."

Sterling flopped down in the water, let it rush over his whole body for the space of twenty heartbeats, and then rose and straggled back to Ark and Zuri…dripping with each step. "I needed that."

Ark waddled to the water's edge. "I might join you, if only—" He peered back at Zuri. "You'll help me get them back on?"

Feeling very much like an over-indulgent father, Zuri waved the Cresta to the water. "Go on. Get wet. I know you've been dying to."

Ark beamed as he tugged off his boots and tossed them aside. He waddled forward and plunged in.

Sterling stood, still dripping, next to Zuri, and watched Ark splash around like a dolphin. "He's really a child under all that blubber."

Zuri glanced aside. "And you?" He leaned against the cave wall. "What're you?"

Sterling raised a finger. "Just a moment. I can't stand another drip. He shimmered and disappeared. Then he reappeared in exactly the same clothes, now perfectly dry. "Much better."

Zuri flung his hand into the air. "So why the dramatic dunk—?"

"You need to look beyond the surface, Ingot." Sterling started for the woods, glanced backward, and beckoned Zuri with a curt wave.

Zuri followed, uneasiness bubbling like a lava flow in his middle.

"I want to speak with you alone." Sterling jutted his jaw toward Ark. "I knew the sight of dripping water would break his resolve."

Tempted to take off his helmet again, if for no other reason than to unbalance Sterling's perfect demeanor, Zuri scratched his exposed neck. "What do you want?"

Sterling frowned like a misunderstood child. "It's not always a matter of *want*. Sometimes it's a *need*. I need you to make Sienna leave—today."

Crossing his arms, Zuri straightened. "I *want* her to leave as much as anyone, but she won't listen to me. She thinks she's protecting Teal—"

"She's more likely to get Teal killed."

Zuri tilted his head and waited. His scalp itched like crazy.

"Ungle is not one to be beaten at his own game. He's deadly serious about studying the interaction between Ishtar and that bloody Chai. He's practically leaking fluids to see them meet the first time."

Zuri rolled his eyes. "I can't stand it!" He swiped his helmet off.

Sterling's gaze snapped to Zuri's head, and he staggered. "By the Div—?"

Zuri gripped him by the arm. "I'm growing hair to impress an Ingot female who thinks that we should return to a more natural state."

Sterling squared his shoulders and tugged his arm free. "Thank you for sharing that with me." He ran his fingers through his own luxurious white locks. "Back to reality, shall we?"

Zuri tucked his helmet under his arm and twirled his hand in the air. "Go on."

"The point is—I want Teal to see Chai and Ishtar up close and personal when the meeting takes place. And I don't want him distracted. That's why I went along with Ungle's suggestion in the first place. But now—"

Walking backward, Ungle plodded into view slightly off balance with his one shortened tentacle. His gaze fixed on Ark plunging in the creek like a salmon trying to swim upstream. He turned, ran into Sterling, and frowned. "Oh, there you are."

Sterling gestured to Zuri. "Here *we* are."

Ungle heaved a disgusted breath. "Yes, of course." He peered at Sterling. "I've told them both—there's no other option. Either she goes or I'll—"

Zuri snorted. "I thought you were worried about that mystery race, the ones who wiped out a third of your planet."

Ungle's face tightened. "Who wouldn't be?"

"Since Sienna supposedly worked for someone who worked for them…maybe you should send her—"

"She says that she was used by the Bhuaci, and she won't make that mistake again."

"Tell her that she's going to get her revenge. She'll use

them this time."

Ungle's gaze slipped from Zuri to Sterling and back to Zuri. "Honestly, I wouldn't have expected such duplicity from you. I thought all Ingots were bred to obey."

"We may have been bred…so to speak. But we still have free will."

"Do you? News to me."

Zuri stomped forward, fury flushing to the roots of his fuzzy, blond hair.

Sterling swept between them, his arms outspread. "Oh, no, you don't! I've got enough on my mind with Teal besotted by that—"

Teal sauntered around the corner, his gaze fixed on Sterling. "Besotted is a strong word…don't you think?" He glanced at Zuri and frowned. "What happened to your—?"

Ungle waved a tentacle. "We're wasting valuable time. Ishtar could be anywhere by now."

Zuri scowled and pulled a datapad from his sleeve. "He's still at the same location." He held the pad up, facing the others. "I've been monitoring him."

Sterling glared at Teal. "That's your job."

Teal folded his arms. "I know exactly where Ishtar is. And I know where Barak, Obed, and Eoban are too."

Ungle swept a tentacle in the air dismissively. "Who cares about them?"

Teal stepped forward. "I think you would—if you really want to understand Chai." He glanced around. "They're heading directly for the stone city—Chai's hometown."

Sterling pursed his lips, his gaze flickering to the cave. "And Sienna?"

Teal turned and started back toward the creek. He called to the water-happy Cresta. "Ark! Time to go!" Glancing back he met Ungle's intense stare. "I sent her back to Lux. She's going to do research."

Sterling closed his eyes and sighed in obvious relief.

Ungle nodded, a glint of pleasure sparkling in his bulbous eyes.

Zuri frowned. “Research—what?”

Teal jogged forward and helped Ark stagger out of the water. He called back. “The origin of our mystery race.”

Zuri dropped his head to his chest and squeezed his eyes shut.

CHAPTER TWENTY-THREE

—MOUNTAINS AND STONE CITY—

BEYOND MERE BARBARISM

Eoban plodded behind Luge. Two of Luge's men flanked him on either side, while Obed and Barak trailed behind. Dark pine trees shaded their path, though bright sunlight filtered through in splotches and slashes. Shadows and light chased each other among the overarching branches. Suddenly, the line of trees stopped abruptly as if a decree had forbidden them beyond an invisible point.

The men crossed the line in silence, leaving the cool green ceiling and the soft mats of brown needles behind.

Obed hissed a deep breath between his lips. "Here comes the hard part."

Luge tromped ahead over gravelly soil, his gaze cast down, his brows wrinkled.

Barak, too, strode forward but looking ahead, not down. A scowl rose across his forehead, warning of an unnamed trouble.

As they wedged themselves between great shoulders of the mountains, Eoban noticed every detail of his surroundings. The sun grew bright and hot, and he wiped away the sweat beading on his face. All bird song faded into the background, leaving an oppressive silence, except for the scuffling of their feet over loose sand. Vultures circled overhead, sending a shiver over his arms. He swallowed. *We should go back.* But he knew he wouldn't. He couldn't.

Barak stumbled.

Eoban turned. “You all right?”

“Thinking of home.”

Frowning, Eoban waved a dismissive hand. “Not a good idea.”

Obed jogged forward, a flush rising over his face. “Not a good idea?” He jabbed Eoban’s shoulder. “You’d advise a married man not to think about his wife and children?”

Eoban picked up the pace, nearly running into Luge. He shrugged Obed away. “No use tormenting himself. He’ll get home when he gets home.” Eoban stopped short. “Besides, I thought you wanted to see fresh lands…experience new things.”

A sparkle glinted in Obed’s eyes. “I do. But that doesn’t mean I’m rude to others.”

Eoban glanced and held Barak’s gaze. “You’re really all right?”

Barak shrugged. “I was tormenting myself.” He wiped his brow and glanced ahead. “How much further?”

Luge, flanked by his men, stopped in the distance. He pointed ahead.

Eoban, Obed, and Barak hustled closer.

They stood, enchanted, and peered over a valley shimmering white and gold in the brilliant summer light. A vast blue expanse stretched over rippling waves of sand.

Set on a distant hill, a walled stone city rose into the sky like a child’s toy ready to be plucked from the earth.

Luge set his jaw, his gaze never straying from the city. “Let’s eat before we seal our fate.”

~~~

Eoban patted his contented stomach as he padded over the sand to the main gate.

Crowds bustled through the narrow entrance with guards asking questions and checking wares. Thick, rectangular
~~~

open windows in the upper stories built directly into the wall allowed Eoban to perceive new depth to the city. Flashes of colored clothing swept beyond the gate. Glimpses of tables piled high with trade goods set his heart pounding.

Like an exuberant child, Eoban led the way, with Luge and his men falling behind Obed and Barak.

Armed soldiers dressed in long tunics and carrying spears strutted down narrow alleyways crisscrossing the main artery through town.

A cacophony of voices—men calling their wares, women hustling noisy children, goats bleating, birds squawking—tingled Eoban's ears.

Luge's labored breathing warned of his anxious state of mind, so Eoban stopped and waited for him to catch up.

Obed hurried next to his clansman and clutched his sleeve like an over-excited child.

Eoban pulled free. "Would you let me be? I feel like my mother is trying to keep me tied to her skirt."

Obed released Eoban's sleeve, his wide eyes roaming the scene. "Sorry, I didn't— It's just . . ."

"You've hardly ever traveled, remember? I'm the one who talked you into this." A chuckle bubbled inside. "Think of what you'd have missed if you stayed at home." Eoban surveyed the bustling crowds. "It'll take every bit of our skills to describe this."

Obed shook his head. "No one'll believe us." He turned in a circle, his arms flapping at his sides. "We'd have to invent new words."

Barak swung his bag high over his shoulder and leaned toward Eoban. "Question is—how are we going to search this city and not attract attention to ourselves?"

With a splutter, exasperation killed Eoban's joy. "Do I have to show you everything? Come on. Do what I say and don't talk too much!"

Obed exchanged an uneasy glance with Barak.

Luge dropped his gaze, groaning.

A burly guard started forward, his eyes narrowing into hard glints. "Where're you from, and where're you bound?"

Huffing like an overwrought trader ready for hearth and home, Eoban threw back his shoulders and puffed out his chest. "I've been in the mountains and am returning home with my goods." He waved at Luge, his men, Obed, and Barak.

The glint in the soldier's eyes testified to his suspicious nature. "Why aren't they tied?"

Eoban leaned in and dropped his voice to a conspiratorial whisper. "They're terrified of me. Already whipped one for rudeness." He tilted his head in Obed's direction.

The guard chewed on this, glanced at Eoban's empty hands, and considered the assembly. "They hardly look fit to trade—much less escape." After scratching the side of his jaw, he spat on the ground not far from Eoban's feet.

Eoban clenched his jaw.

Another guard ambled near and called out. "Better hurry or Gerard'll give your rations to the dogs."

With a quick wave, the guard sent Eoban on his way and marched along the wall.

Eoban marched forward, grinning. He glanced at Obed. "See that wasn't so—"

Suddenly, a piping voice called out from among the raucous din. "You're too late if you want to sell your wares today!" A chubby, red-cheeked youth weaved through the crowd, a grin plastered on his round face.

Turning to his new advisory, Eoban thrust his palm over his heart. "Me? Sell? Oh no, I've just bought these prizes. I'm looking for a place to rest for the night. You wouldn't know of any decent accommodations?"

The boy's eyes widened. "They aren't even bound. How

are you going to keep slaves all night?" He glanced around. "Where're your men?"

Eoban attempted to pat the boy's head, but the youth kept his distance. "I know how to manage my own property. I'll tie them up good and tight."

"With what?"

A storm brewing in his chest, Eoban boomed a hearty laugh. "Stop worrying! I'll manage." He glared at the boy. "Now, what about a place to rest?"

"You'll pay?" The boy's gaze measured Eoban appreciatively.

"Everything you deserve. I assure you." Eoban glanced from Obed to Barak. "Just point me in the right direction."

The boy led them through crooked passages to a wide street and a wine seller's door. "My father lives here. He'll put you up for the night if you have something worthy to offer." His gaze roved over the assembly. He pointed at Barak. "How about that one there? My father needs a new man, someone who'll survive his beatings."

Barak glared in mute fury.

Eoban rubbed his hands together and offered his most ingratiating smile. "Well…that might be a possibility. If he gives me any trouble tonight, we'll work something out."

Barak lifted his hand. "I'm not going to—"

Luge suddenly lunged forward. "My son! I see my son!"

Eoban twisted around, scanning the bustling throng.

Barak unceremoniously shoved the boy to the side and nudged Luge forward. "Go! Follow him." He glanced at Eoban. "Find you later."

Eoban spluttered. The youth's face blazed.

Luge and Barak darted into the crowd.

The boy cupped his hands around his mouth and screamed. "Run away! Run away!"

Plastering his hand over the boy's mouth, Eoban waited until Luge and Barak were out of sight. He pulled his hand away and wiped it on his tunic, peering at the boy. "Sorry, but I'd rather you not tell anyone about my…embarrassing situation. I know those men. They'll be back."

The boy glared, a flush working up his face and his hands perched on his hips.

Eoban leaned in and met the boy's glare head on. "They want to see their families again." He shrugged like an old hand in the slave business. "The big man often thinks he sees his son, but the other one knows to bring him back." Pursing his lips, he glanced at sign decorated with purple grapes hanging over the wine seller's door.

The boy's eyes narrowed, but he bowed in exaggerated friendship. "Certainly. Let me introduce you to my father. He'll enjoy hearing all about your adventures—and slaves who run away and come back of their own accord."

~~~

Eoban awoke from a deep slumber, scratching his tousled hair and rubbing sleep from his eyes. *By the stars, I thought I'd died and*— A cooing sound turned his attention. He rose from his pallet and peered at the nearby figures. Snoring affirmed what he already suspected. The father and son were sleeping. Tiptoeing, he slipped out of the wine seller's house.

After rounding the corner, he called. "Barak?"

Barak hissed. "Here."

Like a blind man, Eoban reached out and slapped Barak's arm. "Where've you been? I had to make up a thousand tales to tell that fool of a boy and his father. I thought they'd get tired and fall asleep like normal people, but no. They wanted nothing more than to stay up half the night and hear me tell one lie after another."

Barak snorted. "Should've felt right at home."

"On the contrary. I wanted to bolt out their hospitable
~~~

door and save my sanity. I've never been asked so many stupid questions in all my life." Eoban's voice simpered as he clasped his hands. "'How many wives do you have? Where do your ancestors sleep? Have you built your tomb yet? What artisans do you employ?' I would've liked to build *their* tombs—"

"Shhh!" Barak waved like a bat ready for takeoff. "Thank you for sharing. I'm fine. Your concern for my welfare is heartwarming. So glad you enjoyed yourself while I risked my life reuniting a father and son."

Mild surprised caught Eoban off guard. "Luge found his son?"

"Not at first. He did see a boy about the right size and age, but when we caught up, he realized it wasn't the right boy. The boy did, however, know of a training ground. He'd also been taken from his family and was inclined to help us. At the training ground, we found a group of slaves, and Luge's son was among them. We managed to get near enough to speak to him. It took an ingenious plot on my part and a great deal of luck, but we got his son separated from the others, and Luge stole him back. They're heading to the mountain pass." Barak gestured to the inn. "Tell his men to go after them."

Muttering under his breath, Eoban returned inside, tiptoed to the back of the dwelling, shook Luge's men awake, untied their ropes, and hustled them outside to Barak, who gave them instructions.

Returning to Barak's side, Eoban propped his hands on his hips.

Barak stroked his chin. "You'll have to come up with a few more lies to explain the loss of your slaves."

Eoban clapped Barak on the shoulder. "Not if we leave now. I'm in no mood—"

"You're forgetting someone."

With more muttering, Eoban traipsed inside, untied

Obed, and shoved him awake.

Once outside, the three jogged away. Obed huffed as he trotted. "There's a certain ironic freedom in being a slave, but would you mind telling me what's going on? I've been tied up for hours."

As the three men hurried along an empty thoroughfare, a streak of pink light appeared on the horizon. They turned right on a side street, jogged between myriad closed shops, and then at a wide intersection, turned left, searching for the main gate. Eoban clenched his jaw at the sight of people stirring at their doors.

Lanky dogs slunk to the shadows, as pigs, a loose goat, and a variety of scrawny hens scuttled out of their way.

As they entered a rougher, older part of the city, they slowed to a gentle amble.

Half-naked children appeared and stared through wide eyes. The stone streets turned to hard baked clay, and the homes diminished to nothing more than waddle huts thrown up against the walls of the city.

Peasants in simple wool and leather garments shuffled by with downcast eyes.

Barak sighed. "I can breathe again."

Eoban nodded through a huff. "I feel as if I've been living in a nightmare. That father and son—"

Obed turned, his mouth dropping open. "You think you can judge them? I heard a great deal as I sat there tied up like a sack. These people have rituals for everything—traditions that go back through generations. Men support more than one wife, they make wonderful trade goods, and their building skills surpasses—"

Eoban halted and stared at Obed.

Obed stared back.

Averting his gaze, Eoban pointed to a grove of trees hovering on the edge of a meandering stream, which flowed down a gentle slope. He started away. "There's a good place. I'm going to get a drink and a rest before I deal with you."

Obed laughed. "Everyone who doesn't see the world through your eyes needs to be dealt with, is that it?"

Barak groaned under his breath.

Each man took a long drink and soon found a soft spot under a large spreading tree.

Obed propped his head on his arm and stretched his legs. "I heard what you told Eoban about Luge, but tell me, Barak, how did you manage to get the boy away?"

With a grin, Barak shrugged. "I hate to say. It was nothing really. I just asked him where we should meet, and he pointed out a place. As the moon rose, we went to the spot and waited. When he reappeared, we walked away."

Obed frowned. "No one was watching?"

"No one dares to cross the desert. After a time of mourning, most people simply accept their fate. The chains weren't so strong—just never tested."

"You mean other slaves could have walked away, but they never tried?"

Barak nodded. "The strongest chains are in the mind."

Shoving himself upright, Eoban clapped his hands free of dirt. "Well, that's a good deed done. Now, Obed, I've a few words—"

Obed waved his hand in protest. "Spare us your judgments. So, you're blind to the magnificence all around you, who cares?"

Feeling like he'd been slapped, Eoban rubbed his jaw. "You have a way of saying things that make the most peaceable man want to knock you down. I wonder how Jonas stands it."

Obed grinned, darting a glance from Barak to Eoban. "She loves me."

Eoban snorted. "That's about what it would take!" He rose and stretched. "Still, I think it's you who are blind.

These people are not great—"

Shooting to his feet, Obed jerked his hand in the direction of the city. "Have you no eyes?"

Eoban crossed his arms over his chest and glared. "The people who live there now are the recipients of other men's intelligence and hard work. Slaves' sweat and broken backs make their lives possible." He stepped closer and peered narrowly at Obed. "They spend time comparing the softness of their clothes, how the colors strike their eyes, and how they feel when reclining on one pillow rather than another." He lifted his hands as if imploring the sky to bear testimony. "Weak with madness, they are."

"The city is well managed. There are guards and warriors in numbers beyond count defend them. They have a well-developed system of trade, buildings for communal storage, magnificent homes for the rulers, and—if you didn't notice—an ornate temple for their god." Obed shook his head. "I doubt our clans could do as much over generations."

Eoban dismissed Obed with a wave. "Why would I want to be like them? Did you learn nothing from Neb and Ishtar? No society can live long when it's built on cruel force."

"Cruel force? You know how many clans live in idle waste and make useless war on each other. Here, at least every man builds to some purpose."

Eoban shook his head as if to clear water from his ears. He turned, peering at Barak while pointing at Obed. "Who am I talking to?"

Barak frowned at his clasped hands. "I'm not sure."

Obed laughed and stomped away. "Stop! So, I'm impressed with these people! I'm amazed that you two are too blind to appreciate the grandness of their design and execution. This city values its artists. They can ponder such novelties such as clothing design and pillow comfort because they have time to do so. They're not sweating for every mouthful or worrying about how to keep their children alive. They've moved beyond the barbarism of mere survival."

Barak straightened and stared at Obed's back. "There is much to be said for the 'barbarism of mere survival.' I work hard to feed my children, but I still have time to think. Is it acceptable to you that this city's grandness is paid for by the forced separation of a father and son? Would you let Onia be taken so that others might enjoy their art?"

Obed leaned on the tree and chewed his lip. "You're right in this point, of course. But you can't deny—they've built some marvelous works."

Eoban snorted. "Anything built on blood is bloody, and I don't admire bloody things!"

Barak lifted his hands. "We have yet to look earnestly for Ishtar in the city. One more day, and we'll head home."

Obed glanced at the towering temple that rose above the city walls. He sighed. "Agreed."

Eoban felt his stomach fall into a black pit. "Agreed."

CHAPTER TWENTY-FOUR

—DESERT—

GOD HELP ME

Tobia watched Ishtar lead the sheep to their watering hole. Exhaustion sapped his strength and sorrow confused his thoughts. A faint light of hope tried to spark, but he could not keep it alight. He glanced down. The pain in his chest should show through…somehow. "Ishtar?"

With his gaze fastened on the sheep, Ishtar coaxed them to the waterhole. "Yes?"

"What happened to Vitus?"

Once the sheep began to lap at the water, Ishtar halted, propped his arm on his staff, and looked at Tobia. "When he lost his mind or when he lost his way in the desert?"

"Both."

A grimace spread over Ishtar's face. "I'm the last person you should ask."

Tobia's eyes glimmered. "But he's dead now—gone forever. I should've kept a closer eye on him."

With a quick shake of his head, Ishtar motioned toward a rocky outcropping. He waited for Tobia to shift into the shade and leaned against the cool wall. "When I first came here, I was a shell of a man, not unlike Vitus. I had neither eyes to see nor ears to hear. I was dead inside. But Matalah's kindness rekindled a spark of life within me."

"Was I not kind enough to Vitus?"

Waving as if to dismiss the thought, Ishtar glanced away. "Matalah gave me the freedom to decide—but I had to make the choice myself. In time, I decided to live and pay back his kindness. Only then could hope flourish." He ran his fingers through his hair. "Apparently, the Creator still has use for me."

Tobia plopped down on the ground and sat cross-legged. "But it was God who struck down Vitus."

"Are you sure?"

"Vitus called—demanded—that God speak with him and then lightning struck…"

Ishtar shook his head. "But He did not kill him, did He? Vitus followed in your footsteps for many a day after that."

"But no one saved him when he wandered into the night. I didn't even know he was gone until—"

Ishtar's expression softened. "Tobia, you're asking what happened between God and Vitus." He peered over the horizon. "I can't say and neither can you. All I know is—Matalah could not have saved me unless I wanted him to, and you could not save Vitus for the same reason."

Pain tightened Tobia's throat, and tears stung his eyes. "Ishtar?"

Ishtar met his gaze. "Yes?"

Longing tore through Tobia. "I want to go home."

As a frolicking lamb nuzzled Ishtar's hand, he patted it. "I'll show you the way."

~~~

Ishtar entered Matalah's tent and bowed low.

Taking Ishtar's hands, Matalah peered into his eyes, his face haggard and lined, looking older than his years. "Though my sons turned to evil, still, I pray on their behalf. May your fortune be better than mine."

Ishtar blinked back tears. "I love you as I could never have loved my own father."

Matalah nodded. "God knows…for I surely needed your love, my son."
~~~

~~~

Ishtar and Tobia marched out of the tent, into the searing rays of a hot sun.

As they crossed camp, Matalah's wife hurried forward, her long dress rippling at her sides. She called Ishtar's name.

Ishtar and Tobia stopped and turned.

Gripping Ishtar's arm, the petite, gentle woman bowed low. "Thank you for everything you've done for our family in our time of distress. I know that you leave with sorrow, but I pray it is not with regret. My husband will never understand his loss, and I'll never stop grieving my sons, but still, we are grateful for your kindness."

Ishtar dropped his gaze, a throbbing ache welling inside.

The woman straightened and her grip tightened. "Evil did not conquer you, and it will not conquer us. Go home now and take our blessings with you."

Ishtar kissed her hands.

With another bow, she turned and hurried away.

Tobia sighed and started forward.

Ishtar circled around the blazing campfire, only glancing at the flames. He turned his gaze to the mountains.

~~~

Lud crushed his son in a tight hug, swallowing back a lump in his throat.

Gilbreth reciprocated the hug with equal intensity.

The two younger children whined and cried, scrambling to get a hold of Lud's arm.

Women worked distractedly in the background, their eyes darting about, their foreheads wrinkled with anxiety.

The men huddled in groups, murmuring in low voices, sharpened weapons in their hands.

Facing his wife, Lud set his jaw against the pain clenching his heart. Unloosing his hands from his children, he wrapped his wife in a gentle embrace and peered over her head. "I was left in charge, and that means in bad times as well as in good. I'll not let these people fall to slavery and death. I must lead them in this fight."

Pulling away, Dinah wrung her hands, her eyes imploring. "We could all flee to the caves."

Lud shook his head. "No, they'd only come looking for us. And I'll not have our warriors backed into a corner."

"I won't go without you."

"Be strong, Dinah, for my sake. Gilbreth will be at your side to help you."

Pounding forward, Gilbreth gripped the knife tied at his waist. "But I'm old enough to fight."

"Then fight selfish desires and learn the power of obedience."

Dinah stared at the distant mountains and clasped her son's shoulder. "Where are they coming from?"

Lud ran his fingers through his hair. "No one knows for certain…but rumors say they started from a city on the other side of the mountain."

Dinah squinted. "That is a very long way."

"They must be a strong people."

Turning, Dinah met her husband's gaze. "Strong once…but the further they get from the mountains, the weaker they become."

Lud considered her words, one eyebrow rising.

"They're far from the source of their strength."

Lud nodded, admiration for his wife's thinking growing by leaps and bounds.

A large gathering of clansmen marched forward, heading straight for Lud.

Taking a deep breath, Lud turned to them. He murmured under his breath. “God, help me.”

CHAPTER TWENTY-FIVE

—STONE CITY—

OUTSIDE THE WALLS

Eoban stood on a hill outside the city walls and watched flames flicker from distant hearths. He rubbed his growling stomach.

With a smile plastered on his face, Obed jogged forward and glanced aside at Barak. "I spoke with a family at the bottom of the hill." He pointed to a small assembly stationed around a stew pot that hung over a modest blaze. "I told them that we're travelers in search of a lost clan member, and they've agreed to let us spend the night. They have plenty of stew, Eoban, and they're willing to share with us."

Shoving off from an ancient tree, Barak rubbed his hands together. "I could certainly use a home-cooked meal." He started after Obed and called back. "Hurry up, Eoban. We're not waiting for you." He and Obed loped down the hill.

Eoban frowned and hesitated. His stomach rumbled again. He blew air between his lips and jogged forward.

As they assembled around the fire, everyone gave way so the three men could partake of the offered stew and fresh bread. Soon, a strong drink was passed around, and in little time, Eoban's mood expanded. After eating and drinking his fill, he flopped on the ground and stretched out between Obed and Barak, who sat cross-legged.

Various community members sat on the ground or on benches drawn back from the fire. Muted conversations flowed in all directions.

Propping himself on one arm, Eoban's only discomfort lay in questions nagging his mind. He licked his tingling lips and launched his words like rocks. "So, how is it that a people who cook so well also ravage and enslave others?"

Deafening silence filled the air. Faces froze and limbs stilled.

Obed whacked Eoban on the side and muttered. "You repay their hospitality with an insult?"

Barak jerked to his knees, scanning the crowd. He met an old man's gaze. "I'm sorry for my rude friend. Clearly, Eoban's had too much to drink. You see, we've been traveling, and he's had many—"

Stumbling to his feet, Eoban waved his arms, cutting off Barak's conciliatory speech. "I can't stand brutality! That's my grievance. It makes me sick. It should make you sick—but you've thrived." He jutted his arm toward the main gate. "Your whole city—"

The old man rose steady and clear-eyed. "My name is Daniel, it means judge. I am the one who settles arguments in our community." He stepped closer to Eoban and fixed his gaze. "You have judged us before knowing the truth."

Moving off to the side and crossing his arms, Obed shook his head. "So often the case with him."

Daniel stepped around Eoban, returning to the central fire. "Perhaps, it's your heart that speaks and not your reason."

A low murmur rumbled through the crowd.

Daniel stared at the flames. "Those who live outside the walls are not the same as those who live inside." He exhaled a long breath. "We are not much better than slaves ourselves. Chains do not bind us, but we're held captive nonetheless. Having no voice, we have no strength to change the laws or fight the armies that protect them."

Barak nodded, his eyes downcast.

Obed glared at Eoban with a told-you-so look.

Eoban returned the glare, his voice rising. "You know the laws are wrong, yet you don't fight them?"

A youth sprang up from the circle. "Knowing something is wrong doesn't put a spear in your hand. They'd kill us—"

Disgust welled inside Eoban, and his words rose like a snarl. "So, not brutes but cowards, then?"

As if in slow motion, Obed marched forward, clenching his fist.

Before he realized what happened, jolting pain seared through Eoban's head, and he felt himself spinning. Darkness swallowed him.

~~~

Barak sat before a waning fire in the early morning light, watching the last stars fade into the brightening sky. Obed slumbered at his right, and Eoban still lay sprawled on the ground where he fell.

After much grunting and groaning and several vain attempts to sit up, Eoban gave a mighty roar and rolled to his knees and then staggered to his feet. He peered around, rubbing his jaw. "I know what happened, so don't pretend."

Barak closed his eyes and dropped his head to his chest, smothering a groan.

"Try as you might, you can't excuse him! Such behavior must be roundly condemned. I hope you did me justice and kept our clan's reputation intact."

Choking, Barak stared wide-eyed at Eoban.

Eoban leaned in, gazing into Barak's eyes. "You and Obed did do me justice—didn't you?"

After rising and stepping a safe distance away, Barak
~~~

peered into Eoban's bloodshot eyes. "It was Obed who knocked you out."

"Obed?" Eoban smoothed his rough chin. "I'll have a word—"

Frustration seizing him, Barak stomped close, gripped Eoban's arm, and tugged him to the summit of the nearby hill.

The glorious white city spread before them, encircled by a wall with tall and short gates facing each direction. Guards marched along the wall, while merchants and villagers started their daily routines. Women opened shops, old men swept dirt from their steps, mothers bustled children to the well with empty jugs, and boys chased flocks into open fields.

Eoban peered at the view and then glanced aside. "What?"

Pointing to a temple roof rising high above the wall, Barak barely controlled his temper. "There! The inhabitants of this metropolis worship a figure that has a man's head, the body of a great cat, and the wings of an eagle. It needs daily sacrifice to keep the city flourishing. Sound familiar?"

Eoban scowled. "Haruz must have studied here. But if Ishtar is in residence, I'm not sure we'll ever get him away."

Clapping his hands together in mute fury, Barak turned away. "Who accused our hosts of being cowards?"

"I've been talking in my sleep…?"

Scrambling footsteps turned their attention.

A twinkling smile in his eyes, Obed sauntered forward. "Have a good sleep, Eoban?" He winked at Barak.

Barak took a step backward.

Returning the smile, Eoban chuckled. "Oh, yes, slept like a baby. Blazing stars exploded in my head when I hit the hard ground—what more could a man ask?" Eoban clenched his fist. "If only you could share my joy." He landed a heavy blow on Obed's chin.

Obed spun backward and sprawled in the dust. He glared at Eoban, his eyes blazing.

Barak stepped over with a hand out, but Eoban blocked him and gripped Obed by the arm and hauled him to his feet. "Now, we're even."

After spitting on the ground, Obed rubbed his jaw, the fire in his eyes dying to embers. "Someone had to shut you up. Or do you think it's generous to insult the people who feed you and treat you with kindness?"

"It was not their kindness I objected to but rather their weak- ness."

Barak lifted his hands and stepped between the two men. "Enough!" He glanced from Eoban to Obed and then pointed to the city. "Or I'll leave you two to kill each other while I go search the temple for Ishtar."

With a snort and a dismissive wave, Obed surveyed the glinting white temple. "Ought to be interesting."

Eoban scrambled down the hill. "Ishtar would end up in a place like that. Let's go." He glanced over his shoulder. "Try not to be too impressed, Obed. We can't bring any of it home."

With a storm cloud rising in his stomach, Barak followed the two men.

CHAPTER TWENTY-SIX

—MOUNTAINS AND VALLEYS—

FOLLOWING IN THEIR FOOTSTEPS

Ishtar and Tobia climbed hills, trudged through mountain passes, and marched day after hot, sticky day, rarely talking and never smiling.

When the outline of a village rose in the distance, Tobia pointed and cleared his throat. "Maybe, we'll finally enjoy a little hospitality."

A memory of the reception he received from Lud's clan flashed through Ishtar's mind. He stumbled, righted himself, and swallowed. "That'd be a welcome change."

As they drew near, Tobia wrinkled his nose. "What's that awful stench?"

Ishtar froze, then his arm jerked out and he gripped Tobia's sleeve. "Wait here a moment." He jogged ahead and circled the first hut. *Oh, God!* Bile rose in his throat as he stared at the remains of a massacre.

Stagnant blood pooled on the ground and splattered across the dwellings. Snarling dogs chewed on unnamed bones.

His stomach heaving, Ishtar ran to a grassy bank and soon retched the contents of his stomach.

Tobia jogged forward, laid his hand on Ishtar's back, and turned away. His voice fell to a whisper. "I would too—if I had anything in me."

Wiping his mouth, Ishtar clenched his jaw and straightened. "Sorry. I should be stronger—with all I've seen." He shook his head. "But it was a shock."

Tobia crept forward, his hand over his mouth and nose. “You think anyone’s still alive?”

Ishtar moved stealthily into the village. “There’s only one way to find out.”

As they searched through the primitive village, a groan rose in the air. Ishtar quickened his pace.

A skinny, toothless old man lay near a grass hut. A bloody cut on his leg, purple bruises on his face, and the way he cradled his left arm, told the tale of recent events.

Tobia glanced around. “You know more about healing, so you can tend to him while I see if I look for others.”

Ishtar knelt at the old man’s side and helped him to sit up.

The old man snatched at Ishtar’s sleeve. “Water!”

A jug near a doorway caught Ishtar’s eye. He grabbed it and jogged around the village, a sour taste still burning in his mouth. A creek bubbled in the distance. He filled the jug, slaked his own thirst, and returned to the old man.

The old man’s hands shook as he slurped great mouthfuls. He wiped his lips with the back of his trembling hand and nodded. “Thank you.”

“What’s your name?”

“Wael. I was the patriarch of this ruined village.”

Leading a dark-skinned, wrinkled old woman and another old man, Tobia wandered back to Ishtar. “I found a few others too weak to rise, but with water and food, they’ll soon recover.”

Ishtar passed the jug to the newcomers and stood, surveying the scene. “Raiders must’ve killed the men and taken the women and children.”

Tobia pointed to the rummy-eyed elders crouching near at hand. “Why leave them?”

Ishtar shrugged. “They’re no threat and no use. It was easier to get what they wanted and leave.”

One old woman groaned. “I wish I were dead.”

Wael shook his head as he surveyed the bodies shriveling in the sun. "Who'll bury them?"

Ishtar glanced at Tobia, and they shared an understanding gaze.

~~~

Tobia relished the cool breeze of evening. Rubbing his aching back, he returned from the burial duty and stood before the strongest of the old women. He wiped his sweaty brow. "We need something to eat."

Her limbs shaking, the old woman rose and limped to a ramshackle hut on the outskirts of the village. Glancing aside, she peered at Tobia. "My name's Olna, and I be the oldest living member of the clan…not much to boast of now, I know. But—" She ambled inside.

Tobia waited, rubbing grit from his eyes.

Wood scraped across dirt and a labored grunt rose.

"If you want to eat, come help me, boy."

Tobia crossed over the threshold and found Olna leaning on a sturdy table.

"Move it over there." She pointed to the east wall.

Dutifully, Tobia shoved the table aside and watched Olna rip a covering of wood from the back wall. From a deep hole, she tugged a large, tightly woven basket.

Tobia gripped the handle and pulled it into the light. "What's this?"

"Our salvation." Olna grinned a nearly toothless smile. "I've seen my share of attacks, and we old women know to keep precious things well hidden."

Flipping back the basket lid, Tobia's heart sang. Uncounted packets lay before his eyes like a sparking stream to a thirsty man. He lifted one and unwrapped the leaves. Inside, grain the color of honey glistened, sending his stomach into spasms and his mouth watering. "Thank God."
~~~

Olna nodded. "And you can thank me, too, while you're at it. No one remembers the old ways and tucks good food aside for bad times—no one but Old Olna."

Tobia wrapped his arm around the old woman and gently hugged her shoulder. "I thank you, indeed."

~~~

Ishtar clasped his hands before his face and pondered the melancholy assembly before him. They were fed for the moment. But their slim resources would not last long. He peered at Olna as she perched on a bench outside her family hut, her hands still, and her gaze unfocused. "What'll you do now, Olna?"

Olna's head lifted a fraction. "What is there now but to die?"

Three old men and two other women crouched around a meager fire. Wael shook his finger at her. "Die then, old woman, but the rest of us" —he waved at other survivors— "we've a mind to live yet a little longer."

Shrugging, Olna turned her gaze to the food basket. "You go on then, Wael, and farm the land, scare up some meat, and pick rations to last us through the season."

Frowning, Wael rose and shuffled to a hut. He grabbed the shovel leaning against the wall. "I'll start now. Don't think I can't."

Ishtar rose and glanced at Tobia, who wrapped a wet cloth around the injured arm of one old man. "You won't survive here, alone. You'll have to come with us."

Olna shook her head. "I don't know that I can leave them…" She peered at the mounds in the distance. "You buried them, but someone should watch over their remains and pray for their spirits."

Wael leaned on the shovel, his eyes glistening. "They would want us to survive." He slapped the shovel. "What
~~~

else did they fight for…but to have someone live…and remember them?"

Tobia stepped forward. "We'll place markers around the mound so that anyone coming through will know of them. Though many perished, they were not forgotten."

Ishtar rose and stepped toward the first hut. "We'll leave tomorrow. But before then, let's gather everything useful—anything you wish to take." He glanced at the setting sun. "Time passes, and we need to move on."

Tobia bit his lip. "Where do you think the raiders have gone?"

Ishtar sucked in a deep breath. "That's what I'm afraid to find out."

~~~

Tobia shared the last of the grain with Olna and the assembly on the third evening of their journey. Everyone settled around a small fire, exhausted after a hard day's march through thick grass under a warm sun.

Olna chuckled as she swished the grains in her mouth, softening them before swallowing.

Startled, Tobia nudged her with his shoulder. "What's so funny?"

After wiping her lips, Olna smiled and stared at the pink horizon. "My granddaughter loved to sit in my lap and hear the old stories. She was never content until I told at least three." She lifted three fingers to clarify and shook her head, her grin fading. "Ay, but there's no one to remember them now."

With a sigh, Tobia shrugged. "Perhaps you can tell them to our children. Though they belong to another clan, we're all related in some measure, created by the same God. The stories belong to all of us—do they not?"

Tears slipped down the old woman's face. "But there's
~~~

few of us old one's left. Those brutes will attack the next village soon."

Jerking upright, Tobia glanced from Ishtar back to the woman. "You know where they're heading?"

"Though they spoke poorly, they questioned us about the nearest clans. We refused to answer…until forced. But the dogs learned what they wanted. This final conquest will be their greatest triumph, they said—"

Rising, Ishtar stepped closer, knelt, and peered into the old woman's eyes. "What direction?"

Olna shrugged. "We're following in their footsteps, I think." Heaving a miserable sigh, she shuddered. "They're far from their homeland…but the leader said they'd soon turn back." She wiped away her tears. "Won't be soon enough for those in their path."

Tobia gripped Ishtar's shoulder. "Could they be heading—?"

Ishtar shook his head. "There's not much between us and home—nothing to turn them aside."

Tobia leapt to his feet, his stomach churning. "We must warn them!"

Meeting Tobia's gaze, Ishtar nodded. "Yes, we must."

Heart pounding, Tobia reached for his staff. "I'll leave right away."

Ishtar grabbed his arm. "You were lost and starved, wandering in the desert not long ago." He glanced at the old people hunch-shouldered and clearly afraid. "They trust you—they need you." He retrieved his own staff. "I'll go."

A ripple of terror washed over Tobia. "But, Ishtar, *you're the enemy*—remember?"

With clenched jaw, Ishtar faced the setting sun. "Not anymore."

Barely controlling his trembling limbs, Tobia watched Ishtar sprint into the diminishing horizon. Vitus' face rose like a specter in his mind. Tears blinded him.

Olna patted his arm. “He’s a strong man, that one. Don’t worry, he’ll be safe.”

Tobia’s throat constricted. “It’s not him I’m worried about.”

Chapter Twenty-Seven

-Lux-

Boiling Lava Rocks

Sienna studied a large hologram rotating before her. Rainbow-colored disks spread across the universe. She tapped the console and squinted. One sector magnified a thousand percent, rolling closer like a storm. She bit her lip and tapped the magnify button again and again. *Beyond the Divide! Where are you?*

A chime rang.

Sienna frowned and turned. "Come in, Kelesta."

The door slid open and the Bhuaci clerk ambled in, a smile wreathing her petite face. "Any success?"

Sienna shook her head. "They're gone…as if they never existed."

Her lips puckering in a childish pout, Kelesta stopped at Sienna's side. "They're just hiding." She waved a languid hand. "They can't hide forever. At some point, their curiosity will get the better of them, and they'll expose themselves to us…or to someone."

A doubt shivered through Sienna. Her gaze slid over to her friend. "Have they shown themselves to you recently?"

Her body stiffening, Kelesta frowned. "Not really. The one who contacted me originally pretended to be human…an old man. I knew, of course."

"And why did he contact you?"

"He said he needed help."

Sienna waited.

"He knew *we* needed help."

Pacing away, Sienna crossed her arms. "An exchange of assistance?"

"We would be each other's ears and eyes."

Sienna turned, her anger building. "And were you?"

Kelesta sighed. "I told Sterling—I told you all—the truth. I thought they were going to protect us…that was the arrangement."

"So you haven't had any contact with them—lately?"

Kelesta cross her arms, her body enlarged and hardened, and a menacing scowl rolling over her face. "No! And I'm not looking to contact them." She reverted to her former petite shape. Sidestepping Sienna, she wandered around the revolving hologram. "There's only one way to keep an eye on such a powerful enemy."

Sienna's eyes followed the Bhuaci. She titled her head. "How?"

"Let them keep an eye on us." She arrived at Sienna's left and tapped the console.

The universe dissolved and reappeared with Earth in the center. "Let's return and discover what it is about humans that fascinates Ungle and the Ingilium so much."

"Crestas are obsessed with science, and Ingots only care about trade."

"More than that..." Kelesta grinned and cast a side-glance at Sienna. "Besides, I'd like to understand Zuri better." She licked her lips. "He's unlike any Ingot I've ever met."

A hot flush worked up Sienna's cheeks. "You're interested in Zuri?"

Kelesta straightened her tunic and tugged at the collar. "Professionally. Certainly. The more I understand our enemies…the safer the Bhuaci will be."

With a shrug, Sienna turned toward the door. "Teal seems to trust him." She stopped. "But Teal wants me to bring information about the mystery race—"

Kelesta nudged her forward. "And you will. Once we get back to Earth and discover what all the fuss is about."

-OldEarth-

Teal, dressed in a patched, sleeveless shirt and gray leggings, stood on the brow of the hill and glanced back at Ark and Zuri. "You two, stay here. I'm going in."

Ark blinked as sweat dripped down the side of his face. "Is that wise?"

Zuri scratched his short blond hair. "You look human enough, but up close…someone might notice differences."

"No one ever has before." Teal peered around. "Where's Sterling?"

Ark glanced at Zuri.

Zuri shuffled his feet. "He's with Ungle." He pointed to a rocky outcropping. "But I don't think Ungle—"

Glowing at the edges, Teal frowned. "I'm tired of tiptoeing around that Cresta's sensibilities."

His eyes alarmingly wide, Ark waved a tentacle. "You may not want to get irritated in front of humans…you're glowing—"

In an instant, Teal returned to his human state—sans the bright outline. He stomped to the enormous boulders.

Sterling sat on a jagged ledge, his hands clasped like a contrite child.

Ungle paced before him, waving his tentacles. "Lux cannot afford to indulge—"

Teal clambered the rest of the way up the incline and glared at Ungle.

Ungle stared back. "This was a private discussion."

Pointing to the stone city below, Teal shrugged. "I don't think they care."

His jaw rotating and bubbles rising, Ungle hissed through his breather helm. "Bothmal was created for such—"

Teal threw up his hands. "Please. No threats. No lectures." He turned and faced Sterling with his hands perched on his hips. "If we're going to learn anything useful, we'd better get down there—now."

Sterling blinked like a mystified child. "*We?*"

Rubbing his neck, Teal kept his eyes fixed on Sterling, dearly wishing he could knock him backward with the force of his gaze. "It'll be a lot easier to pass myself off as a merchant if I have a slave to sell."

Jerking to his feet, Sterling choked. "A slave!" His whole body shimmered. "I never!"

Rejecting Sterling's idiocy, Teal stomped over to Ungle and leaned in close to Ungle's watery orbs. "Do you—or do you not—want to learn about Chai?"

A grin slid over Ungle's face. Wrapping a tentacle around Sterling's shoulder, he led him to the brow of the hill overlooking the city. "If there's a Luxonian alive that can take us beyond murky waters into clear pools, I believe it's you, Sterling."

Sterling's shoulders slumped. With a long shuddering sigh, he shrunk and shriveled, losing stature and weight. His clothes dissolved into mere rags, and his gorgeous locks of hair turned stringy-brown, matted with dirt and lice."

Ungle stepped back hastily, flipping his tentacles out of reach.

Teal frowned. "Don't overdo it. Lose the lice. I want to sell you not drown you."

Grinning, Ungle waddled down the hill and turned toward Zuri and Ark at the bottom. He waved a tentacle in salute. "I'm returning home, so you'll be on your own." He glanced at Sterling. "I want details, Sterling. Colorful details!" He passed Zuri, who stood frowning, and merely patted Ark on the shoulder.

Ark called. “Leaving so soon?”

Ungle chuckled as he headed to the hills. “Mission accomplished!”

Teal nudged Sterling toward the city. “Ours has just begun.”

~~~

Zuri scanned through his datapad, scowling in the bright afternoon light.

Ark flopped down and poured a green liquid into his breather Helm. “By the Divide, I hate waiting.” He glanced over to Zuri. “What’s wrong?” He nudged Zuri. “I thought you’d be thrilled. Sienna’s gone. Ungle’s gone. Granted, we still have to deal with Sterling, but he’ll leave as soon as this temple business is taken care of.”

Zuri’s gaze stayed fixed on the datapad. He rubbed his hand over his short hair. “Oh, blast!”

Ark frowned. “Naughty girlfriend?”

Zuri glanced over. “She liked the picture I sent.” He wiggled his eyebrows and pointed to his head.

Ark licked his lips. “That’s good, right?”

Zuri sighed. “Now she wants to see my hands.”

Tentacles flying to his face, Ark looked every millimeter the blushing, scandalized matron of every-world. “What next I wonder? Your…do we dare think it?” His voice lowered as he leaned in, his gaze dropping to Zuri’s mechanical boots.

Zuri dropped the datapad aside. “This could go places I’m not really prepared—”

A shuffling noise stiffened them both into statuesque poses and complete silence.

A goat trotted forward, sniffed, and bolted back the way it had come.

Ark thrust a tentacle over his chest. “That was too close.”
~~~

Crouching, Zuri scrambled to the outcropping and peered over the edge. In the distance, three children and a flock of goats ambled in their direction. "Boiling lava rocks!"

Ark edged closer. "Please, no ugly images." He peered over the edge. "They're between us and the cave."

"Bet they bring those quadrupeds up here for the season and use that cave for..." His eyes widening, Zuri scrambled for his data pad.

Ark peered at him. "What're you—?"

"Creating a diversion."

An explosion blasted from inside the cave.

Screaming, the children darted down the hill with the goats close at their heels.

Crouching over, Zuri skedaddled for the cave entrance.

Ark lumbered behind, huffing, his gaze searching the perimeter. When he stopped next to Zuri just inside the cave, he patted his chest as if to keep his organs safely inside. "I'm a scientist...not an explorer. I tried to tell them." He glanced at Zuri. "Teal would never've made that mistake. We were just sitting out there for all the world—"

Zuri clambered to his ship, pressed the datapad, and waited while the hatch fell open. "I've been distracted." He climbed the ramp and huffed. "What's your excuse?"

Ark padded behind. "Touchy, aren't we? Just because your girlfriend wants to see you au natural—it isn't any reason to—"

On the main deck, Zuri turned and faced Ark. "I can handle that. One article of bio-ware at a time." He shifted into the helm's seat.

"What then?"

"Sienna's coming back...and she's bringing her Bhuaci friend."

"Boiling lava rocks!"
"Like I said."

CHAPTER TWENTY-EIGHT

—STONE CITY—

HEART SICK

Obed's mouth fell open as he tilted back his head and stared at the enormous, ornate structure. Guards stood posted at the entrance, letting him, Eoban, and Barak pass through without comment.

Inside, carvings covered the walls and statues populated the corners. Strange forms, various mixtures of human and animal, glared down at them. Murals decorated the ceiling and geometric tiles under their feet dazzled their eyes.

Sucking in a deep breath, Obed savored the experience. "Master craftsmen beyond imagination—"

Eoban tapped Obed's lower jaw. "You're drooling. Close your mouth before someone takes you for an idiot." He nudged Barak. "Come over here. I think I see Haruz's god."

Heat flushing over his face, Obed pointedly ignored Eoban and Barak as they strolled out of sight.

As the afternoon sunlight filtered through the elongated windows near the ceiling, Obed wandered from room to room, his attention rapt and his admiration reaching new heights at every turn.

~~~

Barak's hair prickled as he stared at one particularly grotesque figure, a man's lower body attached to a scorpion's upper half. He swallowed back bile and
~~~

imagined his children's terror. Murmuring under his breath, he came up beside Eoban. "Thank the stars we didn't bring Amin to this place."

Images of Ishtar and Haruz's failed sacrifice flashed through Barak's mind. Then, like waves on a stormy lake, memories of every battle he had fought thrust bloody gore before his wide-awake eyes. Shivering, he rubbed his clammy arms. He peered at Eoban. "I need air." Hoping he didn't look as terror-struck as he felt, Barak moved from room to room, zigzagging through the maze-like structure. Once beyond the guards and stepping into the bright sunshine, he gulped fresh air.

~~~

Eoban wandered aimlessly. He watched Barak hustle out, glad the man left before he turned any greener. Eoban started for the next interior entrance and hesitated, doubt clawing up his spine. He scowled. *It's not like I'll get lost.* He glanced at the guards wearing long colorful tunics on each side of the doorway. *Must say, they dress well.* He sighed and peered around. *No sign of Ishtar.*

Entering the next room, Eoban's stomach plummeted to his toes. Around the room, larger-than-life stone carvings depicted half-human, half-animal beasts devouring grimacing human victims. Their silent screams sent terror shivering up his spine. His heart hammering, he glanced around. No table. No altar. No weapons. And most importantly, no victims. Eoban closed his eyes and muttered under his breath. "Time to join Barak. Sensible fellow."

Bumbling passed a guard, he smacked into the wall.

The guard peered at him, irritation drawn across his furrowed brow.

Eoban lifted his hands. "Sorry. No harm done." He
~~~

hurried into the bright sunshine and pounded down the steep steps as fast as his legs could carry him.

~~~

Obed meandered in blissful silence, barely noticing the increase in activity and a chant wafting ever closer in a serpentine fashion through the temple. When horns blasted their shrill notes, he stopped and looked around.

The last of the visitors bustled through the doorway leading to the exit. He pursed his lips. An evening ceremony, perhaps?

With his hands clasped behind his back, Obed sauntered to the guard. "Can I stay and watch?"

Saying nothing, the guard merely retreated to a deeper interior.

Unruffled, Obed wandered back to a strange mural on the back wall and studied the interplay of colored stones and paint with the fading light.

Before he was done inspecting the mosaic, a tall elderly man with a thin beard padded toward him. Obed turned, ready to beg leave to watch to the ceremony.

"We've noticed your rapt attention and obvious admiration, so though we do not usually admit visitors, we'll allow you to stay if you will do as you're told."

A sensuous pleasure swept over Obed.

The old man motioned ahead, and they paced through a series of doorways and down a long, dark hallway lighted only by torches fastened to the walls. At the end of the hall, a reflection of the setting sun poured into a huge interior room, sending shivers of delight over Obed. Seven men, including the old man, stood around the lip of a stone circle. He leaned forward, but in the fading light, he could not see what was in the center of the circle.

Chiming bells, unrecognizable chants, groans, gestures,
~~~

flowing robes, and burning incense formed the bulk of a ritual Obed could not grasp. Confusion and weariness muddled his brain. Finally, an ornate goblet was passed and when it was offered to him, he took a tiny sip, swallowing a grimace from its bitter taste.

Unable to account for his reaction, a skin-crawling terror worked through Obed's body. He shifted a step toward the entrance, panic pounding in his chest.

An undulating shadow rose from the circle, summoning Obed. In a dizzy half-awake stupor, he stepped forward, a deep hole, a cavernous death beckoning. Someone gripped his arm. Sweat dripped down his face. He could hear Jonas beseeching him, calling his name, "Obed!" Jerking, he flailed his arms.

As his grip slipped, the old man demanded, "Obey!"

A searing headache blinded him, but even without sight, Obed knew the distance to the door. He sped through the entrance, crashed against the wall, scrambled upright, and like a wounded animal, limped and clawed toward fresh air.

~~~

Eoban sat on the bottom step, his head in his hands. When Barak plunked down beside him, he sighed. "I couldn't take it anymore."

Barak nodded and peered over his shoulder. "How long before he comes out?"

A sour taste made Eoban wipe his lips. "So long as he doesn't trip over a guard, turn into a statue, or fall into a black hole…" He shrugged and staggered to his feet, rubbing his back.

Barak rose and pointed to a public well and a cluster of food-sellers. He shuffled through the bag wound about his waste. "I've got a little to trade with."
~~~

Eoban nodded. "Food and" —he pointed to a distant tree— "a rest."

"Will Obed find us?"

Eoban chuckled and started forward. "After I get some sleep…I hope."

Soon clouds rolled in and rain fell in sheets.

Eoban cursed under his breath and edged closer to Barak who slept peacefully under the spreading oak tree.

~~~

Obed scampered down the temple steps, his heart pounding, and raced across the city, zigzagging through the narrow streets like a wounded animal fleeing for its life. Sweat and rain poured down his face and into his eyes. He collided against a stone wall and fell in a heap. "Oh, God…oh, God." Rain blanketed him as darkness swept all fear from his mind. Murmuring, he curled into a tight ball and fell into a tormented sleep.

~~~

Eoban, wet and exhausted, opened his blurry eyes and blinked.

Obed stood over him, swaying like a tree in a high wind.

Eoban slapped Barak's sleeping form next to him. "Look who's returned from his midnight merry-making with his temple brothers." Clasping his hands over his knees, he peered up at Obed. "What? No festival leftovers? No tidbits for your hungry, wet, lonely friends?

Obed pointed to the main gate. "Let's go."

Groaning, Eoban stood, his mood turning as nasty as a wounded boar. "Couldn't you even send a short message telling us you would be out . . . or rather *in* all night? I thought we meant more to you than to be left on the wayside by the first religious ceremony that came along."

Rubbing the small of his back, Barak climbed to his feet and grimaced through a smile. "Glad to see you alive, Obed." He shrugged. "I started to worry."

Eoban rolled his eyes. "I was more worried we'd—"

Obed trotted away. "Ishtar's not here. If he ever was—he's dead now."

Eoban leapt ahead and gripped Obed's arm. "Wait a moment! We deserve an explanation."

Glancing back at the temple, Obed shivered. "I have to leave—now!"

Smacking Eoban's hand off Obed, Barak met Eoban's gaze. "Let's go."

The three men trudged along the outer wall until they came to the main gate. Without ceremony, they passed through with a throng of merchants and herdsmen. As they reached the summit of the first hill, Barak peered over his shoulder at the stone city glinting in the morning sun. He glanced at Obed who had halted, his hand tapping nervously at his side. "They perform sacrifices there—don't they?"

Obed swallowed and stared ahead. "Yes." He turned and sprinted in the direction of the mountains.

Barak met Eoban's gaze and they started after Obed shoulder to shoulder.

Eoban shook his head as he ran, his eyes burning and his heart clenched tight.

CHAPTER TWENTY-NINE

—MOUNTAINS AND GRASSLAND—

MADNESS WILL TAKE US ALL

Ishtar ran under a warm sun at an even pace for much of the day, stopping every now and again to rest, gain a view of his surroundings, and get his bearings. He wound his way down a mountainside populated with cedars and pines. The ground, spongy and matted with brown needles, softened the blows to his feet, and the boughs overhead blocked the harshest rays of the sun. The ancient trees comforted him, but with a reserved, haughty demeanor.

By late afternoon, the trees, held back by an invisible command, gave way to scrublands and rounded hillsides. When Ishtar reached the top of one, he considered his surrounding and tried to puzzle out where the raiding clan had come from. He glanced back at the distant mountains and frowned. *Even if they managed to cross the distance, how would they ever get their slaves home safe?* He shook his head. *They'd be mad.* A stab of fear plunged into his gut.

By evening, he spied a group of stocky, muscular hunters passing into the open grasslands. He followed as they chased a fat stag. After a successful kill, they grinned in mute joy and pounded each other on the back. Sucking in a deep breath, Ishtar straightened his shoulders, rose from his grassy shelter, and approached. He lifted his hands high signaling his peaceful intent.

Frowning and circling their kill, they huddled close.

Ishtar spoke slowly, gesturing with each word. "I'm

Ishtar from the grasslands. I'm returning home from a long journey."

Allowing him to step nearer, the shortest and thickest man in the group addressed him. "Ishtar, I'm Butros. We come from the south." He gestured in the general direction, and then swept his hand at the stag. "We return home, too."

Clasping his hands, Ishtar bowed in a sign of respect. "You are skilled hunters." He gestured back the way he had come. "I found a village devastated by raiders. My friend is helping the survivors. But I must warn my people." He stepped closer. "And warn you too. They are a dangerous enemy."

"We've heard of their approach. We hide in the woodlands and when necessary, we move again. In this way, we keep safe."

Ishtar nodded. "Very wise. But have no other clans been attacked? Were none of them your friends?"

Butros glanced at his men before fixing his gaze on Ishtar. "We are too few to fight such a powerful enemy. Their leader is intelligent but mad."

Stiffening, cold shock ran over Ishtar. "Why do you say so?"

Butros shrugged. "His success declares intelligence, but his ambition demonstrates madness."

Rubbing his temple, Ishtar tipped his head. "You are wise indeed." He glanced toward the setting sun. "I must go and warn my people."

Glancing aside, Butros nodded to the stag. "It was kind of you to stop to alert us. Take some meat. You must arrive strong enough to fight…if need be."

Blinking at this unexpected generosity, Ishtar waited while they cut a section of the rump and wrapped it in skin. When he accepted the gift, he bowed low. "If ever the need arises, send a runner to the western grasslands. Call for Ishtar, and I'll come to your aid."

Butros smiled. “If ever the need arises.” He titled his head. “I pray it will not.”

Ishtar turned, but Butros called after him. “Beware of their god! It eats men, devouring them whole.”

Bile rising, Ishtar froze, stunned. He glanced back wide-eyed. “You know this?”

“I know the sound of a man in torment, and I have seen the sacrificial fire.” Butros shook his head. “That’s why we stay far from them.” Peering through haunted eyes, he crossed his arms over his chest. “The danger is too great.”

Turning, Ishtar sprinted away.

~~~

Ishtar rose early the next morning from a short sleep and started again. He soon discovered a wide, beaten trail of travelers who had no desire to hide their steps and held in contempt those who might follow. Under a glaring noon sun, he arrived at an abandoned encampment. Stepping around the remains of an enormous blackened ring, he toed the remains of a feast.

He crouched low, frowning. They had enjoyed roasted deer; the bones and hide scraps lay scattered about. But in the fire pit, the bones did not match the meal. Fresh blood stained a circle of blackened stones. Ishtar’s nose curled, and his stomach squirmed. When he found the remains of a hand, his insides revolted, and he retched in the grass.

With sobbing moans, he wiped bile from his mouth and rose on his haunches. Pounding the dirt, he rocked like a child in torment. Lifting his gaze to the sky, he raised his fist. “Oh, God! How could this happen—again? Is there no evil men will not commit?” He staggered to his feet and stared wild-eyed at the scene. “Madness will take us all.”

A huge black raven flew in low, snatching at the remains. In fury, Ishtar swatted the air, flailing his arms and
~~~

attempting to drive it away. Three more birds arrived, and Ishtar leapt at them, flinging insults and fury.

More birds darted into the pit, and Ishtar, with tears streaming, snatched the hand and what bones he could find. Bundling them in his arms, he ran some distance away, and, using his body as a shield, he dropped the remnant in a heap. He yanked his knife from his belt and scoured the ground, loosening the earth and scrabbling a shallow hole with his fingers. After placing each bone and fleshy piece into the hollow, he covered them dirt and grass.

The birds, unaware or uninterested in his work of mercy, circled above the remaining feast, quarreling for their share.

His hands black and bleeding, his face sweat-and-tear-streaked, Ishtar stepped back and stared from the tiny grave to the angry birds, his mood as black as their feathers.

~~~

Ishtar—exhausted but resolute—loped through the swaying grass and detected a flicker of firelight in the distance. Crouching low, he crept over the uneven ground, his gaze fastened on the assembled throng.

A waning moon rose as one by one, stars blinked into existence. Low clouds spread across the sky like a frayed shawl.

Studying his enemy, Ishtar peered at the beardless, stocky warriors in the bright moonlight. They wore colorful robes dirt stained and ragged but clear reminders of a proud history.

Sentries paced the perimeter and stalwart guards stood at fixed points before a huddled cluster of wretched women and children. The women clutched babies and small
~~~

children in their laps, while adolescent girls and boys huddled with their arms wrapped around their middles, crouching low, their eyes blank and unseeing. On the edges, a few male survivors sat hunched-shouldered, bruised and filthy. The guards smacked them without cause whenever they strode near.

A single tent dominated the scene. Two guards, still as stones, stood on either side of the entrance.

As the glowing moon rose higher, Ishtar's eyes drooped with exhaustion. He dropped his head over his arms, which were wrapped around his knees. His eyes closed.

Suddenly, a commotion jerked him awake. Craning his neck, he peered over the tops of the swaying grass.

A heavyset man, short and broad, with a beardless white face that practically glowed, marched stiff-shouldered from the tent to the center of the assembly. His iridescent robe, thrown back from his shoulders, rippled in the evening breeze. He stood in the center of the assembly and spoke in a confident, commanding tone, all eyes fixed on his face.

Ishtar could not hear the words, but he understood their instructional intent.

The leader pointed, his voice rising.

The assembled warriors lifted their arms, their fists raised to the night sky, chanting, demanding, and affirming. Among raucous sounds, only one resolved itself into a clear word. "Chai."

Sheltered by blackness, Ishtar half-rose and growled in an undertone. "Chai? You and I must meet."

Chai turned and peered in Ishtar's direction, his eyes glowing like a cat's.

A chill racing through his body, Ishtar turned south and fled.

CHAPTER THIRTY

—WOODLAND—

A TERRIBLE MISTAKE

Amin sat on a log before a dead fire and watched Luge's wife, Lydia, trot across the village with an armful of kindling and two children tugging at her skirts.

He whiled away his boredom imagining what he would say to his little brother when he returned home. He pictured Caleb's surprise—his eyes round and wide—as the boy ran into his arms as he always did. Caleb would want him to repeat his adventures over and over and would probably brag to everyone about Amin's journey.

Amin shook his head. *What do I have to brag about?* He stared at the humble village, the rough men and women who hunted and gathered, eking out an existence from the scrubby wilderness. He closed his eyes and pictured his own well-organized village—the craftsmen's homes, women chattering as they spun and wove cloth on looms, children leading herds into distant green hills.

Opening his eyes, he sighed; his shoulders drooped in idle weariness. Scanning the crowd, he saw an old woman scrape a hide with a worn paddle, a man hang strips of meat on a line to dry, and children huddle in circle before an old woman who held at a bowl of nuts in her lap and picked out the shells.

One man attached a sharp stone tip to a long wooden shaft with leather ties. He glanced up and met Amin's gaze.

Amin looked away, a tightening in his throat choked him.

Striding near with hurried steps, Lydia called. "Come, boy. Eat now." She pointed to table placed outside her tent. "We must get everything packed for the move tomorrow."

Frowning, Amin rose and padded to the table. He peered at the tray piled with roasted meat, nuts, and mixed berries. "How can you leave? Luge isn't back yet."

After placing an earthen jug on the table, Lydia wiped the back of her hand over her brow. "I hardly want to." She glanced aside, her brow wrinkled with worry. "But I have to."

Amin tilted his head and peered at her, a spark of interest igniting. "Have to…why?"

Stepping closer, Lydia leaned in, one hand shadowing her mouth as if to hide their conversation. "My husband's brother…" She nodded at a fat, indolent man lying on a soft pallet outside his tent. A man Amin had learned to avoid early on.

"Rueben?" Amin frowned. "He should be helping you."

Snorting, Lydia turned her back to the village and arranged the tray and the jug in perfect symmetry. "He does not work. It's not his way. Nor his wife's." She glanced over her shoulder.

A tiny woman with a tight, flushed face hovered over her husband, flapping her hands like fans, chattering like a child.

Scowling, Amin stared boldly at the man. "In my clan, if a person does not work, he does not eat."

Idly scratching her head, Lydia surveyed the village. "You must be a wise and prosperous people then."

Amin chuckled and shook his head. "If only that were so." His grin faded as Rueben rolled off the pallet and swayed to his feet, his glaring eyes fixed on Lydia.

Amin straightened, annoyance warring with anxiety.

Lydia backed against the table as Rueben drew near.

"Why aren't you seeing to the packing, woman?"

Lydia frowned, wringing her hands. "I've just finished my morning work and made the rounds, telling everyone your plan."

His eyes narrowing, disgust enveloped Amin. The man's stench was unbearable. He flashed a glance at Rueben's wife, who scurried in the background, still fluttering like a leaf in high winds.

Rueben shook an admonishing finger at Lydia. "You know Luge's directions were as clear as the morning sun. He said to move at our appointed time, no matter what."

Amin turned to Lydia. "Why? What harm would it do to wait a little longer?"

Glaring, Rueben grabbed Lydia's wrist and tugged her toward his tent. "The whole clan will starve if we delay. Once the rains come, the roads will be impassible, and winter will have its way with us."

Lydia jerked free and returned to Amin, staring into his bright eyes, leaning in as if to emphasize her words. "It's true. It'll grow cold here soon, and animals will be hard to find. We've already outstayed our welcome." She glanced at the main path leading out of the village. "I was hoping" —she shook herself— "but there's no sense waiting now. Luge will follow us. He knows the way."

Ruben gestured to his wife. "Ulla will help you." He limped to the outdoor pallet and flopped on the ground with a loud, lingering groan.

Lydia lifted her hands in apparent surrender, her gaze sweeping the interior of the tent. "Don't worry, Ulla. You take care of your husband. I'll manage."

As Ulla scampered to her wifely duty, Amin stepped into the tent behind Lydia. He gasped. Discarded clothes, half-eaten food, dirty cups and sticky jugs, ornate decorations, a broken spear, three mangled baskets, and an assortment of other detritus lay strewn about in haphazard fashion. "They're worse than pigs."

Clamping her hand over Amin's mouth, her eyes widened. "Shhh! He's a difficult man when he's feeling well but now that he's sick—"

Amin lifted a jug, sniffed, and wrinkled his nose. His voice dropped low. "Sick or stupid?"

Her hands flashing right and left, Lydia straightened the baskets and tossed salvageable goods into them. The rotten food and broken pottery shards, she threw into a central pit. "His bowels bother him…sometimes he writhes in agony." With a yelp, she jumped back.

Leaning forward, Amin followed her wide-eyed stare and peered in the dark corner where a heap of old clothes lay in a shredded bundle. He gripped the corner and tugged.

Out leapt a litter of rats, which scattered in all directions.

Slapping his thigh, Amin knocked one off his legging and then spat on the ground. "Ugh! Filthy people!"

With a shudder, Lydia grabbed a staff from the corner and swung it at the departing rodents, her own rage flushing across her face. "Luge should never have left me like this! He knows how much I have to do—"

Shocked, Amin froze and stared at her. "He's looking for your son!"

Lydia exhaled a long breath and began tossing articles in the basket again. "I know what he's doing." She glanced at Amin. "But I'm long past such hope."

Using his feet, Amin nudged garbage into the pit. "Still, the boy—"

"I have more than one child, and I must care for those left to me as best I can." Straightening, she rubbed her back. "Besides, I have another coming, and Luge knows how Rueben acts. Impossible man."

For the first time, Amin gazed at the swelling in Lydia's middle. A memory of his mother's rounded belly as she carried Caleb flashed through his mind. He rushed to

Lydia's side. "You should be resting. I didn't realize."

Lydia smiled. "I have time yet, but it's too much work for one woman."

Rueben called from outside. "Lydia, bring me fresh water."

Lifting his hand, Amin rolled his eyes and stepped outside. He glanced from Rueben's supine form to Ulla feeding berries to her husband.

Closing his eyes, Amin snatched the empty jug from against the wall and strode to the stream.

Lydia's two children toddled across his path, calling for their mama.

By the time he returned, Amin's gut churned in fury. He plunked the jug down and perched his hands on his hips.

Lydia stepped out of the tent with one child on her hip, another tugging at her skirt, and a large basket in her other arm. She glanced at Amin. "I need to feed them and then perhaps—"

Amin folded his arms. "I'll help get everything ready."

Blinking back tears, Lydia hurried away with her children clinging to her.

Rueben took a long lingering swallow and then handed the jug to his wife.

Amin glared from one to the other. "What kind of a fool leaves his brother's wife to tend to everything?"

Spluttering, Ulla choked.

Rueben jerked upright, his eyes glassy. He staggered to his feet and towered over the youth. "How dare a mongrel talk to me like that!"

"I'm no mongrel." Amin flapped an open palm at Lydia's tent with her children whining at the door. "She's exhausted and you don't lift a finger to help!"

Raising his arm, Rueben swore to the sky. "By the gods, you have overstayed your welcome! Go and do not follow us on our journey."

Cold fear enveloping him, Amin stiffened. "Luge told me to wait here, so he could find me—"

"Luge is dead, idiot! No one enters the stone city and lives to tell of it." His eyes narrowed. "Leave now before I see fit to beat you and throw you out."

Curling his fingers against the desire to shred Rueben's face with his nails, Amin turned on his heel and stomped to Lydia's tent. He plucked his spear from the wall.

Lydia frowned. "What's happened?"

"Rueben has sent me away." Without another word, Amin charged back into the sun, sweeping along the main path toward the edge of the village.

Stepping out, Lydia gasped and peeled herself away from her children. She trotted to Rueben's side, her tone imploring. "Amin is just a boy! You can't send him into the woods unprotected."

Rueben jerked her clutching fingers off his sleeve. "Since my brother is no longer here, I'm the leader. I do what I think is best for the whole clan." He glared at his wife and gestured to Lydia. "Every moment we waste in idle chatter costs us dearly. Hurry and see to the packing, woman."

Amin stopped and met Lydia's frightened gaze. "I'm not unprotected." He lifted his spear. "I wish I could've helped you." He glanced aside at Rueben. "You're making a terrible mistake." Fury twisting his insides, Amin pounded onto the main path that led into the surrounding woodlands.

Once well outside the village, he stopped and considered his options. Back toward home…or to the mountains? He turned and faced the mountains.

CHAPTER THIRTY-ONE

—WOODLAND—

MY ONE BLINDNESS

Eoban trudged through the wilderness with Barak on his right and Obed in the lead. He muttered, swapping leaves out of his way. "How does he know where he's going? Luge only gave *me*—"

Barak stepped over a log. "Are we going in the wrong direction?"

Eoban shrugged. "Not too much. We might stumble somewhere near it—eventually." He waved at Obed's straight, uncompromising back. "He won't stop to rest…or let us rest. Under the great sky, what put him into such an ugly humor?"

Barak squeezed his eyes shut a moment. "Don't ask."

Nudging Barak's shoulder, Eoban forced him to blink. "Easy for you to say. You don't have to live under his authority. He's the leader of my clan, in case you've forgotten."

Obed halted and faced the two men. "I won't be leader much longer. As soon as we return, I'm giving up leadership. Any man with the desire may take up my role." He stared pointedly at Eoban. "Even you." With a sharp turn, he marched away.

Like an angry stag, Eoban dropped his head, charged forward, and gripped Obed's shoulder. "Oh, no, you don't! You were chosen as the leader, and you've managed your position well enough except for a few lapses when you've contradicted me." He stuck out his chin and peered at

Obed. "Why are you acting like a cat caught in a thorn tree? We" —he gestured toward himself and Barak— "don't even know what happened."

As if he had been struck, Obed rotated his chin and rubbed his hand over his face. "Everything has changed— for me."

Turning his head and glaring out of one fixed eye, Eoban spat his words. "But not for us? You're going to abandon leadership and hope everything just" —he flailed his hands— "works out?" He snorted as bitterness rose in his throat. "We're supposed to let you stew in anger while you lead us?" Eoban waved empathically. "Where are you leading us? Do you even know?"

Startled, Obed licked his lips. "Luge said that he lived on the eastern side near a waterfall. You said there was a waterfall above the foothills on the eastern mount." He glanced from Barak to Eoban. "We're going in that direction. Right?"

Eoban sighed, shaking his head. "For the most part, but I think we need to start coming down a bit."

Obed and Barak nodded, and they trudged on in heavy silence.

~~~

Eoban led the way across the rough terrain, but as the sun lowered, Barak waved a limp hand. "I surrender. Let's rest."

When each man had drunk their fill from a stream and eaten a few morsels from their bags, Barak slumped under a large spreading tree and met Obed's gaze. "I'm afraid this has been a doomed adventure. We certainly didn't find Ishtar, and now you're thinking of—"

Resting against another tree, Obed raised his hand. "I'll explain." He shifted, his gaze sweeping over the ground.
~~~

“I’ve been wrong…about many things. I don’t know where to begin.”

Eoban plunked down between them and chuckled. “Oh, well, if that’s all—”

Barak kicked Eoban’s foot and glared a silent *shut-up.*

Shaking his head, Obed staggered back to his feet and paced before the two men.

An owl hooted in the distance and a breeze stirred the leaves.

Obed exhaled a long breath. “You’re right. I’ve always been so sure of myself…so certain—”

Barak rubbed his head. “Just tell us what happened that night.”

Obed swallowed and stared at the ground. “The temple priests assembled for one of their rituals…and they allowed me to stay.”

Eoban shrugged. “That was generous. I wouldn’t have thought they’d let an outsider watch.”

Obed nodded. “I should’ve been suspicious.” His eyes gleamed in the evening light as he glanced aside. “I should’ve had you with me, Eoban.”

Eoban sniffed and rubbed his nose. “Then neither of us would’ve been there.”

Turning away, Obed strangled a laugh. “Right again.”

Barak searched through his bag. “Was it interesting? Did they do anything…?”

“They offered a sacrifice.”

Barak froze and Eoban leapt to his feet. “By God, you didn’t stand by and watch—”

Sucking in sobbing breath, Obed tottered close and gripped Eoban by the front of his tunic, his eyes bloodshot and glimmering. “They tried to sacrifice me! By all the devils of hell!” He jerked away and pounded to the shadows. “They gave me a drink… it was drugged. I got confused…and weak.”

Obed's breathing grew labored and his face dripped with sweat. "Before I knew what was happening, this…thing." He heaved and bent double. "A shadow…a beast…rose from a pit…strong arms pushed me…I almost got pulled into a damned hole."

Barak dropped his head to his chest and closed his eyes.

Eoban's mouth fell open. With a shake, he stomped forward and peered at Obed's bent head. "How did you get away?"

"I'm not sure." Obed straightened. "I fought them…and I ran. Like a scared rabbit. I ran out of that stone hell and hid in the woods." Shuddering, tears ran down Obed's cheeks. "I've never been so ashamed."

Barak gazed at Obed. "There's no shame in saving your skin."

Obed opened his mouth but no words came.

Eoban placed a gentle hand on Obed's shoulder. A piercing shaft of understanding melted every shred of his anger. "Someone else had to be sacrificed…is that it?"

Dropping his head onto his hands, Obed wept, his shoulders heaving. "God, help me. I knew such things were possible…Neb, Ishtar…Haruz." He wiped his face and straightened, his whole body stiffening. "But I never really felt the evil before…and saw my own blindness."

Obed retreated to a spot under a tree and plunked down.

After a few moments, Eoban rubbed his face and chuckled. "Well, if this doesn't make me happy, nothing will." He stepped over to Obed, crouched before him, and stuck out his hand.

Obed stared, a perplexed frown crowding his forehead.

Eoban's hand remained open and steady. "I want to welcome the new man to the clan. You'll do rather nicely as leader. Just wish you had turned up ages ago."

Obed bit his lip and glanced aside at Barak.

Barak grinned.

Obed clasped Eoban's hand, and Eoban pulled him to his feet. "Now, let's get something to eat."

CHAPTER THIRTY-TWO

—WOODLANDS—

THE HEART

Tobia never before realized how difficult it could be to lead a group of distraught, opinionated old people through the wilderness. If he had, he would have insisted more vehemently to be the one to run ahead.

As he led his unhappy flock, he longed for the days of Vitus' simple obvious insults. These people knew how to provoke each other with color, stealth, and flourish. Olna needled Wael with hints of his past prowess, and he, in turn, badgered the others about their former laziness.

Weary after wandering through summer woodlands, Tobia began to sense a familiarity that made his heart leap. Pleasant memories stirred as his gaze wandered. Like after a spring rain, joy flowered. This was the area he and Vitus had circled when Vitus was trying to expand his trading routes. When they were thoroughly lost, they had retraced their steps to a clan in the area who had treated them with exceptional kindness.

Tobia closed his eyes. *Thank God.*

Once he found the path into the village, so little had changed that he recognized everything.

The six old people traipsed along behind like bedraggled children, limping and hunch-shouldered, wilting in body and spirit.

Glancing around, Tobia swallowed back embarrassment as a flush crept up his cheeks. This was awkward, showing up again in more desperate need than ever.

Like an old acquaintance, Kamila called his name and raced across the village. She stretched out her hands, her face alight and her eyes sparkling. “Tobia! You’ve come back!” She glanced aside at the old people and her smile vanished. “What’s happened? Where’s your friend?”

Without actually giving her a hug, Tobia managed to clasp her hands and grin in relief so palpable he feared his pounding heart might burst through his chest. “There’s much to tell.” He sucked in a deep breath and waved to the broken assembly. “But first, these are the last survivors of a once noble clan that has been ravaged by raiders.” He peered into Kamila’s eyes. “Can anything be done for them?”

Blinking and turning to Olna, Kamila clasped the old gnarled hands. “Most certainly.” She glanced around. “I’ll call my brother. He’ll know what to do.”

A fresh wave of relief flooded Tobia. “I have a strange story to relate. May I speak with Remy, please?”

Kamila nodded, her face sober, and an apprehensive frown wrinkling her brow. “Of course.” She met Tobia’s gaze. “He’s been ill but getting better.” She glanced at a central hut. “He’d like to see you.”

She led the assembly to the hut, stopped before the door, lifted her hand in signal to wait, then darted inside.

Tobia and the ancients stood in the warm sun, peering aside at the adults setting about their business and at a passel of children chasing each other in the afternoon sunshine.

After a few moments, Kamila returned smiling. “He told me to take the women to my home and arrange for the men to lodge in the storage hut until something better can be arranged. There’s enough room for all, and they’ll be well cared for.”

Tobia scratched his head. Images of the old men eating through Remy’s winter supplies flashed through his mind.

Chewing his lip, he led Kamila aside and dropped his voice. "They've been through a great deal…uh…and they tend to…horde things." He swallowed. "And possibly argue…on occasion."

Laughing, Kamila patted Tobia's shoulder. "You underestimate my experience." She glanced at Wael who was wagging his finger in Olna's face. "These aren't the first villagers to be ravaged by disaster. We've taken in others." She grinned. "But thank you for the warning."

Tobia's shoulder tingled at her touch. Without thought, he clasped her hand and met her gaze, his heart pounding. "Thank you, Kamila."

Blushing, Kamila tilted her head toward the open doorway. "You better go in. Remy is waiting."

As Tobia turned to the doorway, he glanced back.

Leading her charges, Kamila wrapped an arm around Olna and listened with a focused gaze to Wael's complaints.

A rush of admiration flowed over Tobia. Swallowing, he hurried inside. The dim interior appeared black for a moment. Tobia froze. "Remy?"

"I'm here. Come in."

As his eyes adjusted, Tobia scanned the room and found Remy sitting on a woven pallet against the back wall. He appeared thinner and his face haggard, but when he smiled, a sparkle in his eyes reassured Tobia.

Remy pointed to another pallet and a folded blanket. "Please, sit. I've thought of you often these past months." He glanced aside. "What happened to your guide—the one who could hardly find his way among the trees?"

With a sigh, Tobia sat against the wall and stretched his legs. He glanced up and met Remy's gaze. "Do you want the whole story…or just a summary?"

Remy waved his hands to encompass his small abode. "I don't have much…but I've got plenty of time."

Clasping his hands, Tobia rested his head against the wall, stared up into the rafters, and told everything that had happened from the morning he stepped out of their village with Vitus to this afternoon when he clasped Kamila's hand.

Never interrupting, Remy sat forward in an attitude of deep thought. After the story, he rested his chin in his hand, his eyes wide with wonder. "You've told me the most remarkable tale I've ever heard, and I don't doubt a word of it." He waved to the door as villagers shuffled passed. "As for the old people, they're welcome. We always take in those in need, though we've become more suspicious of late, as you noticed when you first arrived. We do not suffer fools gladly." He shrugged. "But ancient rules of hospitality demand that we assist the helpless, especially since sickness and old age haunts all our steps."

Leaning forward, Tobia ventured to make his next desperate request. "Could you give me directions home? I'm not sure I know the way."

Remy shook his head. "We're not travelers, and we only met Vitus that one time." He struggled to his feet and limped across the room. "No one has come looking for you, if that's what you hoped. I am sorry."

After a stretch, Tobia sighed and climbed to his feet. "Well, even if you can't give me advice, you've relieved me of a heavy burden." He glanced out the door at the setting sun and snorted a laugh. "Now I can make haste and lose my way that much faster."

Grabbing a pitcher, Remy poured a pink liquid into two wooden bowls. "I never said I wouldn't give advice." He grinned and handed a drink to Tobia. "You're exhausted and confused. Stay with us a few days and regain your strength." He lifted his drink and both he and Tobia sipped from their bowls at the same time.

Remy wiped his lips. "I'll speak to my men and see what

they've heard." His gaze narrowed. "I want to warn them about the threat you've seen." He pointed a finger. "They'll want to hear your story themselves."

Tobia drank the last sip from his bowl and licked his lips, his gaze darting to the door. "I've been gone for so long, and I hate to impose—"

Remy waved his hand and poured more refreshment into Tobia's cup. "There's no imposing. You're our chosen friend." He pressed Tobia's shoulder. "You did a noble thing, caring for the survivors. Many would've let them die."

Kamila strolled by the open doorway, chatting with Olna and another old woman. She darted a glance inside Remy's hut.

Remy grinned and glanced at Tobia.

Tobia hurriedly finished his second drink.

Remy pointed to the pallet. Sleep here tonight. In the morning, we'll talk again." He stepped to the doorway. "I'm going to see to a few things." His gaze swept across the village. "You can take your supper outside with the villagers, or rest and eat alone. Whichever you prefer."

Tobia bit his lip and peered out. "I'd like to join everyone."

Remy stepped aside, smiling. "I thought you might."

~~~

Tobia remained with Remy and his people for two days, resting and regaining a measure of his spent strength. Memories of his travels with Vitus haunted his steps as he remembered things Vitus had said and done, his sneering contempt, his impatience, his complete disregard for other people's feelings. Guilt washed over his mind, clawing at his heart.

Strolling to a large spreading tree by the stream, Tobia
~~~

hunched his shoulders and bowed his head.

Splashing across the shallow stream, Kamila called, "Tobia? She stepped to his side. "Why the sad expression?"

Tobia exhaled a long breath and leaned on the tree. "I feel so old now. So many things have happened. I can't understand…Vitus struck witless and dying in the desert, the nomad family whose sons betrayed their father, the ravaged villagers, and the old ones who nearly worried me to death."

"You've lived lifetimes already. Adventures, some would call them."

With a shrug, Tobia pushed away from the tree and strolled with Kamila along the shore. "I would say so too, except it was too painful. My heart hurts, and my stomach ties itself into knots." As Kamila kept his pace, he met her gaze. "And the worst part is yet to come."

"How so?"

"My friend, Ishtar, was exiled because he offered a human sacrifice—or tried to."

Kamila's eyes rounded in horror.

Tobia fluttered his hands. "He's not that man anymore. His father was—" He shook his head. "Never mind. That's in the past." He peered across the stream. "But few will forget—or forgive. They don't know the man returning to save them from yet another clan of slave raiders." He kicked a stone. "They'll only see the outer face and not the inner heart."

"That's why you must leave—soon?"

Tobia stopped and nodded. "That's why I must leave—tomorrow."

Kamila stood shoulder-to-shoulder with Tobia and stared across the water to the woodland beyond. "I would not have you stay, knowing that your people need you." She glanced in his direction. "Though I wish it were otherwise."

Turning, Tobia met her gaze. He clasped her hands. “You’ve offered me what few ever would—true friendship. My mother sees only her son, and Obed sees a useless child. Vitus and Ishtar—”

Kamila shook her head. “Their vision does not define you.” She glanced away. “Not unless you want it to.”

Straightening, Tobia led Kamila by the hand toward the village, his gaze lighting on the horizon. “I do not know what the future holds, but—I want to return.” He turned and met her eyes. “And see you again.”

Chapter Thirty-Three

-OldEarth-

Intercept Course

Teal leapt over a boulder, scrambled up a rocky incline, and frowned at a loud gasp behind him. He peered over his shoulder.

Sterling lay sprawled on the ground like a broken toy.

Turning on his heel, Teal doubled backed, lifted Sterling by the arms, and dragged him to the shelter of an overhanging cliff. He dropped the ragged figure in the shade without ceremony and fell on his knees, heaving gasps of air.

Sterling sat up and rocked back and forth like a frightened child. "I can't do this anymore. I really will disintegrate."

Falling back on his haunches, Teal leaned on the shaded rock face, his heart pounding, his mind frozen. "I've never seen anything like it. Never."

Sterling lay spread-eagle and sucked in deep draughts of air. "For once…I can write an interesting report…and I won't…have to embellish…a bit of it." He shook his head. His white hair splayed in the dust. "Too bad…it'll be my last."

Disgusted, Teal spared him a glance.

Rising with a groan, Sterling sat up, heaved a deep cleansing breath, and clapped his hands free of dirt and pebbles. "We're not going any further with this study." He shook his finger at the stone city in the distance. "You saw its power. Bothmal! It could've eaten us!"

Clasping his hands steeple-style before his face, Teal stared into the distance. "I don't think it could sense us as clearly as we could sense it. Certainly, the guards only saw us as men…not Luxonians. I doubt it could know—"

"By all that is good and holy, I'm not about to find out what it knows." Climbing to his feet, Sterling ran his hand over his hair and smoothed down his rumbled rags. "You saw them…once they lost the chance to toss Obed into that pit, their eyes fixed right on yours truly." He tapped his chest. "I would've become nothing more than an evening snack for that beast."

Teal rose with a grunt. "Surely, it would've spit you out."

Glaring, Sterling huffed and squared his shoulders. He shimmered and reappeared in his immaculate white tunic and leggings.

Leaning forward, Teal surveyed their desert surroundings. "No one followed. All's clear." He glanced back. "We can leave and meet up with the others—Luxonian-style of course."

Sterling's eyes drooped to half-mast. "I wasn't about to tip-toe over that blasted desert." He shook himself. "I still can't believe I saw an honest-to-goodness demon."

A flush worked over Teal's face. "Honest-to-goodness? You're delirious. Besides, we don't even understand what humans mean by demon. It's a catch-all term to explain any terrifying—"

"Annihilate! Do you deny that fiend was anything but what humans refer to as a demon?"

Startled, Teal drew back. He ran his fingers through his ruffled hair. "I'll never understand you—sir." He met Sterling's gaze. "I thought you considered humans little more than barbarians."

"Even barbarians can be right sometimes. They happen to be right about demons."

Rubbing his chin, Teal considered the rock ceiling.

"How would you define it? Spirit energy? Light force? Dark matter? An unreported—?"

"Oh, it's been reported—by almost every race in the universe. Demons may have different names and come in various forms, but they all inflict the same horror and spread the same destruction." He shuddered. "You and I wouldn't have disintegrated exactly—we would've become subservient to it. Slaves. Dead to ourselves and all free people."

Teal closed his eyes. "I'm glad Obed escaped."

Sterling bobbed his head up and down. "I'm glad *we* escaped!" He stepped forward. "I'm going to recommend that a quarantine be placed around this planet as soon as possible."

Teal gripped Sterling's arm. "But humanity isn't demonic!"

"You saw those men. They are serving it innocent victims every pitiless day."

Pounding into the light, Teal faced the sun. "But not all humanity does so. Some people resist evil." He glared at Sterling. "You said it yourself, Obed escaped. And Ishtar escaped." He exhaled and folded his arms. "Ungle has a point. We have to find Ishtar and watch what happens when he meets Chai."

Sterling snorted. "So we can see him get devoured?" He curled his lips in obvious distaste. "I thought blood-sports disgusted you."

Teal stepped up the rocky incline and pointed to west. "As much as any decent being. We can't defeat evil, but at least we can learn from those who resist it."

~~~

Ark stood at the ship's helm and hid a spreading grin behind a well-placed tentacle. A bubble of enjoyment
~~~

tickled his insides as he watched the drama unfold before his eyes.

Zuri swaggered on deck, explaining with chest-thumping pride each and every instrument panel.

Kelesta practically purred, her eyes glued to Zuri's every move.

Sienna stood near the open bay door, frowning. "Sterling and Teal should return any moment." She glanced at Ark. "Are you quite done?"

Ark cleared his throat, sending bubbles to the surface of his breathing helm. "Oh, yes!" He turned and offered a generous smile. "Young love—I could watch all day and never get bored."

Sienna's gaze shifted to Zuri, roving from his spiked blond hair to his sandaled four-toed feet. "He almost appears human now."

Ark snorted. "That's the idea…or rather to look more Old-World Ingoti."

Sienna crossed her arms and glared at Ark. "So are you going to tell me—or do I have to guess?"

"Zuri's lady friend likes her mates au naturale."

"Zuri has a *mate*?" Sienna's gaze darted to Kelesta.

Unconcerned, Ark waved a tentacle. "I don't suppose it's terribly serious, considering how much time he spends away."

Pursing her lips, Sienna frowned. "Some people are faithful no matter the distance."

A bright light blinked, and Sterling appeared in the middle of the deck with Teal standing behind him.

Zuri turned sharply, and Kelesta tripped, gripping his arm for support.

Without ceremony, Teal glanced around. His eyes stopped on Zuri, and he stepped forward. "Where's Ishtar?"

With a by-your-leave grin, Zuri slipped from Kelesta's

grasp and met Teal in the middle of the deck. "He saw the ravages of Chai's conquests and is hurrying home. Why? What's happened?"

Sterling sauntered closer and shrugged. "We met a demon from hell."

Everyone froze.

Ark giggled and flipped a tentacle over his breathing helm, a flush working up his face. "Sorry. Such a blatantly vivid image—"

Teal stomped to an instrument panel and scanned the surface. "Hardly a laughing matter." He glanced at Zuri.

Zuri padded to the central computer and tapped the surface. A holographic image appeared in the middle of the room.

In colorful detail, Ishtar appeared to be working his way around the coast of a large lake.

Zuri peered up. "He's near home. The women have hidden in caves. He might run into them or someone from his clan soon."

Ark shuffled closer, rubbing two tentacles together. "Bet that'll be fun."

Teal swallowed. "Where's Chai?"

Zuri tapped the console again, his slender fingers flying over the flat surface.

A holographic image showed Chai leading a large band of warriors, with a ragged line of slaves struggling behind, north of Ishtar's position.

Zuri faced Teal. "They're on an intercept course."

Sterling leaned forward scowling. "Who's that coming up behind Chai?"

Teal slapped his forehead. "Oh, the fools. That's Eoban, Barak, and Obed."

Ark frowned, his lips pursed into flabby tubes. "They have no idea what they're about to run into."

The image blurred, and Teal shouted at Zuri. "What're

you doing?"

Zuri shrugged. "I want to know what happened to the boy—Ishtar's son."

Ark snorted.

Zuri tilted his head, his eyes wide. "What? So I have a soft spot for children."

The image refocused on Amin. Sweat poured down his thin face as he struggled through a thick forest, brushing thorns and vines out of his path.

Sienna blinked and shook her head. "Poor thing."

Kelesta squinted at the scene. "There's something following him."

Ark, turning green, glanced away. "I can't watch."

Sterling snarled at Ark. "You're a Cresta scientist—you dissect specimens all the time."

"After they've died!" Ark swiveled about, his tentacles flying in all directions. "Get it through your Luxonian filters—Crestas have to study everything. It's what we do. How we survive. But that hardly makes us cold-hearted."

Teal tapped his fingers together. "Can we debate this another time?" He turned to Zuri. "Want to split up?"

Kelesta's eyes widened as she wiggled next to the Ingot.

Zuri peered down at her hope-filled eyes and rubbed his beardless chin. "Fine. We'll follow Amin."

Teal swiveled toward Ark. "Take Sterling and keep an eye on Ishtar."

Ark grinned, his golden eyes gleaming. "It'll be my pleasure!"

Sterling raised his hand. "When—exactly—did I get demoted?"

Scowling, Teal turned away. "You're doing what Ungle asked—keeping an eye on Ishtar. There's no other place for you to be."

Sienna sauntered over to Teal and wrapped her arm around his. "And we'll follow the three fools?"

Teal shook his head. "They barely escaped the temple demon, and now they're bumbling right into Chai." He exhaled. "I can only pity them."

Ark stood back and appraised the gathering. "If there's one thing I've learned from humans…"

All eyes fixed on the Crestonian.

Ark grinned. "Nothing ever goes as planned."

CHAPTER THIRTY-FOUR

—WOODLANDS AND HILLS—

NOT FOR EVERYONE

Amin sat on the edge of a large, crumbling log and bathed a red scratch on his arm with a wet leaf. He tried to organize his thoughts. A faint noise disturbed his concentration. He tilted his head. The sound of feet thrashing through the woods sent a chill over his arms. His mouth dropped open, and his heart began to pound.

Either a troop of men or a family of wild bears headed in his direction.

A long, wailing screech jerked Amin to his feet, his gaze darting all around.

Soaring low over his head, an owl forced him into a crouch.

Panting, he scurried behind a tree.

Heavy breathing and a grunt drew closer.

Terror ripped through Amin as he sprang to his feet and sprinted away.

Bouncing off a solid body, Amin fell backwards, and knocked the air out of his chest. Choking, he sat up and considered the large figure before him. He blinked.

A large disheveled man peered down, a wide grin spreading across his face. "Amin?"

"Luge?"

"So we meet again, faithful son!" Luge hefted Amin back onto his feet. His smile turned to a puzzled frown. "But why are you so far from home? This is no place to hunt." He glanced around. "Have they started the migration yet?"

Amin swallowed. “N-no. I mean, yes. They’re preparing, but Lydia wanted to wait for you.”

A tall, thin but well-muscled man near Amin’s age stepped closer and stared through wide gray eyes.

Luge tousled the boy’s hair. “Here is my son!” He peered at the boy, his face aglow with happiness. “Lufti, this is Amin, the boy I told you about.” He waved his hands in emphasis. “It’s because of him that I found you.”

Amin blinked. “You found your son? But how—?”

Luge leaned forward as if sharing a secret, his grin wider than ever. “I stole him back!”

A spark of hope ignited in Amin’s chest. “And my father?” He peered at Luge’s men, staring at their impassive faces. “Barak? Obed…Eoban?”

“Brave men, they are.” Luge laid a firm hand on Amin’s shoulder. “But I never saw your father.” He glanced at his son. “It wasn’t safe for us to linger. Still” —he shrugged— “I trust your friends will return with him soon.” With a frown, he waved an open hand. “But why are you here?”

As if he had swallowed a rock, Amin’s throat closed tight. He tried to clear it. “I-I angered your brother…and he sent me away.”

Luge’s eyes narrowed. “Rueben sent you into the wilderness—unprotected?” His jaw hardened. “What happened to my wife? Had she no say?”

“Lydia was busy preparing for the move.”

“What was Rueben doing?”

Amin bit his lip and stared at the ground.

“Why was he angry with you?”

Amin shrugged. “I spoke out of turn…Lydia was already doing so much…” He sighed.

Luge’s eyes narrowed. “I understand.” He turned to his men. “We need to hurry.”

Amin stepped in his way. “But they’ve left by now…on their migration.”

“I know where they’re going.” He glanced at his son. “Lufti, you keep Amin company at the end of the line.” He pointed ahead. “The men and I have much to discuss.”

Nausea wormed into Amin’s stomach as they turned down a well-worn path, away from the mountains.

The two youths marched through the humid forest in silence as the sun climbed to its peak and began its decent.

Finally, Lufti nudged Amin and pointed to a snake dangling from a high branch.

Amin veered to the side, his gaze fixed on the snake.

Lufti shrugged. “It’s not poisonous.”

Amin shuddered. “But it’s big enough to strangle me in my sleep.”

Lufti chuckled. “Now I won’t rest tonight.”

Glancing out of the corner of his eyes, Amin studied his companion. “It must’ve been terrible—being captured and made a slave.”

Lufti nodded. He glanced at the men, talking up ahead. “But it’s over now.” He stepped over a fallen log. “My father told me about you and your search for your father. You’re very brave.”

Choking, Amin staggered before he righted himself. “I’m not brave…just desperate.” He glanced aside. “But you…living in a city among palaces and temples! You must have incredible stories to tell.”

A soft smile wafted over Lufti’s face. “I saw some very beautiful people and places—” His smile vanished, and he closed his eyes. “But terrible things too.”

Amin nodded, swallowing back a gnawing fear.

~~~

Luge jerked awake from a nightmare of temple gods in the shapes of men and animals clawing at his chest. He scrambled to his feet in the early morning light, blinked,
~~~

and gained his bearings.

The sun barely crested the horizon, but the rays sent golden beams through the woods, highlighting dew-speckled spider webs and emerald leaves.

Lufti and the other men rose and gathered their things.

Groaning, Amin stretched and fell in line behind the men, with Lufti at his side.

After heading to the front, Luge rubbed his belly and glanced back. “We’ll eat when we meet up with the clan.” An anxious sickness hurried his steps. In silence, he began the final march home.

Amin peered at Lufti and tapped his arm. “How does he know where to go? They could’ve stopped anywhere.”

Lufti shook his head. “They have a set arrangement about where they go each season.” He peered around. “It would never do to trespass over another clan’s migration path.”

“Ah.” Amin sighed.

By late morning, Luge slowed at the sound of voices ahead. Stopping, he held up his hand in warning. “I want to go alone and see what is happening.”

Lufti and Amin exchanged glances.

Luge frowned. “I fear my brother rules with a heavy hand while I’m gone. I’ll see for myself.”

After pacing ahead, Luge stopped and crouched low. His eyes narrowed as he parted the thick foliage.

In the shade of a temporary shelter, Rueben reclined on a soft pallet while his wife bustled about, offering food and drink, snatching at bits as she did so.

Lydia trudged back and forth across the compound, with her children in tow, clutching a large bundle. The rest of the clan set up shelters and arranged cooking materials.

One man cleared a space for a central fire pit.

A hot flush working up his face, Luge charged from the hedge and marched to his brother, his jaw clenching too tight for words.

Lydia glanced over and gasped. She dropped the blankets in the dirt.

The two children called, writhing in joy, and scampered toward him, their arms outstretched.

Without a word, Luge sidestepped his wife and children and gripped Rueben by the collar. He lifted him off his pallet and forced him to stagger backward until his back slammed against a large tree. Luge pinned his brother against the bark with a tight grip.

Ulla screamed, throwing her hands over her mouth, her eyes wide in terror.

Racing forward, Lydia ran to her husband's side and tugged on his arms. "Luge? What're you doing?"

Luge peered at her, his throat tight, and his arms shaking. "I'm helping my brother get to work!"

Amin appeared at his side along with Lufti.

Lufti laid his hand on his mother's shoulder. "Mother."

Lydia turned and met Lufti's gaze. She froze. Then her eyes grew round as her hands rose to caress his face, her lips trembling. "My son?"

Lufti wrapped his arms around his mother and hugged her tight, murmuring over her shoulder, his eyes filling with tears. "Father brought me home."

Luge dropped Rueben unceremoniously and joined the embrace of his wife and son, the entire village watching, wide-eyed and open-mouthed.

Out of the corner of his eye, Luge saw Rueben scamper aside, practically crawling on all fours. He struck out and grabbed Rueben again and shook him.

Whimpering in terror, Rueben reached for his wife.

Ulla scrambled forward and clung to her husband. "He's a good man, Luge! He's been ill." She glanced around at all the wary faces. "You know the truth of it! He suffers so, and no one helps him."

Amin backed away.

Focusing her gaze, Ulla pointed at Amin. "There's that treacherous child. He dared to challenge Rueben, making accusations, stirring up trouble." She glanced at Lydia. "Some people will trust a fool and leave an honest man to—"

Darting from under Lufti's arm, Lydia charged between Ulla and Amin. "How dare you?" She ran to Amin, gripped his arm, and pulled him forward. "He helped me more than anyone else! And he never once complained." She appealed to her husband. "He told me that you went to look for Lufti, but I had no hope left. I doubted…" Her gaze fell on her son, and she swallowed a sob before returning to her husband. "But he did not doubt. He acted like another son, caring for me as he did."

Stiff and hunch-shouldered, Amin stared at the ground, his face flushing.

Burning rage erupted from Luge as he clasped Rueben by the shoulders and thrust him to the ground. He shook his fist at Ulla. "If you interfere again, I'll throw you both out of this village!"

Rueben cowered, and Ulla fell to her knees wailing.

Turning, Luge faced his people, his arms spread wide. "My people! I've come home, and I bring back our own. I found my son who was stolen from us, and I bring back every man who served me." He swept his gaze over the assembly, avoiding the figure of his brother huddled at his feet. "I've traveled to distant lands and seen great and terrible things."

The clan shuffled closer, their eyes flittering between Luge, Lufti, and Rueben.

Luge lifted one arm. "How is it that no man here protected my wife or this boy?" He pointed at Amin.

Gazes shifted and dropped to the ground.

Lydia wrapped her arms around her husband. "Please, Luge! Don't blame them." She dropped her head on his chest and closed her eyes. "Don't blame anyone. It's over now."

Smoothing back Lydia's hair, Luge peered into her eyes and the fiery knot in his stomach settled into a rough sea. He wrapped his arms protectively around her. "You're right." He glanced aside and nodded to Lufti. "It's over now. We have a reason to celebrate and stories to tell."

Luge and his family stepped around the cowering figures of Rueben and his wife and entered the joy of their reunited village.

~~~

Amin stepped back and folded his arms over his chest. He blinked away tears. The strain in his throat made it difficult to get out his words, even in a whisper. "Not for everyone."
~~~

CHAPTER THIRTY-FIVE

—GRASSLAND—

A STEADFAST HEART

Lud sat on a high ridge overlooking the great lake and scanned the environment. Movement caught his gaze.

A man scrambled among the brush along the eastern edge.

Lud stood and peered down, shading his eyes. He called to one of his clansmen, Jude, who sprinted over and followed the line of his gaze.

The figure worked his way around the lake.

Jude squinted. “A spy?”

Lud shook his head.

The suspect scrambled up the cliff face and slipped twice before he proceeded more slowly.

Rubbing his neck, Lud frowned. “Brave fool maybe…but not necessarily a spy. Could be running from danger or looking for help.” Lud scanned the horizon.

Nothing but birds in the air and a few animals scampering about.

The stranger heaved himself onto a thin ledge and rested, sucking in draughts of air.

Jude smirked. “A fool, sure enough. That’s no place to hide.”

The stranger glanced from side to side, his shoulders squared and his chin sharp and determined.

As his eyes widened in alarm, recognition shuddered through Lud’s body.

~~~

Ishtar surveyed the land. He smiled at the memory of his four-footed friends who had accompanied him along many trails. He glanced at the mountains in the distance. The combination of blue sky, mountains, hills, open grasslands, and a sparking lake refreshed his weary soul.

But in a flash, he saw the view from a different cliff, one where his bleeding feet clutched the edge and a rocky bottom beckoned. He could see Pele's figure floating before his eyes, swaying like a leaf in a gentle wind. He heard her soft words: "Begin again."

A hawk cawed in the distance, a shrill cry, demanding and powerful.

Ishtar closed his eyes. "I yet live."

When he peered up, the bird had retreated into the distance, appearing now as nothing but a speck. With a stretch, he took a deep breath and reached for the next handhold.

As he neared the top edge, he felt eyes watching him. Above, shadows of men waited. Ignoring the sweat pouring into his eyes, he made a final heave and clutched the rocky edge. His foot slipped and in panic, he scrambled for purchase, digging his torn fingers into the stony surface.

A hand clasped his…gripping his wrist.

Taking a deep breath, Ishtar gathered his courage, steadied his footing on the wall face, and leveraged his way up the last few feet.

Another hand reached down and grabbed him by the arm, heaving and pulling him to safety.

When he lay safely on top, he breathed in the scanty grass and the damp earthy dirt.

Two pairs of feet waited near at hand.

Lifting his head, Ishtar peered up.
~~~

Lud stood over him, his eyes wide and his mouth open. He shook his head like a man trying to get his senses to work.

"Ishtar?"

Ishtar climbed to his feet, fixed his attention on Lud, and gripped his shoulder. "I've come home."

Lud stood frozen.

Jude slapped his thigh, a half-smile forming on his lips. "Well, I never—"

Lud reached up and clasped his hand over Ishtar's. "I thought perhaps you—but they thought—so they went looking—but now— you've returned."

Jude thrust his hands on his hips, a puzzled frown puckering between his eyes. "You didn't meet up with the others, then?"

Grinning, Ishtar led Lud and Jude away from the cliff's edge. "I see we have some catching up to do."

As they crossed the plateau, Lud glanced at Ishtar. "Where've you come from? Eoban, Barak and Obed went looking for you with Amin months ago." He paused and glanced back, pointing to the distance. "Toward the mountains. Did you cross paths?"

Searing alarm spread over Ishtar. "Amin went to the mountains…looking for me? When?"

Lud frowned at Ishtar. "Why? What's in the mountains?"

Exasperation eating at his insides, Ishtar raised his hands. "Under the great sky, will you stop asking questions and answer me? I'll tell you my story later, but where are my sons?"

"Amin left with Eoban and the rest, but Caleb is with Milkan and the women at the caves." Lud sighed. "We have troubles of our own."

Swinging his gaze from the village site in the distance to the path leading to the caves, Ishtar chewed his lip. "Before anything else, I must see Caleb."

Lud swallowed and stepped closer. “Certainly. But I have to warn you: an enemy marches near.”

“That’s why I returned. By the will of God, I met Tobia in the desert lands, and as we journeyed home together, we discovered a ruined village. I left the remnant of the clan in his care, while I ran ahead to warn our people. We must make preparations quickly.” He started for the caves. “But first, I’ll see my son.”

Running to keep in step, Lud motioned to Jude to return to his post. He called back, “We’ll return soon.”

They turned north and strode side by side as long afternoon shadows stretched to impossible lengths.

Lud glanced aside, his face flushing. “You seem better…than you were.”

Without breaking his steady pace, Ishtar nodded. “I’m a new man—a better man—I hope.”

“How did you survive?”

“A nomadic patriarch took me in and cared for me.” Ishtar peered into the golden horizon. “In ironic justice, I had a chance to do reparation for my sins when his sons attempted a rebellion. I stayed at the old man’s side and comforted him as I could never have comforted my own father.” He sighed. “But Tobia and the memory of my sons beckoned me home.” He stopped and peered into Lud’s eyes. “I want to be the man I never was…the leader I should’ve been.”

With a strangled voice, Lud pounded forward. “Please, do so! I certainly never wanted leadership.” He sliced his hand through the air. “Barak took good care of your sons, but they couldn’t rest easy not knowing what happened to you. Eoban set his heart on finding you, and Obed sent Tobia with Vitus to—”

Lud halted, his eyes widening. He stopped and turned his full attention on Ishtar. “What happened to Vitus? You said you met Tobia in the desert lands. What about—?”

Ishtar glanced away. "Vitus died in the desert."

Lud's eyes narrowed. "Died—how?"

"It's a long story—one that Tobia can tell better." Grief clutched Ishtar's chest. "Please, it's a haunting memory, and Tobia has suffered more than I can explain."

Rubbing his temple, Lud started away again. "No one is safe from suffering." He shrugged as he jogged over the hard ground. "Truth is…I'm not a leader. I don't know what I'm doing." He blew air between his lips. "It was easy when we were at peace, but now—"

Stepping faster, Ishtar scrambled over the rough terrain. "I've seen the enemy, and it won't set your heart at ease if I describe them to you." Slowing as he neared the triangular cave entrance, Ishtar glanced at Lud. "In order to survive—we need more allies. Many more allies."

Lud dropped his gaze. "I was afraid of that."

Ishtar started to the cave, which opened at the side of a sheer cliff with a heavy mat of moss at the entrance, but Lud lifted his hand, blocking him. "Wait. Let me go first and explain. Your arriving like this…it's a bit of a shock."

Ishtar took two steps back and watched Lud disappear inside the cave. As he paced some distance away, he pictured Caleb's babyish, tear-stained face from the last time he had seen him. The little boy had stood aside, his shoulders shaking, watching his father bury his mother. The bitter image sent Ishtar's heart hammering against his chest. He bit his lip as a film of tears spread over his eyes.

Lud called and waved as he stepped into the light with a tall boy at his side.

A stinging fury enveloped Ishtar. *Why does he bring out his own son?* He called as he pounded forward. "Where's Caleb?"

"Father!" Running full speed with his arms stretched out, Caleb plowed into his father.

Jerking backward on impact, Ishtar choked on a sob and

fell to his knees. He wrapped his arms around his son, who stood taller and stronger than he remembered. Then he shook his head in amazement, his vision blurred. "Caleb?"

Glancing over his shoulder, Caleb shouted to Dinah and Milkan, who also stepped into the light, "Look! My father's home!"

Dinah and Milkan stood at a respectful distance while Lud stepped to the boy's side.

Ishtar composed himself and rose to his feet, his hand firmly on his son's shoulder. He met Lud's gaze. "Thank you." He peered down at the boy. "I can see he has been well cared for."

A scout called from the distance.

Lud and Ishtar jerked their attention to the distant figure of a warrior racing into the village. Lud swallowed hard.

Ishtar exhaled a deep breath. "I will not let us to suffer the fate of other ravaged clans. We must prepare for battle."

Caleb peered up at his father. "But what about Amin? When is he coming home?"

Ishtar glanced from Lud to Milkan and Dinah. "I don't know, but as soon as we defeat the approaching enemy" — he knelt and peered into Celeb's eyes— "you and I will find him together."

Caleb's lips wobbled. "You won't leave me?"

Ishtar stroked the side of his boy's face. "Never again."

~~~

Ishtar perched on a rock as the stars appeared in the night sky, and he waited while Namah, Jonas, Milkan, and Dinah settled in a circle with Lud and other clansmen before a flickering fire.

Lud opened his hands and nodded to Ishtar.

Fixing his gaze on the flames, Ishtar retold his
~~~

adventures from the day he left the clan until he met Lud on the cliff.

Milkan and Dinah nodded alternately, glancing at Ishtar with sympathy in their eyes.

Namah glared at Ishtar, her jaw clenched and her hands in frozen stillness on her lap.

As Jonas focused on the outer darkness, she listened without comment.

When the recital ended, Ishtar peered from one woman to the next. His gaze stopped on Namah. “I have done great evil in my time, and I regret many things, but one of the worst is knowing that I can never make amends to Aram, a man I should’ve treated as a friend and mentor.” His throat tightening, Ishtar all but crawled to Namah’s side and bent his head. “I beg your forgiveness.”

Slowly, Namah’s hand rose, flat palmed as if she would strike.

Ishtar remained in place, humbly waiting, his gaze scraping the dust.

Lifting her hand higher, Namah turned it and let it fall gently on Ishtar’s head. “I forgive you, Ishtar, for in my heart I know that is what Aram would ask of me. I don’t know how you can make up for your evil deeds, but—” She dropped her hand to her side. “You’ve made a good start by returning to your sons.”

Ishtar raised his head, tears burning.

Jonas sighed and faced Ishtar. “I can do no less than my friend and forgive you. However, I will watch and see. A tree is known by its fruit.” She sighed and stared at the black horizon. “But for now, a new enemy approaches.” She met his gaze. “Will you lead your men into battle?”

Ishtar rose and stood before Lud. “You are the leader now. Tell me what you’d have me do, and I’ll do it.”

Lud stood and clasped Ishtar’s arm. “As you said, we need more allies.”

Nodding, Ishtar faced the small assembly. "I have learned through great trial that our best ally is a steadfast heart." A glimmer of hope sparked in his soul. "We already have that."

CHAPTER THIRTY-SIX

—WOODLAND—

HE RAN FASTER

Eoban's legs wobbled. He called for a halt and dropped to his knees before a broken tree trunk and gulped warm, stale water from his skin bag. After wiping his mouth, he glanced from Obed to Barak. "I'm not sure, but Luge's clan might've left for their migration by now. It's past their usual time."

Barak guzzled his water, scowled, and tossed his empty bag aside. "It's past time we went home."

Eoban frowned and took another long drink.

"I think we're close enough now. We could go in either direction." Barak shrugged. "I'm ready to go home."

Obed stepped forward, wiping his lips as he held his bag in a tight grip. "But what about Amin? Surely, you're not suggesting that we leave him behind?"

Barak shook his head. "By no means! I want to find him, but I've a clamoring in my mind, insisting that I go home."

Eoban waved Barak's words away though his stomach twisted, anxiety churning the fluids in his middle. "You worry too much."

Barak slapped his thigh and looked to the sky as if beseeching the heavens for strength.

Obed raised his hand. "I'll find Amin. You two return home and make sure everyone is safe." He raised his eyebrows and tipped his head at Barak. "I'm learning to trust your instincts."

A relieved grin broke over Barak's face.

With a dizzy sensation and a feeling that his world was swiftly falling apart, Eoban pounded over to Barak and shook a finger in the direction of Obed. "You really believe that man can find Amin and make his way home again before the season turns?"

Barak met Eoban's gaze, steady and unblinking. He crossed his arms high over his chest.

Turning, Eoban glared at Obed. "You've never traveled alone! You prefer to sit around and think—"

A small stick smacked Eoban on the nose.

Eoban turned and caught Barak's hard gaze and his fingers still in the flicking position.

Barak dropped his hand and faced Obed. "It's a workable plan. We'll split up. You find Amin. I'll take Eoban, and we'll meet at home."

With a quick nod, Obed turned and began clearing a spot for their evening fire.

Eoban threw up his hands in mock surrender. "Oh, of course. I'm talking nonsense, just being difficult as usual." A flush worked up his face as he indulged in a righteous pout. "I know when I'm not wanted. I've half a mind to go off on my own."

Snorting, Barak bundled kindling into his arms. "And where would you go?"

Eoban ripped into his bag and pulled out a handful of shriveled berries. "I could go anywhere." He tossed the desiccated fruit into his mouth and chewed vigorously. "I could visit friends. I could find new trade routes. I could —"

Barak looked at Obed. "Take him if you want, or he's welcome to come with me, but I think you're right. I can't ignore this inner turmoil any longer. I must get home."

"Inner turmoil?" Eoban rolled his eyes and shook his head. "Now I'll be worried about you, Barak. Obed might get lost, but you'll make yourself sick." He blew air through his teeth. "I'll go with you for Milkan's sake. She'd be devastated if you perished—even though you're enough to drive any man mad."

~~~

Obed rose at daybreak refreshed and ready for adventure. Springing to his feet, he relished the very thought of traveling alone, with its unparalleled level of freedom. Closing his eyes, he sucked in a deep breath of fresh air. At the sound of footsteps, he flicked his eyes open.

Eoban stood three feet away, staring at him through narrowed eyes.

Obed waited, dreading an announcement.

In an unexpected move, Eoban threw his arms out and enveloped Obed in a bear hug. "Since I may never see you again—"

Relief flooding his senses, Obed shoved Eoban away with an awkward laugh. "Likely, I'll make it home with Amin before you and Barak even get out of this trackless wilderness."

Eoban lifted his hands in defeat. "If you say so." He lifted one eyebrow. "I've gone over the directions to Luge's place. Any questions?"

Chuckling, Obed stepped around Eoban and slapped Barak on the shoulder. "Thank you, my friend, for your loyalty to the clan. Best of luck on your return journey." He glanced aside. "I surely have the easier task."

Barak dropped his head to his chest and sighed.

Pursing his lips, Eoban clapped his hands. "Enough blathering." He swung his bag over his shoulder and stomped away.

As Barak trailed after Eoban, he glanced back, met his friend's gaze, and rolled his eyes.

Obed grinned.
~~~

~~~

Obed sauntered over the rough woodland, his arms swinging at his sides, whistling a jaunty tune. Sweat trickled down his back as he swatted insects beyond all possible count. Three times he circled around prickly thickets, and twice he forded meandering creeks and joyfully splashed himself as he went. He reveled in his slow pace and the exuberance of running down an incline with his arms spread wide to catch the breeze. When his stomach rumbled, he stopped to gather berries. By noon, he came upon a large tree with branches hanging low from an abundance of nuts. He pawed through his bag and drew out an empty leather pouch.

He scrambled up the lowest branches and picked to his heart's contentment. When the bag was bulging, he dropped to the ground, toed through the foliage, and found a rock of sufficient size. After smashing a handful of nuts, he rested against the firm, smooth trunk and enjoyed the crunchy, meaty insides.

The filtered sun speckled the ground around him, light and dark dancing like children at play. Birds chirped and flew from branch to branch overhead. A rodent scampered near, sniffed the broken shells, then rose on its haunches and peered at Obed through tiny black eyes.

Grinning and satiated with simple pleasures, Obed relaxed in weariness and closed his eyes.

Pleasurable rest spread through his whole body and cast pretty images of woods and streams in his mind…

Sometime later, strange shuffling, huffing sounds stirred, disturbing Obed's rest. He rubbed open his eyes, yawned, and climbed to his feet. Glancing at the sky, he squinted at the bright rays of sunlight. He gathered his bag and spear and stumped forward. In bemused exhaustion, he trudged
~~~

across a wide, meandering stream and circled around large boulders.

By late afternoon, the air grew thick and his feet dragged. He stumbled twice and then stopped to catch his breath.

Speckled sunlight glimmered through the branches before him.

Pursing his lips, Obed craned his neck around.

Twilight descended behind him.

Frowning, he turned and peered at the low, western sun before him. He rubbed his jaw, his confusion ending in a bemused chuckle. Obed crouched beneath a large spreading tree and murmured, "I can't be lost. It's too ridiculous." He pointed at the sun and grinned, wondering if he was drunk on innocent pleasure. "You're supposed to be behind me." He ran his fingers through his hair. "Maybe I—"

A blurred force of wind and a stone sped by, nicking his face. Confused, he slapped his cheek and glanced aside.

A spear embedded in the tree wavered like an insect tail.

Cold shock drenched Obed.

Crashing, pounding footsteps accompanied by grunts and yells drew close.

Without thought, Obed rushed madly into the woods. As the voices grew more distinct, all strength drained from his limbs.

A gruff voice rose behind him, and a sharp pain on the back of his head sent brilliant lights flashing before his eyes. He fell into blackness.

~~~

Obed awoke with a throbbing headache, barely able to recognize the moon shining down from a star-studded sky. When he tried to rub his stinging neck, he found his arms bound tight. Groaning, he realized that he lay among a
~~~

crowd of people all trussed up like pigs fit for a feast.

His cramped legs ached, demanding a stretch, but when he tried to straighten, his ropes jerked a heat-laden, stinking body close to him.

A groan swelled on his right.

Obed twisted and peered at a scrawny, filthy boy with a rope strung around his neck and waist. When he twisted to the left, his mouth fell open at the sight of half-starved men, women, and children tightly packed all around him.

Sour body odor, stomach leavings, stale urine, and excrement dragged a retching sensation from his stomach. He heaved and realized that there was no place to throw up except upon another person. Squeezing his eyes shut, he fought the upheavals through gritted teeth.

Once he gained mastery over his stomach, he turned his attention to the hot, smothering camp. Flickering flames danced amidst a huddle of armed warriors, who stomped and pounded their spears in rhythm to a low, incessant drumbeat.

In the distance, a whimper rose, followed by a skirmish of shuffling feet and flailing arms.

A murmur flittered among the prisoners, then a gasp and a stifled cry.

The beat grew stronger and more insistent.

A shriveled, ragged figure was dragged before the fire, pleading and whimpering.

A new figure appeared following the first, short sleeved, muscled, straight-backed, and pointing a glinting knife.

Nausea again erupted from Obed's middle, spreading acid through his mouth. He dropped his head to his chest, gasping short breaths. Fear closed his eyes and hunched his shoulders against his ears.

A scream tore through the night air.

Arrows of agony ripped through Obed.

Everyone stiffened. Even the air held its breath.

The cry faltered, slipped to a groan…and died.

Tears flooded Obed's eyes and slipped down his cheeks.

~~~

Obed jolted awake as cold water splashed his face.

A giggle passed on and then a cry, a jerk, and another giggle. Obed swallowed back the sour taste in his mouth, glancing at the dripping figure beside him. He wanted to wipe his own face, but since his hands were restrained, he couldn't reach it.

The man on his left scuttled to a sitting position and wiped his face against his shoulder, peering from the passing guard to Obed. "He generally do like that. Funny he thinks it. Giggles like a maniac every morning. Always the same." He shook his head.

Obed pictured Luge's anxious face when he'd mentioned his lost son. He blinked the drips away and met the other man's gaze. "Where are they from…these slavers?"

Jutting his chin outward, the man glanced away. "Over the mountain some say. Talk of a stone city and glories beyond description." He shrugged. "Demons of hell more like."

Obed peered at the well-armed warrior who stalked among the captives drenching the sleepers, kicking those who didn't budge, and giggling like a fool. *Demons of hell…indeed.*

~~~

Tobia strode with purposeful concentration, relieved of his burden yet anxious to get home. With his back to the setting sun, he charged ahead with dexterous steps, paying little heed to his surroundings.

As evening fell, a strange silence caught his attention. No

birds flittered about, as if an unseen warning held every animal at bay.

Slowing, he turned aside and noticed broken branches and a beaten path across the woodland floor. He crouched low and examined the ground, tracing the prints of feet shod in soft leather and the marks of numerous bare toes.

He rose and rubbed his sweaty neck.

A scream ripped through the air.

Scuttling like a crab, Tobia made his way forward and stopped on the edge of a large assembly gathered around a central fire. His innards twisted into a hard knot.

He circled around the gathering, freezing when the scream rose and fell in torment and finally faded in a pitiful death. After a silent moment, he crawled forward. When his muscles contracted, he stopped before a ragged throng of prisoners. Studying the assembly, his throat tightened and his stomach lurched.

He rubbed his eyes and looked again. Surely his eyes were deceiving him. There, tied to a long line of men, women, and children sat a filthy man with a bowed head. Shadows covered the man's face, but still Tobia recognized him. "Obed?"

Tobia tried to swallow. Had Ishtar failed? Had his people been attacked and overcome? Cursing himself for his stay at Kamila's village, he leaned forward and studied the group. Tears filled his eyes as he frantically searched the crowd for familiar faces.

He frowned even as relief poured over his body. He recognized no one except Obed.

Shaking, he scuttled backward slowly to avoid any undue noise. Stopping some distance away, he crouched on his haunches and considered his options. He glanced back the way he had come. Remy was too far away and unprepared for such a situation. Only the united clans with Eoban and Barak in the lead could hope to make a successful attack.

Scowling, he positioned himself like a man prepared to race like the wind. He turned toward home. A question haunted his mind. *What happened to Ishtar?*

With narrowed his eyes, he darted ahead, his whole body screaming. *Run!*

As he picked up speed, tears blurred his vision. He had not saved his first father or Vitus, and most likely Ishtar had come to a bad end. But still he had a slim chance of saving his second father and his village. His heart hammered against his chest, ready to burst.

He ran faster.

CHAPTER THIRTY-SEVEN

—GRASSLANDS—

YOU CAN ONLY ENDURE

Ishtar walked among his people again. After visiting his son, he returned to the village and sat with the five members of the leadership council.

They welcomed him with smiles.

Perplexed by their obvious joy, Ishtar launched into a full recital of his adventures—including his madness—and concluded with a declaration of his healing through the kindness of Matalah.

The council members continued to smile, their eyes twinkling, their backs straights, and their chins up.

Ishtar considered the line of old men. No deceit there. He dropped his gaze and raked his hand through his hair. "Why do you smile?"

The eldest, Amos, grinned and lifted his hand as if in blessing. "We are glad to see you home safe." He shrugged. "There's nothing mysterious in a clan welcoming their leader—"

Jerking to his feet with a grunt, Ishtar paced away, his voice falling to a whisper. "But I betrayed you."

Amos rose and clasped his hands as if in prayer. "Some may see it so…but not all do." He gazed around the circle and then met Ishtar's wide eyes. "We are warriors and conquerors, descending from a long line of such men. Your father, though he strayed from decency when he lied to us, maintained a close tie to his heritage. When you offered—" He cleared his throat and glanced away. "Attempted to offer a child to the gods, you followed not the will of a woman but the call of our ancestral spirits."

His jaw clenching, Ishtar swallowed and glared. "Spirits I no longer obey."

Amos tipped his head. "You are now your own man." When he lifted his eyes, he took one step closer. "Ishtar, we need your leadership. Now, because of the battles you have fought, you're a stronger, wiser man." A grin reappeared, brightening his face. "And that's why we're glad of your return."

Peering up at the wide blue sky, Ishtar paused. Finally, he sighed, dropped his eyes, and met Amos's unwavering confidence. "May you remain so."

~~~

Ishtar met with leaders from neighboring clans the next day, and they discussed their plans in council with Lud.

Lud approved the plans, and after sending out scouts and closing the meeting, he stared at Ishtar in silence.

Distracted with his plans and anxieties, Lud's fascination merely brushed Ishtar's consciousness. But after a moment, he frowned and met Lud's hard stare. "What's wrong?"

"I think I know what's so different about you. Even when you're worried, you're controlled. Almost at peace."

With a snort, Ishtar snatched up his spear and a whetstone. He ran the stone along the spear tip. "I know now that I can survive madness." He glanced at Lud. "Hope beyond despair is the best kind."

A figure in the distance jogged toward. Ishtar shaded his eyes with his hand. "Who's this now?"

Lud frowned and stepped beside Ishtar.

The sweaty, exhausted young man stumbled to a halt, bent over, and gasped heaving breaths.
~~~

Ishtar leapt forward. "Tobia!" He gripped his friend's arm and glanced around. "Where are—?"

Tobia lifted a hand and huffed his words. "They're with…Remy's clan…safe. But—"

Lud stepped closer and pressed Tobia's shoulder. "Catch your breath. There's no news that can't wait a moment." He glanced aside at Ishtar.

Tobia shook his head and straightened with a wince. "The enemy is at hand, and they've—"

Ishtar shouted to men in the distance and a crowd hurried near. He drew Tobia forward. "Come, sit. Tell us everything."

Tobia lifted both hands. "Listen! There's no time! Obed has been taken. He's tied like a hog ready for slaughter in the midst of a great host."

Warriors with weapons in their hands jostled each other as they closed in, grunting and leaning forward, scowls on every face.

Lud blinked, his face draining of all color. "Where are Barak and Eoban?"

Tobia shook his head, a bewildered expression in his eyes.

Ishtar gripped Tobia's shoulders and stared hard into his eyes. "Where's Amin?"

Tobia's eyes filled with tears. "Isn't he here?"

~~~

Tobia sat before trays piled with bread, fruit, nuts, and berries. He set a bowl of sharp wine aside, feeling bitterness slide down his throat.

After nightfall, Ishtar, Lud, Jonas, Namah, and an assembly of councilmen and warriors huddled in Namah's home and watched his every move.

Closing his eyes, Tobia sat back and sighed. "I can't
~~~

eat…I'm not strong enough yet."

Namah patted his hand. "Take your time. You've been through a great deal."

Tobia opened his eyes and stared at his mother's anxious face. "Obed is still alive…that's the good news." He sniffed and dragged his fingers down his face. "But how he became a prisoner, I have no idea." He sucked in a deep breath. "For a moment I thought that all of you had been—" His lips quivered.

Ishtar nudged the bowl closer. "Take more drink and get some rest. Your descriptions of the host will better prepare us. It's best we know the truth." He sighed and met Tobia's gaze. "I'm glad you made it home alive."

Staring blankly at the back wall, Tobia shrugged. "I don't feel alive."

Namah and Jonas exchanged glances.

Namah rose first. "He'll never sleep with a crowd watching." She started for the door. "You've done well, Tobia. Surviving is no small thing in this world." She crossed into the night air.

The councilmen and warriors rose and followed her example.

As Lud stood in the doorway, he turned and glanced back. "Death is like slavery. You can't stand it, yet you can't escape it." He nodded at Tobia. "You can only endure."

Ishtar climbed to his feet and peered at Tobia. "I'll be just outside…if you need me."

Jonas accompanied Ishtar to the door and dropped her voice low. "He told me about your journey together. I thank you for your service. It wasn't what I looked for—"

Ishtar glanced over Jonas' shoulder and met Tobia's eyes. "He's an extraordinary man." He peered at Jonas. "God asks much of extraordinary men."

As Ishtar passed over the threshold, Jonas stood silent,

staring at the night sky.

Tobia rubbed his aching eyes. “Get some sleep, mother. We’ll need you fresh in the morning.”

Jonas padded to his side and kissed his cheek. “I’m so relieved you’re home.” Her voice caught. “I know Obed will be too.”

Only the sound of her footsteps fading into the next room told Tobia that he was finally alone. Shoving the trays aside, he pulled a blanket close, bundled it under his head, and curled into a ball. Shuddering in the evening air, he closed his eyes and finally let his tears fall.

CHAPTER THIRTY-EIGHT

—WOOD LANDS AND GRASSLANDS—

FOR ALL THE TROUBLE YOU'VE CAUSED

Eoban wiped his sweaty brow and came to a dead halt. "I've made a mistake."

"What?" Tromping in front, Barak waved an insect away.

Eoban cupped his hands over his mouth and shouted, "I made a mistake!"

Barak stopped and turned around, frowning. "About what?"

"I should've gone with Obed. He won't be able to find Amin. He'll wander around the hills for years if I don't help him."

"Are you out of your mind? We've been traveling for hours! Obed is long gone in the opposite direction. Besides, what if there's trouble at home?"

Eoban shook his head, feeling very much like a disgruntled bull. "You'll find the way easily enough from here, and we've plenty of warriors to hold off an enemy until I get back." He peered at the sky. "I'll find Obed and get the boy."

Barak snorted. "Why didn't you say something earlier?"

Eoban shrugged.

"Oh, all right, go on then. But look for Amin first. Frankly, I'll be relieved if you do. I haven't been so sure of Obed ever since he stepped out of that temple. In the meantime, I'm making a beeline for home." Barak sighed as he shoved his bag high over his shoulder. "I'll hold everything together until you return. Lud is probably ready to take my head off for being gone so long."

"Jonas and Milkan, too, I imagine."

"Always ready to offer a bit of comfort, aren't you?"

"It happens to be the truth." Eoban stepped forward and pounded Barak on the back. "Get going! I've lost enough time. It'll be dark soon, and you know what happens in the dark."

Barak swung his staff at a trailing vine. "Sing and nothing with any sense will bother you."

Eoban turned away, muttering. "Who has sense these days?"

Eoban had not traveled far and wide for so many years without learning a few things. The next day, he found Luge's new settlement. When he walked into the village, Luge strode forward, arms extended, ready to greet him.

They embraced like brothers, their eyes dancing in mutual amusement.

Luge called over his shoulder. "Lufti! Go find Amin. Tell him he's finally going home."

Eoban nodded at the boy. "There's a tall handsome youth!"

Luge led the way to his hut, grinning. "Like his father, no doubt."

As Lydia stepped outside, Luge waved at Eoban. "Meet the man who led me to my son!"

Wide-eyed, Lydia wiped her hands on her skirt and glanced from her husband to Eoban, her face flushing. "I owe you my life."

Eoban gripped Luge's shoulder. "Not at all. Your husband did the hard part. I just wandered where wise men wouldn't go." He met Lydia's gaze. "I'm glad my foolishness paid a good return."

Amin raced forward and skidded to a halt in front of

Eoban, water dripping down his body.

Luge laughed. "You could've dried yourself!"

Amin grabbed Eoban's arm, glancing around. "Where's my father? Did you find—?"

Rubbing his forehead, the joy in Eoban faded like a plucked flower. "I'm sorry, Amin. We looked for him in the Stone City and even in the temple…but he wasn't to be found."

Frowning, Amin dropped Eoban's arm. "Where's Obed…and Barak?"

Eoban shrugged. "Obed was supposed to be here—to collect you." He shook his head. "But, as I suspected, he must've gotten lost."

Worry lines formed around Luge's face. "And Barak?"

"He was in a hurry to get home…so he went on ahead." He shifted his gaze to Amin. "There's still light to see by, and I want to find Obed before he's eaten by squirrels. So we best—"

Amin dug his toes into the dirt. "We'll go home without my father?"

Eoban dropped his head onto his chest. "Listen, I've lost just about everyone on this journey." He looked up. "Now I want to find Obed and get you home safe."

With lips pursed tight, Amin nodded.

As they turned to go, Lufti stepped up and handed Amin a beautifully carved spear. "I would not be free today had you not convinced my father to enter the Stone City."

Clasping his fingers around the ornate weapon, Amin's eyes shone. "I didn't do anything except act like a pest." He smiled at Lufti. "But I'm glad you're home safe" —he glanced from Luge's kind face to Lydia's gentle smile—"with your father and mother." He faced Eoban, squaring his shoulders. "I'm ready."

Eoban lifted his hand in salute to Luge. "Keep the enemy at bay and prosper on your next hunt."

Luge's eyes clouded. "There are rumors that the enemy is heading into new territory." He frowned. "Watch your back."

"If I can find my clansmen, I'll die a happy man."

"You do know where you're going?"

"I know the way home. Surely, Obed's headed that way by now. After all, he has eyes and can find the sun, can he not?" Turning, Eoban shifted his bag over his shoulder and flung an arm over Amin's shoulder. "So, my boy, you ready to sing?"

~~~

Eoban marched into his village scowling. "Where is everyone?"

Amin trotted at his side, also scowling. "It's much too quiet."

Suddenly, Tannit pelted across the compound at full speed, shouting. "Eoban, you're home! We've been worried sick."

Dropping his bag to the ground, Eoban crossed his arms like a barricade as the boy skidded to a halt. "What's happened? Where's—?"

Tannit heaved a deep breath. "Enemies are on our doorstep, and the women and children have fled to the caves." He glanced at Amin. "Hi, Amin! Glad you made it home safe." His grin widened. "Your father's been so anxious—"

Eoban choked. "Tannit? Do you realize who this is?"

Pursing his lips primly, Tannit glared at Eoban. "Of course! It's Amin, Ishtar's son." He tipped his head toward the center of the village. "Ishtar's been helping with preparations and watching over Tobia, who's had a rough time of it. What, with Vitus getting himself killed and all. And then Obed being taken captive—"
~~~

Amin's mouth dropped open. He glanced wide-eyed at Eoban.

Eoban, hot, frustrated, and confused, wondered if he would, in fact, boil over like an overheated stew. "Tannit, sometimes you—"

Amin cut in front of Eoban and grabbed Tannit's arm. "Ishtar is here?"

Pointing, Tannit nodded. "Just over there, taking council with Lud."

Eoban wrung his hands like a man practicing to wring a neck. "You said something about Obed?"

"You'd better ask Tobia. He saw Obed trussed up beside other prisoners taken by the enemy."

Gripping Amin's trembling shoulder, Eoban stared hard at Tannit. "Take us to Lud and Ishtar." He swallowed a hard lump in his throat. "Then find Barak. I might need to apologize..."

Tannit waved as he turned. "Lud and Ishtar are over there." He glanced back. "But no one's seen Barak." He winced. "I'm afraid Milkan will have strong words for you two."

Eoban closed his eyes and stomped forward, gripping Amin hard enough to keep the boy from flying ahead.

At the sight of Ishtar and Lud standing together in conversation, Eoban felt the ground shift under his feet. His vision blurred. He gripped Amin's shoulder tighter and leaned down to eye level. "Wait a moment. I want to speak to Ishtar alone first."

Crossing his arms and clenching his jaw, Amin stood his ground. "Make it fast. I have something to say too."

Eoban threw back his shoulders and strode forward.

Ishtar and Lud glanced over. Both sets of eyes widened.

Lud exhaled a long breath and grinned.

Ishtar stood ramrod stiff.

Stepping up, Eoban met Lud's eyes, his tone as dry as

parched corn. "Glad you kept things well in hand while I was gone, Lud."

"I hardly—"

Eoban turned his attention to Ishtar. "Ishtar, I've been looking for you."

Ishtar nodded, his gaze fixed on Amin standing in the background. "So I heard."

Like a dry stick about to snap, Eoban clenched his jaw, his teeth ready to crack under the pressure.

Ishtar turned his full attention to the warrior before him. "Do with me as you will."

Lud stepped back and beckoned to Amin.

Amin ran to Lud's side.

Swallowing, Eoban glared at Ishtar. "What under the sun does that mean? I'd like to beat you to a bloody mess for all the trouble you've caused."

Maintaining their locked gaze, Ishtar nodded, his voice low and humbled. "And well I deserve it." He stepped forward, his arms at his sides. "Beat me."

Flinging his hands in the air, Eoban turned and pounded a few paces away. "By all that is decent and right in the world—do you have to take that tone?" With his head pounding and tears burning, Eoban glanced from Ishtar to Amin. "Do you know what you've done to your sons?"

His jaw clenching into a tight line, Ishtar shook his head. "I'll regret my mistakes for the rest of my life, knowing that I never really can make up—"

Amin leapt forward. "I forgive you, father." Halting right in front of Ishtar, he sucked in a deep breath. "I wanted to tell you that I don't need you—"

Lud, Eoban, and Ishtar stared at the boy.

Amin swallowed and hung his head. "But it's not true. I can't manage on my own. I needed Barak and Luge…and—" He glanced up and met Eoban's eyes. "Even Eoban."

Eoban winced.

Amin peered at his father. "But I need you too. So does Caleb." He glanced around, a frown building. "Where is he?"

Lud gripped Amin's shoulder. "He's safe in the caves with the women and children." Glancing from Ishtar to Amin, Lud smiled. "You must have incredible stories to tell—"

Eoban snorted. "Stories? We've both seen too much!" He pounded his chest. "I don't know about Amin here, but I'm thinking of settling down…maybe with a wife."

Lud choked.

A hint of a grin broke over Ishtar's somber face.

Eoban pursed his lips. "I'll make an excellent husband." He peered at Amin. "Didn't I take good care of you?"

Amin glanced from Eoban to his father. "He tried. It's not his fault that he lost his entire company at one time or another."

Eoban dropped his head onto his chest, exhaling a long, ragged breath.

With a snort, Lud patted Eoban's back. "Don't worry, Eoban. You can regain your honor by leading us to victory." He gestured to the caves. "Jonas and Milkan are waiting. They'll want to know what happened to Obed and Barak. Let's go."

Eoban lifted his head, all strength draining from his limbs. Shuffling along, he muttered. "Couldn't we just go straight into battle?"

Glancing aside, a bittersweet grief made Eoban shake his head.

Ishtar clasped Amin's shoulder and led his son home.

Chapter Thirty-Nine

-OldEarth-

An Honest Weakness

Zuri stood on the hilltop and inhaled a deep breath of air, then exhaled slowly. Exhilaration spread through his limbs. Happiness? Joy? Ecstasy? He couldn't define the emotions soaring like twittering birds through his body. He peered at his tanned, slender fingers. Though they weren't nearly as strong without the mechanical gloves, their sensitivity sent shivers of delight to his brain. He wiggled his toes and shrugged. Not much joy there. Couldn't have everything.

Kelesta sauntered close and wrapped her arm around his waist. "The boy is home now, reunited with his papa, so why don't we do something interesting?"

Peering down at the petite human form, beguiling but deceptive, an image of his previous mate passed through his mind. Jeni used to ask innocent questions when she wanted something. Zuri narrowed his eyes, focusing his lenses. Peering through the human façade, he stared right into the Bhuaci essence.

Kelesta flared and swung away. "If you're going to take x-rays…you should ask permission first."

A hot blush worked up into his cheeks. "Sorry. It's an Ingot defense mechanism."

"You're afraid of me?" Kelesta slapped her hand on her chest in exaggerated shock, her eyes unnaturally wide.

"Not afraid…just—" He turned away from Ishtar's village and stomped down the hill. "After Jeni chose another, I always wonder what she wanted from me in the first place."

Practically dancing alongside, Kelesta flung her arms out wide like a butterfly, each nimble foot bouncing from one spot to the next. "She's the one who wanted you to go primitive, right?"

"She said she wanted me to experience life without all the mechanical hindrances. Talked a lot about freedom and unique personal expression."

"So you do it, and she dumps you?" Kelesta shook her head. "Some beings are brutally cruel." She glanced aside. "But you're left rather naked, aren't you?"

Slipping his datapad from his arm holster, Zuri tapped the keypad. "Turns out, she was doing research. She wanted to gain a position at the Ingoti Magisterium Laboratory. Quite a leap for a fourth tier."

"So, you were attracted to her mind?"

Zuri frowned as he scanned the area. "No. Her mother was actually a reject that slipped through the system but managed to make good by inventing a better detector so other rejects would be caught at an earlier stage." He pointed north. "Chai is that way."

Her mouth hanging open, Kelesta stood frozen a moment before she leapt ahead and grabbed Zuri's arm. "But then she'd be killing others like herself…the ones who might prove the system wrong!"

Zuri nodded. "That's why I found her fascinating." Turning, he stomped northward.

Kelesta crossed her arms high on her chest and scowled as she marched at Zuri's side. "But you still liked her?"

"Not in the least. Fascination is a different experience altogether." He slapped an insect on his neck and wrinkled his nose. "Though I do enjoy the myriad of skin sensations and the exhilaration of freedom from certain mechanical bio-ware, I must admit, coverage had definite advantages."

He held a dead wasp by the wing. “Stings hurt.”

Kelesta stopped short. “So why did you stay with her?”

Halting, Zuri took another scan of the area. “Choose her as a mate, you mean?” He glanced at the flat horizon. “You don’t understand Ingoti culture. Since we are conceived and developed in laboratories, we don’t consider relationships to be anything more than temporary arrangements for emotional, psychological, and physical pleasure.” He snorted. “It’s not like I needed her. Or she needed me. Except…as a test specimen for her lab experiment.”

“You used each other?” Kelesta swallowed and started forward, her gaze sweeping the ground.

Zuri shook his head and paced after her. “Yes. And I don’t see why you’re upset.” He gripped her arm, coming to a standstill. “You’re using me right now.”

Kelesta jerked her arm away, fury flooding her glinting eyes. “How dare you!”

Zuri lifted his arms to the sky beseechingly. “May the Magisterium send me home this very day if I’m wrong. But—” he peered down and zeroed in on Kelesta. “But aren’t you using me to get to Chai? Isn’t that what Ungle asked you to do?”

A hawk soared overhead, and Kelesta followed it with her eyes. “Originally, yes. But I told Sienna the truth. I told everyone the truth. I was being used to get information because I was desperate to protect my people.”

Zuri glanced at his datapad and pointed. “Chai isn’t far.” He shrugged. “When I scanned you, I saw your heightened energy levels. You’re hiding something.”

Kelesta dropped her head onto her chest and closed her eyes. “You’re right.” She peered up and met his gaze. “Even if I tried to explain, you wouldn’t understand.” She sniffed and tapped his naked hand. “Even without all your filters, I wonder if you can ever really love anyone.” She started forward. "Come on! Let's go study a man possessed by demons."

~~~

Ark wiped a tear from his eye.

Sitting on a rock ledge, Sterling glanced at the Cresta beside him and slapped his forehead. "If I'd known you were so emotional, I would've taken the Ingot. He may have a fascination with children, but at least he can hold himself together at a family reunion."

Wringing his tentacles in his lap, Ark felt like a chastened pod. "I just didn't think he had it in him…to be so repentant." He sighed, his shoulders slumping. "It takes courage to ask for forgiveness."

"I wouldn't know."

Ark lumbered to his booted feet, a flash of enlightenment clearing his weary brain. "That may be quite significant!" Waddling down the stony path, he sniffed the air. "There's water near, and I'm desperate for a dunk." He peered at Sterling. "I believe a swim would do us both good."

"Luxonians hardly need—"

A sudden strong wind swirled around them, choking the air with thick dust.

Ark gripped Sterling to keep him upright.

When the air cleared, the two stood frozen, covered in dirt, appearing like mere ghosts of their former selves.

Sterling cleared his throat and wiped grime from his eyes. "Where's that pool you mentioned?"

~~~

Sterling dropped the second boot and watched Ark lumber into a murky green pool surrounded by tall boulders and flimsy grass stems. He wiped his slimy hands on his tunic and stared at the water. *I couldn't possibly. It's much too disgusting. Besides, I can just as easily—*

"Hurry up! It's glorious. Don't be frightened of innocent liquids." Ark splashed a tentacle as he swished from one end of the pond to the other, flipping like an Ingoti eel at each turn.

Thinks I lack courage—eh? Blast him! Taking short, determined breaths, Sterling tiptoed into the water. He winced at the slimy green surface and wrinkled his nose. "Don't take offense if I just bathe my toes." He fingered his long tunic and robe. "I'm hardly dressed for full immersion."

"Toss your robe next to my boots and slip in!" Ark giggled, watching Sterling's every move. "You'll regret being a coward when I tell Teal that you stayed on the edge like a frightened—"

"Oh, shut up!" Sterling flung his robe aside, pinched his nose, and dove into the pond.

Ark rose, his tentacles on his thick middle, his eyes wide, watching bubbles surface.

More bubbles surfaced.

Ark frowned. His tentacles wiggled at his sides.

More bubbles.

Ark's bulbous eyes widened.

The pond stilled, the surface smoothing to reflect the sky.

Ark took a step and leaned forward, anxiety riding like ridges over his skin.

Sterling broke the surface, laughing. Genuine amusement cascaded throughout his whole body. He stared at Ark's open mouth. "I saw everything! You were worried about me, poor dear."

Falling backward and paddling with his arms, Ark maneuvered to the other side. "Was not."

Sterling stood and wagged a wet finger at Ark, drops of water cascading before him. "Oh, please. For all your talk of courage and cowards, you certainly refrain from admitting an honest weakness."

Ark banked against the sandy shore and sat up. "What weakness?"

Sloshing out of the pond, water plants trailing behind, Sterling padded to a smooth boulder. He sat down, letting the water drip onto the sand. "I'm not nearly as obtuse as you think me, Cresta."

Ark leaned back and folded his tentacles over his ample stomach. "Tell me."

"You think that Ishtar's strength lies in his ability to humble himself." Sterling shrugged. "From Teal's early reports, there does seem to be a pattern."

Ark's eyes narrowed as he stared at Sterling.

Sterling clasped his hands together and stared at a flock of birds soaring across the sky. "When Ishtar accepted Eoban's assistance, he broke free from his father's stranglehold. When he accepted Pele's witness, he found the strength to fight the giants."

Ark nodded. He glanced at the whirl of birds and frowned.

"But when his pride was hurt, and he accepted the glory of wealth and a woman who offered escape from shame, he fell into madness."

The birds flew away, becoming mere specks in an endless horizon.

Ark rose and shook himself free of pond plants. "I admire your perception." He waddled closer and crouched by his boots. Snatching them up, he padded to Sterling. "But that's not what I meant by courage."

Sterling stared at the offered boots, pursing his lips, disgust rising from his middle. "What then?"

"When Ishtar met Matalah, he met a new father figure. He could've rejected the very idea. After what he'd been through, I wouldn't have blamed him." He dropped the boots at Sterling's feet. "But he accepted Matalah's kindness and, as we've seen, returned to his own sons." Lifting one of his four-toed feet, Ark balanced himself by gripping Sterling's shoulder. "It takes great courage to trust again…to risk caring. To allow oneself to be helped…to love and be loved."

Lifting his gaze, Sterling met Ark's golden eyes. He swallowed. "By the Divide, you've got me beat, Cresta."

~~~

Teal crouched low in the tall grass and swore under his breath. He fixed his gaze on Obed as he stumbled at the end of a long line of prisoners. Teal turned to Sienna, who crouched next to him and pointed north. "Go and follow Eoban's trail. See if he found the child and made it home."

Sienna glanced from the ragged throng of slaves to the marching warriors and beyond to the stalwart figure leading the assembly. She hissed. "I don't remember pledging obedience to you."

"Remember your promise to Sterling?" He peered into her eyes. "You told him that you'd do whatever it took to become the best healer Lux has ever known."

"To do that, I need to stay close to Chai—not chase after a fool who thinks he can save his people through daring exploits."

"Eoban isn't that shallow."

Sienna stared at Teal, widening her eyes alarmingly.

"All right, maybe he is—sometimes. But he's also brave and resilient. And he knows a thing or two about dealing with injuries and healing emotional wounds. There is a great deal you could learn from him."

"What I need to learn, only Chai can teach me."

His colors flaring, Teal bit off his words. "How to succumb to evil?"
~~~

"How evil holds a person in its grip." Sienna shook her head. "Luxonians were once very sheltered. You know what exposure to the outer world has cost us. We're losing our traditions, our values, our political framework—even our fertility."

Teal dropped his gaze.

Clasping his hand, Sienna shifted closer. "You're one of the last of the old guard, a Luxonian with ambition but without guile. You're so honest, I don't think you're capable of seeing Chai and the power that rules him for what they really are."

"But you can?"

"Let's just say that I'm more ambitious than you."

Teal shook his head. "I'm not about to let you get one step closer to that monster. Even Sterling fears the power it wields."

Sienna sucked in a deep breath. "Have it your way." She nodded decisively. "Someone should check on Eoban, and someone must keep an eye on Chai."

Relief surged through Teal's body, surprising him. He stood and pointed south. "Eoban knows his way around. He probably brought the boy home already. Start at the grassland village and work backwards if you have to. If they're there, stay and wait for me."

Sienna clasped her hands and winked away.

Teal turned and faced Chai. He took two paces before searing pain crashed into his skull and blackness took him.

CHAPTER FORTY

—GRASSLANDS—

WHAT EVIL CAN DO

Obed felt sharp knots chafing his raw skin, burning like fire. Darkness and hot, moaning bodies surrounded him. Dried sweat mixed with dirt stiffened his face into a tight mask. His legs ached and his head throbbed. The hard ground pressed into his buttocks, while pinpricks of stars flickered in a cold, distant sky. He closed his eyes, resting his forehead on his knees.

The stone city and its shimmering temple rose in his mind's eye, sending a chill over his arms. He thought of Ishtar, images flashing like lightning in a summer storm: Ishtar sitting with Joash around an evening fire, Ishtar standing over Neb's bloody body, Ishtar helping to evacuate the burning village, Ishtar with crazed eyes holding a knife over Aram's daughter. Obed's throat tightened. "Oh, God! Ishtar, what possessed you?"

A woman's cry startled him into wakefulness. He lifted his head and stared across the motley throng. A limp child lay like a discarded piece of clothing over the woman's lap. She peered with her head bent low, murmuring soft words.

Another woman leaned in close, attempting to touch the child.

The mother jerked the baby away with a screech.

The child's head lolled to the side, his eyes unnaturally wide, and his body unresisting.

Obed swallowed a hard lump in his throat.

The second woman made another attempt to rouse the

infant and the mother slapped her hand. They quarreled.

An interested guard sauntered near. Crouching on his haunches, deep ravines furrowing his brow, he tapped the baby's cheek. Pursing his lips, he shook his head and muttered sharply at the woman.

She hugged the baby closer, wrapping the ragged cloth tighter around it.

Rising, the guard called to an older warrior who limped over. He scowled at the two women, plucked the baby from the startled mother, and carried it away.

With an animal-like howl, the mother jerked up, but the ropes crippled her. She fell to the ground, screaming.

The other woman, crying, patted the mother's arm and pulled her into an embrace.

Obed watched the limping man drop the baby beside another unresponsive body and hurry to a cluster of warriors clamoring for strong drink.

The mother crumpled, burying her face in the other woman's lap.

Curling into a ball, Obed rocked like a child, wishing for the comfort of his mother…or his wife. Or death itself.

~~~

Ishtar perched on the cliff edge and watched the yellow-pink sunrise. His whole body relaxed between the cool morning air and the smooth rock under him. Though his eyes scanned the horizon for any sign of the enemy, gratitude suffused his heart. He replayed the reunion between Amin and Caleb in his mind and smiled at how they both stood awkwardly for a moment before Caleb rushed into his brother's arms. Nodding, Ishtar applauded his eldest son's nature, especially when the boy's sensitive heart broke all restraint and responded to undiluted love.

Ishtar sighed.
~~~

Footsteps padded near.

Ishtar waited.

Tobia circled around, plunked down on his right, and stretched out. He sniffed in a long breath and exhaled. “Refreshing, isn’t it?”

A grin bubbled up from Ishtar’s insides. “You’re in a good mood—better than I expected—considering everything.”

Staring straight ahead, Tobia shrugged. “I’m not in a good mood, just accepting things as they are. Mother is sick with worry over me and Obed.” He rubbed his nose. “But there’s little anyone can do until the enemy gets here.” He blinked. “I don’t even know if Obed is still alive, or if I’ll survive...”

Ishtar glanced sharply aside. “You’ll survive. The clan needs you, Tobia.”

Tobia met Ishtar’s gaze and held it a moment. With a shiver, he returned to the sunrise. “I wish they’d come, and we could get this over with.”

“The scouts say they are still almost a full day away. They won’t attack until they’re closer and have had a chance to rest before battle.”

Running his fingers through his hair, Tobia lurched forward. “I don’t know what I’ll do till then.”

With a grunt, Ishtar rose and stretched. “Well, I have something to do. I’ll leave you to coordinate with Lud and the rest of the clans.”

Frowning, Tobia climbed to his feet. “What’re you going to do?”

“Free Obed.”

Tobia choked. “You can’t! There isn’t time. You’ll be caught, and then the clan will only have Lud and me.” He gripped Ishtar’s arm. “Let me go instead.”

Ishtar peered into Tobia’s eyes. “You’ve been prepared through great hardship for this trial. Think, Tobia. Your brother died because he chose what he thought was the braver path. But the bravest path of all is the one ordained through circumstance." Ishtar sucked in a deep breath and stepped away from the cliff's edge. "Stay here and be the leader your people need. I must free an innocent man."

~~~

Ishtar crawled on his belly to the border of the enemy camp. Sweat dripped into his eyes, but he didn't dare wipe it away.

The sun shone bright but clouds hovered in the west. No hint of a wind stirred the surrounding grasses.

Three hundred battle-hardened warriors hitched their gear together and strapped weapons to their belts, lacing them tight against the coming march.

Ishtar nodded, muttering under his breath. "You'll arrive at twilight. Very clever." He glanced around.

When his eyes fell on Obed, he sucked in a breath and a whirlwind of emotions struck him: shock, fear, and anger over what had been done to the man. The image of Obed in his prime—a strong and proud warrior—wrestled in his mind with what he saw now. Filthy and hunch-shouldered, Obed sat less than a stone's throw away from Ishtar, but he would not be easy to rescue. He sat with his legs splayed out, his hands tied behind his back, and a rope strung between him and a line of men, women, and children.

Crawling on his elbows and knees, Ishtar slithered forward.

A man on Obed's right glanced over, his eyes rounding at the sight of Ishtar.

Ishtar glanced from the guards only a few feet away to the man and lifted a finger to his lips.

The man continued to stare, his mouth dropping open.

Without further thought, Ishtar scampered over the
~~~

broken grass and hard packed earth, wedging himself between the man and a drooping boy and pressed his knife against the ropes. "Please, make no sound. I'm here to rescue those I can."

Closing his mouth and swallowing, the man glanced to the boy leaning on his arm. "Him first."

Ishtar nodded. He scuttled closer and sawed at the boy's ropes. The man watched, his gaze darting up and around every few moments like a sparrow. When the ropes fell slack, the man grunted and held out his hands. Ishtar gritted his teeth and maneuvered the knife into position.

As the last threads broke, Ishtar gripped the man's arm, squeezing it hard and hissing his words. "Do nothing just yet. Pretend you're still tied and don't watch me. Keep your attention on your boy."

The man nodded.

Crawling to Obed, Ishtar lifted his knife.

Obed glanced at Ishtar, his eyes widening in shock, and jerked away, pulling the ropes attached to his neighbor tight. Yelps of anger and distress rippled along the line.

His mind nearly numb with fear, Ishtar dropped and flattened his body into the crushed grass.

A warrior sauntered by, grunted, and moved on.

Lifting his gaze, Ishtar met Obed's anxiety-ridden face. "Don't be afraid. I'm here to free you. The whole clan is ready for attack."

Licking his cracked lips, Obed's eyes narrowed. "What clan?"

A frustrated whimper escaped Ishtar as he clenched the knife tighter and began sawing the rope fibers. "Your clan…my clan…our people." He glanced at the warriors and then back at Obed. "This must be confusing, but please—by God—trust me and let me cut your ropes."

Shouts rang through camp, and the warriors began assembling into groups. Guards marched along the line, kicking the prisoners. "Get up! Time to move on. Hurry, you lazy mongrels."

Fighting a cramp in his hand, Ishtar sawed the rope around Obed's waist faster.

As the rope fell free, a warrior stomped by, flailing his arms. "To the fires with you! Get moving!"

Obed and Ishtar rose together, their gazes cast down.

As the guard turned to the next group, Ishtar pressed the blade against the ropes binding Obed's hands. The prisoners shuffled forward. Ishtar kept pace, his eyes down, working frantically to break the fibers.

They passed over rough terrain dotted with rises and huge rocks. Ishtar cut the last remaining strings and yanked Obed aside, dragging him into the shaded crevice between two boulders.

Obed fell flat on his face and curled up into a ball.

Ishtar crouched close, shielding Obed's body with his own and prayed for rain.

~~~

Obed started at the sound of drops splattering on the hard ground. He looked up and met Ishtar's gaze. Then he rubbed his eyes. "I can't believe—"

Ishtar grunted. "There were a few clouds on the horizon when I came. I'm grateful for the storm; it'll help hide us…and our footsteps."

Closing his eyes, Obed groaned, stretched, and rubbed his arms and legs. "That's not what I meant."

Darting a glance at the backs of the departing enemy, Ishtar pointed south. "If we head for the cliffs, we can hide in safety, and when they're taking their rest, we can finish our journey and warn Lud and the others."

Heavy with sarcasm, Obed chuckled. "Great plan." With a grimace, he staggered to his feet.
~~~

Ishtar scanned the area again and started forward.

Watching Ishtar, memories flooded Obed's mind: Ishtar holding a knife over Aram's sleeping daughter, his death struggle with his wife, Haruz, and her bloody body laying in the dirt. Fury flushing through his aching body, Obed gripped Ishtar's arm. "Wait! I'm not going anywhere until I understand how you, of all people, happen to be the one to rescue me."

His eyes flashing, Ishtar glared at Obed and waved toward home. "You want me to explain—now? My sons, your wife and children, Barak's family—the whole clan is about to be attacked, and you want me to—"

Obed slammed Ishtar against the rock wall, blind fury burying all reason. "By the devil, I've been through too much to trust you now."

Closing his eyes, Ishtar lifted his hands in an attitude of surrender.

Jerking away, Obed faced the rain.

Dark clouds rumbled overhead, but patches of blue broke through in the west.

Opening his eyes, Ishtar shoved off the wall and spoke to Obed's back. "I slipped into madness, encountered a nomad who cared for me better than I deserved, and regained a sense of decency." Ishtar shrugged. "Perhaps I discovered a decency in me I never knew was there."

Curling his lips through a sneer, Obed turned around and stared Ishtar in the face. "You didn't have to sacrifice anyone?"

"I protected a father from the evil deeds of his sons."

With his eyes fixed on Ishtar, Obed snorted. "Fate or justice?"

"It doesn't matter. I did it for one simple reason."

Obed waited, his teeth clenched so hard his jaw hurt.

"I loved the old man."

A miserable chill seeped through Obed's body.

"I understand your mistrust. But you have no idea what evil can do to a man—if he gets too close."

A sob rose in Obed's chest. "But I do." Relaxing his fists, he straightened and started forward. "Let's go home."

CHAPTER FORTY-ONE

—GRASSLANDS—

ANCIENT ENEMY

Obed peered across the horizon in the morning light and pictured his daughter's face at their parting. Mari had stood tall, her long black hair blowing in the wind and tears streaming down her face.

His son, Onia, had begged to fight at his side, but the expression on Jonas's face convinced him otherwise. He sent his son to the caves to protect the women and children.

Obed swallowed back fear and hate and looked to his men as they lined up ready for battle.

He had limped alongside Ishtar into the village, and a shout rang out that warmed Obed's heart. When he realized that as many men were shouting for Ishtar's safe return as for his own, he had to stifle his irritation. But watching Ishtar work with the men, making plans, calling for weapons, encouraging the fearful and directing the overzealous, soothed Obed's raw emotions. Ishtar was not the same man who had fallen so far from grace.

Eoban gripped Obed's shoulder as he stood next to him. "Did I tell you that I'm glad you're still alive?"

Choking on something between a snort and a scream, Obed peered aside at Eoban. "You said, 'Told you so,' and plodded by, as if I had simply missed dinner."

"You acted like an idiot, and I won't let you forget it." Eoban's gaze roamed to the distant hills. "I wish I knew where Barak ended up."

His stomach tightening, Obed bit his lip. "You should

never have left him."

"Don't blame me if the man can't find his head in the dark." Eoban pointed to the hills. "He probably got confused, circled around a few times, and met Luge. He might've decided to rest a few days."

"Sounds like Barak. A man of leisure."

"Given time, I'll forgive him for being an even bigger idiot than you, but this—" Eoban waved his hand at the sight of a massive assembly drawing near. "I'll never forgive." He spat on the ground.

A shout rang out.

In the distance, a wall of ragged prisoners appeared on the hillside. Most of them were children, and they scuttled forward, prodded from behind.

Obed's stomach turned sour, bile rising.

The enemy was using human beings as shields—to be slaughtered in the first approach.

Ishtar trotted forward. "Everyone's in place."

Eoban glanced at Ishtar. "Your men will circle around?"

With his gaze locked on the approaching enemy, Ishtar nodded and waved to the assembly behind them. "The central throng will meet these children with tenderness. But Lud will approach from the east with his men, and I'll lead mine from the west. Between us, we'll destroy the enemy." He darted away.

As cold hate penetrated Obed's body, he leaned forward, ready to leap ahead. To no one in particular, he said, "Once they're exposed, we rush in and kill them all."

~~~

Eoban wiped sweat from his eyes, huffed deep breaths, and clashed spears with one of the enemy, a short, stocky man who, like the others, wore a knot of black hair on a shaved head.
~~~

Wielding swords and shields with harsh motions and hostile calls, the enemy gained ground. Something aided them that went beyond the realm of mere luck. Most of the children had been spared, but as Ishtar and Lud circled around, the enemy seemed to expect the maneuver and turned with great skill to meet the challenge.

Lud's men were speared and stabbed like sheep led to slaughter.

Ishtar met with little more success. His warriors were more experienced, but time had blunted their abilities.

Screams and shouts filled the air. Carrion circled overhead, and some even landed on the dead and those not yet dead but wishing to be so.

Swallowing back bile, Eoban stared at the descending sun and pleaded like a needy child. "Please, God! Aram, hear my cry…the cries of your people…your friends."

A stout figure with moves quick as lightning came from out of nowhere, pounding toward Lud.

Lud no sooner turned than the man's knife pierced his side.

With a choked breath, Eoban screamed, "No!" and rushed forward, his bloody knife clenched in his hand. Before he made four steps, a new enemy jumped in his path and barred his way.

~~~

Chai chuckled as he stepped back and let the youth fall to his knees before him. This day had been too easy! Tales had been told about this clan, this gathering of clans, and all they had achieved through long years together.

He licked his lips and tasted blood. He peered at Lud, hesitating. "You a man or a boy?"

Grimacing, Lud lurched to his feet and aimed his knife. His hand trembled, and his voice rose to a reedy whisper.
~~~

"I am Lud, the leader of this clan."

Chai grinned, tapping his chest. "I'm Chai. Your leader now." He stepped forward. "Bow before me."

Lud stumbled backward.

The sound of a ram's horn tore through the village, stilling the cries and screams in a hundred throats.

Chai frowned, gazing around, puzzled.

A man bounded to a halt on his right.

Swinging around, Chai faced the blood-splattered warrior.

Lud screamed. "Eoban! Watch out."

The ram's horn sounded again and a dark-haired warrior charged into the confused melee, leading a fresh host of men. A giant man loped alongside at his right hand.

Shock drenched Chai like cold water. Stiffening, he glanced around. His men looked to him for direction, their eyes asking if they should retreat. He shook his head. He never retreated.

Suddenly, a tall, sinewy man with long black hair trailing down his back and blazing eyes turned and stared directly at Chai. Their gazes locked.

Chai blinked. He knew those eyes. He knew that expression. A familiar terror seeped into his bones, and he trembled. He lifted his bloody knife and held it high. "Retreat!"

~~~

Ishtar confronted the mighty invaders, fighting hand-to-hand, stabbing, hitting, and twisting his own body out of harm's way while other horrors rose in his mind. The sightless eyes of countless victims, his father's blood on his hands, and the ghostly apparition of his grandfather crowded him like cavorting devils.

When he saw the enemy leader, he knew with uncanny
~~~

certainty that this man was not merely a battle-hardened warrior or even an intelligent slave trader. An ancient force ruled the mortal before him. Ishtar watched the stalwart leader swoop forward like a bird of prey, his arms outstretched practically enveloping his men in his mighty will—win at all costs.

They retreated now. But they would be back.

~~~

Eoban plunked down on the hard ground before a hut and propped his head on his splayed hands.

An old man fed kindling to a central fire, murmuring a chant under his breath.

A hand pressed Eoban's shoulder. "Resting?"

Eoban stared at Barak in blank amazement. "I always rest after battle—especially after I've spent sleepless nights worrying about my friends."

The old man stepped back from the flickering flames, light chasing shadows across his wizened face.

Barak leaned casually on his spear and shrugged. "I met travelers in the north gathering men to assist us. When Luge heard of our need, he decided to join in. As we approached the village, I saw the danger of a direct attack and decided it was best to come in late and confront the enemy when they were exhausted."

Eoban tilted his head at the irony of Barak's thinking.

Barak nudged him in the shoulder with the butt of his spear. "It worked to good effect, don't you think?"

Pursing his lips Eoban nodded. "Just about killed us, but yes."

His arm bleeding and his clothes ragged, Obed limped forward. Without a word, he dropped to the ground, leaned against the shed, and shut his eyes.

Ishtar strode up, pointing north. "They'll hide in the hills
~~~

for a few days…but they'll return."

A man called. "Ishtar! Come!"

Without hesitation, Ishtar sprinted away.

Eoban glanced from Obed to Barak. He waved his fingers airily. "Some of us are much too clean."

His eyes widening, Barak sat next to Obed. "You think I should've rushed in to look heroic and been overwhelmed with everyone else?"

Eoban raised his hands in protest. "I'm too tired to argue. Wait till later."

Obed groaned. "It's like being back in the wilderness with you two all over again."

Ishtar hustled back and stood before them, his eyes grave and serious.

Sitting up, nauseous and weary, Eoban lifted his gaze. "What?"

"The healers can't stop Lud's bleeding. We need Jonas and the other women."

Barak slapped Eoban's leg. "Let's go."

Struggling to his feet, Eoban glanced around. "Where's Tobia?"

Turning in a circle, Ishtar's eyes widened in alarm. "Last time I saw him, he was running—" He glanced north.

Obed moaned. "Could he have run into the enemy line?"

Barak shook his head, frowning. "He's too smart for that."

Bouncing a glance off Obed, Eoban looked away.

Ishtar stepped aside, gazing at the hills. "He must have had a reason."

Trying to rise, Obed faltered. "I'll go after him."

"Sit still." Eoban pressed Obed back to the ground. "You need to recover your strength." Grimacing, he rubbed his back and faced the hills. Night soon turned everything into blackness. "I'll be back before morning."

"Barak's eyebrows rose. "You don't look too good yourself."

"I never look good." Eoban sucked in a deep breath and patted Barak on the back. "You're a decent man, Barak. Remember I said that. It may come in useful. Besides, you and Obed need to get the women." He waved his finger at them admonishingly. "No one is to follow me." Hunch-shouldered and sick at heart, Eoban plodded away.

Ishtar stepped beside Eoban and matched his pace. "Except me."

Eoban nodded in exhaustion. "Except you."

CHAPTER FORTY-TWO

—HILLS—

ISHTAR BY GOD

Ishtar crawled to the edge of a clearing surrounded by distant trees and stared at the flickering flames of a huge central bonfire. Images of the many fires he had watched flashed before his mind: Neb's elaborate feasts to celebrate victory, the humble cooking fires he sat around with friends and family, the fire that had reflected his wife's blood, the fire pit burned to embers outside Matalah's tent…

Eoban grabbed Ishtar's shoulder and hissed in his ear. "I said you could come with me, not run ahead and throw yourself at the enemy."

Ishtar glared at Eoban.

Eoban glared back.

A large ornate tent was pitched before the huge fire and slump-shouldered warriors sat like thick, sallow-faced mounds. They chomped on their rations and murmured a few words back and forth, their gazes glancing nervously at the tent. The surviving prisoners huddled in a ragged line to the west as guards strode along the perimeter, grunting and swearing.

As a figure exited the tent, all conversation stopped. All motion halted. A lone man strode to the fire, holding an ornate bowl above his head. He chanted in a hoarse voice. "Chai calls, spirit. Be our guide. Lead us to victory. Burning flames engulf us; take us! Make us yours. Forever yours."

Ishtar stood up, a surprising calm embracing his body.

Clawing at Ishtar, Eoban tugged on his tunic. "Get down, idiot!"

Shoulders back and head high, Ishtar stepped into the flickering firelight.

Eoban's smothered groan followed him.

Ishtar stopped before the fire and peered through the flames at his enemy. "I am here, Chai."

Roused out of their stupor, every warrior focused on Ishtar, their hands clenching their weapons.

After lowering the bowl, Chai took a slow sip and peered over the rim. He tossed the bowl aside and grinned. "You know me?"

Eoban scuttled forward and nudged between the prisoners as if he were one of them. He slipped his knife from his belt and cut the bonds of the nearest prisoner.

Once freed, the prisoner motioned for Eoban's knife. Quickly, Eoban slipped an extra knife into the man's hands.

Glimpsing Eoban's actions out of the corner of his eye, Ishtar refused to be deterred and focused his attention on Chai. "Lud told me about you."

"The boy?" Chai laughed. "Did he die with my name on his lips?"

"Lud lives, but the dead cry out."

A myriad of eyes shifted away from Ishtar and landed on Chai.

Striding around the fire, Chai chuckled. "The dead do not cry out. Their voices are stilled. They are consumed by the spirit who offers us victory and life."

Ishtar matched Chai's stride and kept the fire between himself and his enemy. He peered through the flames. "Your spirit offers only lies, not life."

As if annoyed that Ishtar had matched his pace, Chai stopped and thrust his hands on his hips. "I know the god

I worship. He has led me here. He will consume you before the break of dawn."

"Does your god serve you…or do you serve your god? Pass through the fire, and we will see."

The watching crowd of warriors stiffened.

Freed prisoners shuffled forward.

A child cried out.

Still cutting bonds, Eoban sucked in a deep breath.

His eyes fixed on his opponent; Chai stepped closer to the fire. "Who are you to direct me?"

Ishtar paced away, turned, and crouched low. "I am Ishtar, by God!" He sprang forward and leapt through the flames.

Startled, Chai stumbled and fell on his back.

Landing solid on his feet, Ishtar stood over Chai, his heart exultant. "I have passed through fire and am not consumed."

Scrambling to his feet, Chai eyed his men.

In a lightning-fast move, Ishtar gripped his enemy by the arms and whipped him around to the very edge of the flames.

Chai fought and writhed.

Eoban leapt forward and stood at Ishtar's back with his arms wide, blocking any interference. "Take one step, and he'll feed your master to the flames."

A shadow loomed.

The crowd shrunk back from the sight.

Chai called out as he struggled. "My men will follow me to death and beyond!"

Ishtar glanced at the hesitating throng. "Will they?"

Like a dam freed from all restraints, an enraged thickset man barreled in from outside the circle and thrust every person aside, Obed's knife in his hand. Screaming, he leapt on Chai and stabbed him repeatedly. "My wife! My children lie dead—to hell with you!"

As if waking from a stupor, a warrior started toward the attacker but two freed prisoners stepping from the shadows held him at bay.

More warriors advanced, shock blanching their faces, but the ragged, inflamed prisoners advanced too. Shrieking, shouting, and darting erratically, the prisoners attacked.

Ishtar caught Chai's body as he slumped to the ground.

Bursting from the darkness, Barak with Luge and their men pounded into the fray and fought the bewildered, furious warriors who were now backed against the flames.

Nearly collapsing, Ishtar pulled Chai away from the flames. He stared into the unfocused eyes of his enemy…a stark reminder of his father as he lay dying.

Chai's head dropped onto Ishtar's arm, like a child cradled in his mother's embrace. Swallowing convulsively, he stared at the star-strewn sky before riveting his gaze upon Ishtar. "I came to conquer." He choked and blood trickled from his mouth. "You defeated me."

Tears filled Ishtar's eyes. "You gave me little choice. Evil devours itself…in the end."

Chai shuddered and cried out, clutching Ishtar's arm. "Don't let the demon take me!"

With his emotions breaking like shattered pottery, Ishtar gasped. "I have no say over such things."

"Please!"

Screams and grunts of fighting men and women swirled all around them. A young warrior fell into the fire and the flames flared.

The shadow grew, blocking the moon and twinkling stars.

Chai whimpered and clutched Ishtar tighter. "Not me!"

Ishtar slipped free of Chai's grip and whipped off his cloak. He flung it on the fire and smothered the flames enough to grab the fallen warrior and pull him free. He bit off his words, glancing at the shadow, “No more…victims…today.”

Eoban ran forward and tossed a bowlful of water on the young man, sending an angry hiss into the air. He shook his head as he stared at the unconscious warrior who was little more than a boy. “What a waste.”

After a last mighty shudder, Chai lay still, his arms flung out, and his eyes glassy, staring sightlessly at the brilliant night sky.

Ishtar watched the defeated enemy shuffle to one side of the smoldering fire and drop their weapons.

Luge strode before them and ordered his men to tie them together.

Kneeling beside the body of Chai, Ishtar wept.

CHAPTER FORTY-THREE

—GRASSLANDS—

TO YOUR HEART'S CONTENT

Tobia scanned the sky as a vulture swooped down upon an unlucky prey, a victim of the dwindling battle. He surveyed the area and frowned. Sharp black mountains loomed on the horizon while blue foothills softened the landscape. Short grass with tufts of weeds covered the ground, but rocks and boulders broke through the surface, refusing to be forgotten and ignored. This was a hard land no matter how green the foliage.

A familiar figure appeared in the distance. Tobia's voice dropped to a husky whisper. "Remy?"

Remy?

Springing forward, Tobia squinted. How could Remy be here? Three warriors surrounded the man, knocking him to the ground. Tobia's heart tightened into a painful knot.

A yell scattered Tobia's attention. He glanced aside.

The enemy leader called for retreat. A thrill ran through Tobia. He glanced at Remy, who now lay defenseless on the ground. Tobia choked and sprinted faster, his whole body aching and his heart pounding.

Tobia rushed between Remy and the three warriors, his pent-up fury exploding from his body as he jabbed his spear wildly at the three men.

Taken aback, the warriors glanced from the whirlwind before them to their retreating clansmen. After venting their frustration with bone-crushing blows to Tobia's head and chest, they abandoned the immediate fight.

As the warriors loped away, Tobia staggered and felt every bit of strength leak from his body. He collapsed into a black pit of despair beside the body of his friend.

~~~

Obed limped among the hundreds of dead and wounded, calling Tobia's name. His head ached and his stomach churned. *Where could the boy be?* Two figures lay separate from the main battle. Clenching his jaw into a tight grimace, he hobbled to the site. Bile rose in his throat as he knelt down.

The man beside Tobia lifted his head. "I'll be all right, but Tobia

needs help. He saved my life."

Swallowing back a sob, Obed bent low and pulled Tobia's limp form over his shoulder. He bit back the pain in his shoulder and faced the stranger. "I'll send help soon."

"Tell him—Remy will be waiting for him."

With a curt nod, Obed staggered away.

~~~

Tobia awoke to the blurry image of his mother staring down at him.

With a smile, Jonas whisked a stray lock of hair from Tobia's eyes.

Tobia tried to speak, but a searing ache stabbed his throat, and he grimaced.

Jonas turned away and soon returned with a cup of water. Lifting his head with her hand, she helped him sip more than he spilled.

With a satisfied nod, Tobia lay back against the thick pillow. Weariness weighed on his body and squeezed his heart. Using determination and will power, he lifted an arm and rubbed a raw spot on his temple.

Jonas wrinkled her nose and tried to brush his hand aside. "Leave it so it can heal."

"I don't even know where I'm injured." Tobia peered at his mother, irritation warring with pain. "You probably know every bruise and cut on me."

Wringing her hands in her lap, Jonas nodded. "They're not so very serious…just numerous."

"So, did we win?"

Jonas's smile faltered. "Of course. The battle is long over, and the enemy is defeated." Rising, she retreated to the other end of the room and straightened a line of towels and bowls. "They didn't find their efforts well rewarded. Even their slaves are freed."

Despite the cheerful news, Tobia felt a black hole beckoning to him. "I never received any reward for my efforts either. Vitus is dead. All our goods are lost. I left a whole company of old people at the door of a friend who later came to rescue me but only met death in the end."

Turning abruptly, Jonas frowned. "Your friend is not dead. Remy is resting nearby, and you can see him when you're well rested. Besides that, you came home alive. That's all that matters to me."

Tobia heaved a long sigh, relief flooding his body as he remembered Remy with his arm around Kamila. *Thank God.* "I'm glad. That's good news." His gaze roved to his mother. "But there is much that isn't good. Your husband was made a slave, and innocent men, women, and children are now dead. And for what reason? Evil has had its way with us. Where is the good in that? I gained nothing."

Sitting at his side, Jonas clasped her son's hand. "Neither Vitus nor Obed was your responsibility. Wars and battle are part of life, and evil hounds our steps." An exhausted smile wavered on her lips. "But evil is only one choice.

Ishtar has returned home a new man, and your old people have found a fresh start, thanks to your efforts. You, like Ishtar, chose a different path."

Squeezing his eyes shut, Tobia shook his head. "My path has led me here—weak and injured."

Jonas patted her son's hand. "But you're not dead. You're a young man with your whole life ahead of you." She touched his chin and lifted his face.

Reluctantly, Tobia opened his eyes.

"You said I could see all your wounds, but that's not true. You're wounded in places I can't see. So I can't heal you. You must heal on your own." Standing as if ready for the next task, Jonas clasped her hands. "The truth is, Tobia, I need you. This clan needs you…and apparently your friend, Remy, needs you. He hasn't stopped asking after you."

A spark ignited in Tobia's middle. "He wants me?" A weak hope flared to life. He threw back his blanket and tried to rise.

Rushing to his side, Jonas pushed him back onto his pallet. "Not yet!" She flicked the blanket over his legs. "When you can smile again, I'll send him in." She waved an admonishing finger. "But not a moment sooner." She picked up a tray and turned to the door.

His heart tightening, Tobia called out. "And Obed?"

With a tilt of her head, Jonas stared at her son. "He's fine. He's changed too." She bit her lip. "He left a piece of wood for you on the bench…with a new carving knife."

A shiver ran down Tobia's spine. "For me?"

"He said there are worse things than dreams…." A smile played on her lips as she shook her head. She stepped over the threshold. "I'll get your supper."

After Jonas left, Tobia settled back on the pillows. His body ached and his head hurt, but his heart unclenched.

CHAPTER FORTY-FOUR

—GRASSLANDS—

YOU'RE NOT GOD

Ishtar entered Jonas' dwelling and peered through the slanting rays of golden light. His attention wandered from a half-eaten meal of barley bread with roasted fish to a sharp carving knife resting on a piece of wood. No wood shavings littered the floor.

Tobia slept curled up on his pallet, his chest barely stirring, though his bruised face still showed the marks of recent events. The bandages wrapped around his hand and arm told the tale of wounds he took in the battle.

Jonas tiptoed up to Ishtar and lifted a finger to her lips.

With a nod of understanding, Ishtar backed over the threshold.

Jonas followed.

Strolling to the shady side of the house, Ishtar perched on the bench. "Where's Obed?"

Flicking a glance to the distant hills, Jonas wrinkled her brow. "He's helping a shepherd who can't keep track of his sheep."

Amusement coursed through Ishtar as he remembered his own flock on the other side of the distant mountains. "Sheep are not always as compliant as one might think. There are some…" His gaze drifted away.

Jonas drummed her fingers on the stout framework of the house. "Something is upsetting Tobia." She jutted her chin toward the hills. "Anxiety weighs him down."

"Even when we live beyond trial, the horror still clings

to us."

Squinting, Jonas shaded her eyes from the bright sun. "But you defeated your enemy when you killed your father and again when you killed Chai." She bit her lip. "Tobia suffers from an enemy he can't defeat."

Irritation flushed through Ishtar. "I didn't defeat my father or Chai. They succumbed to the evil fate they created for themselves. I merely endured their self-destruction." He rose and paced in front of Jonas. "Tobia faces the same enemy we all face: despair."

Coming to a halt, Ishtar pointed to fresh grave mounds. "Men died defending us. Women lost their husbands and children lost their fathers. Though slaves were freed, many have no families to return to." He glanced at Jonas. "Homes and villages can be repaired, but lost innocence can never be found again."

Setting her jaw in a firm line, Jonas scowled. "You think I don't know that?" She pointed to the great lake. "I lost Tobia's father and my eldest son in the battle with the giants. Tobia was there. He's known both evil and courage." She shook her head and turned away. "But this time…"

Ishtar frowned. "What about his carving?"

Jonas shrugged. "Obed gave him a new knife and a beautiful piece of wood, but Tobia hasn't touched them." She flung her hands in the air. "He seemed so excited when he heard that Remy was here, asked to see him and smiled when they met. But then—"

A sudden memory riveted Ishtar in place—the first time he beheld a beautiful woman. He pursed his lips. "Tobia once mentioned that Remy has a very kind sister."

Jonas met Ishtar's gaze. "A woman?"

"Tobia is a man."

Swallowing, Jonas leaned on the wall and slid onto the bench. "You think—?"

A shout in the distance turned their attention.

Eoban stood between Obed and Barak, calling, “Ishtar, Jonas, come say goodbye to Luge, the man who made our success possible!”

Ishtar held Jonas’s eye a moment and tipped his head.

Sucking in a deep breath, Jonas marched forward.

~~~

Tobia stirred and rubbed his bleary eyes. His stomach rumbled, and as he scratched his head, he became aware that someone else was in the room.

Ishtar sat in the doorway, carving a piece of wood. His piece of wood. Tobia sat up and frowned. “Obed gave that to me.”

Nodding, Ishtar’s gaze fixed on a long wood shaving that curled around the knife. “Jonas told me.”

Tobia bit his bottom lip. He glanced at the dish of bread. “I’m hungry.” He licked his lips. “And thirsty.”

With a shrug, Ishtar continued his work. “There’s wine in the jug and bread on the table.”

Mild complaints issued from his joints as he stood, but Tobia ignored them and hobbled to the food. He swiped the jug from the shelf, pulled out the stopper, and took a long swig. He eyed Ishtar. “What’re you making?”

“A boy.”

After smacking the jug on the table, Tobia ripped off a broken piece of flat bread and took a bite. He talked around a chew and stepped closer. “Why?”

“I am going to replace the son that Matalah lost.”

Tobia stared at Ishtar’s bowed head of shining black hair and snorted. “Matalah won’t laugh at your joke.”

Ishtar glanced up, his eyes wide with wonder. “I’m not joking.”

Tobia scowled and bit off another piece.
~~~

"I only want to heal a terrible injury. Is that wrong?"

Dropping the bread, Tobia slapped the wood out of Ishtar's hand. "You can no more make a man than I can."

"I made my sons."

"Not from wood! And you didn't make them. Your wife conceived them by the will of God."

Picking up the wood with a disinterested shrug, Ishtar appeared to inspect it for flaws. "After I make Matalah a son, I'm going to make a new Vitus."

Hot fury flushed Tobia's face. "Damn you!"

After laying the wood and the knife aside in slow, precise motions, Ishtar stepped into the evening air.

As if pulled by a cord, Tobia followed. His breath jerked at the coolness, and he flushed with hot shame. "I—I didn't mean that." He stopped on the threshold. "You don't understand. Nothing is funny to me. Everything hurts too much." He closed his eyes. "I'll never laugh again."

A hand pressed on his shoulder, and Tobia opened his eyes.

Ishtar met Tobia's gaze. "You'll never love again?"

Shoving off the frame, Tobia hobbled across the compound toward the grave mounds by the rolling river.

Ishtar followed at an even pace.

When Tobia halted, a shiver spread over his body. "I've died inside. I'm old. Too old. I can't marry and have children…because I already know how it'll end. Some invader will come. I'll do battle and die. My sons will die. My wife and daughters will become enslaved or die of sickness or starvation—"

Ishtar clapped his hands together and gasped. "Tobia! Stop. You'll depress the fish in the river, and I'll want to kill myself before nightfall." A grin played on his face.

Burning in rage, Tobia flung himself on Ishtar and beat his chest. "It's not funny! Damn you—I mean it now. How can you joke?"

Ishtar grappled with Tobia. Clutching his arms to his chest and shoving Tobia's back against a tree, he stilled his raging fury. "I'm not laughing at you, Tobia. Only at the horror that you must leave behind."

Tobia writhed, attempting to free himself. "It won't leave!"

"It will—if you let it go." Ishtar held Tobia's gaze and tightened his grip.

Gulping air, Tobia calmed into a shaky acceptance. "Let me go."

"Stop fighting your pain. It's making you mad. You think you're doomed because pain blinds you to any other possibility."

"What other possibility is there?"

"Evil is only one option, Tobia." Ishtar let go and turned away. "I know what you fear, for I've feared it too. Even when I turned from Neb's evil ways, I could not really succeed because I never accepted the truth."

Rubbing his arms, Tobia spat his words. "What truth?

"That there's more to life than this world and the evil we must endure here. I've passed through madness into a new hope. Life does not end there." He pointed to the grave mounds. "Aram does not live in the dirt. There are more worlds than the ones we see."

Burning indignation rose from Tobia's middle. "I never deserved to suffer like I did."

"And I never deserved forgiveness."

Tobia's rage tripped and fell, but questions still pounded his mind. He looked Ishtar in the eye. "And Vitus?"

"How do we know what he deserved?"

Tobia dropped his head onto his chest with a sigh.

"The beginning of wisdom is to realize—God exists—but you are not Him."

Ishtar stepped over to the doorway and picked up the piece of wood and the carving knife. He held them out.

With the last flicker of his anger dying like a flame in a summer rain, Tobia accepted them.

Chapter Forty-Five

-OldEarth-

We All Make Choices

Sienna watched Kelesta out of the corner of her eye as she stood at the control dashboard and tapped the directional sequence for planet Helm. "Would you stop pacing? I'm getting dizzy."

Kelesta swung around, crossing her arms over her chest. "You don't have to watch me like a hawk."

"Not a hawk…more like an interested bystander."

Clomping forward in oversized sandals, Kelesta shook her head. "Bystander? I hardly think that's a fit description. Not after you zapped Teal and practically stole a place in the inner ring."

With a shrug, Sienna stepped to the holograph pad and tapped in new coordinates. A swirling universe appeared before her eyes. She grinned. "I did get a nice view." She peered aside. "I must say, Ishtar's daring rivals Teal's."

"Teal would probably like to see you evaporate."

"You mean disintegrate?" Sienna laughed. "He's angry, but he'll get over it, and Sterling was seriously impressed. I'll have no problem in getting sixth-year status now."

"And I thought I was ambitious!" Kelesta stomped to the door. "At least when I use someone, I still care about them. I don't knock them unconscious to get what I want."

"Like you used Zuri?" Sienna licked her lips. "He told me all about your interest in his previous relationships and how you feigned personal interest, so he'd take you to observe Chai."

"It wasn't feigned! I actually like Zuri."

"But you like Chai better."

Narrowing her eyes, Kelesta marched to Sienna, flung her hands on her hips, and stared her in the eyes. "Chai wasn't really Chai. He allowed himself to become used by a force he couldn't control. We never actually encountered Chai…we only perceived a man wearing his skin."

Sienna nodded. "I agree. Though he was a free man when he let it take him." She swished the hologram around and pointed to a dark sector. "Not to change the subject, but our mysterious friends—the ones who nearly decimated Crestar—have been adding to their black hole."

Kelesta frowned. "I'm not sure I'm done arguing with you about Zuri and Teal."

The door swished open, and Sterling swept onto the bridge. "Ah, I thought I'd find you two here. Playing nice, I hope."

Kelesta met Sienna's gaze. She whispered under her breath. "I'm not done—"

Sienna waved the comment away and strode around the hologram. She beckoned Sterling forward. "I found something I believe you'll find interesting, Judge Sterling."

"Using formal titles, are we? Impressive." He grinned. "Though I always find you impressive."

"Except when you're trying to kill her."

Sterling flicked a glance at Kelesta. "Especially then." He focused his attention on Sienna. "What are you so eager to show me?" He stepped closer but kept one hand raised in a defensive posture.

Startled but unwilling to lapse into rude curiosity, Sienna focused on the elongated black hole. "It's growing. Getting longer." She bit her lip. "If it keeps going at this rate, it'll" —she tapped the console and the holographic image reshaped. Now the black hole appeared as a thick black line in space— "divide us from a large portion of the universe."

"They must be on the other side." Kelesta glanced at Sterling.

Sterling tilted his head. "Perceptive, my Bhuaci friend." He glanced from one woman to the other. "I'll call you Impressive and you Perceptive from now on, so I don't get you mixed up." He peered at Sienna. "Promise not to stun me, so I can put my hand down?"

Sienna rolled her eyes.

Swinging his arm, Sterling gestured to the door. "Where's Teal?"

"He's avoiding me."

"Wise man."

"He's a fool. I would've missed seeing the greatest exchange of wills since Arkolopus and Hugunt battled for supremacy on Ingilium."

"A mere folk tale, nothing more." Sterling frowned. "As a sixth-year you should know better." He strode around the hologram. "Besides, Teal was my choice for guardian on Earth." He tapped the black hole, and his finger went right through it. "You overstepped the line, and I'm afraid there will have to be consequences."

A hot flush burned Sienna's face. "I did what I thought was best for all concerned!" She chortled in his face. "You know what Ungle would've done!"

Kelesta shook her head and stepped away. "Ungle was there. Well—as good as." She tapped the console, and the universe vanished. In its place, the scene between Ishtar and Chai replayed in all its fire-lit glory.

"Zuri informed Ungle when we arrived on the scene, and the wise Cresta insisted on a direct feed." A grin brightened Kelesta's eyes. "Zuri's good about that kind of thing—set it up so no one was the wiser. They thought we were prisoners along with all the rest."

Sterling snorted. "No one followed directions. You were supposed to watch Amin."

The door swished open, and Zuri stepped in. He peered from Sienna to Sterling, and then his gaze wandered to Kelesta. With a smile, his attention flickered to the holographic image. "Like it?" He strode forward and waved a hand. "Saved for further study. Ungle's idea—"

A ka-boom blasted eardrums and fragments of the door exploded though the air. Zuri dropped to the ground, pulling Kelesta with him. Sterling toppled over. Sienna crouched under the main console.

Ark stood in the broken doorway with a Dustbuster held limply in one tentacle, his bulbous eyes huge and frightened.

A gray cloud of dust and tiny debris floated through the air, and a sharp stench curled up Sienna's nose. Swallowing her disgust, she crawled to Sterling who lay face down on the floor and placed her hand on his back. "Are you—?"

Sterling lifted his head. "Alive…for the moment." He peered back, and Sienna followed his gaze.

Zuri had thrown himself over Kelesta, protecting her. They both stirred.

Sienna snorted, rose, and wiped her hands on her long dress. "So he does care."

Sterling stomped toward Ark and snatched the Dustbuster from his tentacle. "What are you doing?"

Ark shuffled forward, his head hanging low. "Ungle ordered me to. He wants you all dead before the sun sets."

Choking, Sienna yanked the Dustbuster from Sterling's grip and pointed it at Ark. "Why?"

Ark lifted his tentacles helplessly. "I wasn't aiming to kill. I shot high so as to make it look good. Though, I'm sure Ungle is monitoring us…" His gaze swiveled around the deck.

Zuri scrambled to the main console, and his fingers flew over the board. He glanced up. "Not anymore!" Crossing his arms, he glared at Ark. "You mind telling us why Ungle wants to kill us…especially after we fulfilled his every request?"

Sterling glanced at Zuri. "I suspect that's exactly why." He returned his attention to Ark. "He got what he wanted, and now he'd like to clear the planet of unnecessary elements—perhaps?"

Shuffling to a wide chair, Ark plopped down and dropped his tentacles in his lap. "Truth is, we're at war."

His eyes widening, Zuri stepped forward and leaned in toward Ark. "Crestar is at war with—?"

"Ingilium and Lux." He glanced at Kelesta. "Sorry, the Cresta Ingal do not consider the Bhuaci a sufficient threat to declare war on them. Though if you interfere…they may change their minds."

Sienna gripped the railing that led to the upper deck. "If we're at war…then you're" —she clenched her jaw— "the enemy."

Sterling stepped between Sienna and Ark. "I can't believe I'm saying this, but I wish Teal were here."

"I am." Taking each step slowly and deliberately, Teal descended to the central floor. "I've seen everything."

Heat worked over Sienna's body, and she glowed at the edges. "I wondered where you'd got to."

Sterling cleared his throat as he glanced from her to Teal. "You could've warned us about Ark and his dramatic entrance." He turned and peered at Ark. "I read Ungle's transmission. You're a master liar."

Ark bowed as if accepting a compliment.

Zuri tapped his fingers together nervously. "So are we really at war with Crestar?"

Sterling nodded. "Crestar has sent out a formal declaration that all foreign elements are to leave Earth immediately or be eliminated."

Sienna flashed a frown at Ark. "Crestonians are as foreign as the rest of us."

Sterling waved his hands. "That's beside the point. What Ungle hopes to achieve is more to our interest."

Ark sighed. "He was severely disappointed with Ishtar—and Chai for that matter. He was hoping that Ishtar would destroy the thing that controlled Chai. But Ishtar not only ignored it, he appeared to grieve the loss of a thoroughly despicable man."

Zuri wrapped an arm around Kelesta and leaned on the wall, pulling her close. "What did he think Ishtar would do? He doesn't have a Dustbuster or advanced weapons. Obviously, a force that strong couldn't be destroyed through primitive means."

As Kelesta nestled comfortably in Zuri's embrace, she frowned at Ark. "Bhuaci may not be a match for Crestonians, but we'll see the annexation of this planet as an act of aggression and fight to maintain our interest here."

Ark pointed to the hologram. "If you'd be so kind, refigure that thing to focus on the growing Divide between us and our mystery friends."

Sienna tapped the console and brought up the same image she had used earlier. "It's still growing."

"That's what frightened Ungle and our entire planet into panic." Ark rose with a groan. "I don't agree that abandoning Earth will save us from the evil that beset Chai and almost destroyed Ishtar. That same force can bedevil the heart of every being this side of the Divide…and perhaps the other side as well."

Sienna shook her head. "So what are we going to do?"

Sterling stepped to the blasted door—nothing more than a ragged frame. "I need to discuss the matter with the Supreme Judges." He peered from Sienna to Teal. "Make ready to leave as soon as possible."

Zuri glanced from Sterling to Ark. "You aren't going to take your enemy as hostage?"

Sterling grinned. "I don't see an enemy, do you?" He started to step through the door and shook his head. "By every star in Heaven, I almost forgot…never mind." With a flick of his hand, he flashed out of sight.

Kelesta peered up at Zuri. "What are you going to do?"

Zuri caressed her cheek and peered into her eyes. "I'm going to do my duty and report home." His thumb ran under her chin. "Just like you're going to do when you return to Helm."

Kelesta's voice rose in panic. "You're going to leave me?"

Teal cleared his throat. "Could you two have that discussion somewhere else?"

Sienna glanced at Teal. "We could be having the same discussion."

Teal shook his head. "No. We couldn't." He nudged Ark. "You'll have to return to Lux with me. I hardly think your misfire today will go unnoticed."

Zuri glanced over. "We'll bring Kelesta to Helm first and then swing by Lux and drop you two off before I head home."

Like a body blow, Sienna suddenly understood what the term heartbreak meant. Her mouth dropped open. "You mean you're not going to forgive and forget? Like Ishtar? Like Aram and all your wonderful human heroes?"

Teal frowned. "Forgiving doesn't mean I turn a blind eye to reality. I hold no animosity toward you. I just can't trust you." He turned away and nodded to Zuri. "I'll study the Divide phenomena on the upper deck. Call me if you need anything." He turned and ascended the steps.

Zuri took Kelesta's hand and led her through the blasted doorway. "We're going to be—"

Ark waved them on. “I don’t need details.”

Sienna watched Teal’s booted feet disappear on the upper landing. She plunked down on a chair before the main console.

Ark reached out and wrapped a tentacle around her shoulder. “We all make choices.”

Sienna blinked, her heart falling to the ground. “Apparently, I’ve made mine.”

CHAPTER FORTY-SIX

—GRASSLANDS AND HILL LANDS—

A NEW LIGHT

Tobia sat next to Remy before a glowing fire with Remy's men, Jonas, Obed, Onia, and his little sister, Mari, seated in a semicircle on the other side.

A full moon rose in the evening sky. Birds sang their goodnight songs from nests built among the swaying grasses as a refreshing breeze swept through.

Laughter erupted between Remy's men as they discussed their return trip home the next morning. Remy listened and laughed along with them, sampling from various platters of barley bread, roasted quail, wild rice, and early onions. Flasks of thick mead sat within arm's reach.

After swigging down a bowlful of mead and eating enough to fill his belly, Remy tapped Tobia playfully on the shoulder. "So, when will you come visit me and my sister, eh?"

"I'm not at my full strength yet." A blush burned in Tobia's cheeks. "And my family needs me…"

Remy's men chuckled, sweeping glances between Remy and Tobia. One man spoke for the rest. "If Remy had his way, he'd race us all home. But since he's so old and worn out now, we'll have to carry him the distance."

Flicking a twig at the man, Remy laughed. "I'll have had a long night's rest by the time you stagger in."

Obed snorted and took a swig from his bowl.

Jonas frowned and turned to her guest. "I want to thank you again for all the aid you gave Tobia. You've been a valuable friend. More than we can ever repay."

A sly gleam entered Remy's eye as he focused his gaze on Tobia. "Oh, he can repay our kindness any time he wants."

Obed wiped his mouth, his eyes narrowing. "How?"

Tobia stiffened.

"I happen to have a very beautiful and good-hearted sister…and she's taken a liking to your son."

Tobia glanced around and met a dozen eyes staring at him. He sighed, his shoulders slumping as he stared at his scarred hands.

Obed reached over and teasingly smacked Tobia on the shoulder. "Why didn't you tell us?"

"I hardly know—"

Obed rose shakily and swung his bowl into the air. "I propose that we invite Remy and his sister to return for a feast in three months—"

Jonas tugged on Obed's legging. "Stop! You can't do that. It's rude to ask them to travel here again so soon. They've already done so much."

Obed swayed, his voice slurring. "You're right!" He glanced at Tobia. "Stand up, son."

Tobia swallowed back a bitter taste rising in his throat and stood beside Obed.

Obed flopped his arm around Tobia and gazed into his son's eyes. "She's beautiful?" he asked, his breath pungent.

Tobia clenched his jaw and looked down as the men around him chuckled and his little sister giggled. "Yes, and kind. And I'd like to see—"

"Then next full moon, we'll visit Remy's village! As your father, I should meet the family." He nudged Tobia in the chest. "This'll give you cause to rebuild your strength." He refilled Remy's bowl.

Remy rose and saluted Obed, sloshing the mead. "I look

forward to that day. The preparations shall begin the moment I get home." He beamed at Tobia. "Kamila will rejoice."

Remy's men stood and cheered, pounding their spears.

Jonas climbed to her feet, gripping Tobia's shoulder. Her eyes locked onto her son.

His heart tearing in pain, Tobia clenched his hands at his sides and forced a smile.

~~~

Eoban shrugged. "Whatever makes you happy, Jonas. I'll do my best." A dead weight settled in his gut as he watched her hurry back to her dwelling in the bright light of a new day.

Heading home, Obed strolled by, glanced in Eoban's direction, and changed trajectory, intercepting his friend.

A flock of geese flew overhead in perfect formation, honking as they went.

Eoban exhaled, threw back his shoulders, and mentally prepared himself. He muttered under his breath. "Should've gone hunting." He acknowledged Obed's nod with a nod of his own.

"What did Jonas want?"

"She wants me to go with you to Remy's village."

His eyes still bloodshot from the previous night's revelry, Obed's jaw clenched as he flashed a glance at Jonas hanging fish on a line. "Why?"

"You know Jonas. She worries."

"She thinks I'll get lost or captured?"

Eoban rubbed his neck and wished he could fly away with the geese. "I think she's worried about Tobia, and that—"

"His father will push him into something he's not ready for?"
~~~

Eoban held his tongue in check.

Obed's eyes traveled to the hills, where dots of black and white sheep grazed and stick-like boys played on the grass. "In that case, I'll take Onia with me. Perhaps I can be trusted with *one* of my sons."

Two emaciated dogs quarreled over a bone, creating a racket.

Eoban frowned and raised his voice. "Listen, Obed. Jonas loves you. She worried the whole time you were a prisoner. She's a mother too, and she can't divide her emotions up into reasonable parts. She's been afraid for so long, it's become a way of life. Don't be angry that she wants an extra man to help out in case there's trouble." He shrugged. "There could be trouble."

"Barak isn't coming?"

"No sane man would ask Milkan to let him go."

With a snort, Obed nudged Eoban. "You're right. I'm being unreasonable."

Eoban dropped his gaze. "Truth is…you and Tobia may behave yourselves on this trip…but I don't know about Remy."

Obed scowled. "Why? He's an exceptional fighter and a strong leader."

"Yes, but he's a terrible singer." Eoban whapped Obed on the back and called over his shoulder as he strolled away. "It'll be up to you to lead the chant during the wedding ceremony."

~~~

Tobia woke early on the morning of their departure and forced down a breakfast of roasted fish, rice, and toasted grains mixed with fruit and nuts.

Onia stood near, shuffling from foot to foot.

Tobia swallowed his last bite and wiped his mouth.
~~~

"What's wrong with you? Aren't you going to eat?"

Onia shook his head, one hand gripping his lean belly. "I can't." He glanced toward the hills. "When are we going to start?"

With a bulging bag slung over his shoulder, Obed marched toward them.

Tobia wiped his hands and stood, willing himself strength he did not feel. The thought of Obed meeting Kamila turned his legs to water. One sidelong wink, and Kamila would know what his father really thought of him.

Grim-faced, Jonas paced close at Obed's side.

"We'll leave soon enough." Tobia dropped his tone to a whisper. "You'll soon wish you were home again."

Onia frowned and stepped aside.

Obed stopped beside his brother and nodded at the crumb-strewn tray. "You'll get a stomach ache walking off all that food."

Jonas squeezed her husband's arm and peered at her son. "He's young. He could eat a whole hog and then run till the sun sets." She glanced from Onia to Tobia. "You're ready?"

Onia's legs jiggled in the anxious waiting.

Obed frowned. "Calm down. You'll wear yourself out before you even leave."

From the far side of the village, Eoban hustled forward. As he neared, the glint in his eye shone brighter. "Everyone ready?" He jutted his chin at Obed's bulky bag. "What've you got there?"

"Just a few items to trade, if they're interested." Obed nudged Onia. "Get that other sack I filled."

A frown deepened between Jonas's brows. "I thought this was just a friendly visit?"

"Trade is friendly." Obed pulled her close, kissed her cheek, and whispered in her ear. "Don't worry. We'll be fine." He glanced up as Onia jogged forward with the second, larger bag. "Come on; the sun won't wait, and Remy will think we've forgotten our promise."

Eoban snorted. "Once he sees those bags and Tobia's smiling face, he'll forgive any delay."

All eyes turned to Tobia.

Forcing a grin, Tobia nodded and pointed to the hills. "Let's go."

Eoban tapped Onia on the shoulder. "Get in front. Might as well learn how to lead when you don't know where you're going. I do it all the time."

Jonas stared at Tobia, their gazes joined in understanding. She kissed his cheek and let him go.

Tobia stepped forward, glancing back at Obed's bulging sack, feeling the weight of it on his shoulder. "We'll take a direct path this time and perhaps we won't lose anyone."

~~~

Tobia saw Kamila first. Though the journey had been swift and direct, the return to a site associated with so many painful memories wearied him. Only her smile encouraged his lagging feet the last steps.

Remy sprinted to him, his arms wide in welcome. The whole village surrounded the visitors, grins on every face.

Thrusting his bag into Eoban's arms, Obed jogged forward and gripped Remy's hand. "Well met!" He surveyed the crowd and stopped at Kamila who stood at Remy's side. "This must be the beauty everyone told me about!"

Standing next to Eoban and watching the scene, Tobia clenched his jaw.

Eoban pressed the young man's shoulder. "Obed is just showing off. Don't get impatient."

They waited and watched.

As Obed chatted with Remy, Kamila peered around his
~~~

shoulder. She met Tobia's gaze.

A flush worked over Tobia, embarrassment fighting with irritation. He marched to Obed's side and nodded to Remy first. "Good to see you again."

Remy laughed and pulled him into a bear hug. "Well met indeed!" He turned to the watching crowd. "Let the feasting begin!"

Tobia's attention shifted to Kamila, and their eyes met.

Twisting her hands, she blushed and glanced at the villagers. Everyone scurried to attend to food-laden tables and a dressed goat roasting over an open fire pit.

Tobia shuffled in place and bit his lip.

Eoban shoved Onia toward the tables. "Go help out and get me a snack. I'm famished." He strode to Tobia, nodded at Kamila, and grinned. "You two take a walk somewhere. Find out if there are any enemies ready to attack."

Kamila's eyes widened.

Tobia snorted and took Kamila's hand. "We better go before my father and Remy take notice and—"

Kamila gripped his hand, and they darted into the woods.

~~~

Tobia's spirits rose to new heights and his full stomach settled in contentment as a full moon rose in the night sky. Kamila grinned at him with her usual confident composure, and Obed had not touched his trade goods.

After helping the women clear the dishes and trays away, Kamila returned and perched on a log next to Tobia. She pointed to three new huts on the west side of the village. "Remy and the men built homes for our new elders. They've earned their keep in a hundred ways since they came, watching the children, nursing the sick, assisting new mothers."

Tobia shook his head in wonder. "I'd never have thought
~~~

they had it in them to be helpful. They were so anxious and troublesome on the journey." He glanced at her. "I felt terrible leaving here…just dropping them into your hands for safekeeping."

Kamila tilted her head, her dark eyes sparkling in the firelight. "You've had troubles of your own, Tobia. Too many troubles for one so young."

Sudden tears startled Tobia. How could she see into his heavy heart and understand his grief? He swallowed and took a firm grip of his emotions. "I'm not young…not really. My mother said I grew old the day my father died."

Reaching out, Kamila placed her hand over Tobia's. "I lost my parents at a young age, too. I understand." She nodded at Remy, who laughed at something Obed said. "He's been father, mother, as well as brother ever since they died."

Tobia laced his fingers into Kamila's. "I'm sorry. I forget that others have lost more than—"

Sliding off the log and sitting next to Tobia, Kamila leaned in. "It's not like that. There's no comparison. We all grieve our losses and endure painful trials. But helping others makes us less lonely along the way."

"Can I help you, Kamila?"

A smile twitched on her lips. "I think so—"

A shout turned their heads.

Onia stood hunched with both trade sacks over his shoulders.

Obed nudged his youngest forward while glancing at Remy. "See what I've brought, my friend." He turned and waved the crowd closer. "Come and see if there's anything you'd like to trade for. My clan wants to embrace you all as brothers and sisters. Let's exchange goods."

Tobia dropped his head to his chest. "By the stars. He's becoming more like Eoban every day."

Eoban stepped up and pressed Tobia's shoulder. "I was

never so obvious."

With a shrug, Kamila laughed. "He's happy. Making deals and showing off his wares is like medicine to a man. Besides, trade with the wider world will do us no harm. And it's a natural preparation for the wedding exchange."

Cold fear swept over Tobia. He glanced at Kamila's serene face. *How does she do it?*

Obed's face glowed, reflecting of the firelight, and Remy laughed uproariously at a joke Onia cracked. Obed clapped Onia on the shoulder and never once looked at Tobia.

Kamila peered through the dim light. "You don't look well." She stood and tugged Tobia's hand. "You need a different kind of medicine."

Glancing at Eoban, Tobia's heart jumped to his throat as he climbed to his feet.

Eoban nodded to an empty hut on the edge of the village. "A little hug won't hurt. Mind you, I said a *little* hug. Go on. Take your time. I'll make sure they stay occupied."

Stepping into the shadows, Kamila grinned and beckoned Tobia to follow.

Tobia halted and glanced from his father and the villagers clustered together, to Eoban who crossed his arms and turned away, to Kamila who waited with one inviting hand extended. Warmth spread over his body, and thunder, like an impending storm, roared in his ears. He gripped Kamila's hand.

CHAPTER FORTY-SEVEN

—GRASSLANDS—

FOR THE SAKE OF YOUR SON

Ishtar tossed the last shovelful of earth aside and stared at the long, deep trench. He wiped sweat from his brow, laid the shovel aside, and plopped down, leaning back on his hands.

A glorious breeze ruffled his long hair, and children called in the distance. He glanced up.

Eoban and Obed marched toward him with Barak trudging along behind.

Ishtar scrambled to his weary feet, his gaze level as the men approached. "To what do I owe this honor? Three dignitaries coming to view my" —he glanced aside and shrugged— "ditches."

Obed laughed. "That's why we've come. Word reached us that you're digging canals to carry water to your village."

"It's just an idea…something I saw while traveling."

Barak shaded his eyes and surveyed the long trench meandering from the base of the hill to the edge of the village. "You saw this?"

"I saw how water travels down from the hills. And sometimes it reaches the people. Sometimes not." He rubbed his chin. "It seemed that a little assistance might give us what we need in dry spells."

Eoban glanced at Obed. "It's a brilliant idea. Surprised you didn't think of it."

"Wish I did." Obed turned to Ishtar. "But it's all yours.

Except…" He laughed. "I might steal it and do something similar in my village."

"Feel free. I'm too—"

Amin sprinted into view, jogged around stray sheep, and stopped with gasping breaths before his father.

Eoban gripped the young man's shoulder. "What in the world are you eating, boy? Whole hogs? You've grown twice your former size!"

Ishtar's smile broadened.

Obed nodded his agreement. "You'll be ready to take the mantle of leadership off Ishtar's shoulders soon."

Barak frowned. "What is the matter, Amin? You look upset."

Gulping his breath, Amin gazed from one man to another. "It's Caleb. He's not feeling well." He turned to his father. "I told him to rest. I'll do his work today."

With a nod, Ishtar's joy dimmed. "Fine. It was good of you to think of it." He pointed to his efforts. "I'll show them my grand scheme and come home in a bit."

Amin glanced at the field and nodded. "I'll get to work but keep an eye on Caleb too." He stepped away.

Ishtar waved toward the base of the hill. "Let's go. I can show you what I've done. You might have ideas to add."

Eoban and Obed fell in line behind Ishtar.

Barak stopped and peered back at Amin. "You think he'll be all right?"

Ishtar grinned. "Caleb is a wonderful child…but sometimes he doesn't like to work, and Amin is more than generous." He bit his lip. "I'll have a talk with the boy."

The three trudged upland to a natural land basin where Ishtar had enlarged the width and depth and added a channel leading toward the village.

As the sun descended, Lud and Gilbreth joined them, and they followed the trench into the village, making suggestions and exchanging ideas.

As he loped along, Eoban scratched his head. "Looks like Gilbreth has grown as much as Amin. What do you feed your children these days?"

Barak chuckled. "Anything and everything. Boys are always hungry. Ask Milkan."

Rubbing his stomach, Eoban winced. "Speaking of food…"

Glancing from Eoban to the other men, Lud laughed. "That's why I was sent…to tell you that a repast awaits at my home, if you'd like to join us."

Eoban leapt ahead like a yearling goat. "Don't be sluggards! The boys will eat it all, if we don't hurry."

~~~

Ishtar reclined on the ground after the repast, and everyone grew quiet as they sat around a modest fire. The warm evening air stilled, and songbirds settled in for the night.

Eoban glanced at each of the men. "So much has changed since we first met."

His eyes widening, Lud sucked in his breath. "More than words could ever say."

Barak nodded. "Aram has been gone for so long, I forget his face but never his strength. I only hope that the future will bring us more peace and less anxiety."

Ishtar watched the flames flicker and the sparks intertwine as they rose into the sky. "I, too, hope we will know peace, but I wouldn't wish to live without burdens or trials. It was a heavy burden that brought me to a place I could not run from. It was a painful trial that forced me to face the spirits that haunted me." He sat up. "We must continually strive to become better than our former selves, or we stagnate and corrupt. I pity the man who is satisfied with himself."
~~~

Barak shifted, his voice dropping low. "Even Aram struggled to become a better leader. He never really knew how good he was."

Lud dropped another log on the fire. "As a father, I agree. One is never done learning."

Stretching, Eoban yawned. "Since I am neither married nor have children, it seems that I have an easy life, but I tell you—in truth—I'm married to the entire village. I'm father to the young, brother to my men, servant to every woman who needs an extra hand, and uncle to the children near and far. I am the most married man I know!"

Chuckles rose with Eoban as he staggered to his feet.

The setting sun spread a pink and lavender glow over the village. The rest of the company stood, said their goodbyes, and started to their homes. Silence, the companion of each, framed the village in quiet slumber.

Ishtar strode along the trail with his heart at peace and knew that, for once, joy united them.

~~~

Amin raced up to Ishtar in the darkness outside his house, his heart clenched into a tight ball both furious and afraid. "Caleb is worse. I've done everything I can think of. Water, wine, broth, food…but nothing helps. He vomits everything." He wrung his hands as he trotted at his father's side. "He said his belly hurt, but I can't see any wound."

Ishtar peered through the darkness as he stopped before the doorway. "Did you call for the healer?"

Amin nodded. "She made him swallow an herbal brew, and he fell asleep."

Ishtar paced to Caleb's side and knelt on the hard ground.

Sweat beaded Caleb's forehead. His cheeks were flushed an angry red, and he tossed with his arms flailing.
~~~

Ishtar stroked his son's head, but Caleb brushed his hand away. Swallowing hard, Ishtar turned to Amin. "I'll get Jonas. If anyone can understand what's wrong, she can."

Amin nodded, terror biting at his insides as Ishtar hurried outside. He dropped to his knees, clasped his little brother's sweaty hands, and watched his every move.

Time slowed to a standstill. An owl hooted in the distance and a wild dog howled.

Caleb fell into a deep slumber, his body stilled, and his skin paled to a deathly white.

Amin's eyelids grew heavy. His head dropped onto the edge of the bed and exhaustion took him.

When a bird chirped, Amin jerked awake and rubbed his eyes. A sliver of gold edged the horizon and the sound of shuffling feet drew him upright. He stood and faced the door.

Ishtar ushered Jonas inside.

Striding to Caleb's side, Jonas touched the little boy's face and arms, and then carefully worked her way down his body, peering intently at each limb.

Ishtar tossed kindling onto the dying fire, flaring it into renewed life.

Jonas beckoned Amin closer. "Did he fall? Any accidents?"

Amin shook his head, his stomach churning. "He was fine up until a couple days ago. Then he said he felt sick and didn't want to eat. After a time, he said his side hurt…and then his middle. He got so weak he could hardly stand." Amin glanced at the rising sun, tears filling his eyes. "The more I tried to get him to eat, the sicker he got. Once the fever set in, he didn't even know me."

Jonas rose, soaked a cloth with cool water, and sponged Caleb's head and wiped down his body."

Ishtar crouched at her side and watched her every move.

Amin paced away and added fuel to the fire.

As brilliant rays of light streaked over the horizon, Caleb awoke. Appearing calmer, he peered through red-rimmed eyes.

Jonas backed away and let Ishtar kneel closer. "Caleb?"

With a weak smile, Caleb grinned as his father took his hand. "I felt terrible. But I'm…better now." He glanced aside. "Amin?"

Amin shifted near, kneeling by his father. "I'm here."

Caleb blinked and frowned. "It's so dark, I can't see you." His voice dropped to a whisper. "But I can hear you."

Choking on strangling grief, Amin stifled a sob. Tears flooded his eyes. "I'm here, Caleb."

Caleb closed his eyes, murmuring. "Father's back, you know… So glad." He gasped a rattling breath and exhaled slowly.

Amin squeezed his brother's hand, but it felt cold and lifeless.

Caleb's head drifted to the side, his whole body falling limp.

Amin shrieked. "Caleb!"

Trembling, Ishtar wrapped his arm around Amin and held Caleb's fingers in his own.

Jonas nudged in closer and pressed her ear to Caleb's chest, her eyes wide and staring.

Tears rolled down Ishtar's cheeks, as a low groan escaped. "Please…"

Jonas blinked back tears. "He's gone."

Dropping his head onto Caleb's chest, Ishtar sobbed.

A stabbing pain pierced Amin's chest. He rose and fled into the searing light of day.

~~~

Ishtar sat outside his dwelling staring at a gray fire pit mounded with dead ashes. Beyond that, in the distance, a
~~~

small grave lay covered with large flat stones.

Footsteps shuffled near and a shadow crossed over him. Tobia knelt at Ishtar's side. "May I sit with you?"

Hollow as a drum, Ishtar didn't care who came or went.

"The wedding ceremony was beautiful. Obed outdid himself. Even Eoban behaved well." Tobia crossed his legs. "Wish you'd been there."

With a feeble effort, Ishtar waved him off. "Kamila was with you. That's all that matters." He closed his eyes. "I'm very tired." He stretched out on the bench and clasped his hands over his chest, lying like a dead man.

Something small and hard pressed on his chest.

Ishtar opened his eyes and peered down.

A little wooden boy with his arms outstretched lay over his beating heart. Ishtar choked and struggled for control as he sat up and clasped the figure in his hand.

Tobia peered into the distance, his voice as steady as if he were telling an evening story by firelight. "Long ago, Eymard told me that our mighty Creator made this world and took all life back to Himself when he willed it. It sounded good and made losing my father easier to bear. But when Vitus died, and I saw so much death and horror, I shoved Eymard's story away and grew angry at God."

He paused, as if the words stuck in his throat. "Did our Creator have the right to punish Vitus for his foolish pride? Did the elders deserve to see the last of their line suffer imprisonment and death? Who was this terrible God I prayed to?"

Ishtar peered into the azure sky and blinked back tears.

Tobia's voice rose. "But then someone told me that I was thinking like a man and not like God. Someone said that no one knows what goes on between a soul and his Maker."

Dropping his face onto his hands, Ishtar rocked in misery.

“Pele lives beyond our sight. The same is true for Aram. Is it not true for Caleb too?”

Dragging his fingers down his face, Ishtar lifted his gaze and met Tobia’s honest eyes. “Caleb showed great promise. He would’ve grown up to be an honorable man—perhaps a leader among men. Why was he taken and not I?”

Tobia peered at the horizon. “I can’t answer your question. And neither can you.” He glanced aside. “Repentance brought you home, Ishtar. Let hope keep you here, for your sake and the sake of your other son.”

Straightening, Ishtar nodded. “You are honest and true, my friend. I’ll be a man again, but—”

Tobia turned to leave. “God did not abandon Matalah. He will not abandon you.” With a nod, Tobia paced away.

Rising, Ishtar gripped the figure in his hand and let the sun pour over him as fresh tears fell.

CHAPTER FORTY-EIGHT

—GRASSLAND—

IF YOU DARE ENOUGH

Namah watched a spider weave its web in the corner of her home while the sun set in crimson and gold. A conviction that she would never see such a sight again spread through her.

After an uneventful night's sleep, she stood in the doorway and watched the morning's sunrise, feeling mildly surprised that she had lived to see a new day. She glanced in the corner. The spider was nowhere in sight, but the web sparkled in a shaft of sunbeam.

She stepped outside and began her morning routine. Pouring water from a large basin, she washed her hands and face and then stirred the outdoor fire and added kindling to the pink-centered coals, drawing life from the gray heap.

After a simple breakfast of mixed grains and goat's milk, she called next door for her daughter, Gizah, to attend her.

Living with her sister, Bethal, and her brother, Bararam, Gizah fit herself to the role of servant to all. She hurried to her mother with a beaming smile and clasped her hand. "Morning!"

Namah's heart clenched and then expanded as she smiled back. Squeezing her child's hand, she peered into the young woman's laughing eyes. "You are the treasure of the family, child."

Gizah giggled. "Treasure that some lucky man is just waiting to possess, no doubt!"

"No doubt, indeed. Your line will prosper like no other. I've seen it in my mind's eye." A return of foreboding clutched at Namah's chest. "Tell your sister and brother I want to see them. I have things to give them before I go."

All hint of laughter fled from Gizah's face. "Why? Where are you going?"

"Not for me to say or you to know just yet. Do as I say, girl. Tell them to come before sunset, or it'll be too late."

A frown flittering over her face, Gizah turned and entered her sister's home.

Namah returned to her own home and poked among the shelves. She found a clay pot with an intricate design fashioned along the sides. She laid it aside and then tugged at her finest cloak until it fell free from a high hook and landed softly in her hands. Caressing the fine fibers, she eyed the bright colors and detailed edging that made it one of the finest wraps in the whole village. She had made it for Aram. He had told her to keep it for her burial.

Shaking her head, she mumbled under her breath, "And you were buried in nothing but your tunic and that old wrap with the torn edging." She sniffed and chuckled. "I wanted to disobey you, but I didn't. I loved you that much."

Rubbing her back, she rifled through her possessions again, fingering toys for the children—and grandchildren—she hoped. She set certain objects to the left and others to the right and only two lay on the ground before her feet.

When the sun had risen to its peak, Bethal and Bararam appeared in her doorway.

Namah beckoned them forward, her gaze darting to Gizah, who shuffled in behind them. Stepping back, she opened her arms to the objects laid before them. "Today you must take what I give you so there will be no confusion after I'm gone."

Tall and muscled with a head of rich black hair, Bararam

towered above the women, but his surprised grin hinted at his mischievous side. "Where are you going, mother, that you offer us such gifts?"

"I go where you cannot follow…at least not yet." She pointed to the pile on the left. "These are for you two and your families when you have them."

Bethal gasped and knelt before a decorated pot, a pile of colored beads, and a sharp knife. Picking up the child's toy, she caressed it in her fingers. "I remember this. It was my favorite." She glanced up. "Why give us these now? Why not wait until I'm married and settled?"

"I may not be here then. And I want you to know…I offer these with all my love." She nodded to the right. "And you, Gizah, will take this house and these other things: the pillow, the blanket, and my best rope for your own."

Opening her mouth but unable to speak, Gizah stepped toward her mother and stopped suddenly at the middle pile. Her eyes widened as she stared at the fine cloak and the carved figure of a man.

Namah lifted the cloak and the wooden figure and pressed them into Gizah's hands. "Wrap me in this, as was your father's wish, and lay Tobia's gift in my hands when you bury my body." A smile quivered on her lips. "I know well enough that it is not my husband but only a likeness of his figure. But Tobia comforted me during my loss, and I want to comfort him. We will always be together like good friends."

Voices rose across the village, and mothers called little ones to supper.

Bethal glanced at her brother.

Bararam gathered the objects in his arms and shook his head. "There's no hurry. You'll live many long years yet. But we'll keep them safe in our house—until you wish them back again."

Namah raised her eyebrows in command to her youngest daughter.

In shy obedience, Gizah bundled her gifts in her arms and followed her sister to the doorway.

Stopping on the threshold, Namah called after them. "Remember, the greatest treasure I have given you—is each other."

Namah watched them pace to their home next-door and returned to her own abode. Fixing a light supper, she sat outside and enjoyed a cool breeze that rose with the night. A distant bird warbled and two owls hooted back and forth as in their usual evening conversation.

Memories of her first journey to the lake made her gaze shift over the water. Twinkling lights flickered in the last sunbeams as they slanted across the rippling surface.

When her chest tightened, as it usually did at night, Namah pulled herself to her feet and dragged herself to her bed. Laying her weary head on her pillow, she remembered Aram's face, Barak's stern countenance, Irad's last words, her fall from the cliff, meeting Jonas for the first time, her daughters' births, her son's laughter, Aram's hand clasping her own, and her trust in the unseen God. She closed her eyes and sighed in contentment.

~~~

Gizah tiptoed into her mother's house with a bundle in her arms. She laid it aside and knelt at the bedside. She clasped the old woman's cold hands and pressed them to her cheek. Then she kissed the gnarled fingers and held them against her breast. "Best of mothers, I will miss you forever."

Namah did not stir.

Bowing her head, Gizah reached back and tugged the cloak free. She unfolded the cloth and laid it gently over her mother's body. Then she reached deep into a pocket of her tunic and drew forth the wooden figure. She kissed it
~~~

and laid it on her mother's breast.

~~~

Barak exhaled a long breath and wrapped his arm around his wife as they lay in bed.

Milkan rolled onto her side and peered into Barak's eyes. "You miss her so very much?"

"I miss many people."

Milkan snuggled closer, drawing the blanket over her shoulders. "I wonder…is she with Aram now?"

His eyes widening, Barak stared at the thatched ceiling. "I don't know."

Milkan laid her head on his chest. "I wonder which of us will die first."

Spluttering, Barak coughed. "I can't say."

"Well, anyway, I'm glad I knew Aram and Namah, and I'll always miss them, but I can never be too sad when you're with me."

As if grief had been shoved to the side, Barak's heart stirred with overwhelming love. Warmth spread through his body. He wrapped his wife in his arms. "I am blessed among men." He leaned down to kiss her.

A baby cried out and an older child whined, "Mama!"

With a low groan, Milkan threw the blanket aside, heaved a deep breath, and rose to her feet.

Barak watched her, his heart swelling.

Milkan turned back and laughed. "You're much too comfortable!"

"I will be—as soon as you return to bed."

The cry rose a decibel to a high-pitched shriek.

Milkan stumbled away.

The crying stopped abruptly.

Milkan plodded back to bed and plunked the baby on Barak's chest.
~~~

A whimper broke the still air.

Milkan paced away and returned with a whimpering little boy. She tucked the child under Barak's arm, swung the baby to her chest, and lay down in bed, nudging Barak over a bit. She glanced at him. "Comfortable?"

"Not in the least."

Milkan stared and opened her mouth.

Barak leaned over and kissed her. "But happy nonetheless."

~~~

Jonas watched Onia saunter out of the village with a heavy bag slung over his shoulder, and her heart soared. No anxiety tugged at her heart as he wandered away to trade among their neighboring clans. He was so well liked and trusted that Obed said he could trade a sunbeam for a loaf of bread. Jonas didn't doubt it.

Laughter turned her attention. Mari helped one of Ishtar's men string the day's catch of fish on the line. The girl was always laughing—too spirited for her own good. Jonas shrugged. She had her father's nature.

Her gaze wandered to the edge of the village, to where her first husband's grave had melted into the earth and could only be seen by the mound of stones on top. "You are not there, love." She placed her hand on her heart. "You're right here."

An arm slid around Jonas' middle, and she shivered. She peered into Obed's alert, sober eyes.

Obed glanced from the grave to Onia. "He's off again?"

Jonas nodded. "He's taking some of Tobia's carvings this time. Said there's a growing market for such things."

With his shepherd's staff clutched one hand, Obed led Jonas toward the shady side of their house. "Sit and rest a moment. You rose before the sun."
~~~

Jonas perched on the edge of a bench. "Only to catch up with you."

His gaze traveled around their neat and prosperous village, Obed sighed as Tobia strode toward him with Kamila walking at his side. "I'm glad that Tobia's settled into married life and started carving again. He seems too old for one so young."

Tobia stopped before his mother and nodded respectfully. Kamila did the same but with a smile spreading across her face.

Obed scrunched his brows together. "Where's that figure of Caleb you made? I want Jonas to see it."

Tobia shrugged. "I gave it to Ishtar."

"Oh." Disappointment washed over Obed's face as he leaned on his staff.

Her heart bursting with joy, Jonas clasped Obed's hand. "But I did see it. Ishtar carries it everywhere, and he showed it to Eoban. Eoban told me about it, and when I saw Ishtar, I asked about it." Pride swelled in Jonas as she nodded at her son. "It's your finest work yet."

Obed glanced from his wife to Tobia. "I never saw a man change as much as Ishtar. I thought that once evil had hold, there was no turning back."

A hot flush worked up Jonas's cheeks.

Obed pressed her hand playfully. "But I've learned."

Jonas peered into her husband's eyes. "What have you learned?"

Obed gripped his shepherd's staff and looked to the hills. "If you dare enough—there's always hope."

~~~

Lud paced silently through the wheat field, slicing weeds at their roots. As sweat poured down his face, he straightened, wiped his brow, and glanced at Dinah and the
~~~

children working in their garden patch. He smiled.

The sun blazed with mid-day strength. Thirst stung his throat. Time to go home and rest. Swinging his hoe over his shoulder, he started down the incline.

A flock of birds sailed before him, twisting and turning, and then fluttering high into the sky.

Lud shook his head. The vision of Pele's face as she peered at the wide blue expanse flashed before his eyes. He never could see what she saw. He stopped and wiped his brow again. He didn't have to. He had seen her, and that was enough.

Gilbreth called, Dinah grinned, and Lud's heart soared like the birds.

~~~

Eoban perched on the edge of a log as a full moon floated overhead, shrouded in wispy clouds. A fresh breeze rustled the high branches of distant trees. Lud and Gilbreth sat cross-legged on each side of while Deli dangled on his left knee, and Ham nestled contentedly in the crook of his arm.

Dinah bustled before the fire, preparing a dinner of spiced rice and rabbit with vegetables and fresh bread.

Eoban's mouth watered.

Gilbreth glanced over. "Any stories to tell, Eoban?"

Shifting to keep his blood in circulation, Eoban met the challenge. "Well, once on a night very much like this one, there was a boy about as big as Gilbreth there, named Kilbreth."

Deli gasped and turned wide-eyes on her brother.

Eoban patted her arm reassuringly. "Yes, similar names. Hadn't realized. Anyway, this boy was brave and strong, but no one knew it because he never left his parents' sides. He pined to see the world, so he left home and traveled far and wide.
~~~

"Time passed quickly—as it does in stories—and after many years, Kilbreth returned home much bigger and swaggering with a bounty of knowledge. The whole village welcomed him with a grand feast."

Deli wiggled. "Like we're going to have?"

Eoban nodded and pressed on. "But tragically, he'd forgotten everyone. His mother and father tried to pretend it wasn't so, but he called everyone by the wrong name and, worst of all, he spent the whole night telling his family about all the fine people he met, and he never once asked about his own clan."

Ham yawned, and Deli kicked her legs.

Lud shook his head in definite admonishment. "Foolish boy."

Gilbreth peered through the darkness. "What happened to him?

Eoban straightened up. "Well…one dark night, he fell into a hole. He called and screamed, but no one came—remember—he had forgotten all their names."

Deli smacked her hand against her cheek. "Uh-oh."

Eoban shifted. "Right. Eventually, his father heard him, got the neighbors, and they hauled him out."

Gilbreth's eyes twinkled in the firelight. "Did Kilbreth learn his lesson?"

Eoban laid Deli in her brother's arm and scooted Ham to the ground. "From then on, Kilbreth traveled the world, telling everyone about his own marvelous clan—and he called them each by name."

Dinah raised her head and smiled. "Supper is ready."

Shuffling to his feet and rubbing his back, Eoban glanced at Gilbreth. "Thank the stars above. I'm about worn out. Now let's do justice to your mother's cooking. There's no one who can make a feast as well as she."

Dinah waved Eoban along. "Come eat then."

As they crossed the threshold, Lud chuckled. "And no

one tells a tale like Eoban!"

As he stepped inside, Eoban grinned. "And later, we'll all sing!"

~~~

Ishtar stripped to the waist and wrapped a cloth tight around his head, holding his hair away from his face.

In the pre-dawn light, a fire blazed before him with a tripod fixed over the flames. Nearby, perched on a flat rock, sat bowls filled with different colored substances. A cauldron hung from the center of the tripod.

Working methodically, Ishtar sifted the ingredients and poured a little of each into the pot. After it melted, he tugged a mold into place and poured the mixture into it. Then he added another substance, waited for it to melt, and poured the thick liquid into a second mold. After he had several molds lined up beside the fire pit, he sat back and wiped his forehead.

The sounds of the waking village drew his gaze. Two of his men passed and nodded. He nodded back.

When the first mold cooled, he took a hammer and knocked the frame away. Then he peered at the metal piece narrowly, looking for tiny bubbles and weak spots. Satisfied, he laid it on the flat rock and hammered it until it fell apart. He gathered up the pieces and threw them back into the cauldron. As he reached for one of the bowls, Amin shuffled by.

Ishtar sucked in his breath. "Amin, come and help me a moment."

With his head down and his shoulders drooping, Amin took the necessary steps and halted before Ishtar. "Yes?"

"Help me sift the ore. I'm trying different kinds and amounts…your sharp eyes would—"

"I'm not a metal worker, Father."
~~~

"You could be."

"I don't care to be."

"What do you care to be?"

Amin shifted from one foot to another and glanced aside.

Concerned, Ishtar stood and motioned his son to the fire pit. "Sit with me and watch awhile. You might find it interesting."

"I won't find metal work interesting any more than I found trading and traveling interesting."

Ishtar's jaw clenched. "Why are you still angry at me?" He swallowed hard and blinked as he stared at the glowing horizon. "He was my son as well as your brother."

"You've found other things to interest you. I'm not so easily amused."

With a swift motion, Ishtar swept up a handful of the dirty ore. "Do you see this?"

Stiff and unyielding, Amin merely raised an eyebrow.

"It's what the Creator gives us to work with. Dirt. And with this dirt" —Ishtar snatched up a metal tray behind him and held it out— "we can make beautiful things." He tossed the dirt and tray aside. "But it'll never happen without a willing mind and a dedicated heart to shape it." He peered into Amin's eyes. "The tray is worth nothing if no one cares for beauty."

Amin spat his words. "Caleb was worth more than a tray!"

Ishtar leaned in. "But Caleb would've seen the beauty and cared." Ishtar waved a broken piece of metal before Amin's face. "Impurities must be driven out by fire and hammer." He turned and peered at the mountains "Like ore, we are shaped by things that burn and beat us, and we think we'll never recover. But in the end, we're transformed."

Amin closed his eyes, his lips trembling. After a moment, he met Ishtar's gaze. "Without Caleb, I feel so…dead."

Ishtar gripped Amin's shoulder. "Hold on—even in the depths of despair. Only then can true faith be born."

Wrapping his arm around his son, Ishtar turned the boy from the mountains and the fire. Together, they faced the rising sun.

Chapter Forty-Nine

-Lux-

No Doubt at All

Teal stared at a cluster of luminescent red blossoms in a field of yellow stalks and shook his head. *Why?* Who planted them didn't bother him so much as why they planted them. He lifted his gaze and considered the expanse before him. A whole field of Calif, enough to feed the entire Luxonian capital, stretched out before him. Then, in one corner of the field, a bunch of unrelated red flowers—as unexpected as a fully armored Ingot in a Crestonian pool.

He bit his lip and started down the path that led back to the bustling city and Sterling's high-rise. Loneliness enveloped him. In such a busy world, no one would even notice such an oddity. And if they did…no one would care to wonder why.

With his head bowed, he trudged along and hoped the suffocating ache in his heart would lighten and allow him a little breathing room.

~~~

Teal's gaze flickered to the purple vine on the windowsill as he entered Sterling's office. He froze. The effervescent fronds had grown to mammoth size and fluttered in a gentle breeze. When he bypassed Sterling standing at his white oval desk and strode to the window, the plant seemed to wiggle its stalks in welcome. A tiny spark of joy kindled
~~~

deep within him.

Sterling stopped at his side, nearly touching his elbow. "Oh look. She's happy to see you. Waving like an old friend."

Teal glanced aside at Sterling. *Irritated or pleased?*

Irritated.

Teal patted the fronds, shouldered his duty, and faced his superior. "You asked to see me, sir."

"I had to. It's been over three cycles, and you've hardly spoken to me."

"There didn't seem to be anything to discuss, sir."

"Stop with the sir. I'm rising but not so high that you can't talk to me without using a formal address to punctuate every sentence."

"Yes, s—" Teal swallowed and peered at the frond. He could swear that it humped in indignation.

"So, is there anything to discuss?"

"You need to go back to work."

A lightning bolt of hope shot through Teal. "I can return to Earth?"

Sterling waved his hands as if terrified by hasty assumptions. "Now, don't zip off just yet. I told you that this whole Crestonian cold war was a mere bluff, but even bluffs can have disastrous consequences if not treated respectfully. In order to settle matters to our satisfaction, we need a few friends on our side first."

"Friends?"

"As in a certain Uanyi representative who just happens to enjoy OldEarth delicacies—delicious broiled vegetables with cracked wheat bread and virgin olive oil." Sterling licked his lips, emphasizing his point.

An involuntary cringe curled inside Teal. "Uanyi are insectine, correct?"

Sterling waved a hand over his desk console and a holographic image of a large-chested, small-waisted Uanyi male dressed in a white one-piece body suit rotated on the surface before them. “They have rubbery exoskeletons and internal bones.” He leaned in, enlarged the face, and glanced at Teal. “How do you like those eye bulbs? Bigger than Cresta orbs aren’t they?”

“I can see why certain races use them in precautionary tales to scare their young into good behavior.” Teal envisioned a particularly gruesome large-eyed arachnid that tormented his dreams as a child. He shivered.

Sterling chuckled. “Those mandibles aren’t for eating people, my friend. They’re nearly all vegetarians, though some have adapted to a more varied diet. I’ve heard they’ve taken a liking to boiled sea urchins.”

Teal winced. “And the breathing mask?”

“After so many civil wars, they’ve nearly decimated their home world, certainly the air. So breathing masks are a part of everyday wear at home or off planet.”

Teal flicked a glance at his superior. “So why are you show—?”

“Because I need you to go to Sectine and make friends with the Ultra High Command.”

“Why would they listen to me? I’m hardly an expert on their culture, and I have no associations with any of their kind.” Teal shrugged. “I don’t even know one word of their language.”

“Ah! Don’t worry about that. Despite their appearances, Uanyi are exceptionally bright and have a gift for communication. They’re highly proficient in every known language this side of the Divide.”

“Speaking of the—”

“We weren’t—so drop it. Focus, would you?”

Teal worked his way around the desk and returned to the window. He stared at the glorious Luxonian sunset. “I still don’t see how I’m going to convince them to work with us.”

"You probably won't, but I'm sending Ark with you. He can be very persuasive."

Rounding on Sterling, Teal stomped back to the desk, his mood rumbling like an active volcano. "He's still on Lux?"

"You think he wants to return to Crestar for execution?" Sterling held Teal in a steely gaze.

Teal broke away first. "Fine. Ark and I'll go to Sectine and try to negotiate an agreement. You have any idea of the conditions for this supposed treaty?"

Sterling tapped the console and drew up a holographic document image written in five languages. "Certainly. Zuri has it all written down and translated perfectly."

"Zuri?"

"Only fitting, since you three were best buddies on Earth. Besides, he can represent Ingilum interests, and Ark can work in possible arrangements for Crestar that might allow him—one day—to live among his own kind again."

"And Kelesta?

"The Bhuaci spy?"

"She wasn't a spy…for long."

Sterling chuckled and ambled away. "We'll see about her…but in the meantime, let me tell you a little story."

Teal squeezed his eyes shut and clenched his hands.

Sterling stepped to a desk drawer, opened it, and made a snipping sound.

Teal opened his eyes.

Waving a scissors, Sterling chuckled. "A few days ago, I went to the open air Bhuaci music festival. I thought a little amusement after all that brouhaha with Crestar would do my circulatory system good." He ambled to a large wall cabinet, flung open a large door, and started shuffling about, pulling red and green objects aside and shoving something decidedly pink to the back.

"I missed the first song, but the second…do you know what the gloriously handsome Bhuaci lead sang?"

Teal sighed and continued to watch Sterling's haphazard trail through the cabinet.

"Well, it started…'I woke up and my head was a mess, so I combed my hair. Then I felt my insides rumble, so I drank some Shang Slew.'" Sterling frowned like a seriously disturbed beverage authority. "Do you have any idea what Shag Slew will do to a person early in the morning?"

Teal swallowed back bile.

"I doubt he'd live to see the afternoon. Not sober and alert anyway. That stuff will muddle the mind no matter how carefully you try—" Sterling waved the thought away. "And then another singer started in. I couldn't understand a word he said."

Teal rubbed his forehead. "I can only pray that there's a point—somewhere."

"Ah ha!" Sterling lifted a white pot from the cabinet and cradled it in his arms like a newborn. He grinned. "There's always a point to my stories." He strolled to the window. "Despite the absurdities, I couldn't stop myself. I tapped my toes and swayed to the rhythm. I was taken in. Completely. I adored those singers."

"But you hated the lyrics?"

"Every nonsensical word."

Halting before the window, Sterling drew a small table close and placed the pot in the center. With precise movements, he cut a slender rectangle of dirt from the windowsill pot.

The purple plant practically stood up as its more-developed tendrils swung like enraged trees in a hurricane.

Alarm ripped through Teal's body.

Sterling dug out tiny clusters of roots and gently nestled them in the bowl. He smiled like a loving father. "Sweet thing. But you've got to let your little ones go, so they can grow big like you."

With a choking gasp, Teal peered at Sterling's handiwork. "What are you doing?"

Sterling pressed the white pot into Teal's hands. "It's a parting gift." He led Teal to the door. "Humanity will be fine while you go to Sectine and find a way to protect Earth from a universe they're not ready for."

"And the Bhuaci singers?"

"Oh, that. Yes." Sterling swayed his hips and hummed. "Just remember, your words won't convince an audience as much as your passion."

~~~

Teal strode along the Sectine walkway with Ark on his left and Zuri on his right.

A brilliant orange sun hung in the pale green sky, without a cloud in sight. Huge reddish anthill-like buildings rose from the sand-colored environment.

Uanyi bustled from one establishment to another over well-trod roads, scampering on their long legs or using scooters that hovered just over the hard-packed surface.

Zuri wiped beaded sweat from his reddened face. "It's dry, but the heat's enough to kill me."

Teal considered Zuri's beautiful shoulder-length locks of blond hair, his ocean-blue eyes, and the mechanical outerwear ending in sandaled feet. "You're still going forward with the return-to-nature scheme?"

Ark gurgled. "Kelesta convinced him to hold on to what technological advantages he has." Ark peered around Zuri as he padded forward, his eyebrows wiggling, and his words laden with heavy emphasis. "Her entire family has a *thing* for mechanical exoskeletons."

Teal snorted. "That's so counterintuitive, I don't even know where to start."

Zuri shrugged. "She's a good woman, working from
~~~

home to convince the Regent of Song that Lux has a more sensible plan than Crestar. After all, quarantine only lasts as long as everyone obeys the rules. But without the mystery race in the game…there's no telling."

Teal sidestepped a mother Uanyi pushing an infant in a stroller. He glanced at the baby, frowned, and blinked back to Zuri. "So you and Kelesta are still together?"

Ark rolled his eyes. "Like stanzas of Bhuaci poetry."

Zuri shoved Ark off the path and glanced at Teal. "You and Sienna?"

Teal picked up his pace. "Don't ask."

Zuri pulled a tottering Ark back onto the path and held his gaze.

Ark nodded.

Teal glanced from one to the other. "What?"

Zuri ducked his head and nudged Ark.

Wrapping his tentacles behind his back like a well-behaved pod, Ark shrugged. "Nothing. Especially. We're just glad to be with you on this mission."

Teal stopped and glared from the Cresta to the Ingot. "What?"

"Well, we happened to get a little, tiny—" Zuri pinched two slender fingers within millimeters of each other—"preview of the Uanyi representative we're meeting today."

"How'd you manage that? Sterling wouldn't give me anything but her name. Jasmine. Of all the ridiculous—"

Ark slipped his tentacle around Teal's arm. "You never know what'll happen when you open negotiations. Things can get interesting. Very interesting, indeed."

Exhaling a long, drawn-out sigh, Teal fell in step with his two friends. "With you two along, I've no doubt. No doubt at all."

About the Author

A. K. Frailey, an author of a historical sci-fi and science fiction series, short story collections, inspirational non-fiction books, a children's book, and a poetry collection, has been writing for over ten years and has published 17 books.

Her novels expand from the OldEarth world to the Newearth universe-where deception rules but truth prevails. Her nonfiction work focuses on the intersection of motherhood, widowhood, practicing gratitude, and rediscovering joy.

As a teacher with a degree in Elementary Education, she has taught in Milwaukee, Chicago, L. A., and WoodRiver, and was a teacher trainer in the Philippines for Peace Corps. She earned a Master of Fine Arts Degree in Creative Writing for Entertainment from Full Sail University.

Ann homeschooled all eight of her children. She manages her rural homestead with her kids and their numerous critters. In her spare time, she serves as an election judge, a literacy tutor, and secretary/treasurer of her small town's cemetery.